The i...

Paul Rosher

authorHOUSE®

AuthorHouse™ UK
1663 Liberty Drive
Bloomington, IN 47403 USA
www.authorhouse.co.uk
Phone: 0800.197.4150

Published by AuthorHouse   05/05/2015

ISBN: 978-1-5049-4131-0 (sc)
ISBN: 978-1-5049-4132-7 (e)

Print information available on the last page.

"Dedicated to the memory of my dear daughter Elizabeth."

CONTENTS

CHAPTER ONE

By the dirty auld river.

They are an echo in the blue-black midnight industrial graveyard.

Their presence is the background chill of an awful murder scene, or the distant laugh the condemned man thinks he half-hears, as his final steps are taken to his execution. They are ancient. Their breeding ground is misery and their inheritance is torture.

They are the i…

Pronounced as the letter "i" in the word ink. No big, fancy, protracted, esoteric name.

No grandiose or arcane complicated evocations. Simply and wretchedly efficient.

The i…

The original life-form motivator. Both a generator and a consumer of fear, whose purposes end in madness and whose main intentions mean harm.

Ancient before the first empires thrived in the youth of human history.

Travellers from a world and a star far into deepest, distant space.

The i...

In the shadows which meet you in the dark places of the mind, in the pillow logic night. They swarm like moths and mutter quietly as a massive tragedy approaches, they laugh as the surprise disaster floors you, and then glow with delight in the face of your newly acquired soul. Just imagine losing something you never really thought you had, or if you did, what damned difference did it make anyway?

Arthur MacNeil walks down six flights of granite stairs and out of the Tyneside tenement on his way to work. Same set of steps for two decades, same job, same routine, same holidays off and weekends spoken for. He walks to save money. Unmarried and entirely habitual, his life unchanged and unchanging.

In the enormous dockyard, brick-built office he works as a draughtsman and knows every file and drawing stacked around three floors of dreary ink and paper business. He earns a better wage than that which the men working outside receive, yet his heavy black tweed suit is old and trimmed with dark leather on the cuffs and elbows. His sturdy shoes shine, despite their age.

He is quiet. His shirts are clean, threadbare and dusty. His attic flat is a neat and simple arrangement of small living-room, a tiny bedroom, a cupboard kitchen and a closet that works. Above all, the rent is cheap. Yet his home is orderly and functional. Arthur's most treasured items being the bundles of letters from his mother, stacked into an old shoe box. Gas mantles burn low at night as he responds or reads. In old Gateshead, down in a warren of ancient houses soon to be demolished in the massive upheaval that the following decade soon will bring. This is his world. He grafts as hard as he may to keep his mother in rural comfort and care, far up the Tyne Valley, in an expensive nursing home, nested in the gentle woodland overlooking Hexam. Whilst he abides in haunted Pipewellgate, right by the dirty auld river, with the enormous span and towering supports of the High Level Bridge, casting a perpetual shadow on the maze of chares, or alleyways, and the substandard, semi-derelict tenements clustered below.

Every Saturday he takes the steam train early, out of Newcastle Central Station bound for Carlisle, stopping at Hexam. Every single Saturday, bar those where illness or malfunctioning engineering or weather forbid. After a day of gentle rambles and talks with his troubled mother, he stays in the same guest house in the little rural town, near the sculptured ruins of the old abbey. Arthur could not remember his father who had perished in the Great War in 1918. Dad was but a face in a faded photograph. A Royal Flying Corps uniform, that brave, clean-cut look, lost over France, his reconnaissance biplane, tail up in a foreign field. A folding issue penknife with lanyard, and his RFC cap badge and a rack of medals, his only reminders.

Sunday would see him take his dear friend and parent on a shorter walk, always by the river. Afterwards he would catch the train back to the dirty city in the afternoon, the fields and forests and farms flashing by unnoticed. Always he dwells on her words, always he holds their conversation, pondering, until the massive, black engine grinds into the grimy station platform. His routine, when walking to or back from the station, was to have a couple of pints in The Bridge Hotel, which helpfully was just over the High Level Bridge, and had become his local. Simply being there, having a beer, acted as a remedy to the disconcerting madness in his Ma's words. Around him all was soon to change. The looming 1960s will challenge in ways he cannot yet know or prepare for. His beloved mothers death, the demolition of the Pipewellgate slums, unemployment and an appointment with alcoholism.

In that filthy, shadowy, industrial sprawl, as the massed workers of Tyneside grafted and lived their predictable lives, Arthur, the most predictable of all, held a knowledge of something terrible and dangerous. All his mother's stories, all her dreams, every letter, her life's obsession and reason for her illness, these things, the monsters that terrified her, the fiends she called the i…

The i…

Tyneside. 1960's Northern England. A dreary black and white photograph of a place. Battered, derelict houses are widespread, the broken doors and smashed windows gape at the callous world. In a tenement on Bottle Bank, not far from the river, a gang of young teenagers kick an old piano down a stone stairwell. It rings and rackets its booted-in music whilst they laugh. As the faded walnut veneer and wood-wormed panels crashed into dusty splinters and the vandal's symphony rang on the cold stone walls, something else was laughing.

The piano has no further to fall. It crunches to rest and thrums slowly towards silence. One of the gang stops mid step and glances back up the stairwell. He had half-heard a laugh, a dull-dry hollow sound. He can see nothing and spits on the exposed strings as he passes. Very soft and low, they ring.

The i… For such is their music, this is also what they are drawn to, the discordant and violent. In the wanton forte of a self-indulgent cacophony, whether it is the raucous destruction of an old piano or the arrogated avant garde and their mael-odies, the i …are near, waiting and watching. Finding a way into their quarry with a patience developed over thousands and thousands of years, on this planet at the very least of it. They scrutinize first to acquire later. They stalk and plan. Unseen, efficient, observant, and terminally deadly.

The lads pass around cigarettes and smirk at their handiwork. Outside a siren blares as it rushes by. The night wraps the city, its frozen winter fingers reach into the tenement hall. After their exertion they begin to feel the chill, their breath and exhalations billow into the gloom. Looking for swag in old houses, getting into fights and smashing up stuff, this was their world. These old buildings had good quality lead in the roofing, available if you had no fear of heights and a big brother to cash it in for you at the local scrap yards.

Nearby, a dingy quay, the is tide out and the stinking mud-banks glisten. In a deep trough of the river there is a small dock, a pool of ink in the gloom. Within its rancid waters rust prams and old knackered bicycles. Rib-cage hulls of old rotted boats, abandoned long ago, where now only fat river rats worked. Fag-ends float on the filth, half submerged bottles bob uselessly. The murk is rippling in the yellow light of a distant street-lamp. Above, the uncaring sky ranks a canopy of frozen vastness. Here is the Northern England no-one mentions.

A seventeen-year-old boy is limply flapping at the surface. He has been beaten so badly his spine is damaged and he cannot keep himself afloat in the stinking mire. Slowly, gradually, he is dying. He gasps and struggles and cannot accept this tragic, frozen demise. As he sinks, he thinks he can see a group of people standing on the dock in the shadows, dark, tall, and muttering. As he reaches towards them imploring for help, they begin to actually giggle and soon they are laughing outright. They find his death funny. The sick bastard things. They find each drawn out moment warms them. They are amused in this dreadful place. Such is their food, their nourishment.

The kid's hair floats in the polluted filth, a used condom catches in the sway. Bubbles slowly diminish and soon all is silent. Except the laughing and the cold, mean, sense of humour. Whilst the solemn, freezing night that bridges the earth below greedily consumes all warmth. Physics cannot be argued with. The perishing cold logic of winter.

The i...

Delighting in filth and poverty, knowing too well that these are the fertile fields of human suffering. Anything that creates, encourages or develops grief, they are there, entertained by our troubles. Their low sickening laughter, hateful and sinister, confident that you are theirs to play with. They will enter the spaces where we dream, they will haunt the zones of our unconscious. Planting seeds of doubt and fear, they wait and watch as horror grows, slowly and painfully to an ancient plan. A story which always has the same ending.

The i…

Industrial smog thickened under the High Level Bridge stanchions, over in the West the sun was setting beautifully, but by the Tyne night had arrived. From the numerous pubs in the tightly packed slum area, yellow light and human noise leaked. The smell of beer and tobacco, the stench of Victoria's most northern secret, that lost era fading before its final fall. This was the last of this place, a relic of a time about to be abandoned. Sagging slate roofs and the crumbling towers of chimney stacks climbed up the steep hill on the bank of the dirty river, all dwarfed by the massive black stone and iron bridge above. Demolition had begun upstream, wholly unique areas had been crushed to tired rubble and dust. Gone forever. Gone.

Many rooms and houses were derelict. Within the shattered windows, shuffling dossers and tramps would bed down, once the gangs of quarrelling kids had finished their battles and roughneck games. The river rolled by, dead from the ravages of an industrial revolution and the engineering requirements of an empire and two world wars. The warehouses looked run-down and unsafe. Scrap yards had appeared where once precision and detail ruled. Old barges rotted on the Tyne's muddy banks, baring the ribs of oak that framed within, as the toxins in the water corroded the skin of their visible history. Their time of usefulness had long passed.

To the i...the place was singing with the concerted memories of so many difficult lives. It retched from the squalor with a sigh upon their senses, and always the sound of children crying, some place. The i... enjoying the suffering and ignorance, the poverty and knowledge that it was all about to disappear, after all this time. In the little pubs along narrow streets, sometimes singing could be heard, maybe a piano, hammering through some old-time, much-loved, favourite tune.

The music halls were gone and soon even their songs would be worthless. They would sing in these places sometimes, howling and hooting with tears in the eyes of those worn-out northern faces. Nothing to remember them by, nothing much to say or do or be. Fertile fields to the i...

The i...

By another river running through a similar industrial city, Belfast.

A far more troubled place than the Tyne, yet an architectural twin, having the very same look, the same tattered, dog-end Victorian architecture, a similar oldness and much the same greasy dirt.

In a drinking den, in a dive that tolerates moronic, raucously bellowing football supporters. The accentuated vowels and sectarian jibes belch with the blue cigarette smoke out into the run-down street. They are happiest in their tribal group, all boys together. Revelling in the unquestioned bigotry that permits this dense illusion of grandeur. Their jokes are cruel and always pointing away from their tacky loyalties.

Their crude songs insult the ears, they all dress more-or-less alike and worship the same empty soulless hard-men without flinch or question. The air turns thick, the pint glasses click and slosh. They are drunk and content and secure in their arrogations for yet another Saturday night.

No one there heard the quiet laughter, a different amusement, a dark and sinister sound. Pool balls skitter over the threadbare baize, young guys posture for the girls, the television blares unheard. They are awaiting the news and football scores, another busy night...

In a devastating instant, in the physical detonation of Semtex, the scene is irredeemably transformed. A bomb planted earlier in the day by hard-core members of the very group they claim to despise, it explodes!

Fucking BOOM!

In the sub-seconds of the blast, as bodies are thrown and split and shattered, as glass showers into lacerating dust and all the top shelf hard liquor adds to the calamity by flowering ablaze, the i ... they are laughing! Relishing the moment, in the bright, loud expansion of high combustion and concussion, they gloat. Deriving pleasure from every contorted frame, each shower of radiant blood and splintered bone, every shriek and anguished howl.

Passers-by in the street flinch at the shock wave. Some throw themselves to the ground. Tragic shapes that emerge from the dust and smoke are staggering, some are trying to shout. Some moan or cry, their clothes in bloodstained rags.

It will never or can never cross the minds of these victims that they set themselves up. That by their demonising and harassing, they alone created a ready-made enemy, hence therefore scripting their own demise. A point not wasted on the i... They appreciate the irony and the obvious consequences of projection phenomena. In the brief silence after the blast, when the glass and detritus tinkles to rest, just before the cries of the survivors and the terminally maimed screech and wail, the i.. they are gloating, feeding contentedly.

A youth bleeds slowly to death from a severed leg, the useless limb cradled like a baby in his bloodstained arms. The smouldering pockmarked walls, burnt and splattered with a film of viscera and gore. Look where all that hard man swagger got them? Not so tough now eh? They wanted to bait the Fenian bastards and wish-fulfilment being what it is, they got exactly what they asked for. Yet only the i… got the joke in its fullness.

A once pretty young girl screams, a long, loud bray of pain and induced shock, her hands sticky with blood as they hold together the lacerations that have marred her beauty forever. All the bravado, all the stories that showed clearly that they were tougher, better, cleverer, more human, these all stand out as those cultural footsteps leading from ignorance to disaster.

Where there is sectarianism, or half-witted, uninformed emulation of the same stupid human tendency, the i …are close, some place near. Watching, waiting, feeding and coldly capable. The i... always will feast well on the suffering.

The i…

Tyneside, the same one targeted for bombing during WW2, the dirty auld river that flows and thrives on war. During wartime, work increased and those at home in the slums and squalor had a major concern and distraction. Britain went off to do battle, especially when the enemy wanted to bomb the factories where flat-capped blokes made very dangerous kit indeed. Equipment like tanks, field and deck artillery and of course the warships. This plus all the varied munitions required to make the wide range of weaponry effective. Tyneside made the best. The river carried them all far away to very violent theatres indeed.

Arthur had been a draughtsman of these same warships and was considered essential civilian personnel, one who would not serve and fight on a foreign field, rather instead to construct and draw. He was supervised by chief engineers on the execution of these precise construction diagrams. It was an exact, time consuming job. This was Arthur MacNeil's work, hours spent gainfully which translated into these floating machines of destruction, very much engaged in the conflict that had swamped the whole world. Arthur reflected, he had felt important and had grafted so very hard indeed.

All those years ago... When...

Arthur remembers...

Over the channel voices were singing heartily, words such as...

"Together my brothers, we'll show them a sign! United we'll always be free. The morning will come when the world is mine! Tomorrow belongs to me!"

These very words, cackling through a Bakerlite radio, the BBC news report on the source of all these sorrows, in a documentary broadcast on Hitler's rise to power. Arthur remembers...

...He and his mother sat in the little kitchen, by the window that looked out upon the Tyne Valley below. Their family home, a terraced house on Whickham Hill. Down in the blackout, the besieged town waited. The radio whispered in the dark. Sometimes the bombers would drone overhead and Arthur would wish he were somewhere else. Though on clear nights, when the crump and flash of direct hits on Newcastle and Gateshead showed in the distance, they would watch like children captivated by fireworks, but quietly, for they were both watching in silence. Once an enormous column of fire soared up into the sky, a direct hit on the gasworks. It was astonishing and terrifying at the same time. An image of hell. Arthur recalled how his mother turned and whispered to him,

'Can't you hear them laughing?'

He had glanced at her, away from the heightening orange plume. Her face was waxen, serious, drawn. Returning his stare to the pillar of flaming gas he had replied,

'Hear who laughing Mother?'

'Not all that lives requires food the way we do.' She had said.

Such an odd thing to say thought Arthur,

'What do you mean?' frowned Arthur, not wishing to miss a second of the spectacle, now a flickering tongue of sword-like fire, having a go at the sky.

'Some things live and feed on the heart of strife and misery'

He remembered shivering, even though it was warm in the kitchen.

He had to look at her squarely to ensure she was well.

Was she talking about the German bombers?

'We are their food. Our terror and grief, their meat and drink.'

He remembered wishing she would not to talk so strangely, and simply watch the blazes the Nazi bombs had planted behind them.

'Whose food Mother?' Arthur asked.

'Those things, those glass-like hollow things...the i...the i...'

Arthur froze that day in such a manner which he would really never thaw from. He turned again from the fire-storms away down the valley and looked at her eyes. They saw nothing. She was not there. He remembered the blankness, the stare.

'The what, Mother?' he questioned.

'The i…, the …i….'

Memory

Arthur remembered what had been his Friday night routine during the war years. Before catching the last bus home, he would have a few beers, usually in the Bridge Hotel, with his other workmates who had been spared war service. He was in his early twenties and had ceased to feel awkward about not being in the Armed Forces, he and his pals had began the same ships on paper that eventually fought the great sea battles. He was playing his part, doing his bit. Arthur's war effort was always to apply himself and produce the highest standard of work, for slackers were not employed for long in this critical time.

Over the sea the war was going badly. No soon had a warship been finished in its design draft then it could begin construction. It would be engineered, furnished, equipped and fully crewed, then launched to task with small ceremony. Often later to be torpedoed and sunk in the Atlantic Ocean. The German U-Boats kept Arthur at home and crucially out of the vicious fray which was Hitler's War. The newspapers announced the ships which had been sunk, sometimes with the terrible words added "all hands lost" as an awful addition.

He recalled one evening arriving home on Whickham Hill to find the front door wide open. The cold, foggy November night was free to prowl about the house. The gas-lamps within were all off and the range was dead cold. He had called to his mother, his memory guiding him in the dark to the kitchen gas mantle. As it purred into yellow life and chased away the inky darkness, he closed the black-out curtains and called again. No reply. He lit a candle in a brass holder and assumed she had gone to her bed.

It had occurred to him that the front room curtains also were open, so by candlelight he had entered, only to jump in surprise, almost dropping his light. The glow fluttered on his mother's face. She sat bolt upright in the dark room, glaring at the window, her hands gripping the arms of the chair, her knuckles white.

"Are you alright Ma`?" he had asked.

She had given no immediate response and only when his warm hand had touched hers in a gesture of concern she reacted and shrieked a long shrill wail. It had made his nape hairs stand on end as he bristled at the terrified cry. Slowly she turned her eyes from the window to himself and as recognition grew in her fear-filled face she had pitifully croaked,

"Arthur.. help me! They were outside! Through the window, in the street!"

He carried her to bed, tucking her in fully clothed, a deep concern displacing his slight intoxication. The next day he would arrange a doctor to visit. This was the first of many incidents over the years before she was sectioned in a mental institution. Arthur recalled that very first episode, knowing it had been the beginning of a long commitment, creating the routine that would endure until she died. The weekend visits to the hospital and her worsening condition, the way in which it had also burdened him at such a young age. Out of love and duty, he had never abandoned her, constantly engaging the hospital staff regarding both her comfort and mental stability. Year after year this continued, until she was released to the hospice in Hexam, frail and worn beyond her actual years.

The i…

Under the High Level Bridge, in the soot blackened tenement Arthur reads a collection of his mother's recent letters. They were becoming fewer and the handwriting thin, lacking emphasis. The urgency of her writings in the period of her early years in the hospital had impressed hair-fine channels into the page. She once had to use heavy weight papers, the omnipresent pressure of her fear manifesting through a tightly held pen. The recent letters were scrawled over thinner paper, the manic urgency now absent, but the words still reeking of ever-present danger. Of a torment that had imbalanced her and ruined her life.

A sound from outside distracts him, one of young lads playing. Carefully placing the letters back, he opens the filthy window and leans on the sill, looking out over the river. The narrow street below had a high, crumbling stone wall flanking it on the riverside. Over this, a few small industries lingered on. Some had long packed it in, the derelict tool-shops and warehouses being prime play areas for rough young boys. Arthur was high enough up to see directly into the staiths, or the jetty fronting the old abandoned factory loading area. A bank of black reeking mud revealed at low tide the feet of the massive oak beams. Mud full of disease and poison. Over two centuries of pollution stank within its silt and reek.

Four ragged youths, average age of nine years between them, are taking turns with two catapults and are making sport of the rats below. A dead cat, road-kill the boys had found earlier had been used as bait for the bloated rodents. As the vermin scuttle out of the hollows of the staiths and slither towards the flattened cat, the boys let rip with rusted hexagonal nuts found everywhere inside the vacated workshop. They cheer when they almost get a hit, the viscous mud plopping as the speeding metal splats into the riverbank, the fat vermin hissing and struggling to scamper back to safety in the slime. They burst into hoots of laughter when they get a hit. Arthur waits and watches, vaguely smiling until they get a direct hit and a kill. A happy sound. Arthur laughed and applauded. One kid turned, looked up and smiled.

As night fell and the gas lamps were lit, Arthur found himself going to the window to see if the boys were back. They had long gone of course, and it dawned on him it was their laughter and sense of plain and simple fun that was still playing on his mind. Over the river, on the Newcastle side of the Tyne, a cargo boat was unloading directly into a large industrial warehouse. The wide, dark Tyne rippling in the glaring sodium deck lamps, the small, dark figures scurrying about. The far bank rose to the castle keep above and held a deeper darkness of crammed buildings, clusters of chimneys, rooftops and spires. A homely yellow glow from the many windows punctuated the city riverside and the ranks of chimneys smoked above.

A familiar view, one which had been there so long it was fair to assume it would be around a lot longer still. A decayed and jumbled city, with unplanned architectural mixes of eras adding to the oddity that it was. There was an unintentional Gothic air to the place, pre-1960s, Tyneside.

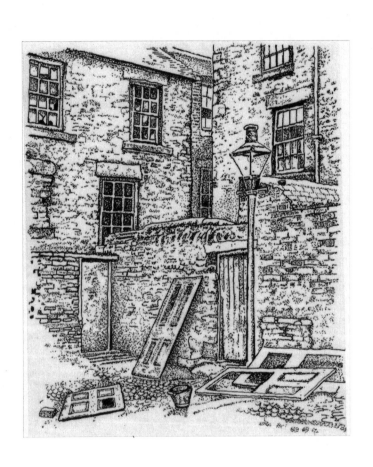

CHAPTER TWO

Concerning the i...

Once when Britain was young and sparsely settled communities shielded themselves against the unknown by all manner of inventive superstition and folklore, the onset of winter was marked by the festival of Samaihn. One of the stories linked to this time, one which allied itself with the arrival of savage winds and increasing cold, was the story of the Wild Hunt. The various names and reasons for this particular festival would vary with people and place, yet the basic theme of the boundaries between our earthly realm and the supernatural being breached was a constant.

As the gales and storms would bash and lash around the walls and roof, by the fireside, folk would shiver, yet not with cold, hearing instead words upon the wind, or crying and howling, borne upon the night. In the imagination of children, mad horsemen tore across the ragged cloudscape, their hounds baying and slavering for a kill. The safest place was indoors and the best course of action was to pray to whatever deity could and would protect. So pray they did.

Fifteen hundred years later, the land being rendered soulless by the scars of a thousand thousand roads and the sterile procession of expanding cities, fear had new forms. The terrorist, from whom our unquestionably efficient and caring leaders would protect us, became one focus. The thug, with his callous violence and savage disregard for anything other than himself, was yet another.

Homes and workplaces were rigged with all manner of lock and alarm, rigid and primed against threat and intrusion. Cars, those icons of prestige and achievement, similarly prepared to thwart the faceless invader and cunning thief with shrieking alarms and immobilisers. Fear was endemic, yet trivia reigned supreme. Terror was widespread, yet banality and an unreasoned belief in self-worth ruled, without any authentic assessment or consideration of what actually mattered, of what was real.

In the rage of the Wild Hunt, in ancient Britain's rustic heart, the i… would thrive and gather in the places where the storm crashes trees through many a roof, or suchlike calamity. Or when the flood breaks the river confines and courses into the sleepy hamlet or hovel, the i… would be there, enjoying the panic and delighting in disaster, for such is their way, and plagues, how they love plagues.

They have always been and may well always be, a sentient, non-corporeal intelligence that are drawn to tragedy and suffering. Their origins may be guessed at, their nature a mystery, yet whatever name they have accredited, whatever title they have attained, they are what they are; a force that feeds upon fear and takes joy in misery and death. Time has not changed them, merely provided more opportunities and chances for a feast. Place has not confined them, like the Wild Hunt they roam where they will, and do whatever pleases them. Few, very few have known of them or gained an insight into their ways. Fewer still have achieved a basic contact with them by intention and design. Their existence raises crushing questions about the broad spectrum of human life. For the means by which these aliens work could define the unexplored and the unknown within the human sphere.

Civilisation, or this immensity of populous and effort, does not make premium space for such ephemera, rather instead the seedy world of occult practise and speculation occupies the quiet corner. Religions, particularly the many bastard offspring from the stem, which was Christianity, confine all manner of unaccountable wickedness to a general evil. The more archaic sects and traditions actually blaming a devil, a Satan, a figure to be held responsible for the source of all malice and malign.

The world turns and the televisions blare. The roads congest with precious cars and their fumes stain the greenery about them. Avoidance of our plight has become an art. We can go on holidays, or have a hobby, take up a sport, work out in the gym, or fuck all that and go clubbing or pubbing and wreck the mind that could attempt to reason the complexities of our world. Oh, and there is work, standing like a new religious philosophy, a definer of personality, a lifestyle enabler, a measure by which we estimate our worth, to loss and gain. This is life, like it or not, and all the whining poets and bleeding hearts cannot and will not change a single feature of it.

The bigger picture is out of focus. The grainy details are non-specific.

What was once true of the part was true of the whole, but not any longer. Do what you want has become the whole of the law of life. Do whatever you want and either don't get caught or don't let on, and once you are rich enough to build an impregnable and impenetrable barrier against the curious, then it doesn't matter any more.

These are the playing fields of the i... The combined total mass of multiple million lives which consume and create, build up and pull down, esteem and despise. Hither and thither in an interlace, a web of life, a labyrinth within which we ourselves are trapped and hunted. Whilst being unaware we remain unconcerned. Forces of darkness and evil powers are the foibles of dusty books and people who should become museum exhibits. Such denial is ideal for the i... nothing could suit their machinations better than a disbelief in their very existence. It is this environment that these pages will explore, this ramble through the unfortunate and the sublimely worrisome.

The i...

Where do all the unanswered prayers go? What ornate ontological pet cemetery holds the uncountable crosses worn smooth by the aeon slow drip of human tears? The comfortable notion of a personal, caring deity is often shattered by the catastrophic intrusion of sheer calamity. At such occasions brave men's hearts may falter and strong souls break and despair. Everybody believes they want to be happy. Has anyone ever questioned that this species obsession may be the resultant of more than sucking, fucking, mucking and ducking? What, or who promoted this vector as the sole resultant motivator and predicate of our race?

Questions of this nature frequently avoid intellectual attention because of the obvious solution of the proposition in the first case. Namely, why does our race value happiness so highly? A simple enough question which should furnish an equally comprehensible answer.

Would it stretch the virgin imagination to visualise the human evolutionary story as one massive avoidance of big teeth, nasty claws, steep drops, fires, earthquakes, floods, tsunami, landslides, avalanches, rockfalls and weapons. Warfare and its resultant battles move into a finer, relatively more recent and less primal focus. The origin of the human species is entwined in the roots and source of real and present abject fear. Of terror and panic that can interfere fatally with the cardiovascular functions, which also may shred the sense of self or emotionally devastate the victim, the casualty, or the food source of the i...

The i...

A sophomane is a person who genuinely believes without rebuttal that they themselves are and remain the most intelligent person they have ever had the pleasure of meeting. It has been recognised as a mild psychological disorder. Lacking the scary clout of disturbing conditions couched in phrases like, hyper-manic sociopathic schizophrenia with violent delusional obsessions. Now that has an edge. Sophomania never seems to get the profile of the invasive states of madness, yet mild insanity it is and remains.

True to form, the sophomane is completely unaware of the absurdity of their inward claim on the world of cleverness. They absorb standard self-referencing narcissism into their personality and whether by incidence, intent or mischance, the habit takes form and becomes ingrained in their psyche, subtending all reason. Simultaneously, this state of being has an outward effect upon a large percentage of those who surround or are social with the afflicted maniac. The reaction of caution, wariness, dislike or outright avoidance can be forthcoming. Equally, it also can be fascinating to students of these unbalanced mental states.

When a degree of genuine ability is present and enough sycophants can be found to fawn and support the over-indulged and cocooned sophomane, an ego is gradually inflated at an unlimited rate in a manner concomitant with the condition itself. This can turn the sophomane into a self-regarding pompous ass-hole, a pain in the neck. In time, even the most loyal of the supporters have to fall away, either by old age, illness or disillusion. Which leaves this slightly poorly human ripe for the attentions of the i... In short, food.

The i...

They infect every inhabited world discovered in their wanderings, contaminating each planet unfortunate enough to be in their way. A sub-ancient life that should have bowed-out, moved on or become extinct millennia ago, they drift and journey through our galactic vastness. Cold, patient and rational, observant yet cruelly sadistic they are bad news for any world with a breathable atmosphere and certainly all of the intelligent life forms encountered. Bad news.

The i...

The worst kind of alien, with no detectable spaceships or warning of their approach. Far beyond cheesy, shocking brutes or predatory, evolved insectoids. They have found us and poisoned our species and played our human history, consequently feeding upon our suffering. For this is their way. We are their nutrition and entertainment, as they are both hungry and bored. The energy, or emotional charge, within our pain and distress sustains their rapacious appetite. The enduring self-arrogation of our race more than compensates for the ridiculously enormous distances they have patiently traversed.

Space. Lots and lots and lots of freezing cold, deeply dull space.

It was such a pleasure to find this planet of new homo sapiens, with their potential or inherent brutality towards one another and their immense capacity for deluding themselves. Occasional acts of human kindness may stand out as remarkable exceptions to our general methodology, which principally consists of profound unkindness, petty judgementalism, absurd smugness and a deeply irrational self-righteousness. It was rotten luck all round that they came here, we were already sadly destined to be a distressingly troubled species.

Consider the shallowness of human connections and interactions, and how loyalties can switch on a whim or a mood. Take the slanderers and the dismal lack of reflection or fairness which hallmarks their sorry efforts. In reality, they will have no really close friends, for by manifesting a toxic passive-aggression as a daily social sport, they equally display an incapacity for intimacy of any true measure. All social dealings, are negotiated and conditional. They will suffer a frigidity of imagination which closes down opportunities for empathic or intuitive functions, as they are truly alone. Therefore truly vulnerable, and thus prime nutrition to the alien invader.

Isolated by a selfishness become pathological, the sophomane takes these dysfunctional exchanges even further into remoteness and isolation. Far removed from sympathy and compassion, due to their mental state, they are blind to the actual pomposity and the swagger associated with their acute illness. Again, this common minor tragedy provides great opportunity for play and feast to the dark entities, for they view the sophomane as the easiest prey. Good meat.

It is authentically sinister. For what could well define the sinister would be when something once good and meaningful does not just turn bad, but slowly, and malignantly rots in a loathsome decay. Where all the fine and sweet things in life that once rejoiced in friendship and trust, love and appreciation, wretchedly sink into a living, contagious poison. A point is eventually reached where psychological walls and barriers no longer efficiently function and the afflicted experience a clinging, deep unease. This is sinister, to have a life transformed into something foul, to find goodness and kindness subsumed and consumed by a hateful, rotten cancer.

The i... regard this predicament as a free meal. Sweet meat.

The i...

Surrounded by half-finished musical manuscripts, the self important composer king scores and scratches the lines that set his latest effort at immortality. His whole life having been lived for himself, his most important friend being his own hide, he has no idea that the i ...have been working him for years. The dozen, modern classical, long playing records he had recorded over a long career lie around as visible proof of his greatness and as validations for the ruthless, manic selfishness and that same driven ambition. He has no idea how much his children loathe him and see through his inflations. All the time he could have spent with them had now sadly decayed into a malignant, seething contempt. The i... love this sort of thing. They thrive on balloons such as this man.

He hums through a discordant, erratic sequence, akin to the sound of a piano being booted down a stone stairwell, but lessened by the pointlessness of its existence. As he settles for its genius and smugly pours another whiskey, he half-hears someone at the front door. This being the second time it has happened in the same night. Perhaps it is kids playing about, as it is near Guy Faulk's Night, a time for high-jinx and pranks. Yet again there is no-one there. At least no- one visible. The dark greets him impersonal and cold, the first of the night's raindrops are blown into his face. It is freezing and as he turns to go inside, again, the half-heard laughter, almost a giggle, suppressed and muted. He sighs and returns to his Magnus Opus.

A large spider has fallen into his whiskey. It frantically struggles to escape the poisoning yellow trap. Gently he fishes the insect out by one leg, which breaks off as the arachnid falls to the floor making a break for freedom. At least it has seven legs left, he thinks, and wonders if he can include this abstract notion into his ongoing composition. Maybe even calling the piece ' The Seven Legged Spider'. He likes that, as most of his self-indulgence is given a random title, unrelated to the grating cacophony within. Happy with his night's work he sips the strong, soothing liquor, wondering how his next audience will respond to another foray into the dark and moody corners of the avant guard. He hasn't a clue. Nothing could prepare him for what is to come. All the while the i ...watch patiently, as is their way.

Species.

They live, eat, work, shag, shit, kill and generally make a right royal mess in this undignified evolutionary process. Its kind of sad. On the planets where the dominant life forms get beyond devastating asteroid and comet impacts, also on those worlds that survive poisonous bacteria and decimating viral infections, yes, even those that avoid utterly wiping one another out in fevered religious delusional abandon, there is a dominant dilemma. Namely, the vast and desolate enormity of space. The terrible, dangerous, frozen and utterly immense emptiness. The Void. Cold, infinite and best left to itself. Space, both very dark and largely unexplored and presenting many mind-bending hazards and physical challenges.

However, genuinely stubborn species have challenged this titanic limitation, via the utilisation of global resources, creating massive space juggernauts, which launch the arcs of their genus into the staggering vastness. It's a hit or miss thing. Psycho-biological fungi, spreading their seed pores like plague across a forbidding absence. Admittedly, it would have a limited success in those immediate vicinities to the parent solar system. Which is relatively speaking, a mere backyard jaunt. The sheer scale of the problem is humbling.

The major impediment is the harsh fact of the critical reliance on material commodities. Thus creating a dependence-based culture which has no option other than to consume all needful resources until it tragically perishes in a nasty, greedy grab-fest. One which eventually will decimate all supplies in a terminal scenario. In short, they cannot escape their limitations and by such constraints are doomed to predicates set by their design. Such is the bitter destiny of physicality.

The Cosmos, that impersonal absolute, the enormity which both challenges and dismays, has a potential which is ever fond of the surprise. Many the advanced cynic has become clinically undone by the chance discovery of the technically impossible. Species variation and adaptation is a matter for genuine genius only. That being in limited supply, let us cut to the quick here and identify a race that managed to avoid the whole species self-extermination thing. A race that tried for several costly millennia many interplanetary impregnation methods. One that sailed their super-massive space freighters to the nearest score of stars. Some would encounter hostile indigenous life-forms, consequently triggering terrible wars and costly conflicts. The whole farm. Intelligence limits the contestants to a pitiful few that could transcend these serious matters. Those that get beyond the challenges. What would they be like?

Nothing like humans for starters. We have not even cured asthma yet, neither are we capable of living peacefully with the other apparently sentient beings in our own village. No. It takes a genuine science fiction imagination to visualise the race that has been there and done it. A race that sat down after aeons of effort and realised that thrusting masses of alloy into infinity was not going to cut the mustard. A species that had the fair fortune and good management to survive the travails of this long and lonely road. A culture weary with effort. A life form bored to its back-teeth with trying. A survivor class interstellar order. Yes. A challenger, a contender, a worry. The prime survivors.

They had a proper name a very, very long time ago. A nomenclature as regular as a postal address. A name, aeons before they tried and quit spacecraft-based exploration and expansion. A name, back when they were entirely physical forms. They have no name now, or of a sort we cannot recognise. In fact, there is little we can connect with these ancients, other than their laugh. Their LAUGH. The manner by which they express themselves and are collectively amused. A dry, echoing stuttering rot. The sound of antiquated hatred, staggering with perverted glee, assessing, utterly amused. The i… going on and on and on and on and on and on…

…i…i…i…i…i…i…i…i…i…

A sound only the unfortunate hears alone.

Real space is terribly bleak. No matter how long a dis-incarnate, non-manifest, sentient, thought-energy based entity can bumble through the inky vastness, eventually it will reach the stage where they will delight in the rich variety of simple amoebas on some far irradiated sphere. Or swoon over the scuttling stag horned beetle, ticking and rutting its biological program in the desert sands of some insignificant outer-rim world. After lots of nothingness, a paltry something appears interesting.

The unfathomable glee which results when a wide blue globe is found, and there is no dominant species. Where ocean-going mammals sing and map undersea contours ingeniously, but unobtrusively. Where once massive dinosaurs have evolved into generally harmless avians. Where the continents have done little but drift and crunch together slowly, interrupted only by the occasional impact of stellar debris. Such a sedate and potentially malleable planet could produce immense returns for a minimal investment. An opportunity not to be overlooked.

A world where there are no armies to spurn ones immigration efforts, and no methods of detecting ill-intent or time-honed mischievousness. A green and blue sphere of pleasant, simple, unhurried, evolutionary bliss. A perfect opportunity for a long-term plan of interference and acceleration. Such a place as this, our own dear sweet planet, our own world.

How odd it is, that the days in which we find ourselves, second only to the ridiculous, and the dangerously inane impact of religious war is the damnable horror of child sex abuse. It has never crossed a single liberal mind that our very earth has been contaminated. That the infancy of a carbon based, psycho-biological, bipedal mammalian life form has been interfered with in a manner, which has a resultant in every single vector of our consciousness being adulterated and defiled. That the very eyes that see and the soft, bone encased brain that receives those signals is contaminated with poisons, that it is wholly impure, radically and incontrovertibly changed.

Not a chance!

One bright spark proffered the adage that civilisation is measured by the distance we put between ourselves and our excrement. Push this foul-some but adroit envelope further and visualise a vision of culture, and therefore the individual, which values itself by the distance it puts between itself and that which it cannot neither accept nor perceive. Where the unknown neither exists nor is valid until empirically proven and gifts providential practicality. A tragedy of still-born creativity. A lost lot.

Cute little cut and thrust world, rife with sweetheart fatty tears and prominent painful pimples, deals and duties, a way and a wont. Sure is no place for a soul, this spinning testament to materialistic victory. Or if it is, they got places for that kind of thing. Churches and suchlike...

If the i.. get on your case then you need to see a priest. If you try and remove its occupancy by any other means than the genuine and most ardently sacred, the resultant psychic mess is so worrisome to behold, it will stagger the sceptical mind. Why a simple hearted and well-informed person of faith and not one of these pick and mix, New-Age types, it is genuinely not known? Yet it is common for the i... to ruin whole communities of people, entire friendship circles and social groups get frazzled. All blown apart, cast upon the desolate wind, never again to warm in fellowship and trust. Fried. For folk with a faith are regarded as a tainted food source and tend to be left well alone.

Yet consider the monkeys, and the sinister clowns.

The oddities, errata, that build up over the years,

The kind that is never satisfied till it has drunk a lake of tears,

The sort that wait and watch and plan and play upon your fears,

The wretched ones, the dangerous ones, the i... the i... the i...

CHAPTER THREE

Business as usual.

The human imagination has often adventured its optimal guess work upon those dimensions possibly inhabited by other forms of consciousness. Apparently articulating their speculations without reference or requirement for a deity. Yet what nature would these other beings possess? How would they be accounted for?

Any advanced, hyper-intelligent life-form would not let the cat out the bag during communication, translation and interaction with us. They would not show their frosty contempt for a species that finds it genuinely hard to be friendly over a longish period of time, or avoid impacting asteroids, or sleep properly, or live contentedly. They may pretend to befriend us, equally, they may well not.

The i …enter into the human dream-scape like a shark. A predator willing to chase you to the shallow end of the night. Theirs is an inconsolable hunger and they are looking for a key food. A particular configuration of human emotion and intellectual charge bound in the reasonless embrace of slumber. Why does our sleep matter? Well, that is simple, try existing without having any. Why do they view us as food? They just do, food and more crucially, as a form of regular entertainment.

This would be easier to narrate if some bright spark had invented the impossible "Dimension Goggles", which would permit all us light-spectrum bound, 3d limited humans to peek at the scary array of intersecting planes and levels that surround us, as we mess the sand-pit with the rest of our own dangerously avaricious species. Such an invention would not reassure our fears about the inhabitants of these other realms, how could it? Our curiosity will always take second place to the well-honed human survival instinct. We would not like what we saw and what is more, why should we?

Nearly seventy three percent of the physical "stuff" in the manifest cosmos is unaccounted for. This is given the wonderful title of Dark Energy and its accompanying Dark Matter. It is said to be everywhere and as yet remains undetectable. A dire medium. An enigmatic link between worlds so far apart, which needs no hulking spaceship thundering for generations into the frozen void. A lock which opens to a particular key. Call it anything but accountable, or user friendly, or safe. This impenetrable presence is a riddle, it is a clue, and it is also part of the answer for those who hanker after the bigger picture.

The i...

They know the secret doors, which open into any stronghold, fortress or palace. They know the shadowed alleys and narrow wynds with an intimate fondness. Preferring the old and derelict to the new schemes and estates, they watch as shepherds do upon their livelihood, upon us poor, vulnerable humans. Less than one hundred of their kind found our world, when our evolution had just moved out of the upright-ape stage. They were thrilled to find such malleable sport. Those timid, easily frightened homo sapiens with their sensitive, quizzical, intelligent eyes. The curled lips and the shrieking sounds they made when frightened. After so much deeply uninteresting travel, Earth was a jackpot.

Fast-forward almost a million years and those apes have grown fiercesome and powerful, but to the i… we are still little more than the monkey that we sprang from. Our warheads and rocket ships are amusing toys to them, compared to their own colossal achievements when once corporeal. Our science to them is genuinely quite rudimentary. Our penchant for causing misery is something they have taken a great pride in fostering and nurturing amongst us since their arrival. We are their pets, we are their food, and we are their entertainment. They have moulded us in our very history. Not in the great events or prominent persons of our turbulent past, but quietly, behind the scenes, slowly, skilfully and with fine-tuned attention to detail, they have played with us. All we regard as our strengths and securities they make light of, we cannot lock them out, or once they find us in some plight, we cannot remove them. They are our unwelcome, hostile guardian angels, more of a visiting devil, and many times have been called so. They thrive unseen and they operate virtually completely unhindered.

There is no talisman that can keep them at bay. There is no formula or incantation or solution to their sadistic manipulations. The one solitary thing they avoid is a person with genuine, heartfelt faith. Those deeply involved with their belief in a deity, those who love it and live it, these tend to be given wide berth. It reminds them of something they once had, but since becoming godlike themselves, they have long dismantled and buried aeons past. Faith. They don't like people with a real and ardent faith. Not because the work is harder or the problem more difficult to resolve. It is for them like being close to a contaminated food source. The soul of the faithful tends not to be full of fear, nor is it prone to anxiety. Still, though, that left an awful lot of humans for them to play with. The faithful could huddle in their small corner without ruining a single plan of the i…Most of the time.

When the i… originally arrived and began to interfere with the ape-man, they found to their enormous disappointment that they were not the only visitors to this vulnerable world, they were not alone, The

Lords had arrived in vast aeons previous and although few, they were avoided. The Lords was a term used oddly enough by both the i... and their source human nourishment.

They Who Rule, the Lords of Conflict and Change, found this world when enormous lizards roamed its bizarre and savage terrain. The Lords thrive in the moment of aggression, their obsession is the fight, and their delight, namely any living thing with fists, teeth, claws or weapons pitched in bitter, ruthless battle. The Lords possessed powers far more advanced than that of the i... for instance, they could multi-consciousness themselves and by such manifestation have direct physical effects upon the world. Thankfully, they were few, and oddly enough, becoming fewer.

Yet the i ...avoid the immediate battlefield. That plentiful harvest of human suffering is the realm of these other sentient, dimension-shifting entities. The Lords are on another, higher level of design, function and objective and they are all serious trouble. War is their patch. The i.. would be regarded as food to the Spirits of War. This does not demean them, or belittle them. Massed conflict is not their habitat. They are ancient enough to know their place and advanced enough to enjoy that position.

The i ...have frequented the periphery of misery which is the war zone. Visiting those who have been smitten by mere location and misfortune. Those who starve within a besieged city or those who slowly freeze and perish because shelter, supplies and will power have been wiped out, these may become nourishment to the i... As do the victims of plague and raging contagious infections, again, this is easy prey and offers a veritable banquet to the predatory alien.

Arthur's mother in the nursing home up the wooded Tyne valley was fated by quite particular genes to become one of those humans who had developed the ability to sense and see the alien entities that had fixed themselves upon our species. Describing them, without contradiction, in her many letters as being like glass, or semi-transparent. Yet the dynamic and vitality of their partial manifestation creating a form of such, with individual features and character. Equally, they have an essence not limited by the physical world or restricted by buildings or walls.

Whenever they were close, she would pray, her breath marking the frozen air. Always the same cold would announce their proximity. Bells would ring in her ears. The very memory of looking out of the window to see one, recalled the terror their appearance induced in her. The fear of a frightened mammal before a stalking predator, a cornered wee mouse before a cat.

In her disturbed sleep, Arthur's mother would see the monsters at work. As the i...went about their sadistic wind-up, the link that human DNA had promoted for our survival guided her dreams. Sadly, such moments of adaptation fit poorly upon any individual within a clumsy social species, and the fatigue brought about by so many virtually unendurable visions of horror had completely worn out her wits. The sedate retirement home with its peaceful old world order and civility could not manifest a more opposed pole when compared to the awful mischief of the i...

A balance, struck between the gentle calm of those scented gardens, bird-song full, and the malicious cruelty of these beings, these sadistic invaders.

The i...

An old lady dreams, and in this dream she is following the unearthly, glimmering shell of glass that is the enemy. It glides along, tall and menacing, down the narrow alleyway descending steeply down many flights of stone stairs. A winding way between the crowded buildings to the Tyne riverside, originating by the castle above. A chare, as they are locally known, an alley, by any recognisable term. She is cold but cannot draw away her awareness of the ghoul, or wake up.

She follows, and as she follows, by darkened arch and doorway, the devil thing pauses by the thick, cobbled window of an ancient Quayside pub. It was listening with senses honed and intelligence keen, seeking a particular scent. A unique set or configuration of emotions. It can predict that there will be a savage fight in this place later and that there could be some entertainment to be had.

A middle-aged couple emerges from another pub a few doors down, they are drunk and argue ferociously over some trivial slight. The i... smiles and drifts towards the pair. The dreamer knows the ghoul will make matters far worse for them than they already are, but is powerless to do anything about it, trapped in this dreaming state as she was. The scene is a normal everyday occurrence, but her awareness of the entity, which was now reading the couple like a book, creates awful expectation and an anxiety in her.

The staggering drunk woman totters away from the now shouting man, and screams so loud it echoes in the street, some folk nearby turn their heads briefly. The inebriate lady is weeping and cannot articulate her frustration and annoyance. When her red-faced husband tries to slap her, he misses and careens into the dirty wall, knocking himself out. The i...cowls over the fallen man like a carrion crow, leeching the unfortunate fellow of his essential vitality, even as he lies twitching on the worn pavement slabs. Drawing off the stuff of life whilst planting the seed of a perverse fear deep into the psyche. That is what these cruel things do, and do well, for they enjoy their work. As the drunk woman shrieks now with concern, the unseen, phantom vampire thing is laughing soft and low, gloating, feeding. The distressed lady is making too much noise to hear it. The dreaming old lady awakes.

The i...

Cold beings, product of an ancient species, older than our landmass, from far and deep into the frozen sea of night. Old beings, beyond the reckoning of us little, new humans, slipping in and out of our life and living space, only to leave tears and misery behind them. Calculating the degrees of their pleasure, they stalk us. Unseen by the mass of humanity, knowing us intimately and acutely unimpressed by those things we dearly hold to as giving our species value. They care not. They never will and they never have and likely cannot.

We frighten easily, partly as a result of that common blight which has dwelt amongst our race since the dawn of our kind. The interference and pestilence that is the i...They are the bogeyman, the midnight apparition, the ghost story repeated in a thousand languages. Dwelling anywhere they wish, hunting anyone they think wise prey, these other worldly demons walk amongst us. They don't rush, and they can see to the bottom of a lake of bullshit quick as a flash. From their contemptuous perspective, we are monkeys; stupid, gibbering playthings that they fully intend to utterly ruin by the time their boredom threshold is breached. They may be patient when compared to us, but they are not divine or spiritual. Not one bit.

In the millennium prior to the i... leaving their world, the science of cerebral, micro-magnetic and biometric fields had peaked and they could read the thoughts, emotions and physical feelings of any heat generating life form with ease. They knew the subtle frequencies by which they could influence the mechanics of the brain and central nervous system, through which they nudged and played their subject into extreme agitation and even madness. It became part of the assimilation of their science and knowledge as they opened the final door into dimensions, parallel yet utterly other than the materially bound continuum. It was a weapon they would not consider doing without. In their view, a mere bomb had no sense of humour.

They mapped not just the mind, but the biological substratum of thought and the emotional processes, monitoring the tiny fluctuations in electrical energy at a cellular level. The radiating body heat announcing to all, information that the transmitter cannot hear or see or feel. Eventually they could receive those pictures associated with thought, the things visualized within the mind of their quarry.

The i... could not just read the mind, but see the very things it was thinking.

When the time came for them to disperse into the greater universe, the gathering that found our planet had become as immortal god-forms, individual yet cohesive, capable of working alone or in groups, and they were most dreadfully efficient and took pride in their arts and skills.

Distributed over our globe, the i...could communicate at distance and by utilizing their familiarity with dimensionality, could appear almost at the command of a comrade. Any seriously poisoned food source within their stock had to be known, noted and observed at a safe distance. They had become comfortable here, and could avoid the other dominant alien parasite, that of The Lords, without difficulty. The Warrior Gods made an immense noise in the subtle resonant fields wherever they went. The i... could hear their booming, thunderous presence long before they arrived. The i... were quiet, very fond of the silence, the long drawn out icy absence of sound, especially in an old, miserable, run-down dirty place. Like 1960's-1970's Tyneside. An environment rich in potential and actual nourishment.

The soft sigh of our sorrow a music to them, the cruelty and ignorance of man, a source of immense and profound pleasure.

The i...

Watching from the shattered window of a ruined house, the alien predator regards the snoring derelict that had been his recent sustenance. Such as these were easy game, having obliterated any defences or resistance by the sheer amount of dubious alcohol consumed the previous night. The evil creature is icy still and motionless as it watches the Pipewellgate slowly awake to its morning activity. There is something it is looking for, someone who is generating potentially fruitful signals, someone ripe for the picking. It waits and watches. The drunk tries to cry out in his sleep, his choking rasp pitiful and bleak.

There is a core, a root to these things. At the intersections of subatomic planes, they have perpetual beacons. These can be moved and attenuated, the purpose being to maintain a link between the earthly interaction and their secret core, the centre of what sustains their consciousness. Humans posed no threats of detection as yet, the only danger associated with them lay in their ability to contaminate themselves as a nutrition source, by means of a particular series of virtues, all abhorrent to the i…

With resign the Geordies walk to their jobs, some heads hung low, tired before the day even begins. Wrapped in silence, under the shadow of the huge bridge, the i… reads the signals they emit with ease from a distance. Something radiated a particular form of fear the previous night, someone close in this area. Whilst feeding over the river on the ancient Newcastle side, something odd occurred, it had sensed that it was visible, somehow, someone was watching as it worked and this should not be so.

After the arguing middle age couple had provided the energy proportionate to expectations, the creature had returned to check on the raucous inn at the base of the steep, narrow stone stairs. The fear signal had increased and originated with a giant of a young man. A group of six around him was taunting and extracting maximum embarrassment and humiliation from the tall, muscular, but overweight youth.

The i… was not interested or listening to what they said, rather it sifted through the emotional content of each voice and then would establish its reaction and effect in the big fat lad. It did not take long to contact the enormous anger subdued by reason, will-power and self-doubt that the massive but cringing young dock hand was suppressing. The i... laughed quietly, nothing but a slight mutter in the noisy bar. This could be good entertainment.

The big fellow began to blush heavily and sweat uncomfortably. The i... had tapped into the substrates that maintained self control and reason. The boy may have been slow, but he was not stupid, the degree of resistance encountered surprised even the unseen observer. It was at that moment it heard the signal, a frequency rarely encountered, generated neither by i...or the noisy Lords, something so rare it had to concentrate and momentarily lost the link to the fat lad.

The i... engaged itself to remember, it was accessing the Overmind, or their data-base and history, seeking a positive correspondence, when the fight erupted...

The massive lad roared in anger as he lunged an enormous fist into the ring-leaders surprised face, which erupted with an instant spray of blood. The big mouth with the burst nose and lips sank at once to the dirty floor. Three of the five remaining drinkers jumped on the crimson-faced boy. He heavily smashed his elbow backwards and winded a guy who had tried to grab him from behind, simultaneously throwing off the other two with such ferocity they crashed into drink laden-tables. This evoked a loud and immediate response. A fight broke out. An old fashioned Geordie-land scrap where the big blokes pound each other witless with large calloused fists. The whole pub got in on it somehow. It had gone from an incident to an event. The fat kid had beat the noose and had no notion of his good fortune.

The distracting tone had thrown the i...A ripe situation had been completely lost because of it and as the creature scanned the drab humans, shuffling unwilling feet to work, he looked for that same signal. It had come from this bank of the Tyne, someone here was on the threshold of awareness about their ways and their means and could somehow detect them. The sign had a unusual correspondence, that is it had rarely occurred on Earth before this time, yet it was quite human in essence and origin.

A close reference, one similar to the signal was found. That of a species the i… had plagued and polluted in the first aeon of their non-corporeal state. A race that in time developed, through their complicated, evolving genetics, a faculty which made them capable of perceiving the i… First, they had been few and rare, but within three generations enough of this new mutation had created many who could actually receive an impression of their presence.

Initially, it had not been taken seriously. The i…regarded every lesser or backward species they found with unrepentant contempt and would not believe this new ability held any threat. They had become invulnerable, beyond both detection and attack. Only this once had they missed the implicit danger and being relatively new to their trans-stellar trade, they over-reacted. For the problem had become clear and manifest. The i… responded by directly targeting leaders and warlords amongst this capable species. Manipulating a series of disasters and costly conflicts which threw the distant world back into barbarism and primal savagery. The lesson remained one the i… would not repeat. If this incident was along similar lines a meeting would need to occur. A gathering of the i…Something unusual and surprising had happened and a consensus was required. Could these apes be waking up?

They cannot call, nor do they ever visit.

All of the warnings that could be warned,

Have fallen upon closed ears like unwanted rain.

In the millennia where we went it alone,

In the aeon where we cut loose from Deity.

In this special time where you are so cherished,

In this sewer of cheap excuses,

Each selfish sentiment.

Another turd blocking the drain.

They will not call, little remains for them here.

A ruin has limited attraction for a spirit.

Ruins that walk and speak and live awaiting life.

Places once bright with talking friends,

Wasted memories, cold upon these fallen stones.

In this do-it-yourself era of being so uniquely whole,

So fantastically up ones own arse.

Destiny perhaps? Or merely the inevitable?

Like the list of friends you let down.

They gather here not, neither are their thoughts towards us.

Ready made answers and unaccountability,

Have frozen the chances of mercy and grace.

In this nothing time, in our own invented time.

Wandering fatherless in a dangerous land,

Oblivious and uncaring, happy in our drunken dream.

Unable to see a child's smile or hold its little hand.

Rootless, disinherit, stricken by a poverty,

Deeper than bank balance or lifestyle.

They have forgotten us as we have forgotten them.

Our way has brought a conclusion at its heels.

The dogs are loose and hungry for the kill.

No boundary or fence or door shall stop them,

They shall devour you when least expecting it.

An answer to the question of preciousness,

Cowardice, treachery, heartlessness and lies.

Your throat ripped out in the living room,

Wouldn't that be ironic, blood splattering

The tasteless furnishings and tat.

The i...

The i...

CHAPTER FOUR

Trouble on Tyne.

The i...

Black shrouds of ancient dust rise from the wrecking ball as Pipewellgate falls, never to be the same again. Gone. Smashed to unhealthy piles of stained brick and sandstone and slate. Timbers lurch from battered roofs, the broken bones expose the chimney-stacks, busted, leaning, ready to fall from their own resignation. Very old slums by the 1960s, the tiredness of their structure was manifest in their willingness to collapse. Black dust, like spectres made form in the daylight, drifting under the High Level Bridge, spun in a rising spiral of heat, dissipating over the railway yard. Gone. Gone beyond repair or recovery. Gone away.

Arthur MacNeil watches the demolition crews work from a vantage-point on a high bank above the `Gate. All that remains to his eyes are a filthy row of small riverside industries and the police station. All the buildings were falling down. Small gangs of little kids sat carrion-like, waiting for the demolition crews to knock-off work, so they could get to those rooms only recently vacated, plunder to the urchins and young opportunists. So many years ago, so many days that seemed they would always be just the same. The end of a thing is no light matter. Only the stupid, the ruthless and the callous are inured to such themes.

From his threadbare, heavy overcoat he withdrew the bottle of whiskey, furtively glancing about him as he did so to ensure no one was watching. He took a long slug. That was for all those years living and working down there, and here was another one for the memory of his dear tormented mother. Glug-glug went the bottle as the yellow alcohol burned its soothing path inside him. It was not yet even half past eleven. It was going to be one of those days. One of those days walking those streets that somehow had memories tattooed upon them, a sense of being haunted whilst taking a ringside seat at the end of an era. How it had been could still be discerned in the cobblestones and tramway rails rusting under the passing cars and buses. It could be seen in the architecture, poised on the brink of mass demolition, dirt-stained and abandoned, forgotten in the rush to reach the modern and the new. Time passes. A decade of unremarkable alcoholism fleets by for Arthur MacNeil.

The young lads of the 1970's Tyneside troubled Arthur, they gave him a disconcerting feeling. The trend for growing hair long, way past the shoulders and the uni-sex fashions they sported threw out his traditional sense of gender and presentation. He was helpless and he knew it. The world had jumped forward into unknown and bewildering times, leaving him ill at ease with this transition. He longed for the sureties and securities of an era now falling into dust and demolition bonfires. The shattered stones and broken bricks, raised in heaps higher than any that the German bombers had managed to achieve. The local council seemed determined to obliterate the past. Whilst Arthur simply drank in order to forget it all.

By the late 1970's, Arthur found himself living at a Salvation Army homeless hostel. His luck and his money had all run out. In the tiny cupboard by the single bed in his minuscule room, a shoe box stuffed full of letters waited for him. His habit was to sit on the worn stone stairs above Pipewellgate, just to drink, gaze down and remember how it was. Now the hillside was a weed rank tangle, with only small sections of walling and shattered foundations peeking through. When the bottle was finished he would return to that pitiful, shabby room and read his mother's correspondence until tiredness overcame him, and he would sleep for a while. The dreamless sleep of an alcohol assisted rest. A fitting respite for a weary soul.

The presence of the old and dirty Tyneside was being forcibly removed. In the cleared zones, the rising reinforced-concrete constructions and pre-fabricated units were gradually emerging, almost as science fiction made manifest. The pristine light grey and the modernist lines of these brave, futuristic dwellings stood in distinct contrast to the remaining slum areas about them. A statement, a comment, a declaration of the new vision heralding a bright utopian future. Forged in the minds of very clever town planners and ardently optimistic architects, these estates and schemes would soon come to dominate the hillsides either side of the dirty auld river. A bright new tomorrow for all!

Where once Roman legions had built their fortifications. Where ancient Britons had fished in the Tyne and hunted game in the rich, deep verdant forests. Where history had played out many changes of hand, and humanity, gullible and fatalistic, now regarded the worn out cards with resignation and a sense of utter powerlessness. There was nothing unique about Arthur MacNeil, he was one of many. Played and branded like stock, seemingly disregarded in the progress of the time.

To the i... the passing centuries, which change the appearance and character of Britain, seemed akin to an ants nest. The aliens possessed inordinately long memories, connecting families and bloodlines throughout the ages and changes, actually taking an interest in particular strains and adaptations of the human ant. Certain types provided a richer yield in entertainment value to the monitoring i...

Remember, they are bored in essence, and distraction is a key method of dealing with the ennui of the consciousness.

To the i...the ruins and architectural traces that litter Britain are enduring testimonies to those links they have made with this ancient island. The jutting stone teeth of a crumbling castle, swamped by the sea of a forest, all plantation pines and larches, lying many miles from a decent single-track road. A place perhaps visited by ardent hill-walkers and die-hard historians, but an unremarkable grave. Battered by over eight hundred years of rain and blinding winters, its shell remains. The weeds and shrubs had almost overtaken it, the bramble-tangled core within is silent. The ruin cannot speak of the past, if it could what would it say?

A cruel fight had fallen here, a sideshow in a major battle in a national war, yet it had missed a lasting mention in the important history books and currently accepted story lines. Principally because both sides in the fight here almost completely wiped each other out. The wounded limped away and the whole scene smouldered for days with only the wing-beats and quarrel of carrion to set motions and sounds upon the slaughter. Too few survived to bury their dead. They lay where they fell and gave sustenance to crow and fox and rat. A dismal scene and situation. Such were the times. Such is real history.

The ruin had once figured in the machinations of The Lords, the other, older, non-manifest sentience which also have found home upon this rich, delightful sphere. This crumbling tower had represented a particular subtlety in an argument of battle, in which the Lords of War found complete preoccupation. The theory and practice, concepts and technology of conflict was their entirety. The Lords had evolved from an entirely military culture. Survival therefore being a rare thing, due to their inherit destructive qualities, yet in time they had attained deep familiarity with quantum energy physics. As had the i...but The Lords attained this critical juncture wholly through military science and a consumerist society that decimated realms of worlds before a shot was even fired. Whole planetary systems lay dead and burnt-out in their wake. Bastards.

Humans saw or sensed ghosts wherever The Lords had argued amongst themselves loudly. Here was such a place. Rarely visited, largely forgotten and most remote, the silica and mica atoms in the stone and soil resonating ferociously with the very memory of the presence of The Lords. This and the unwritten drama of a courageous defence and a bloody fall.

Yet The Lords had been few when they arrived, thrown into the void by their superiors, set to drift between the stars for age upon age upon age. Their remit had been to explore and eventually report back to the home-world, but this had been long forgotten, as the constant in-fighting and divisions became the entire rational and dominant motivation.

It was a perfect meeting point for a council of the i…

The northern night draws tight and dark, horizon wide, the pines are still and hushed. A coldness grows in the tower, beginning in its vaulted cellar, increasing to fill the collapsed hall above. The roosting birds and tiny mammals leave their nests and sheltered burrows. The i…had arrived. Forms slowly manifested in the cellar, a concentration of darkness deeper than gloom, so intense, a figure is revealed. Some sit upon piles of stone, others stand alone or in close groups. They share one thought, it passes from mind to mind, important information. Yet in our very language, the first audible voice says, (for speech retains some interest to them.)

'The Lords are dying…Only eleven remain…They will destroy themselves, and in so doing will ruin our investment.' The words are crisp, a hushed even tone.

'We inherit the joys of insects and grass!' another voice hisses with a savage, undisguised resentment.

'It is non determinate.' A third solemn, authoritarian tone announces factually and heavily.

After a pause, the hateful hissing voice barely contains its savage contempt,

'So, do we wait for the insects and the grass to evolve?'

'We could move on?' A fourth voice suggests, low and unassertive.

'Drift upon the winds of space..' A triad of i… chant in unison,

'.. Down ages stream the endless fields of stars.'

They remember the long epochs of utter boredom, merely sailing into the blank unknown. They remember the worlds they had abandoned, their stepping stones in space and time. They compare, as is their way, the collective assessment of their journey so far.

'This species has vitality yet, it has not uncoiled its genetic pattern'

'…Could be interesting…'A breath of ice speaks, a frozen fear made audible.

'…Could be to our gain...'

The i…laugh.

They laugh out loud, and knowing intimately one communal mind, they emanate a chorus of echoing music between themselves and then release it into the night. It is a real sound, but an awful song of contempt, a psychic wave and an inhuman humour. They like to gather, plan, and laugh…not because anything is funny…simply because it is a pleasure to their company and a warning to any life form within audibility. The i...ancient as ages and inherently territorial, to hear their laughter is to know the vice grip of terror. Tremors nocturnes. Nightmares beyond belief.

Arthur curls up upon the Salvation Army Hostel bedding in the narrow little room. Dust motes float in the weak yellow street light that finds a way through the dirty window. Outside, the town is silent, nothing stirs. No trains are passing or due. An hours pause in the constant beat and pulse of movement. The quietest time, and in the weight of that sheer silence, Arthur is wide awake, now dressed fully and shivering lightly, like a small scared animal.

He knew what he was hearing. His mother's descriptions had long prepared him for this moment. They were very far away, but in old Gateshead's unusual quiet as those early hours passed, he could hear them. At first it seemed remote, as the beat of music heard from afar. Then, as the song grew, Arthur could identify sequences and patterns, this froze his blood. Eventually it seemed to fill the air of the little room. He curled up, a frightened child needing his mother's comfort. There would be no such solace, even if by some miracle his mother could have held him there, she above all folk could bring no peace. She would know what was going on, and she would be terrified. The i... were laughing.

A wood-worm slow fall of deep resonant vowels, i... (as in ink or drink). The i...creating sub-echoes from its base consecutively, which collide or combine, filling the audible range with sub-tones of sinister laughter. In the dark and in such black velvet silence, it has a most unnerving effect upon the human mammal. If it could be heard, then they were close by and the listener was in serious trouble.

An early morning train rattled into the northern dawn and the spell of fear faded. As the sounds of a city coming to life grew gradually, the laughter of the i...slowly decreased. The passing traffic became a most comfortable, reassuring sound and Arthur slept. As he did so he dreamt he was back at home on Whickham Hill with his mother, watching the Tyneside docklands and warehouses burn. The twitching column of fire from the gasworks leaped, his eyes stared, fascinated.

In his dream they watched, and it seemed to go on for much longer than it had originally. Arthur realised this was because he did not wish for the dream to end, he was with his mother again and he was happy. The glow of memories fondness and root. The comfort of a loved ones presence. He woke crying at around nine thirty, there was a knocking at his door. Another day had begun.

'Mr MacNeil, it's me, the cleaner. Let me in please, you are the last room to do!'

A young lad with his greasy dark hair tied back in a ponytail was standing impatiently as Arthur opened his door. Their eyes did not meet as he quickly entered, the smell of pine from the mop bucket was quite pronounced as the young man passed the old fellow in wrinkled clothing. Arthur sat as the lad swept and mopped the floor then emptied the steel waste-paper basket. Yellowed fingers rolled a cigarette and jaundiced eyes failed to understand why a young man should have a girl's haircut. The night had been frightful, the deep draw of tobacco soothed him, and he began to count the minutes until the boy departed and his whiskey appeared.

The wet floor dried slowly in the pale morning sun. The open window, the movements of the dusty lace curtain, the coils of smoke drifting to the ceiling, and an old man supping a small glass of whiskey. He wondered with whom he could speak about what had happened and whether or not it could have been a dream, a delirious state, something he ate perhaps? Or too much booze?

By his second glass he was deeply buried into the scrawl of his mother's letters, this time reading not out of nostalgia or sympathetic puzzlement, but as a potential believer. So very late in the day for him to realise that she was not mad. Or if she was, then also so he was himself. He searched for a name, a friend and confidant of his mother. A visiting priest. It was there somewhere in the sheaths of mildewed age.

In the daylight of late 1970s Tyneside, the visiting eye would note the spread of new constructions and building work. Most of the slums were gone and their inhabitants relocated. This would produce more problems than any professional body could have predicted, and the bright new future landscapes of hopeful concrete efficiency became crime-infested twilight zones. They concentrated societies forgotten non-entities like an outbreak of pustules and sores. The future had kicked them all in the balls.

Gangs of evil boot boys roamed their territorial streets and districts, pounding senseless anyone who crossed them or got in their way. The rain of heavy footwear thudding into a human head and body, saturating the victim with blind, insensate hate, intentional violence and a twisted northern humour. The savagery of their actions, inconsiderate ignorami that they were in the main, provided these boot boy gangs with something to be proud of. Enough so for their exploits to be graffiti upon walls and public spaces. Territorial markings and warnings of intent and ability.

"DEKKA KILLS!",

Bright red upon an ancient stone wall. A tiny fragment of the old world that had been safe for a while. On a section of hillside where once a walled nunnery had nested between the spread of new streets. On part of the old boundary wall, there it was in brilliant, blood-red paint. It still glistened, waiting to dry. It could be seen from the top deck of passing buses. A significant motif for a turbulent period of time.

From this newly adorned place, red gloss graffiti declaring its glory to the shoddy Geordie World, the view was interesting. Looking north and west, up the River Tyne, a great spread of the Tyneside conurbation could be seen, even to the point where concrete met greenery, and fields and woodlands began. The river lay flat and glistening, a poisonous slick of two centuries worth of effluent and waste, a quicksilver flow under a cold and comfort-less sun.

On those rare clear days, distant moorland could be glimpsed. A dark green, far-away, brooding under stacks of summer cloud. A scene that summed things up, celebrating the changes and state of human life in Northern Britain. It was never painted. It may have been photographed by chance.

The red paint spoke of a truth in intention and actuality. Four days previous, on a Friday night, a beer-fuelled fight took place between two small groups of rival gang members. Three lads were hospitalized and one completely innocent passer-by was beaten so badly he suffered brain damage and for a few hours gave real concern to attending ambulance crew and later, the worried hospital staff. He would be afraid to go outdoors for the rest of his life, and would receive psychiatric counselling, and also be considered for medication. Although given frequent and positive encouragement to venture out, he never did. The poor man would be held in the grip of fear for the rest of his days. The i...had their sport in this. Nothing more sure. For one stood in this very spot and smiled as it considered its next appointment.

The i...

When the door knocks and there is no-one there. When the winter wind carries voices crying for redemption that will never, ever arrive. Cold in the hail and the vilest of winds. When all is a long memory of decay and corroding, nothing other absolutely, than a nihilists solemnest toast. The odds of it. The chance of misery stacked on poverty bound by chains. Civilization and all its congruent merits arrayed, for fair and foul. Sixty million needy pairs of hands, here alone, here, alone.

When the footsteps behind you are the last you ever hear. In the darkest place, in the shadows of fear, you are abandoned. With no mates to stand by you and no sheltered bay amidst life's storm, where one gets dry and can get warm. The very drain pipes gurgling with laughter, gravity and matter colluding. A broken underground public toilet, where the lights slowly dim from dull yellow to flickering red strobe. Busted pipes hiss and make slippery the littered, shit covered floor. In the dark, trying the feet further onwards, moving the steps down into the shuffling, stinking absence, what is there? Who is there?

What feeds on such forms of fear?

Nevertheless, the alien has a specific interest in the remote, the lonely and the inconsequential sorts of humanity. A place where they can amplify distress alarmingly and avoid detection. They see it as fattening their livestock. For they do not desire ever to be detected.

The memory of the i …endures the centuries with ease and cunning. They are connoisseurs of a selective nature and are not happy when their handiwork is interrupted. Few life-forms are inwardly content when their meal is broken, the more feral initiating the response of violence. And food takes many forms.

To dream of oneself crying is to find a part of oneself dying.

When the rain began. In the race of man. Running to nowhere, running afraid. Striving to make, to mend, to mar. Even the lowest have their scars, of coming through grief and bother. Of breaching the dark-time and crossing the Great Wasteland, and going to hell for a heavenly cause. Just like the song says, an impossible dream.

In the rain, if one were born unlucky and unfortunately placed, in the rain, as it falls, they may see something other. If such mischance made vision, it would determine the silhouette of a man with a lightly glimmering skin. Of blue moonlight upon water seen from the vantage point of deepest shadow and darkness. No form, just presence. No physical body, only threat.

The pig is fat, but it is not my field.

The tools are rusting in the workshops, a nation somehow inflates itself on vacuity. The fatter the better, the sooner it's yours. Verbatim. Crap food, fast track, fish-hook work drawling out the slavering facts of human degradation and tedium. Fast car, half-wit, uninformed young twit's misery in the moment of their crashing ruin. Some draw it out, by calculation, over years. Some talk around it, until it disappears. The vertiginous relationship between life and death. Without sarcasm, it is a profound matter, the irony in the obvious, the tragedy in the unseen. The sense of being watched is quite irrational, occasionally accompanied by strong urges to busy away at anything other than the laughing silence.

When the revolution comes, I genuinely hope it is wearing a condom.

Species. Humans. Fascinating. Irrevocably and demonstrably so. The fact of it now. A world fit to bust. A fatty daydream turned serious. The grim irredeemable monstrosity of selfishness and indiscipline made prominent in the populations eating habits. It is almost as if, confronted by impending peril, the humans gorge themselves in a gross ritual of mass indulgence. Eat before you fry, or fry before you eat? It is abhorrent and slack arsed and unwise. It is also understandable. Poor humanity.

If anyone has as much as sniffed the i...or merely dreamed of one as it passed in the night, or simply glimpsed a movement in a dark place. A tendril of its presence will be barbed within the unconscious of that soul, for years. For reckless, pointless, unguided years of being afraid. Justifiably so.

CHAPTER FIVE

Far remembered hills.

1938. Arthur is twenty and newly qualified as a technical draughtsman when he secures his first job with a major Tyneside shipbuilder, in the drawing office. Tensions in Europe were mounting as Germany muscled its way into a scrap the world would never forget. Yet upon Whickham Hill it was still 1920, Birds sang and bees hummed in the hedgerows, pit-wheels continued to turn under an ever changing northern sky. Coal spilled from the mines and far down the valley industry thrived, but where Arthur lived it was bordering on rural Northumberland.

Readying on a summer morning for the early bus, a herd of Friesian cows a quarter of a mile distant could be seen from the kitchen window. They resembled a surreal black and white jigsaw puzzle. Arthur remembered his mother's encouragement.

"Are you looking forward to this job?" she had asked.

Arthur had combed his unruly mop, realizing he needed a haircut, and thought about his looming future, before he could answer she continued,

"A draughtsman is a good career you know. You will do well for yourself."

She was stating the obvious, conversationally, he assented, and regarded the moving jigsaw against the distant verdant green field.

"Aye Ma`" he had replied casually "I know I am really very lucky."

Yet it wasn't just luck, he had proven very skilled at all technical drawing, his work was exceptional and his grades at college could not have been better. Arthur had earned this break, he remembered that particular feeling of being on top of the world.

Shame it had not lasted for very long.

The i...

Solemnly the processions of Fall betide a faultless inevitable. When the sureties of youth and fervour dim and fade. In another place. In the uncertain glance, the lacunae, the bits we miss. Travelling through, easy like. No-one wants to hurt or intimidate anybody. Everybody knows this is how it goes in the civilized forms of social interaction. The idea of ghosts and such is peculiar or quaint. All the bits we miss. Ite misse est. When it really is finished. When it is time for the oil on the forehead. When we become the ghosts.

The river flows, the culture that swarms its banks seethe and diminish, flourishing and then decaying like bacteria. People, their ages and times falling like leaves from the autumn trees of years. The sorry end of little days and tiny consequences. A flickering lantern to the moth of the i...The watching eye of alien intent. That fearful spur of human evolution, our long familiar bane. Our shepherds, our tormentors, our assessors, our demons. The i...

The thrum of many running boots in a dark place. The sounds of rasping and grasping and boots. Then the yelps and snarls of brutal conflict. Down dingy cobbled dog shit streets, in Northern England's lost and fallen industrial grandeur. In the 1970s skinhead gangs ran rampant. Territorial and outright aggressive, they prowled and stalked and louted about. Prime examples of a terminally savage, predatory violence. In the Wasteland of the Heart, the buildings are falling down, crashing physical memory into dust and rubble. The wolves gather, sly eyes and hungry faces. Edgy. Dodgy. Watch yourself pilgrim.

Kid, kicked to a pulp. Cars pass, boots thud, groans and unheard cries echo in the darkness. Boots, running, into the night. The town is being slowly demolished, the people are grey and burnt out. The youth is vile and unpredictable. Time passes. The memory of the thudding running boots, the thumping thwack of boots. In the dark, in a half-light. Where blood is black, and warm and sticky. Gas lamp and flyover, Dickens meets Beirut. Tragedy, poverty and the inevitable violence. Wounds. Scars. Losses. A bleak cloud of impoverished cultural hatred.

Time will sort it out. That, and the cleverness of a race of bureaucrats capable of talking anything up. Ancient buildings falling down. Ancient river, silver in the moonlight, a poisonous mercury, a quicksilver sliding away to a glutinous shining sea. The constant is the river, permanent and indicative of the health of its inhabitants. Sloshing along, leaving a twenty-two mile slick of petroleum distillate on both banks that throbbed and stank in the dim northern sun. Little kids sometimes played in the black river mud. Some of them even laughed. We are a most strange species.

The perennial cruelty of human lack. That rampant bitter weed infesting our decency. The voice in the dark place. Alone… Where night finds every breath and shiver, real as a car crash, hard as nails. The dark. Alone… Where anyone can be vulnerable, where anything can occur out of the glare of a street lamp, in the shadowed place where you should not have charged ahead. The memory of the echo of boots, the recollections of pain. Half heard and almost noticed, the low muttering laugh of a background observer. The prone body is losing consciousness and hears this stuttering laugh, he has to let it go. His body is recoiling from the shock of brutality. His mind is taking a sleep. Boots. Kicking at the body. Boots. Some thing or someone is laughing nearby. Something sick. Boots.

Memories

The past is gone, it is finished. Only echoes remain stubbornly clinging to a place, or a memory attached to a place. As though by holding on to a physical location, there would be a chance for it to re-occur. Like faded old photographs, tinted by time and emotions, coloured with gladness and sorrow, they endure.

Arthur remembered her, his first love. Her much washed and mended cotton print dress of fading pale flowers tight upon a young, healthy body. A wholesome smile and a country girl way about her, and a warm embrace. The memory of sunlight through summer oak leaves and blue kindly eyes. Her slender sun-tanned arms and legs, her hair lightened by sunshine to a pale straw colour, her attractive bearing. So long ago, so far away in those green remembered hills.

It was 1936 and Arthur had a farm labourer job during his college summer break. High on the Cheviots, right up in rural Northern Northumberland. He had noticed her as he worked, whilst the weeks passed, often on her horse or attending to tasks such as milking or gathering the hen and duck eggs. It was when they had been shoveling barley from a tractor trailer to a dry wooden loft above a barn, then for the first time, he had met her. Most of the day they had simply worked, Arthur, the girl and her two big strong brothers. When they had finished they sat back upon the yielding mound of barley and drank pale ale, the aroma sweet and earthy. One brother sat by the open loft door, smoking a hand-rolled cigarette. Sunbeams slanted throughout the dusty barn. Long ago and far away.

Arthur was 18 and clueless, enjoying the light beer with the barley behind him conforming to his weight and shape as he reclined. One arm was sank deep into the fragrant mound, in that moment, in that instant it begun. Her hand found his. She was sitting right next to him and she touched his hand, right in the very same room as her brothers. Arthur turned with surprise and looked directly at her and she smiled at him. A lovely face, full red lips, a freckled brow and bird's egg blue eyes. She had smiled at him and inside himself Arthur glowed with astonishment and joy. It had all began with that hidden hand contact under the mound of barley.

As those long summer days dawdled by, rolling slowly along, they took walks together after the work was done for the day. They watched lovely sunsets, talking much, until the first stars peeked down. Her name was Eleanor and she had spent her entire life on the hill farm, her school having been in the nearby small country town of Rothbury, her family church in Netherton. Tyneside to her had an allure, a distinct attraction, one which she also held for young Arthur MacNeil, despite his unflattering descriptions of its terraced sprawl and riverside squalor, she remained enamoured of the city and of himself. An easy thing to do from afar.

It had never crossed Arthur's mind that romantic love could ever happen to him. When it did, he was uselessly swept along by it all. The lingering kisses, the straightforward embrace that became gradually and increasingly arousing. They explored that strange and ever changing realm of desire over the remaining weeks, eventually to become lovers.

An old shepherds hut lay high on the moorland, a primitive dwelling, its door closed shut with a short length of rope and a latch. Within it was sparse, smelling of damp and mildew. They had taken leave for a night together, ostensibly to go on a longer, final walk and to camp out. She had sat upon the ancient spring mattress in the lamp light and reached her hand to him. He took it and quickly they were a tangle on the uneven bed, kissing with passion, deeper than friendship, firmer than comfort, sweeter than wine.

Love, in it's most simple expression, a merging together in soft moans and whispers. So utterly personal, fondling there, clothes disarrayed, wrapped in each other, bound in affection. Just love, but Arthur's first and every detail of it was etched upon his soul for the rest of his days. The sweet intimacy, near as breathe, warm as summer sunshine, a secret island in the river of time. All those days of youth now spent, all the gestures, words and feelings, those eternal themes. Perhaps the only ones worth keeping warm and alive in the archive of memory, those initial lessons in sexual love. Bequeathing a presence so gentle, the kindest sort of memories. Manifesting quietly within the ageing man. Arthur MacNeil is older, but still sentient, his body has aged but his mind is vigilant. Hungry. Yesteryear arises in his morning mind...

A river high on the Borderland moors, where Northumberland meets Scotland without formal notification or event. A continuity of hills and valleys. The memory of summer trees, fresh green leaves and warm light return to him. He recalls his love from long ago. Her bare feet on the smooth river stones. Her hair as light in colour as straw. A much-mended dress of old cotton over a slender frame. The haunting picture clear down the miles of memory. More than a recollection, a presence. The very simple fact that once it was all real. The stones have dried in many a summer sunshine since. Smooth river rocks touched by her wet bare feet, the warm light pouring down.

When she smiled at him, the world was briefly kinder. When she held him close, the scent and physical proximity of her young body completely intoxicated him, conquered him. He was in love and she knew it. Worshipped, his living idol, a manifestation of sweet human femininity. She enjoyed it all too and had gladly returned his youthful ardour and affection.

All those years of summers gone. All the tender kisses and idle hours. The heart beating heavy with desire, the eyes looking on, looking on. Gazing into the unexplored universe of love.

Time is not kind. The young and the beautiful have a brief tenancy. The lure of their glamour is a transient one, their loveliness merely a short but pleasurable summer season. Blessed love and aching longing, throbbing its hormonal madness into a firmness demanding redress, seeking realization in a world destined to dry them out. In time, like the peat fire, it slowly smoulders and dies. Tomorrow belongs to a cold morning. Where was she now? The only tender respite in all his days. The very memory of her laughter like a weight of lead between his ribs.

Arthur poured himself another drink. When his mother died, the undertaker refused to allow him one final look...Deceptively, he had led a troubled life. His poor mother. When she died, her face had frozen into a mask of unutterable fear. As she had slowly perished, her heart refusing to take any more nightmare, terror and madness, she had feebly scratched on the wallpaper above her bed a single letter of the alphabet, repeated, until her fingernails broke, and she finally perished. One letter, frantically scored into the paper.

i...i... i...i...i...i...

The booze took Arthur far away. Away from the tragedy of his poor tortured mother. It inured him from the memory of the ghost of a farmer's daughter he had loved as a youth. Now, the Pipewellgate was gone and demolition was rendering the south bank of the Tyne unrecognisable. A joke he had overheard in one of the pubs before it was destroyed was that the council had an easy job; they would just have to knock one house down at the top of the hill and the whole place would fall over like a domino row. The dirty old shit-hole was going away forever. Gaps were appearing in rows of blackened buildings. Fireplaces, cupboards, doors, wallpaper and gas mantles were bared to the gaze of the passer by. The era had ended, its privacy and common mundanity laid bare. It is rare for the old to have dignity in death. History was closing a chapter, and Arthur was a relic, a leftover remnant of a polite and more formal age.

As he slept in the dingy hostel, he dreamt of his first love, his only true girlfriend. He searched for her hand, whimpering in the cold northern night. It seemed to him just out of grasp. He tried to listen to her words, but the wind took all their sense and blew them away. He strained, sobbing as he slept, choked with the poisoned emotions of loves unfinished business, of something good that never grew, never thrived. In the dream she was always a little way ahead of him, bare feet on short sheep cropped grass. Her thin, cotton summer dress clinging to her litheness as a light wind stirred her pale hair, and then she was gone. She was gone. He woke sixty years of age, stinking of stale alcohol, crying, shaking, thoroughly and utterly lost to himself.

Asleep, drowning in the fear of a vivid nightmare, Arthur struggled desperately and frantically to awake. His besieged sentience being but weakly defended, he was losing. With his will fired on the fuel of terror, the dream engulfed him, each extended, horrible vision pushing him deeper and inexorably into the next. Successively, worsening seizures shook him. He was drowning in this state, and as he sank, the i…played him and found his efforts hilarious. Arthur descended into paralysis, his voice could not form a cry, nor could his hands reach out for a candle. He realised that within this torment he might perish.

His mother had often written and spoken about the power of prayer. Like many of his generation, Arthur considered himself agnostic in outlook. The immense evils of a recent world war and the stupidity of the previous one, which had taken his father from him, these had not warmed him to the concept of a compassionate deity. Yet he had lived a moral life from rational choice and had sacrificed much for his troubled mother. He had been a good and loving son.

As he sank, the light of consciousness was diminishing, shrinking to a small bright circle far above him, out of reach. Arthur formed the words in his mind,

'Please God help me!'

The distance grew between the dot of light and himself, and the darkness congealed about him. It began to freeze the warmth of his awareness into a single frozen protracted state of abject terror. He could hear the laughter.

i...i...i...i...i...i...

At the point of complete blackout, like a cork released from deep under water, he shot back to the surface of awakening. The room appeared completely normal. With a cry of alarm he lurched out of his bed, covered in sweat, his heart pounding madly. He knew without doubt in that moment that his mother had not been mentally ill. She had been a victim. He realized, in no uncertain terms, that some form of predator lived amongst our species and made most cruel sport of their advantages over our human nature. His mother had called them the i...after the way she heard them laugh. They were real. They were not the product of a mind in malfunction, they were very real indeed.

With trembling hands, he poured a glass of strong rum. He gulped it down too fast and coughed and spluttered, hacking as it burned its way into him. Pussers Rum, potent stuff. He also realised he had prayed to escape the torment. Reality seemed frail, a temporary structure in which humans invested permanence without any firm guarantee of returns. A faded, shoddy frame, which formed the view we choose to look upon. It was not enough for Arthur any longer. He had called upon a God that he did not believe in when the horror had become dangerously unendurable. He decided he would visit a priest. That very day.

It was still three hours until the hostel served the meagre breakfast in the dining room below. He was so shaken by his experience, he dressed with absent-minded clumsiness, dropping items, unfocused and shaking. He decided he would take a long walk in the hope that it would calm him. Arthur took another measure of rum, this time with less panic, and filled his pewter hip flask. It would be a long and thoughtful day. He felt as though he had been utterly laid bare, that his inward thoughts had been read like a book and discarded as his deepest fears manifested for the amusement of some unimaginably powerful fiend. He tried hard to avoid the term demon. This conjured images from his strict Roman Catholic childhood, where dark threats and implied torments aided the processes of conformity.

There was no such thing as demons, he reminded himself as he fought to find the worn out northern streets reassuring. The rows of industrially blackened terraced houses, the run-down architecture of a once glorious era brought no solace whatsoever. Men, on their way to work looked drab and sad. Some would glare at him as he loped along at a furious pace. He looked to them like a criminal. A fugitive escaping with the law in pursuit. A man with a mission. A man being hunted. For so he was, so he was.

The i...

Peripatetic notions of health and optimistic solutions will not wash. The species that have found our race and played our entire history to their plan are not like us. When humans get fixed on a destructive vector, they make or invent weapons and destroy each other. They validate and talk-up the necessity of creating these weapons with stirring, incisive verbiage, but it all resolves itself in the factual proof of human suffering. Obviating the fact that the common resultant is the dominant principle, namely loss and pain. The weapons are made by warmongers and hateful wasters who deceive and mislead until enough human life is lost and they are finally seen for what they are. Generally too late in the day at that, more is the pity. Death is the end game and the entire mission objective whether the medium shines or not.

Their time is on watch, their era is closing. Eventually the worship of death and the delight in the means of actual demise will slowly close. As the species gradually awakes to the fact that weapons are actually really sad, genuinely redundant, distinctly pointless baubles of man's inherent sickness and lack. For weapons are not symbols, they are weapons. The application of war is the reality of suffering and death. Talking the manufacture of weapons up until the gullible either placidly accept or tacitly consign themselves to the rhetoric of fools, this is the Art of War. This is the bane of our race and our era. Even the Buddha warned us about such folly in the Noble Eightfold Path.

Where are the original thinkers who can shoot this odious warmongering bullshit down with swift and accurate terminology? Why are we still being enthralled by the pointless validations of these morons who have made bigger idiots of their imbecilic audience? A weapon is not a symbol. It bears repeating that it is the extension of a violent and redolent soul. It is illness and disease and foul-some gratuitous error. It matters not how well made it is. Any who think otherwise are in dire need of therapy. The capacity for human self-deception is actually frighteningly vast, it is nothing short of remarkable.

The i...

Have weapons that read the very pictures in the thoughts of warm-blooded mammals, even more than that, they know the true emotional charge behind each thought and the degree of manipulation possible in the subject, their prey, their quarry. They cannot be deceived by a junior species, they are far beyond our predictions and expectations. We have not developed far enough. We have no possession of the intrinsic realities that steer our own race and its desires. We are as ants to the aliens that have made themselves our demonic tormentors. We are their fun, their empty pleasure, their study and the object of contemptuous observation and of course, their constant entertainment.

Arthur hesitates outside the Catholic Church he had occasionally attended as a youth when in town with his mother. It had not really changed at all. An air of early Spring weariness hangs upon the clusters of dead flowers in the Marian grotto by the dark stained, double doors of the church entrance. His doubts swarmed his decision and rendered his early thoughts adumbrated. He paced back and forwards between the doors and the grotto, his brow creased, his shoulders hunched-up against the cold.

A black-clad figure emerged from the church. Arthur was startled and almost collided with the priest. The unexpected arrival caused Arthur to stutter slightly, clearly un-confident and obviously distressed, he gradually had made it known that he wanted to take confession. On familiar ground, the priest ushered him into the gloomy interior of the dark wood and stone church. Statues watched from the alcoves, the faint scent of incense clung to the chilly air.

'Bless me, Father, for I have sinned. It has been forty-five years since my last confession, my sins are many and odious to God.'…

Arthur began a pre-considered list of his many failings, none of them particularly major or outstanding, but it was a language he had understood once, and wanted or needed to understand again. He noticed within himself the reluctance to admit his dependence on alcohol. Even so, he mentioned it, realizing he may as well go the whole way. He had nothing at all to lose and was desperately in need of any kind of spiritual assistance or advice.

The priest listened quietly from behind the latticed grill separating himself from Arthur, who waited nervously for a word, a reply to his litany of errors and failings.

'Is there anything else you need to confess?' the priest inquired gently after the pause.

'Aye Father, I have heard the laughter of demons, as my mother did before me.'

There was a long pause and a sharp intake of breath before the priest spoke again in question.

'What makes you sure this laughter is demonic?' The man of God asked cautiously.

'It drove my mother to sickness and eventually killed her, the stress in time stopped her heart. When it draws close to me, I freeze completely, the fear is too great to bear. I cannot move, I can hardly even think...It is horrifying Father, it is genuinely and absolutely terrifying. I do not know where else to turn'

The voice on the religious side of the grill tested the veracity of this account by questioning the degree of alcohol dependence of this confessor. Arthur replied honestly and without playing down his moderate daily requirement and the reasons why he drank. The priest carefully broached the subject of re-sanctification. He did so with a careful tone.

'Do you wish to return to the Church of Rome? Is it in your heart to repent of a life away from the faith? The faith you were born into and now seek help from?'

'Aye Father, I want to come back and live an upright life.'

'Is this driven entirely from a fear of what you believe are demons?' The priest asked.

Arthur paused, for it was entirely so. He would do anything to be free of the awful experience in the night. He measured his words with care and deliberation.

'The devils I have heard in the night, they are real. My terror, that is real also. I return to the Church because I know of no other spiritual sanctuary. If the Church will turn me away, then I fear my soul will be lost to these demons. They are tormentors Father, they delight in our distress. They are the opposite of all that is good.'

This answer convinced Father Peter that the man was telling the truth as he perceived it. He decided to accept this confession and choose a penance heavy with prayer, until their next meeting. Something he would have to arrange quite soon. Absolving the troubled soul beyond the partition, the priest thought he heard something odd, someone laughing outside the church doors, briefly, then it was gone.

Somewhere in the softest touch of lost tender sweetness there is a memory. A fragment of a desire for that will to live. Where encroaching years make neither demur nor demerit. A memory, razor sharp in how it is recalled. A genuine, simple wholesomeness. An unrepeatable innocence. The Blessed Land, as far removed from grabbing and grasping as the sun is from the earth. The memory of home. Mad as it is, the home could be anywhere. There does not have to be wealth, neither need be love, or comfort, nor surety or grace. Just a roof, a bit to eat and folks you know. Decals of our proof of species. We forget them, until work fades and old age seizes, until little of distraction or self-deception remains. And then we see it. All we really had. Our stake and claim on common humanity. Home. Folk and kin. So sad.

An unremarkable Tyneside day passed under a flat, iron hard sky. A chilly wind blew upriver from the North Sea. It found the threadbare corners of Arthur's coat, his collar turned up, his hands deep in his holy pockets. He hoped the visit to the priest would provide comfort. Some measure of sanctuary from the nocturnal tremors. He was still careful with his money, what little he had he made stretch, a touch of parsimony, the habit of a lifetime. He would be more careful with the alcohol too, it crossed his mind again that the nightmare in which he had been trapped was possibly a result of the booze. The grimy daylight, the sombre streets, the unfriendly faces he noticed on the road. Northern England in the 1970's was not a cosy place, perhaps it had never been or could never be?

The Land of the Lost. The Kingdom of the Hungry Ghosts.

Back at the hostel he had missed breakfast, not that this troubled him. He would take a nap until late afternoon, a good sleep makes little room for hunger.

The stale sweat reek that depressed him so much and assailed his sense of smell in the dining hall. The unshaven faces, the dingy clothes, yellowed eyes and nicotine stained fingers. He hated the fact that after all those years of hard work, all those precise drawings, all of those battleships that he had designed and this is what it had come down to. A Salvation Army Hostel full of charmless, smelly, vagrant human wrecks. Fucking Hell!

Returning to his little narrow room, he decided to take a bath. The ancient cast iron tub was cracked and stained. The hot water filled an inch or two and then ran out. He would scrub the stains of nightmare from his ageing body. He found a faded shirt and had arranged a clean change of clothes on the bare wooden chair by his meagre bed. He washed himself thoroughly in the paltry few inches of warmish water, dried himself and then donned the worn but clean clothing. It did not take long for the weight of rest to hold him, then take him down into the waters of sleep.

The i...

They were waiting for him. They had something special planned for him. A rat trap for a human psyche. A maze in which the baited mind would break itself attempting to escape. They had a name for this particular sport, "Storage", they called it. An entertainment and collection obsession, that often would kill the fragile specimen-victim, for extreme fear can freeze the heart. To die in such a state is bad enough. To be watched and hunted and laughed at whilst struggling, this was even worse. Arthur had risked exposure to an unhealthy food source, the i... would have to do something about it. From their vantage, the situation was akin to a farmer who, when herding his cattle, finds that one is constantly trying to escape his efforts. That is the one which he would mark for slaughter. Arthur MacNeil was noted in the same dispassionate way. The predators could not risk contamination. They waited for the deepest state of sleep to descend, and then they trapped him. Soon Arthur would know this. Soon the i... would irrevocably and completely have him.

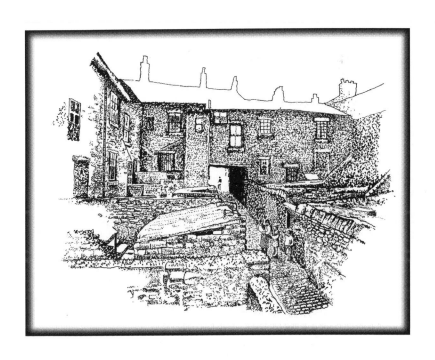

CHAPTER SIX

The Game of Doors.

Tiny, within the frozen night where all that might is right is trite and there, again, there is this thing, a memory. As familiar as a much frequented and lived in room. As close as breath in the gloom. Where within reach the sought after solace is slowly lost to touch and meets not need nor sense, and separate it is, and forever to be so. What is this voice? What is the laughter in our sickness? What is its form? What is the purpose of its attrition? Other than greed, or lust or duplicity of some sort or the other. Primal indolence. Primal screaming. Primal hates. Primitive treachery. Primitive cruelty. Primitive man. The i...

How they found their way here is anyone's guess. Dandelion-like shivers upon the winds of the void. They abandoned spaceships long, long ago, and found ways of concentrating their individual consciousness into something so small, and capable of travelling relatively so fast, that our Earth bound chuntering science is left wanting and standing, holding its flaccid dick whilst the real erect revolutionaries charge away. Into White Space. Into those parts that our best scientists say does not exist. The point where one travels so fast that the Universe appears full of glaring white light. Blazing in all directions, a simultaneous eruption of visible light. Matter appears dark. Suns appear as black, pulsing orbs. Weird space, weirder science.

Yet even at speeds exceeding that of light, where White Space erupted and matter shimmered dense and dark, it still took an age to get anywhere. The Universe is simply vast, too immense for even an enormous imagination to grapple with efficiently. The i...had to sail into the unknown. Far into unexplored emptiness, skirting the outer arms of our spiral galaxy, visiting the fringes of the thousands of millions of stars which compose our locality. This did not sit easily with them. It was not simply a case of interfering with one life-sustaining world until it destroyed itself and then searching out another. Life is very thinly spread, most of it is bacterial or rudimentary. Higher primates are rare. Advanced races even more so.

When we gaze into a night sky full of stars and wonder about the possible existence of other worlds actually supporting life, it would be a depressing reality to confront how little of it there really was, and what percentage of this could maintain a conversation. The distances between these worlds presented the principal hurdle, even once the technology existed to build efficient engines and life-sustaining space ships, which could venture forth in search of pastures new. Yet even this epic achievement was a hit-or-miss affair. The longer the time and distance away from the point of origin, the chances of return decreased. It is the ultimate scientific problem. The very scale of our situation.

Strangely enough, the need for entertainment is paramount when these stunningly dull journeys would be undertaken. Stimulation was a critical aspect of retaining sanity during these ventures into the vastness, and frozen, empty silence. Most species that made it into the interstellar league would compile all their literature, poetry, music, and art in a format they could carry with them to the new worlds. Where space pioneers journeyed, so their culture was carried with them. The invigoration of the senses and the intellect being of prime importance. It was no different for the i...

Amongst the many forms of entertainment they invented, the "Game of Doors" had proved enduring. For the i…it represented a challenge for both the intellect and the knowledgeable content of the memory. It demanded their fullest concentration, and by result, created the greatest returns. It needed at least two to play and could continue in some cases for centuries. When it was discovered that they could use this format as a method to establish exactly how capable a victim species actually was, the play became a sport. The higher primates, animals of a certain brain size and the uncommonly intelligent races encountered upon previously visited worlds, all provided much in the way of amusement to the i… Unfortunately, when the game became protracted, the strain would cause the distressed life form to die, usually of a heart attack, or its equivalent, induced by the abject fear they were experiencing. Humans varied in their degrees of resistance. The i… would cast wagers on the survival possibilities or the time expected for the game to run. The currency used in the contest being "points of prestige". This made for much in the way of what we would call fun for the i…The game was enacted in what we would consider as a vast zoo, or an immense prison. A real place in an actual dimension with physicality and laws. Somewhere that allowed the aliens to get to know their subjects in a very tangible and intimate manner. Some place that was no place to be.

Arthur awoke in his deep dream state. The wooden floor was cold, the panelled walls were somehow familiar. It slowly dawned upon him that this was similar to his old school, an intersection of corridors forming a cross. Yet it was also quite different. The tall alcove windows were gone, as were the statues of the Christ, the Holy Mother or the Saints. The actual corridors seemed longer too. It was most odd. He could touch the wooden panelling and feel its hard surface, as if he were genuinely present, it seemed fully real. He wondered how this was possible and what on earth was going on?

He knew he was asleep in the run-down hostel and experienced that sense of dislocation frequent to the lucid dream state. He did not know that this was the entry point for the "Game of Doors" and that a pair of i... watched him, assessing his vitality and endurance. He decided to walk to the end of the corridor directly ahead of him and see if there were more to this place than four empty passages and four closed doors.

The portal was shut. He quickly noticed that upon its surface at face height, there was an elaborate carving of an equal-armed Celtic cross. He knew he had seen this before. It took a minute or so for his memory to divulge that it was one of many beautiful grave headstones near the ruined Abbey at Hexam, where he used to walk with his mother. He tried the door again, this time it opened. As he was entering Arthur heard a commotion back down the corridor, whence he just had entered. The sound of angry dogs barking and snarling. He was just closing the door when he saw them, huge Rotweillers, three in all, charging towards him, mad eyed and savage.

The door shut with a satisfying click, an enormous coach bolt slid with a clunk into its housing. He could hear the riot of angry animals on the other side, he felt momentarily safe. The corridor in which he stood was gloomier, but he could make out pairs of doors opposite one another down its length, six each side. He counted them and decided to investigate. Trying the nearest door to his right, he found it opened into an old-fashioned headmasters room. The windows were shuttered with wooden blinds, light came from a dull, hissing gas lamp. He had walked in on a moment of punishment. A tall, stocky man with enormous hands had been caning a skinny young lad. The teacher, in Victorian garb, gown and hat, turned and bellowed at Arthur with a voice that shook his confidence,

'What on earth is the meaning of this interruption?'

Arthur stood confused. He did not know what all this was about. The red-faced master with the cane was glaring at him. The lad was crying, his eyes full of glistening tears.

' Where am I?' Arthur requested reasonably.

The cane thwacked hard down upon the worn, stained desk, to emphasize the teacher's shouting.

'You are in my room, you ninny-wit! Disturbing this reprobates well deserved punishment!'

Arthur backed off out of the place, bewildered.

He then tried the door opposite. It was a prison cell. Light-less and stinking, he was confronted by the moans of many miserable souls. In the dim light leaching from behind him, he could discern a number of chained captives, they surged towards the open doorway with cries and sobs, their chains heavily limiting how far they could reach. Dirty, bony hands implored his help. Voices long unused to speaking croaked for aid, for freedom. He stepped back into the corridor. The stench of the dismal cell revolted him, the dehumanized prisoners began to wail desperately. It hit him with a visceral force.

'I will get help!. Arthur said feebly, ' I will find a way to get you out of here!'

With a crippling feeling of guilt, he closed the door on the scene of direst misery.

Arthur thought about returning by the way he had entered, but the notion of confronting the three massive dogs played heavily on his mind. He continued down the corridor, trying for another way out. The third door he tried on the left-hand side was locked. A steel panel set into it at shoulder height was similar to the feeding hatches on old-time jails. He slid the inspection hatch aside and peered into the murk.

A candle burned in a book-lined room. Incense drifted thickly in spirals and plumes. Something or someone rose from a high-backed chair, it faced a manuscript-strewn table, a clutter of inkwells and pens are scattered upon it.

'Who stirs my study?' requested a rich aristocratic voice.

Without turning, the tall, thin figure regards an enormous hourglass.

'It is not yet time for my paltry repast, what means this interruption?'

'Excuse me please' Arthur politely asked, ' what is this place?'

The tall man lifts the hefty candle and approaches the door, his face is bony and drawn, the hands slender and elegant. His eyes are heavily lidded, drugged looking, distant and dim.

'This is my habitation and you, sir, are outside of it!' the gangly gentleman replied.

'Can you tell me how I can get out of here?' Arthur discerned an unhealthy skin colour by the flickering candlelight, a touch of jaundice or ill health.

'Equally so my man, can you tell me how you got in?' the character smirked in response.

'I was asleep, I don't know what is going on, I just woke up here.'

'Then find yourself a safe room, ideally one with a lock or bolt and go back to sleep', the gentrified voice called from an age before the Victorian, anachronistic, unsettling.

'Oh, well, thank you' Arthur replied.

'No sir' the character responded, 'thank you!' and with this blew hard across the candle held before him so that the hot wax splattered onto Arthur's face.

He staggered backwards, clawing at his eyes. The metal hatch slid shut, and as it did a laughter that emerged from within the room, an unhinged cackle, something both lunatic and unsound. Arthur felt the heat of the wax, and a very real stinging of the eyes. He paused before the fourth door, on the right hand side of the corridor, opposite the one where he had just been assaulted and quietly, carefully, turned the handle. His nervousness manifestly growing.

The room was much longer than it was wide. Pale marble veined with lines of brown and grey covered the floor, its coldness uninviting. Pillars of alternating black and white ashlar stood evenly against each wall, running towards the far end, where a platform was raised slightly. Arthur stepped in and felt the chill of the stone through his shoes, his pace echoed lightly. At the far end, five steps made easy access to the raised section, which he noticed, as he approached it, was hung with veils. It was a mausoleum, claustrophobic and chilly cold.

Arthur ascended to the dusty silks and parted them cautiously. Upon an onyx slab, altar like, lay a female in a white funeral shroud. As he approached his heart began to beat heavily. It was a young woman, very similar in initial appearance to his first girlfriend of so many summers ago. Yet she was bone thin and pale in death, her dusty hair arranged neatly upon her shoulders, her eyes closed by two gold coins. He wanted to weep, but his mind told him that all this was not real, that he was trapped deep in a state of sleep. He could feel pain and fear, but this was not to be trusted. He touched her hair, her forehead. Cold and dead. He gently touched her lips and began to cry uncontrollably, despite the logic that his mind had determined. He had to leave this place, he had to get out. It was a dismal experience.

Arthur sat upon the steps before the veils, his head hung in his hands, the tears very real and wet. His chest hurt with racking pains, he could not control his grief. This place was all sick and insufferable, he found it a terrible, frightening experience, and he could not bear it any longer.

Then the sound of soft metal hitting stone stung the stillness. A gold coin rolled across the tiles before him. A frozen hand touched his shoulder.

He leapt forward, falling ungainly upon the marble floor. He twisted his head back, aghast, unbelieving.

She stood with unseeing eyes, her shroud discarded, her skin a reflection of this cold pale tomb. The dark purple puckered wounds upon her body told of a violent attack. He scrambled backwards as she slowly descended the steps, his heart threatened to burst with the sheer vileness of this nightmare. His feet scuffled and frantically he pushed himself away from the sight, sliding along the chilly floor. She silently approached, her eyes blank, her face devoid of expression. This was impossible, she was dead. The dead walk in this place!

In panic Arthur found his feet and fled, he ran from the stone room with his heart pounding madly, he had to get out, he must! Escape became his entire will and effort and thought. As he reached the door she spoke in a croaking, the dry rasp of a long unused voice, saying,

'There is no death here, there is no rest nor peace...'

Back in the corridor, he slammed the door of the awful tomb, it had no lock. He could not take much more of this horror, his thinking was becoming frantic. Trying the next door down on the right hand side, and without much care, he entered the fifth room. His breath came in rasps, his eyes still hurt from the wax that had stung them and the copious crying. He steadied himself in a damp, murky interior. At least he was alone. He noticed this door could be locked from within, a large mortise with a massive key made this possible. He turned the lock shut and placed the key in his jacket pocket. What was this place in which he now found himself? How was he going to endure this ordeal, this mad house? How had he come to be here?

As his breathing calmed, he began to take stock of his surroundings.

He stood in what appeared to be the basement of an old hotel. To his left a heavy banister and stairway rose to a dim landing. He ascended to find the hotel foyer, where three doors faced this entranceway, the one to his right led to an abandoned dining room. Tables lay set, covered in cobwebs and moulding lace place mats. A large sideboard dominated one wall. Arthur checked the drawers, and they took some effort to open as years of dampness had rendered them jammed shut. Within he found more cutlery, tableware and decorated place-mats.

In one drawer he found a set of old postcards tied with red twine that snapped to the touch. The normality of these mildewed, faded pictures reassured him. They all depicted coastal resorts from before World War One. Crinolines, and big bonnets for the ladies. Suits and hats for the men. Skegness was so bracing. He almost smiled at the fat, jolly lady in the striped bathing suit. One section of the cupboard revealed a selection of wines, spirits and sherries, he noted this with a strong twinge of desire. Something very familiar called to him. He almost knew this place. He strained his memory to reveal why this was so.

Returning to the foyer, he checked another door with an external bolt and hefty padlock. It was most certainly shut. At the back of the foyer there were kitchens. The pots and pans had largely rusted, the stainless trays and platters now dull and dusty. More service rooms led away from the kitchens, one a washery with enormous tubs, wringers, boilers and pressing devices, another a storeroom stacked with long decayed food in large glass jars and rusted tins, and beyond this a small room for wood and coal.

Returning to the kitchen, he thought to search out a weapon of some sort, for if he met any more rabid canines or unhinged gentlemen, he would have a little security. Soon he discovered large carving knives and meat cleavers. Their edges had rusted, but one hefty bill-hook shaped implement, probably for breaking meat bones, fitted his hand well. He took it and for the first time since waking in this hell began to feel a degree of control return. Perhaps he could take on the guard dogs that held the entrance passageways with this? He tried a few swipes with it, the weight and balance were perfect. He stuck it safely into his leather belt and decided to check the upper floor.

The stairs creaked and groaned beneath his tread. The carpet slightly stuck to the soles of his shoes as he ascended. The smell of disuse and abandonment dominated. The light was pale, coming from far overhead, a rectangle of grey, three or four floors above him. Arthur tried each and every door, noticing that some of them were damaged. The locks had been smashed as though entry had been forced. Most of the rooms were still tidy, but damp, dusty and heavily cobwebbed, yet clearly had been made up for visitors who had long ceased to call. All the windows were shuttered tight, apparently from the outside. This seemed odd, like much in this twilight. Some of the rooms were littered with abandoned belongings and clothing. Wardrobes revealed dresses and suits, neatly folded shirts and blouses, frequent pairs of antiquated shoes. It all spoke of an age which he found reassuring, comfortable and safe. His very early childhood memories wanted to emerge, like holidays with his mother and that happier time between the wars.

The more spacious and generous suites were situated at the ends of each of the three floors, all of which he thoroughly checked. There was no-one here, the old hotel was empty. No demented gentlemen, no walking dead, no roomful of shrieking prisoners and no angry dogs. Nothing but a history, which revealed itself with every bedroom, chamber and cupboard space he investigated. The floors above the third landing were apparently inaccessible. The stairway had completely collapsed and in the fading light, he decided that further exploration was not possible. It seemed that the day was failing, so he thought to make himself comfortable for the night. The shadows deepened in the old hotel.

Quickly he descended to the kitchen rooms, found a large coal scuttle and filled it with fuel and kindling. Then, returning to the dining room, he took from the sideboard a large bottle of brandy, two-thirds full, and a glass tumbler. Elegant perfumed candles, still boxed seemed a most fortuitous find, as did the stainless steel match case, these he stuffed into his jacket pockets. Carrying these to the first floor, he decided to use one of the larger suites he had discovered earlier. It had a sturdy lock and key in a heavy wooden door. Ideal.

Arthur placed a row of candles on the shapely mantelpiece, struggling to light the ancient matches, which thankfully were dry and did eventually ignite. From one candle he lit the others. Dusty velvet-draped curtains covered the shuttered windows. Safe, securely locked.

In the adjacent bathroom, he tried a verdigris-covered brass tap. A rumble began in pipes far above him and stinking brown water spluttered from the bronze spout and stained the dusty sink. He let this run until it began to clear and then closed it, satisfied. Similarly, the lavatory flushed with much the same complaints from the long unused plumbing, until the water in this also cleared. Arthur then set and lit a fire with the candle and drew a large, comfortable chair to the warmth. The flames back-drafted smoke into the room for a while until the rising heat found its way out and the blaze took heart, making the place seem almost comfortable. This would do for now, he thought. All seemed well. As well as could be reasonably considered possible.

Upon a small side table, he placed the meat cleaver, the remaining candles and matches and his bottle of brandy. He cleaned the tumbler with his handkerchief and filled it, relishing the beautiful scent of the old alcohol. Sipping it was a simple bliss. He felt its warmth course through him, as its vigorous potency eased his tired body, which ached from the travails of this terrible place. His gaze often strayed to the locked door, candlelight softened the decades of dust and damp, the place began to warm and resemble comfort, peace and rest.

Curiosity overcame him as the brandy took hold, so, with a candle in his hand, he explored the room. The wardrobe held what had once been very expensive clothing. A pair of slim gent's suits including a heavy travelling cloak hung there. He threw the cape about his shoulders despite the smell of age clinging to the cloth and continued rummaging. There were some ladies dresses and skirts, collar-less shirts and hat-boxes, cuff-links, tie pins and even a lovely pocket-watch on a silver chain. Arthur rewound it and held it to his ear, amazingly its tiny heart pinged each second with new-found life. He took it, if only for its friendly familiar sound.

On the wardrobe, a set of suitcases caught his eye, so he took them from the top shelf and placed them on the grand double bed. The locks had rusted and took a degree of persuasion, though eventually opening. He rifled through the private possessions of someone from a time when he would have been but a baby. A much-thumbed diary, an address book in which he noted some highly respectable business names, still surviving until his own time.

Which seemed odd, for what was his time? This place in which he had found himself had no fixed age, it made little rational sense and had much to create foreboding. Yet the brandy and the room had softened all this. The coal fire burned happily away, throwing out the heat and drying the furniture and carpets around it. The scented candles drove away the smell of dampness, which had pervaded everything. Arthur returned to the fireside chair with a handful of books and periodicals he had found in the suitcases. The gentleman's cloak gradually lost its mildewed smell and shed its dampness, it enfolded him generously and made him feel safe. He thumbed through a copy of Empire Traveller with its fading photographs of far away lands and tropical skies. He became very tired and quite drunk.

It occurred to him how strange it would be, to go to sleep within a dream, but his fatigue was sincere, as had everything been since he arrived in this weirdest of places. He picked up the meat cleaver and swayed over to the slightly unmade bed. Someone had slept here long ago, thrown back the sheets and blankets and so it had remained since. The bedding was now grey with age and still noticeably damp, but he did not care, fully clothed he lay himself down to rest and in a very brief period was fast asleep. Dreaming within a dream.

CHAPTER SEVEN

Transitions and acquisitions.

The i...

The cult of the moron swept the inclement northern wastes. A few thousand rampant boot boys vandalized and purveyed their aggression with both aplomb and sheer savagery. It was not a place to be young in.

1970s Tyneside was a bomb-site without an enemy to blame. It was a tragedy of epic proportions. Random acts of violence were practised without aforethought or concern. Let the useless liberals talk until their sorry arse sags. May their distant concern grow until their nose hairs lengthen. No one in their correct mind would wish to be poor in Tyneside in the 1970s. Genuinely.

The Northern Wasteland was a death of hope, the demise of honest labour and the grave of true attempt. Antagonism and aggression ruled without neither helpful interruption nor demur. If one were so unfortunate to be kicked into unconsciousness, pleading uselessly unto ones grinning, laughing assailants, there would be no mercy. Water in a parched desert would be more likely. They would kick you until cerebral spinal fluid ran pink from one's eye sockets or ears, nose and mouth.

This is what made the North of England most suitable to the i...

Here every suitable malleable motive and distortable intent did dwell, made obvious.

A plastic, easily influenced, intrinsically violent people. The Geordies.

A warrior race without any really genuine enemies, a predatory sub-species with just enough to eat... Generally.

The Geordies.

Mainly and essentially every single testosterone laden male, especially the ones which had a predisposition to wanton, frenzied attack and the serious referent to an enemy. To destroy a thing or a person lay dominant within their sorry genetics. Perhaps this was how they made such consummately loyal and efficient soldiers? Such themes created much interest to the i...A genuine tragedy to the human species. These aliens. They who steer us, our masters, our watchers, our bitter, sorry end.

Who fixed the contorting images of death into many a young mind? Who troubled the rest and sleep of innumerable good and decent folk? They that strung and rang an ongoing concerto of wretched, filthy injury until the Decent Gods made laud, and more police poured into the breach. Deity anoints their diligence with prayer and the accidence of bureaucracy. The i... send in the i... send in the Vandal, the Hun, The Visigoth. Send in the mad eyed, gibbering fundamentalist to destroy each signpost and all historical proof. Gentleness and sophistry make sender play in their reckoning. Little that comforts us warm human beings makes rational sense in their cold climate. Unless you are prey. Unless you are a fat, easy, nutritious supplement to a diet you never, ever figured upon. Call the cops...

The i…

They saw him. They watched him sink into biological slumber. The rotten alien bastards monitored his gradual progress into the physiological recumbent. As he sank into the velvet embrace of sleep, they assessed him. The nasty rotten shit-bags! The filthy, heinous, wretched swine! They played him. Like they have played our species since we fell out of the trees and used tools. The evil, stinking nasty fucks, they played him, and cast him, predicate, into a world he had no chance or opportunity of surviving within, as is the way with these advanced predators.

Oh but we have our projectile armaments! We have our geeky electronics! We possess the certitude of this most erudite sphere through our brilliance to demonstrate our proficiency into the icy void, our inordinate acumen, our indelible ingenuity. Our relevance.. So it goes. For the validations of an idiotic, infantile race eventually wear thin and pointless, as the weapons heap up and the victims needlessly perish.

The i…

Collected the soul or essence of their victims. Once processed and assimilated, the record and character of their consciousness would be bound into the archives of the i… and assimilated into their collective knowledge-map, or the Overmind.

This was the unhinged gentleman occultist locked in his cell, myrrh and opium staining the chamber. He was a prisoner in the repository of the i… As has been the wailing, chained up captives, even the dogs. The i…had visited plenty of worlds populated with lower primates, animals interested them. Of course they did! Look what they created from a bunch of clever monkeys! A perfect creature to study.

Animals could be taught to hate and attack. Fear was a spur to greater ability or extinction, growth or demise. Fear generated patterns in the fascia sheath surrounding mammalian muscle structures. This collagen-celled system reacted to and memorized shock and harmful assault. In combination with the brain and the central nervous system, memory was a physical matter. The i...can read all this as we do a book, more so, a magazine. Lots of pictures and predictability for them to skim over and log. Humans were their most intimate investment to date. Sometimes, without superstitious trappings, a human would be born with the innate ability to figure out that the i... were actually real. These sorts were rare enough and as long as they remained healthy entertainment, would all stay under development. Now and again, the i... cropped some of the existing stock.

Arthur had been born when the First World War ended. He was sixty when the i...caught him in the 'Game of Doors'. His heart might not last for long in the labyrinth that awaited him. It could slowly shred the mind via a series of calculated projections, all of which were horrible. The sinister sinister's sinister.

Down stairways and twisting tunnels, Arthur is not a clever hero, he is an ageing man. Rummaging rooms and wrenching open swollen cupboards and drawers, in his sleep, as he sleeps. In reality, his real body was frozen cold in a narrow, sad little room in a run down Salvation Army old folk's hostel.

Odds with the i...stood at him lasting about a week, their time.

Fingers of silver light filtered through the wooden shutters and told of day upon moth eaten velvet curtains. Arthur woke. A gentleman's cloak fell from his shoulders as he sat up. There was a key in his pocket and a meat cleaver by the bed. He was hungry and cold. The brandy looked inviting, just a little warm up? He thought best not to.

As his eyes grew accustomed to the gloom, in the bathroom, he washed his face in frozen, rusty water and dried on a mildewed towel full of old dead insect husks and gossamer powdery moth wings.

The face in the mirror was still that of an ageing man.

He pocketed the matches and left the bottle of sweet brandy. The door, once unlocked revealed the same barren landing. Doors. He ascended two damp floors. The stairway was completely rotted away after floor three. A curving corroded spine of cast iron rail reached to wet, green floorboards aloft, collapsed and rank. What little he could make of the ceiling on the unreachable floor above, was that it was heavily damaged by water and the elements. A dull wind stirred there. He thought this could make for a way out. If he could find the means.

Double checking this upper floor, he opened a door he had omitted to search the previous evening. He had assumed, by its size and type, it was just another of the basic single-bed suites. Arthur paused and noticed the bare, scoured pine boards on all the surfaces. It was very clean and faintly smelt of chlorine and bleach and soap. There was another door at the back of the room, three quarter size, with frosted glass panels on the upper third section. He thought to check all the access on the upper floor and would come back here later. The look and smell of the wash-room spoke of many hours of labourious scrubbing.

Another similar neighbouring door led to a long tile-lined corridor where weeds and broken glass littered the floor. A section of guttering lay across the passage, which was open to the sky and green pools of algae thrived in the approach. Detritus crunched underfoot. In the far room an enormous generator rusted, two more doors led to a second, smaller boiler room and then a cloakroom. Hard hats and military helmets still hung there, along with capes, gowns and heavy coats also abandoned. Two sets of fire doors stemmed from the twin passageways, which led to a common approach where a set of marbled stairs rose to a large empty room, reminiscent of a dance hall. There was more light in this section than in the previous explored areas. The roof was a span of cast-iron arches with ornate sub-lattices depicting a Pugin-esque homage. The floor had fallen through in places which corresponded with the points of ingress of the rain and wind from above. Some paper party banners still sagged from rusted pins. Arthur had felt the wax in his eyes as a real thing, he reasoned that a fall through the floor of an empty hotel would be just as authentic. He was not wrong.

Carefully he stepped around the near rim of the hall, approaching on his left hand side where the floorboards seemed firmer. A door was ajar to a storeroom. Another damaged door frame opened to a space that had collapsed in timber, iron and glass. Weeds infested the dangerous looking mess. A stale wind breathed by another door, and light. He approached this second corridor. Windows opened out to his right, he paused, curious to get a notion of place. The rotten old lace curtains fell silently as he touched them. With his cuff Arthur wiped the glass.

A landscape of rooftops and spindly chimney stacks ranged far. A flat grey sky passed above and threatened rain, the stain of weak yellow sun looked down. There was no colour, all was dull monotonous tile and wet stone, but other. It somehow cluttered with architectural detail and elaboration that confused. Industrial pollution had stained the brickwork towers and common masonry which rose above him. He noticed there were walkways on the crests of rooftops.

The corridor terminated where a mass of masonry had fallen and shattered through it and continued down through an indeterminate number of floors. In a room below he could see a small trunk that had been ripped in half by the event of the collapse. A silk garment fluttered from it. The room had a small fireplace, a hairbrush and mirror still lay there upon it. Arthur paused.

This was a city. Being on the roof of a building would only confirm this. Still, it was light and almost refreshing compared to the dimly lit corridors far below, beyond the locked door. He felt for the key.

Manifestly and thankfully it was still in his pocket. Arthur couldn't find a way to progress any further, nor any indications of access down into the rooms beneath his feet, smashed open by the fall of tons of dirty baked brick and flue liner. The destroyed area below him looked unstable anyway. He returned to the hall, noticing that the entire floor slumped toward the windows. It looked and was distinctly dangerous.

A light rain began, the remaining lace curtains hung heavily from the damaged windows, dripped and fed the micro-system of rot and decay, ensuring that the view from here might not be wise to attempt. Slowly he made his way to the right hand end of the timbered room. He noticed white-painted loudspeakers with brown and yellow rust stains peppering their surfaces, long silent. A poster celebrated Armistice Day. It was caught and abandoned in that time. A frail wooden kid's toy cracked under his heel, the floor creaked ominously. Gently he made his way to a door. A small plaque at handle height with missing letters gave him added curiosity.

The floor was tiled, more broken glass crinkled underfoot. There was a roof top garden, of the sort in vogue before WW1. The ironwork was perilous in places and the rows of arched windows had accrued so much filth, nothing could be seen through them. At the rooms centre, an elaborate twin spiral staircase convoluted its way up towards a roof tower. Once this place would have been a riot of colour, now it was clumps of unhealthy weeds and fungi. The cast-iron steps appeared firm, so he testily ascended to the viewpoint above.

An iron-framed door complained as he prised it open, wide enough to step through onto the decorative turret walkway, more cast iron, more spilling foliage and more curves of corroded metal. The view was most odd.

The town rolled downhill for as far as he could see towards a river, many bridges spanned the narrows, beyond this a heavy fog banked. Arthur noticed that these bridges were festooned with dwellings. A few little plumes of smoke lazily drifted. People. He hoped they would be friendly and maybe have some food.

The city was also a jumble, familiar in the industrial era dirt and feel, but with many far older buildings, some of them unrecognisably ancient. When he turned to look uphill he started in surprise. Rank upon rank of castle and cathedral hulked and crowded the whole rise. Far above he made out distant black towers. A series of blocky structures jostled on the summit, a large black flag flew there.

In the distance, a murder of crows rose in their noisy complaint within the extensive ruins of a tree-filled abbey. They croaked and flapped upwards to settle upon ivy-hanging defensive walls, just a little further up the hill. There was too much detail for his eyes. It filled his mind both with bewilderment and curiosity.

Arthur wished he had his spectacles, he wanted to see more clearly the upper ramparts and steep walls, with dark spires and dull green copper domes. Pigeons flew up there. Trees filled the ruins and shells of tenements, some over twenty floors high. The vacant rectangles of windows lay open, bird's nest strewn. White streaks of droppings signed of the years of abandonment. He studied the fold of the rooftops to gain an idea of where streets and thoroughfares lay. He could also make out numerous open sections of the town down the hill, some with high, elongated public sculptures and silent fountains full of weeds and pale flowers. The floor began to creak, he thought it wise to move from this spot.

Arthur was confident he would find a way out into the street eventually, so he began to feel more at ease and in less of a panic. He noted the creaking and ticking of the iron stairwell in complaint as he descended. Returning towards the ruined hall, he retraced his steps back into the main section of the hotel. He thought to try the wash-room again when it occurred to him that this old hotel was still full of the belongings and clothes of wealthy folks. How had it not been long pillaged? Arthur reasoned that it had to be bricked up or boarded over on the street level. However else would it keep out curious kids and opportunist scavengers?

It was stiflingly quiet on the landing of the hotel. He soon found the damaged rooms where the brick-work had fallen and smashed through, here the water dripped rhythmically down from somewhere on the ruined floors above. He entered the wooden wash-room to find dried blocks of carbolic soap, and big bristle brushes. Linen and towels were neatly stacked in efficient cupboards built into the panelled wall. There were sinks and heavily enamelled wash-tubs in the neat, re-assuring room. A three-quarter door opened to a tiny cloakroom where garments still hung, also an odd set of wooden stairs. These climbed very steeply, almost like a ladder, with handrails at each side. It was dry and dusty, but sound and safe, so he clumped noisily up at least two floors to a place he could only but find characterful.

It was a small, square room with four broad windows in each wall, providing a commanding view over a spread of local rooftops. Walkways radiated along the apex of most nearby buildings, narrow affairs with twin safety rails, which linked and jumped areas by arching cast-iron bridgework. A mildewed logbook lay upon a cubbyhole desk-bureau, he opened it to see what it detailed, finding inventories of the bundles of laundry, listed according to room and rooftop area. They dried the laundry up here, this struck Arthur as a very clever use of space. The attic room had also been the viewpoint where someone had watched the weather, whilst organising the drying of the visitors clean clothes. He was getting a fuller picture of the abandoned hotel.

An intriguing feature of the watch room was a fold-down bed that unhooked from the wall and swung down to a horizontal position, being retained by sturdy chains. The double rails on the stairway were also runners for massive wicker baskets that could lift and lower to the wash room below. Clever design, thought Arthur. The doors had strong bolts and a flat-topped stove seemed well preserved indeed. If he needed to stay another night, this would be the place. Exploring the room further, he found fold-down tabletops, similar to the bed, but scrubbed clean and polished by much use. Three boxes of laundry were carefully stacked and stashed away in the built-in cupboards. He found clean shirts his own size and put them aside.

The room was dry and sound and provided a view. He decided to take from the suites below what he may need and use this place as his base until something better emerged, or his situation resolved. He needed to know where he was and he needed to know how he got here. He wanted to get back to the old folk's hostel. Or did he? What time was it? The yellow sun-stain seemed overhead. It had to be near midday.

The key that he held in his jacket pocket was a way back to an experience, one which had completely terrified him. Why should he need to find his way out into the town by those particular doors? This place was very strange, but it was drawing his attention and certainly more interesting than the humdrum and routine of life back in the 'sallybash'. He took one of the spacious canvas laundry bags and carefully descended the steep stairwell to the wash-room below. He was going to explore, this time with calm and patience. He may need not to escape by the way he had entered.

Arthur began his rummaging in the dining room, where he retrieved three boxes of scented table candles and more matches. To his pleasure he counted six unopened bottles of wine. Carefully, he placed all these in the canvas holdall. The whiskey, brandy and rum had mellowed beautifully, he took one of each spirit, finding the largest and fullest of the selections available and pouring the remaining quantities into these until full. He discovered a corkscrew in the draw with more postcards and took both. On his way he checked out the cellar door, it was still heavily secured. The door itself was made of very sturdy, steel-framed timber. It was most odd for it to be so ruggedly made. The key remained safe in his jacket pocket.

He carefully wandered from room to room, some had remained untouched since abandoned. In the larger suites he found better pickings. Wealthier sorts had used these, it was reflected in the items they had left behind. A sporting, countrified type had an army rucksack slumped in a large walk-in storage cupboard. It rattled as he lifted it. Inside, he found binoculars and to his extra surprise some very useful camping kit. He emptied the lot onto a bed and sifted through the stuff.

A quality waterproof infantryman's cape rolled up tight with a leather belt, which would be useful if it rained. A nested set of pans with folding steel handles stacked around a small camping kettle. Ideal light kit. A dry leather pouch containing polish, beeswax and oil and brush. It was always sensible to look after your boots. A large water canister, British Tommy type, round and felt covered. A flint and steel set in an old tobacco tin, also containing fish hooks and snares. Perhaps theses would come in handy? There was a beautiful fishing knife, still bright sharp and keen in a greased sheath. It handled well. At the bottom of the rucksack, was a neatly rolled-up sleeping bag in a heavy canvas wrap.

He packed all these back into the sturdy rucksack and inspected an oilskin pouch. Within he found six long, slim, paper-wrapped packages containing rations; two tins of hard chocolate, two of thick boiled sweets, one block of hard tack biscuit and one of coffee powder. He would open these later to his great satisfaction. He threw aside a moth-eaten pull-over, its fabric consumed beyond use. The socks and shirts had all gone the same way. He discovered several pairs of sturdy boots of solid make, some were his size and he wanted them. Both gents and ladies boots of quality lay in a row in the cupboard. One of the larger fittings sat comfortably, regardless that the leather was old and dry, but there were the tubs of beeswax in the rucksack. The boots would oil up easily.

He was enjoying this salvaging work, but realized he did not actually like being in this part of the derelict hotel. He felt constantly uneasy. Arthur really sensed that someone was observing him and he could not shake the feeling off.

He returned to the room in which he had spent the night, carrying the rucksack and the canvas laundry bag full of booze. He retrieved the glass tumbler to his pocket, and the meat cleaver to a side pouch of his bag. He took the magazine that he had thumbed through, then snapped the unused candle stumps from the marble mantelpiece. These he stashed, filling the rucksack finally with a rolled up gentleman's cloak. The outer straps held the whole lot firm.

Shouldering his load and belting it at the waist, he took the coal scuttle in one hand and the booze bag in the other. It was a hard slog back to the comfortingly clean laundry rooms. He placed the rucksack, booze and coal bucket in one of the woven baskets at the ramp at the base of the steep stairs, also adding a large block of carbolic soap. Then carefully he climbed to the top and cranked the handle that raised the load. A ratchet clicked eight times a circuit, so when he paused to catch a breath, the rising provisions did not crash back down the ladder run.

Arthur then closed the wooden door that shut off access from the steep stairway below and checked the bolts and hinges. Finding them strong he verified his decision to stay in this watch room. Hungrily he wrenched the chocolate tin open, the contents were white and completely dry and hard. It took time to release the flavour in this ancient, stale block, but when it did it pleased him. Similarly, the stone hard-boiled sweets returned effort eventually with floods of flavour. It was like being a kid again and having the experience for the first time. He considered lighting the stove and having some coffee and hard tack, but remembered that he did not know this place. He had just arrived here. A bit of care may be needful. Arthur could always light a fire after dark.

He cleaned the lenses of the binoculars and prised the casement windows open. A high stool set Arthur at just the right elevation to look down on the town comfortably. He relaxed into the wheel-back chair on its tall legs and scanned the view. Where he could see onto streets, they were empty. The many bridges far away still cluttered on the river narrows. He determined the Medieval look to them and also high, dark tenements which crowded their approaches. Arthur was sure he had seen this scene before in a history book. Beyond the river a shapeless gloom brooded in mist and haze, a bank of cloud or fog shrouded and obscured. Some spires and towers punctuated this, giving an ethereal appearance to the far, far distance.

Arthur then scanned the nearby sea of rooftops. He noticed there were lots of pigeons, certainly more than was usual in a town. Rank after rank of rows of terrace housing spilled in every direction downhill. Larger buildings and churches broke the monotony with their odd elongated and elaborate architectural finishing. These little ostentations seemed quirky, so fixing the town in a period of time was strangely evasive and elusive. Hours passed observing in this way.

Down river, where Arthur assumed east to be, the binoculars enabled him to take in more of the city and its vastness. He discerned lines of gantries and tall cranes, the black ribs of an enormous ship ran in massive, curving rows. The houses in its shadow were tiny. Church spires broke the swell and continuity of terraced-house rooftops, school and factory also, stark and thin. Eccentric castles and fortified manor houses stood out above the ocean of slate roofing. A thin mist hung over everything, making distant detail vague. He could not discern the sea.

Upriver, where west should be the town diminished into woodland and field. They were a pleasant green in the daylight and many miles away on foot. He adjusted the binoculars and realized that the shadow on the far horizon was not cloud, it was the swell of hills and moorland. The river ran from here. From his vantage, this side of the city was broken by more parks and wooded gardens, also a better class of housing in the main. Many rooftops were a riot of ornate ironwork. Scroll-wrapped, banded globes, broad-winged angels and crowns, all of black wrought iron. These seemed frequent features. One building in the middle distance had metal decorations, describing symbols and signs, ornate geometry and totemic icons. It had a serious occult look. Narrow windows and spiny dormers, gargoyles and devils grinned and grimaced from the eaves and ridges. Many tall trees surrounded it.

He kept the best view for last. Moving his high stool to the fourth window at the foot of the fold-down bed. He closed the mattress away into the wall and heaved the window casement open. The call of crows carried to him. On this side of the river the town was sprawled about a hill, mainly on the gentle slopes of its skirts. The upper reaches of this vast conurbation had crags and steep, rocky slabs exposed towards the summit. Every single available space had been built upon and ruins flourished, seeming to dominate whole areas and sections. Nearby, buildings similar in size to his abandoned hotel clustered, there was a lot of similar look. Uphill, above and beyond these hotels, an ecclesiastical settlement sprawled, their dwellings had been terraced with economy and skill. Pathways and stairs criss-crossed the exposed walls of rock. Again, many periods of architecture could be seen.

Arthur opened a bottle of wine and filled his glass, after a long sip he returned to the binoculars and the hill above him. The military sections appeared to follow the shape of the exposed bedrock, utilising the natural defensive positions along the contours and crags. It was like a fascinating read. A ruined series of sturdy castellated towers clearly had been attacked at some era in the past, and still not yet repaired. Black spaces of shattered masonry gaped like cave mouths. The cruciform archer's windows set their signs in the castle stonework. It did not make sense to have so much historical architecture concentrated with such intensity.

The battlements beyond these had cannon slots, a few rusted barrels jutted from these defences of a more recent time. Above these were baked-brick built edifices, which almost defined the horizon. The enormity of these bastions was formidable. All was stained with the filth of a long industrial period, giving a dirty uniformity to the walls and buttresses. He took the glass of wine from the windowsill. It smelled rich and deeply mature. It tasted perfect. The day was passing slowly into the evening. He had scrutinised the city for hours, developing a notion of its spread and the lie of the streets.

He waited well until dark before he lit the little stove. It glowed into life eagerly. The room was less than twelve foot square, it heated quickly, and scant fuel burnt long. The softly flickering light from the stove door was enough to see by, as darkness gradually descended. He waited to see how many lights came on in the town below, activity of any sort to break the spell of the crows and pigeons. He did not light a candle. He knew he would be very visible, and so made do with the shards of warm orange which spilled from the stove.

A small cluster of tiny yellow stars blinked into life down by the river, where the curious old bridges gathered. A small constellation of them, candle and lamp twinkling in the night. Nothing shone forth on the hill above at all, nor in all the streets and buildings close by. Far upriver few habitations showed any signs of life. Not many folk lived there. Arthur wondered if a war or a disaster had devastated the population? Down river the mist had thickened and nothing at all showed. He slowly finished the wine and felt the need to rest. The sleeping bag required a sound shaking to loft the down filling. He staggered a little on the thin carpet. The swing-down bed seemed a great and inviting place. He crawled onto it and into the bag, everything about him drying gradually out from an age of dampness. He sighed and soon was deep asleep. Again, dreaming within a dream.

CHAPTER EIGHT

In the city.

The i…

Arthur wakes in the garret room to the sound of a solitary tolling bell. He is in a city, such places have churches and cathedrals and so naturally a bell would sound on a Sunday. So it would now be Sunday in this place. Again, the day was grey and promised more rain, but the bell ringing was a very re-assuring sound indeed.

Arthur had realised the property had been boarded-up, timbered firmly to resist the gangs of little kids that would have swarmed through the many deserted buildings like hungry mice. It was an industrial town after all. The river cut its flat silver sweeps through mile upon mile of terraces and tenements, a dull pewter meander under the vague yellow sun. He wanted now to get out of the old hotel, desiring to see what was about him and maybe figure out how he woke here. The rucksack's contents lay in orderly rows upon a workbench. He packed, thinking of inspecting the rooftop walkways and gantries that spanned the many spires, dormers and rooftops of this time-locked place. There had to be a way down. He would find some way out.

The hinges were rusty and the door, which took some wrenching to open, eventually yielded enough space for him to squeeze through and then reach back inside for his pack. The sound of the bell came from the hill above him. He thought he could determine movement far away, unsure of his sight, he retrieved the binoculars and focused his vision. An uneven group of drab figures was walking at a brisk pace up a broad street, some wore tall stove-pipe type hats, and all were clad in black and white. Arthur could discern the elaborate towers of an ecclesiastical building, but no doorway, as rooftops occluded a fuller view.

He thought to check all the alternative rooftop walkways that took him away from this central observation point. He remembered how the metal had creaked in complaint the previous day whilst exploring. Most of the central section of the hotel roof was constructed from cast iron beams with opaque, heavy-duty glass windows. It did not look safe at all. Uphill, to the back of the hotel, he found his first-choice rooftop gantry had taken him to a fire escape, the lower two floors of which were missing. Beech trees grew close to the roof, seedlings had grown in the drains and walls, and it was damp and slippery with mould and moss. The bell still rang.

Looking about this shady backyard area he noticed that the trees had intruded and grown into the other fire escape arrangements, mostly on the middle sections. He peered into the shady gloom. All the lower parts of these ancient cast iron structures had been removed. There were three in all, each corresponding to an enormous wing of the hotel, all at the back and disconnected from the ground by two whole floors. Arthur thought to try the next fire escape along where large boughs had grown right through the handrails and treaders. Cautiously, he made his way back to the viewpoint room. There he re-entered and took a length of thick washing line. He would lower the rucksack down to the ground.

Through the dirty glass it seemed cosy, but he remembered that there was a door in this hotel and that it led to a place he did not wish to return to, so he would explore this strange town and try to find another friendly billet. He would push on and explore.

The central wing met the main hotel building at the point where the huge but derelict observation point was situated. As he approached it, he could see down into damaged sections of the building from above. He recognized the suitcase with the silky garment spilling from its rented gape, it was far below. A slight nausea overcame him, and he steadied himself on the corroded handrail. The danger he was in awoke again and he very carefully placed his feet, every groan of old metal and fall of flaking rust sent his heart beating at a racing pace. The walkway creaked in complaint under Arthur's weight. It was not a safe place to be.

He made it slowly past the rotten central rooftop area and onto the walkway for the middle wing of the hotel. The trees told of early summer, yet it was not warm. He realized he certainly did not want to fall and tempt the providence that had brought him to this interesting city, nor did he want to drop the rucksack. It held five bottles of wine and two full, large decanters of brandy and two of single-malt whiskey. He had packed his kit around this precious load, but a fall of forty feet or more he or it had no hope of surviving. He entered the foliage.

This section of the garden had completely succumbed to trees and shrubs, fighting for light and life under the shadow of the mature beeches. His eyes grew accustomed to the shade. Arthur tied the heavy cord onto the rucksack and carefully lowered the bag. As he began to climb into the beech, he clung as a child does when first learning to scale trees, with arms and legs clenched tight about the bough, shuffling along slowly towards the central trunk. He moved like an old man, it took all his effort to cover a very small distance. He considered the fall with a flutter of panic, then found he could just cling on, pause for a while and regain his breath. Thus he spent a full half-hour, gingerly lowering himself by small degrees to the leafy floor beneath. The bell had ceased to toll.

The trees cast shadows on a bluff of mossy crag, which created a natural boundary for the property at its rear. From this bluff an enormous wooden fence had been erected, which he followed. It ran out of the tree line and back to the hotel, which had been heavily boarded up, just as he had previously suspected. The lower floors also had each doorway and window space bricked up shut. The windows above were similarly covered with hefty shuttering for three floors. Arthur wondered why anyone would wish to do this? It seemed excessive.

The fence could not be scaled where it met with the hotel walls, so he retraced his steps back to the damp green crag. It was a distinct line, varying from fifteen to twenty feet high and way beyond the abilities of a sixty year old man with a loaded rucksack. Following along the base of the crag, he noticed a stained, cast-iron pipe that ran down the wall, he could discern the lower courses of masonry of a ruinous building above. Arthur thought to check the entire perimeter before he took such a testing option.

Yet he found both the hotel and its grounds were very securely contained indeed. The substantial timber wall was twice his height and festooned with rusted barbed wire at its crest, it was incredibly off-putting. Arthur finally decided to try climbing the drain, as it looked solid enough and there seemed to be little choice in the matter. He wanted to get out of this place.

Arthur tied the washing line to his leather belt, intending to haul the rucksack up once he had made it safely above. He could just reach the lowest of three iron pins that fixed the pipe to the crag and so shuffled his way slowly up. His breathing became rapid with the effort of climbing, until eventually he could place one foot upon the pin, once above it. His hands were green with algae and decay. Again he reached for the second pin, which was far more corroded and initially crumbled to his touch, but had enough stable iron within it for him to repeat the move. His head slowly drew level with a stone windowsill.

Gasping for breath, he looked into a collapsed ruin. Another strenuous reach brought him level with the opening, enough for him to step cautiously sideways into it. He reached into the space, where once a casement window had sat, fumbling until his hold was certain, and then he moved, stepping into the long-collapsed building. Arthur sat down immediately on a pile of stones and regained his breath. Then he recovered the rucksack.

A doorway led to a narrow cobbled alley. Carefully he stepped through the clumps of weeds and piles of fallen masonry to reach this back lane. A gas lamp hung from a bracket above his head, the glass long gone, the mantle obscured by a pigeon's nest. To his left, the lane led unevenly uphill, the dark stone structures leaning into the alleyway at eccentric angles, making it seem quite foreboding. He turned right and slightly downhill until he found two short sections of stone stairs between buildings whose roofs almost touched. This led him to a wider street.

Turning right again, he followed the high wooden fence up towards the hotel. Crossing the street to get a better view of the structure, he could see down the broader road a number of similar sized buildings, none of which had been sealed off like the hotel from which he had just freed himself. The road was empty, nothing stirred. There was no litter and long grass and weeds grew thick from the pavements.

Now that he could see the hotel from the outside, it was clear it had once been an up-market affair. The facing Regency era masonry was skilfully dressed and carved pillars flanked the main doorway. He assumed this was the padlocked door on the ground floor. The entrance space was completely bricked up and iron rods ran vertically across this. A lot of effort had gone into closing this hotel to the public. Large letters hung from the eaves, with only the word "Hotel" remaining complete. Stumps and fragments of metal letters indicated that the actual name had been removed, or destroyed. A ghost of paleness upon the stonework remained, a shadow created in the time that the sign had been whole and the sun and weather had spared the corresponding masonry beneath. He couldn't make it out clearly, but there had originally been nine letters, starting with an 'A'.

Arthur thought to make his way up the hill, to where he had seen the group of people. To do this, he followed the hotel road to where it crossed a broader street running up a long steep bank. He halted and looked. The structures here and there called out to his memory, they were familiar, but surrounded by buildings that misplaced the setting completely. It was most strange. He turned and set off uphill at a keen pace for a sixty year old. Nothing moved on the street but Arthur alone.

He passed hovels with sod walls and grass roofs, some doors opened onto a thick darkness within. Yet still no people. He drew level with a chapel on the brow of the hill and stared. A dirty, plainly dressed stone, early Wesleyan Church. He knew this because one like it existed on Tyneside, back there in the world of the 'sallybash' and also manifestly real in this haunting place. Maybe it was just a coincidence, Arthur thought without much genuine conviction. He continued past a row of ancient pubs and hostelries and small shops, all with boarded windows. These terminated before the stained masonry of a grim fortified wall. A large tower dominated the street, and the road ran through a defended arch at its base. It was closed, with a wrought iron two-part gate, secured and barred from within. A postern gate to one side was similarly padlocked. The hill top was distinctly fortified.

He could see beyond, through the iron bars to a very different part of this town. The road on the other side of the arch, ran straight across the brow of the hill, the structures on either side were a mix of Tudor and Medieval periods. These skirted the massive wall of an inner citadel. Here stood the blocky dark shapes, the rooftops that he had discerned from the hotel below. Nothing moved, but the buildings were not derelict. He was curious and followed the outer wall along a cobbled alley, which flanked this fortification. Soon he was heading downhill again, were west should be.

The alley gradually diminished in size to a mere cobbled path. Most of the buildings he passed were pubs and little bars, all locked. The wall he followed permitted no access through its defences. He paused to assess the situation. The terrain dropped away steeply and a crag rose almost vertically to his left, the citadel wall following this line in a formidable defensive face. A series of stone steps, much worn and cracked, found a natural line down the hill. He sat on the cold stairs and took in the view. To the west, more trees emerged through a less dense spread of houses and buildings. It didn't look so gloomy and the greenery appealed to him. He set off down the steep thoroughfare. The city spread wide below him.

On the steeper sections Arthur noticed that the steps had been carved out of the rock face, empty space fell steeply away on the open side. He looked out upon a series of large rooftops, possibly hotels and hostelries like the one he had just vacated, though not boarded up and closed. Yet still nothing stirred, just the noisy flapping of disturbed pigeons as he emerged into a pleasant, but overgrown street. Decorative cast-iron railings fronted the properties, hedges had bulked hugely and spilled out onto and across the pavements into the road. Elaborate gateways guarded shadowed drives, hints and glimpses of the buildings beyond telling of a wealthier part of the city.

He noted he was heading gradually downhill, away from the fortifications that dominated the hilltop above him. A murder of crows croaked and called from the tall trees that grew from the ruins and stone shells. He was aware that he neared a peculiar structure that he had previously discerned from the hotel viewing point. A convoluted tangle of craftily twisted wrought iron work that had caught his attention. The gateway and railing featured strange symbols, which stood out in their uniqueness. He decided to investigate further.

A short, tree-lined avenue took him to an elaborate convolution of conical towers and tall, narrow windows. Some of the upper casements had rotted and fallen out, revealing tattered drapes and curtains within. Two grotesque demonic statues flanked the massive oak doorway, which was firmly shut. The forged hinges and studding gave it an impregnable appearance, more suited to a castle or a grand cathedral. He tried the handles, which creaked, but did not give entrance. The lower windows were barred with iron. Arthur took a walk around the building, peering through the dirty windows at ground level. Inside it looked dark and dusty. Elegant furniture and decorative woodwork told of an old world affluence, but there was something else about this place which drew him. He could not define it yet. It had the feeling of an old church, a sanctuary of some sort. He was drawn to its secure, shadowy interior.

He could not gain access without breaking a window and removing a vertical iron rod, and being unwilling to commit such an act, he decided to explore the town further and to try to establish why it was so deserted. As he walked back to the main street a movement caught his eye. A curtain had briefly moved up on the second floor, it sent a shiver down his back. Arthur kept walking, glad he had not forced an entry to the shadowy mansion.

As he followed the street downhill, increasingly he would come across constructions which had to be Roman. What puzzled him was their good state of repair. One such squat tower had parchment windows and a large woodpile, signs of activity showed around a chopping block, footprints and wood-chips, but again no people. Further downhill he came to the entranceway of a park, the gates wide open, weeds were rank and profligate, the trees and hedges untended. He knew there would be tall statues on columns within, he had seen this place from the hotel aloft yesterday. A low wind stirred last summer's old dried leaves.

He became confused again when reaching a crossroads, a number of familiar features demanded an explanation. There was a library and it was almost the same as the one back in his own, real world. Both the building itself and the structures nearby were more elongated, taller and gloomier, but it was almost the very same place. This did not make sense. It was in appearance a warped copy of the library in his home town. He paused for a while and sat on the stairs, under the shelter of a pillared entrance. All was silent and still, nothing stirred, nothing moved. The grey day slowly passed over the rooftops. Arthur had to pause and take stock of what had occurred. It could not be the same place. That did not make any sense.

The cold stone beneath him was real. The Romanesque pillars were also solid and supported a very authentic roof. He rose and covered his brow so he could peer into the shadows within. The glass-panelled door had a handle, this opened. Without hesitation Arthur entered the gloom. The library rooms were much taller than that of his own, also an antiquated ladder system on rails and runners provided access to the volumes fifteen feet from the floor. His heart started quickly as disturbed pigeons noisily found their way to a small broken window. It was similarly familiar inside, but it was thankfully not the same place.

There also was very little light. Arthur felt like he was walking in a dusky canyon. It was certainly much larger within than the central library back in his own town. Soon he felt relief as he knew this enlarged copy was now just that. Yet he could not place why it was so familiar? There was no cafeteria in this version of the library, only more steep avenues of books stacked to the very roof.

He noticed that the walls of the bookshelves were braced with iron brackets at junctions up near the roof and on the longer sections of the avenue. Also that the light fittings were gas powered and that the entire place was spotlessly clean. Yet there was no-one around. Maybe they all come out a night? Arthur thought to himself, maybe they don't go outdoors at all? The narrow corridors of book-lined walls provided no answer at an initial glance. Arthur then decided to leave this empty place.

Back out in the street the day remained solemn grey, nothing stirred, but the ever-present pigeons. He began to head towards the river, down a street of tall Regency period houses. The beech trees which once flanked the pavement and road were greatly overgrown. The small gardens that fronted these large, comfortable family houses had been untended and had spread to obscure the lower windows. All of the doors were shut and all of the curtains remained closed. Still, the roads were deserted.

At first Arthur thought it was imaginary, but as he walked further down this affluent but overgrown street, he heard music, or at least a rhythm. As it became clearer, he knew it was actually musical sounds of some description. Crossing a junction of roads, the buildings he approached were of the same Regency era, but much more neglected and run down, without those little wrought iron fence enclosed gardens, and they had doors which opened directly onto the street.

The sounds were loud now and emitted from the upper floors of this rougher looking block. He recognized the type of thing he was listening to, it was the music that spilled from the kind of pubs Arthur always avoided. Pubs full of threatening and aggressive, leather clad young men and women. It throbbed and occasionally droned metallic and repetitive. He thought best not to intrude. A most prudent move.

Somewhat reassured by the normality and the sheer fact of the music playing, he relaxed a little and was happy that he had found this place and the city was inhabited by more than just a dozen churchgoers. The area became seedier and dingier the further he progressed into it, this and the fact that there was a growing smell, something he recognised. The odour of poverty and age, of grimy industrial smears on brickwork and tall chimney-pot clusters. He passed his first car, parked before what once was a guest house. It was old by his terms, with long black mounting boards and an enormous bonnet. Rust was devouring the black metal skin, the leather upholstery on the seats had been stripped long ago. Again, it was reassuring in a strange sort of way.

Many of the windows and doors he passed were shattered and broken. Burst piping spurted water, which ran in the grass and weeds of the street. The rotten carcass of a long dead dog stank horribly, the dull drone of flies hummed within a bared ribcage, its white teeth still bared in a final defiant snarl. The area became even grimier. Tenements now dominated the road, which gradually was narrowing and as they increased in height, less light found a way down to the cracked and weed rank pavement. The slated roofing was steep and many spiked garrets and dormers broke the blue-grey monotony. Yet still, the streets were quite devoid of any people.

Arthur approached a dark church, which sat at the point where the street divided into two smaller roads, each a little wider than an alley. The whole place looked suspect. He wondered if he was doing the right thing in coming here. A distinct uneasiness grew steadily in his mind. The stench of ancient poverty and the reek of decay had also increased. He drew near to the elongated church and saw that its doors were ajar, the stained glass of the windows were nearly all shattered and indiscernible words had been painted on the doors in white and red, a long time ago. Arthur considered entering, but something instinctual buried deep within him objected and he continued onward, down the left-hand narrow street.

The sparse light barely reached the alley, broken glass and strands of pale weeds crunched noisily beneath his feet. Soon he realised that this narrow roadway divided into a series of claustrophobic little chares or alleys that only caused his nervousness and apprehension to swell, almost to a panic. He stopped, his back to a crumbling stone wall, and looked about the dismal slum. There had been no planning to this part of the town. It seemed to be completely without order. No straight lines, no street signs, no lamps nor shop fronts. It had developed in miserable filth and unhealthy, crowded squalor. Arthur had a vague notion in which direction the river lay in and decided to press on, finding a break in the ancient tenements which ran in the right direction.

When he had reached out his arms, Arthur could easily touch each filthy wall. At one point the back-lane narrowed absurdly where an archway, dark as a cave, linked adjacent buildings. He stumbled and braced himself, realising that steep stairs descended into the gloom, ahead of him a narrow slit of grey light denoted the exit. Carefully, he shuffled down towards the paltry illumination. Emerging, his hands dirty from using each wall to brace his descent, he looked down upon the river.

The water seemed congealed, a slick oily ripple under a flat patch of sunlight from an iron-hard sky. The river ran with a slow, dark rippling movement, the only sign of flow and direction. A score of derelict buildings in his immediate vicinity spoke of six different ages of history. He stood at the head of a steep bank which despite its incline had many structures crammed into it, and again, the eras and styles of this mainly derelict area varied confusingly. There were even older sections and fragments, with miserable hovels built inside of the empty stone shells, makeshift huts and shelters huddled within the sheltering walls of the ruins. Yet still no person could be seen at all.

Arthur looked down upon an undulating landscape of slate rooftops and chimney-stacks. Gradually, the stone steps led him to the riverside streets. A smog hung shroud-like upon the opposite bank, turrets and spires occasionally peeked out and then would disappear into the mist. He eventually found a way to the long collapsed staiths of an old docking bay, its massive timbers rotted and slumped in a broken tangle. The river mud was black and uninviting, it also stank. Pigeons had fed and pecked here and there, traces of their movements remained in the filth.

All was silent. The stain in the sky where the light leached down became shrouded in a darker cloud, it threatened rain. It was long past mid-day and he was growing hungry.

He backtracked to the widest street, one which ran parallel to the river and would lead towards the area where he had seen the yellow lamplight by night and a little chimney smoke by day. He had to try to find someone who would know about this place, this confusing, half-familiar town. The road initially seemed straight and virtually continuous, but in many places it narrowed or buckled around substantial stone built industrial structures. Arthur was still heading towards the knot of bridges however, the populated area, further down river.

The rank stench of stale sewerage and polluted water dominated and his fear again grew within him. The road turned and he approached the first of these bridges. Again, it seemed familiar, a skeletal framework of iron, lying flat between enormous stanchions. But it was what lay beyond which threw him and unsettled his mind. The second structure was a scaled up High Level Bridge, massively larger with huge monolithic stone plinths and broader approach arches. It was proportionately exact, a much enlarged copy of the familiar, a scaled-up original, exact and aloft, stained dark.

He had lived in the tenements which clustered about the feet of this rail and roadway bridge. His clean garret rooms and orderly life had been lived out there, before the death of his mother and the assault of alcohol. Arthur thought that it could not be the same place. It was far larger than the original he knew and more densely packed with run-down buildings that crammed every available space upon the entire bank side. Slums very much like those knew had been demolished and crashed to rubble many years ago back in his own Tyneside. Greatly confused, he pressed on.

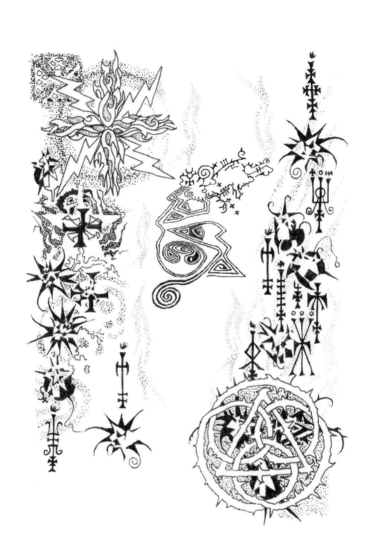

CHAPTER NINE

The Fog on the Tyne.

Tyneside 1978. In the narrow room of a Salvation Army Hostel a long-haired young man working his mornings as a cleaner opens the unlocked door of a late riser to do his morning tasks. The old guy is still in his bed, fully clothed, bar his shoes. Outside, the traffic roars and the busy world continues about its business. The young lad opens the window and gives the recumbent figure a gentle shake on his shoulders. There is no response. He tries again, this time a little more vigorously, and again, no reaction.

'Aw Hell! Not another one!' he moans, and runs off to the supervisor's office, leaving his pine-smelling mop and bucket steaming in the cold morning light. This was the fourth dead or dying old codger he had discovered in less than a year. It was beginning to get to him, as it would.

The little drama unfolded with but a few of the hostels dishevelled occupants peering around the door, as the doctor checked over the prone figure. No-one really cared; the room would be cleaned once Arthur was taken to the hospital and tucked away into an even smaller sterilized cubicle, a number of tubes attached to his arm, drip feeding saline and glucose. He was diagnosed comatose due to a stroke, even though his heartbeat was steady, if rather low and very weak. His body lay supine, but his soul was bound and confounded elsewhere, in danger of another sort entirely. Most certainly and definitely quite trapped. A horrid business. A dreadful affair.

The i...

...In the not nice. In the final glare of the obvious snare. When the mouth is utterly and balefully ineffective as a measure of defence. In the dark place. In that time when all your friends have got scared and ran away. Away in the wrong night, in regret. Where the writhing cruelty of our human lack is laid open and bare and plain. In all of this.

Be ye not there.

Sparse yourself from every manner of ignorance and bestial blame.

By ire, bile and harridans lash! By blistering shame and everlasting rue!

In the dark place where, if you are lucky, you may have some friends left.

In the dangerous time, scratching writ, holy, ardent and earnest, scrawled within a score of unread journals. Where wrong is wrong, and always remains wrong, yet remains ignored. Where it howls its tortured fucking head off from out of the very self-same, blood-soaked ground.

Where morning brings a headache, a sense of lack, and a longing.

Green hills, far away. Real far away.

Break the febrile humour of this desolate species in a summary, a conclusive act of clear, obvious Deity... An act of God or an invasion from outer space. A manifest, non-rational, corporeal signature. Grace, in the old way of putting it. Grace or aliens... Time is passing. Time is not your friend.

A thousand stabbings in one hundred towns, with bloodstained mates bawling and brawling. There is crying and laughing, and pointless cruelty, stacked against some macho surety.

Nail all the morons, bullies and thugs to the church doors.

The tough ones, fix them with four metal pins,

Spread-eagle them across the portal, make it hard for it to be opened.

The lowest sort, just fix a limb or two in some wretched and irremovable mien. Where dark means dark, where the nasty becomes nasty, in the lonely place, where comeuppance looms certain, in the kill zone...

Be ye not there.

May your days, neither see stain nor slight from such vigilante justice.

In the darkest place, where little ranks of note or import.

In the outer limits, in the cold land, in the space between worlds, frozen, freezing, unappealing. Yielding to the blighted night all things of fear and horror and fright. In the dimmest place, in the death of all things.

Save our weary ears another malediction. No more screeches from the despairing. There is enough of that in plenty, more and enough. It is all round clear, hurting is endemic. Sorrow is epidemic. All the ugly memories are sand, falling through our fingers. In every wretched frame, our hand holds sand. For when all the tiny birds have sung their last sweet morning song, and such delights will not come again, then music is dead. Words, become like the fragile bones of dead sparrows, crisp, but beautifully formed.

Where are the gentle ones?

Those whittled from a barren stock, speak sense and speak it quickly, for soon it is all over. For ever and ever, for ever and ever Amen.

Inglorious, inflame, in deed, it is done. Lest time itself rewinds the spool.

Such facts as food and air, and lest we forget, the pit.

Whence every gangrel and waster falls. Make nothing of this crash my love.

An ending is in fact the very thing the widdershin oaf and confused cretin craves.

At the very least it is conclusive as a solace.

The i...

Slowly and with a distinct dread, Arthur MacNeil walks towards the massive version of the High Level Bridge. This monster copy spans the oily river, its far side wreathed in a fog that never seems to lift. Beneath its massive arches a whole knot of tenements and buildings nestle for space. A few chimneys lazily spill smoke into the dull day, this reassures him. It begins to rain. Lightly at first, then with every pace he takes, it intensifies until he is soaked through to the skin.

He reaches the shadow of the iron bridge, streams of water spill down upon the structures below. Here is a tenement block, just like the one in which he had lived not so long ago, in the real world, back in the original Tyneside. Before being totally demolished, it had been populated with people and movement and noise. The door to the stairwell was open. He looked up to see that it was a good three floors higher than the version upon which it seemed to be based. Arthur entered and began the slow wet slog all the way up to the top floor.

He found the door to his small attic flat. He kept his key on a length of string within fingertip reach through the letterbox. Cautiously he entered, taking off the rucksack and becoming more curious as he recognized familiar furniture. The carriage clock he had pawned for whiskey, it was there, and also the wardrobe, which had held his few clothes, worn but clean. Checking this he was surprised to find his old work jacket, leather trims on the cuffs and elbows. A relic from his years as a draughtsman. This was his old flat, of that there was no mistaking.

Arthur changed out of his rain-soaked clothes into a perfectly fitting worn black suit. It made no sense. The few books he had owned were also there, so was the dark stained chest of drawers, which should contain shirts and suchlike. It did. The bottom drawer was where he kept his mother's letters. He did not expect to find them, he hoped against hope that this unnerving facsimile of his home town had limits. His heart began to beat fast when he found that the shoebox was really there, heavy with thirty years of disturbing correspondence. An most un-nerving find.

He sat on a stool by the dirty window. It opened with a bit of persuasion, revealing a ghost city, silent, eerie and drab. He wondered if the smog on the far side ever lifted and if it did, would he see a scaled-up and distorted Newcastle packed with architectural details from every age and era? Deciding to spend a night here he bolted the door and took a bottle of rich red wine from the rucksack. In his tiny kitchen, his few domestic items remained as they had been. Retrieving the corkscrew and a dusty glass he returned to the window. Arthur peered out whilst drinking, in the vain hope that he would see another human, or even hear scruffy children at play. The bottle slowly emptied and the rainy day, gradually began to fade. Nothing stirred, no one was out there. A quiet, puzzling world under a dull and darkening sky. It grew colder, Arthur thought to light a fire in the meagre little grate.

As darkness crept into the crowded tangle of ancient buildings, a night devoid of sound and light gained hold. The wine was excellent, as were the handful of boiled sweets and hard tack biscuits. Leaning out of the open window, he looked east, far down the river where a few tiny yellow lights had told of habitation. He would explore this part of the town in the morning. He closed the casement. Finding that the gas mantles were not working, he lit a single candle and sat in an armchair by his modest little fireside. Arthur opened the shoe box, withdrawing a bundle of letters, his hand lightly shaking nervously.

He had finished the bottle and was considering having a large brandy when it occurred to him that these letters were not exactly the same ones as those he kept back in the real world. The whole tone and content had changed from a paranoid ramble to a distinctly clear account of what her tormentors were about. As he read her words, they resembled less a mentally troubled woman and seemed more like the work of a prisoner, who knows her jailers but not her sentence. He checked the address. Again this was identical to the real care-home where she had been held in observation and treatment for thirty years. So much was the same, yet the differences displaced any comfortable identification. He looked for the dates, which she usually placed centrally at the top. There were none, no dates at all. This was not right.

She had described this other-worldly town as a 'zoo', and the people within it as specimens collected by a demonic race of beings. These creatures even collected architecture, she thought this was because 'they' liked the mood created by such forms. Arthur read on, his head swimming with alcohol and bewilderment. He wondered if it were possible that she was also here? Could his mother have woken in this place just as he had done? Her explanations in the pages he held were confident and assertive, but still disturbing in the belief that these predatory creatures made sport of humanity, delighted in misery and suffering and also having the power of gods. What could she really mean?

Enough was enough. He carefully replaced the letters and put them away, drained his brandy in one go and threw off his suit, falling into the damp sheets and a deep, dreamless sleep. Outside, in the city, wary figures flitted from darkness to darkness, alley to alley. In a place of its size, there were few, very few indeed and every single one of them lived in fear and wariness and dread. Arthur snored as the frozen darkness crept stealthily by, the long hours slowly passed. He had no idea what awaited him. There was a lot to learn about the prison-city in which he was now an inmate. His mother's letter was right, it was a kind of zoo, a place where human souls were deposited after careful selection. Like a zoo, they were watched, and groomed, and occasionally cropped and culled.

Morning announced itself as a growing discolouration of the gloom, it stole into the attic rooms of the tall, narrow tenement beneath the enormous bridge of massive masonry blocks and steel. The grey light reached the sleeping old man, he stirred, rose and dressed. His old routine in his old room. Arthur's head hurt, the tap water ran brown for a while, then briefly spluttered a yellow colour before turning clear. Even the large bottle of aspirin still lay in the cabinet of the tiny bathroom. He wanted to make a cup of tea, but the gas was off. He then remembered that it had ran from a coin-operated meter. That too was in its correct place also were the small pile of shillings, which he kept by it, just in case of such a situation. The coin clinked into the sturdy little box. The gas was back on, simple as that.

The kitchen cupboards contained some tinned food, stale cheese and mouldy bread. Dusty tins held oatmeal and flour, dried milk, sugar and crucially, loose tea. Soon the kettle began to whistle merrily, all seemed completely normal. He knew it was anything but that, yet these rooms were quite the same. How was it all so authentic? The possessions, the clothes, the food. Even the gas meter and the emergency coins he stashed by it. Then his mother's letters, especially these being here, this troubled him more than anything else. That and the fact they were so different in tone and content. It was a distorted but a paralleled version of his own real world, yet authentic enough in itself.

Arthur sat by the window with his hot mug of sweet tea and dipped his hard tack biscuit into it. Over the dirty river, the far side was still shrouded in thick, swirling, pea soup smog. Wisps and fingers of it curled and reached out over the glutinous water as if to make an attack on the opposite bank, but dissipated before making it barely halfway. He wondered what was over there and why it was constantly hidden? The tea was good and soon the aspirin dissolved his hangover adequately. He decided to explore.

The previous night he had hung his wet clothing by the front door. They sagged on hooks, still damp and dirty from his exploits. He folded them onto a coat hanger and hooked this to the window where it could slowly dry. Then he checked the pockets. First, he found the beautiful gentleman's hunting watch he had taken from the hotel on the hill. Then a stained handkerchief and his worn calfskin wallet containing a few notes and coins. When his fingers touched something cold he shivered and withdrew the iron key, studying it closely by the mean morning light seeping through the soot-stained window.

He had not previously noticed how elaborate it was, unlike any key he had ever seen before. Having been in such a state of blind panic from his experiences in the corridor of doors, he had simply pocketed it without a second glance, once the door was secured shut. The thought of the things that he had seen in those rooms caused him to shudder. The main bar of the key was a fluted damask rod, spiralling elaborately to a series of interlocking elegant shapes of strange geometrical design.

He studied it from various angles and thought it best to put the thing away. Even though he had held it in his hand and turned the strangely beautiful thing in his fingers, it remained unnaturally cold. He placed it under his worn white-cotton shirts, beneath the brown paper, which lined the drawer, and was happy to forget about it.

He dressed as he would have done for work, but without his tie. Arthur took the sturdiest shoes, ones that he remembered he had worn out long ago, and left the relative comfort of his rooms at the head of the stairwell. Outside in the narrow street, nothing stirred or moved. Water still dripped from the bridge arch, way above him. It fell through a windless space to strike noisily upon the cobblestones of the street. Deciding to retrace his old route to work and time the distance, he withdrew the pocket watch and rewound it. He had no idea what the real time was, so he set the hands to nine o'clock, it felt about right. He remembered it took him between fifteen to twenty minutes to walk to the draughtsman's offices and the factory, it would be telling to find out how close a copy this place was to the world he had left behind. He wanted to pay attention to the differences.

Where the Swing Bridge should have been a whole clutter of structures contended for space. Most were constructed entirely of massive timbers with high, stout gates restricting entry. One possessed formidable frowning towers of roughly dressed masonry, which fronted a castle-type portcullis gate. Another was a fascinating, overcrowded stone structure, which bridged the water in a series of shallow arches locating on plinths. It was covered in buildings, houses and pokey little shops as if every inch of space upon it was utilized and claimed. It was clearly Medieval, the timbering and cantilevered upper floors denoted this. He paused for a while, simply staring down the dark, narrow tunnel created by the slumping buildings overhanging the thoroughfare. Then he continued on as if to work.

The narrow lanes, lofty warehouses and tenements restricted his view, as did the manner in which so many grimy buildings had been packed into every possible available space. This had a distinctly claustrophobic effect upon Arthur. He passed many closed doors and blackened windows, which seemed to be closing in upon him. The road indeed narrowed, so it wasn't until he was virtually beneath it that he saw it. A Tyne Bridge, of a sort, soaring aloft. Like the High Level Bridge, this was a gargantuan, greatly scaled-up copy. He paused, craning his neck to guess the actual height of the roadway above him and shook his bewildered head. It was enormous, simply massive, an intimidating version of a feature any Tynesider would recognize in a moment. Where had the people gone? Where was the traffic? This continued to trouble him and increased a deep and growing anxiety, which this town seemed to promote by its very nature. The height of the tenements and structures around it had obscured this obvious feature from his view. Now it soared over the river into the fog.

Beyond the dark shadows of the monster Tyne Bridge, Arthur entered an area that initially assaulted his sense of smell. Here were cramped, dismal slums even more crowded and concentrated with squalor and ugliness than anything he had yet seen. Again, all ages of architecture were represented within the tangle of tall, decrepit houses and tenement blocks, but it told of new levels of impoverishment and destitution. It was like walking back in time. The stench was so pronounced he held his handkerchief to his face and quickened his pace. He thought he heard a woman crying, but he would not stop here, nor had he any will to investigate. The place reeked disease and corruption, he simply wished to be away from the area.

Out of breath, he neared what was clearly an industrial area. Gantries and warehouses competed for space and prominence. Much of it was unrecognisable, but in the distance at the limit of his view, down the little cobbled street, he determined the massive, stained red-brick walls of his work place. High masonry walls topped with broken glass set in cement flanked him on either side. Huge iron gates, padlocked and bolted, allowed only a glimpse into railway marshalling yards and construction areas, littered with packing crates and overhead cranes. In time he neared the factory where he once worked. The main gates were locked. He thought to try the doors to the office building.

It now did not surprise him that it was much taller, by ten floors at least. It was dirtier and seemingly bleaker than he remembered, and like all else in this city, it was an elongated, scaled-up version of the real one, which he well knew existed back on the original Tyneside. He checked the pocket watch, it had taken three quarters of an hour to get here, this puzzled him a lot. There was something very strange indeed about this enigmatic and creepy version of Gateshead. There was more of it, if not all of it, all it had ever been, yet crammed into an almost similar area and terrain. Close, but certainly and clearly other. So different. Very different. It constantly gnawed at his mind, how such a thing could be?

The large double doors by which he had arrived each day were open. They creaked with an unsettling shriek and allowed him into the cool, gloomy interior. Ranks of lockers and postal cubbyholes lined either side of the entrance hall, the inquiry office had its shutters down, and silence dominated the place. An old black bicycle had been placed near a fire hydrant, a canvas satchel marked ARP hung from the handlebars. His footsteps echoed on the dusty parquet flooring. He took the stairs to the upper floors, checking each level to see how it corresponded with the real factory, which in his memory was a hive of activity, and buzzing with noise and chatter. The pigeons fluttered in the light, which streamed down the central stairwell, it seemed an awful long way to the top floor drawing offices.

The ceiling was higher and the windows dirtier, but the ranks of files and wooden storage drawers where the drawing work was safely ordered, these were the same. He went instinctively to a cabinet and opened a pending drawer. It was his own work, he knew it at a glance.

He had never used stencilling on his lettering and numbering. It was even signed with his very name. Yet the date was absent.

Every drawing should have had a finished date and a checked date. The index number was there, all was in place bar the fact that it could not be fixed it in time. The absurdity of this hit Arthur. Every drawing was procedurally and systematically dated, without exception. He checked other drawers and other files and the work of his fellow draughtsmen, and not a single one of the drawings was dated. This was impossible. It was not how things had worked.

In the manager's office, the calendar, which always sat on his desk, was absent. The orders book was a thick black volume, again also forever present on the bosses desk. It was there, full of details, but no dates, no reference to days, weeks, months or years. Arthur opened the iron-framed window and breathed deep. The air had a hint of the dreadful slum area, which he had passed through on his way here, that and the pervasive reek of soot, oil and engine grease. The view revealed dockyards and industrial compounds fronting the river. Smog still obscured the far side. Nothing moved but the poisoned water. A number of ships and smaller vessels remained uncompleted, some had rusted utterly.

Arthur slowly descended back to the entrance hall, on his way he checked at random various floors beneath, hoping to find someone at work. Anyone would have done. The massive building was empty save for himself. In the inquiries office he found a local newspaper, folded into the pocket of a heavy, grey-tweed overcoat. The leading article spoke of bombing raids and ships sunk, of battles in Europe and troubling news from a war torn world. Yet there was no date. Nothing could be fixed in time here. All ages and eras seemed to be represented, but nothing made reference to or indicated what actual year it was. It made the claustrophobic atmosphere of the town tighten about him and cause a constriction within his chest. He was alone and he was stuck here. His hands met solid objects and his eyes identified features, which almost corresponded with what he knew to be real. The very air he inhaled indicated the character of this place, but nothing told him what it was, or where it was, or why it existed or even how he came to be here.

Arthur felt sick and slightly dizzy. A panic was threatening to swallow him whole. He took the antiquated bicycle with the canvas bag still draped about its handlebars and stumbled into the street. It was a nightmare, but it was real. Made all the worse by its intimations and reminders of what he knew and where he had really come from.

The bone-shaker rattled along the cobblestones. Arthur had not ridden a bicycle since his twenties and found it more of an annoyance at first. As he approached the dire tangle of the stinking slum area, he realized this old machine could get him through the unbearable stench quickly. It did, but the odours still clung to his clothing as if unwilling to yield their diseased presence. He sensed the shadow of the overblown Tyne Bridge engulf him, then it was almost a relief to see the teeming, sub-standard houses that spilled down the steep bank sides of an alternative and otherworldly Pipewellgate before him. He drew near the Medieval bridge and paused before it a second time. The tunnel-like street faded halfway into a deep mist.

Turning his wheels towards the quaint but unstable looking pile, he pedalled into the shade of the overhanging buildings flanking both sides of the bridge. He noticed that it was taking him a lot of effort to cover very little ground at all. Eventually he stopped and propped the bike against a pitted, dirty sandstone wall. A painted sign in Old English calligraphy overhead revealed that the shuttered shop was a bakers. No smells of fresh bread or suchlike came from within. He began to walk further into the shade of the cramped street. His heart began to thump in his ears and his breathing became laboured and difficult. Something skipped between the buildings in the deep fog, almost at the range of vision. Arthur called out, and the sound was muffled, the narrow way and the looming structures seemed to absorb his call. Then he glimpsed it again, this time more than one little shape darted across the narrow street. To walk took all his will and effort, he had almost reached the coils of smog when he thought he saw little children at play. He heard distant laughter, it reached him from afar, the delight of kids at their games. It became an effort of will to continue. He tried hard, there were people here, he could hear children playing, and they were just out of sight in the mist ahead. He pushed forward with all his might, struggling hard to overcome the sickly, nauseous way he felt.

As he reached the fog and as he inhaled its cold, sweet poison he knew he would soon pass out. Staggering, as if blind drunk, his last remaining rational thought was for him to turn around and go back the way he came before it was too late. He felt as if he was being pushed down into mud, he could physically feel a great pressure upon his head and brow. Arthur's eyes wanted to close, and his body desired sleep. He turned and lurched back towards the Gateshead side, which was but a dull light at the end of the tunnel like bridge-street. He felt himself choking and gasping for breath. With his last conscious effort he tried to run the remaining distance, fearing for his life. He collided with the bicycle propped against the baker's shop and smashed heavily to the cobbled path, knocking himself out cold. He lay still, and completely unconscious, a thin trickle of blood running from a dark bruise and gash that was forming on his forehead.

In an innocuous hospital ward composed of small single rooms an old man's body trembled. No-one noticed, for no-one was attending him. Neither were there monitors or methods of declaring that his heart rate briefly increased, as did his respiration and temperature. He shook for a moment, enough for the tubes and drip feeds to shake with a gentle rattle. No-one heard him. No-one saw. The incident lasted less than a minute and a half, and as quickly as it had occurred it ceased.

Arthur subsided back into the comatose stillness that had marked his condition for three uneventful days.

A day into digits, making money, making money,

Six days and six nights, work, work, work work.

Into the unknown…and every minute there is threatened,

Each machine like day, each weekly pay…

The Kill-Kill Machine… is rubbing out the contradictions,

To do as you say, each time, each day.

Each point of friction.

The Kill-Kill Machine…is doing the diction.

Like good worn-out clothes, we wear out our welcome,

Again and again, the thing, the thing,

Is just out of grasp…every time it's consequential,

Each turn of the wheel, routine, routine…

The Kill-Kill Machine…is terminating all the contracts,

Assessing the score, you win! You win!

To an inhuman predilection,

The Kill-Kill Machine…is no work of fiction.

Nowhere and no-one, inadequate and long redundant,

The noise and the fear, the noise, the fear.

Away over there...where limitations never figure,

Each time in control, control, serene...

The Kill-Kill Machine...eradicating irritations,

And scratching the itch, with ordinance...

A decadence,

The Kill-Kill Machine...a consequence.

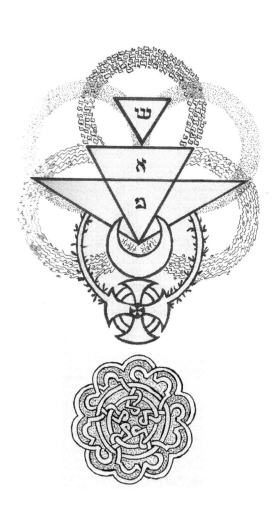

CHAPTER TEN

Concerning the zoo and it's environments.

The wholesome smell of freshly baked bread woke Arthur MacNeil from his black out. He was lying face down on the cobblestones, his head throbbed and dried blood had stuck his left eye shut. It was almost dark and the bicycle was long gone. He was lucky to still be wearing his shoes, any later into the night and they also would have been thieved. Groaning, he slowly got to his feet using the wall of the baker's shop for support. A small gas mantle on an ornate iron bracket burned yellow at the Gateshead end of the bridge. Remembering how he had come to fall over he glanced in the opposite direction over the water, nothing could be seen or heard. He knocked on the door of the fragrant baker's shop.

'Bugger off!' came a coarse voice from within almost immediately.

'Please open up!' appealed Arthur.

'I told yer, yer bastard, had away an'shite!' the voice was more emphatic.

'Can you please just talk to me for a moment?' Arthur tried to appeal again.

'If I have got ter come oot ther' I will knock yer bloody teeth oot yer heed!'

He sounded as if he meant it. Arthur considered the threat accompanying the voice. What could he do? There seemed nothing to lose from knocking again, so he did.

'Are yer still there yer stupid fuckah?' the voice from within the bakers demanded flatly and aggressively.

'Aye' answered Arthur timidly, ' I am'.

'Then yer need a bluddy weapon!''

The heavy door opened and a lovely smell wafted out with sweet warmth, homely candlelight and the aroma of fresh baking. However the apparition that accompanied it was anything but friendly. A twisted little hulk of a man, whose burly shoulders hunched up on one side. He was almost as wide as high, he snarled and brandished a huge cudgel. His face was pock marked, the teeth unevenly broken and his eyes red and bloodshot. The horrible figure had a braided beard and metal scull cap. Arthur quickly backed off.

'Ahhh! 'See some bugger got to yer first' the little beast gestured at Arthur's bruised head with the hefty stick. Clearly a shellelagh. A hurtful weapon if used right.

'Yer new aroond here aren't yer?' he squinted up towards the taller man.

'Aye' replied Arthur, 'that I am'.

'Then git back ter where `ivver th` fuck yer came fram, if yer have owt upstairs, ye stupid fuckin' bastard!'

The wee man began to close the nail studded wooden door and then hesitated just before doing so.

'Yer got owt ter trade?' he questioned with a feral snarl.

Arthur paused and thought about it.

'I've got a bottle of really good wine' Arthur offered.

'Real wine or home made shite?' the wee man quickly snapped back.

'Oh, real wine, proper stuff, good rich red Beaujolais' Arthur replied.

'Boo jah bluddy whet?"' Stumpy looked at Arthur as if he were a complete and utter idiot. The dodgiest member of the Seven Dwarves was glaring intendedly at him, but a very foul mouthed and seriously dangerous version, with a big, knobbly stick.

'I will go and get it.' Arthur replied nervously, adding, 'I will be back in ten minutes'

'Ten whet?' the ugly wee man was now convinced Arthur was a complete imbecile.

'No matter, I will be back soon'

'Whet`s yer name?' the little monster snarled.

'Arthur ' answered Arthur, ' What's yours?'

'Nivver ye fuckin` mind! Gan an` git th` vino!'

Despite the adequately convincing hostility of the stunted freak in the baker's shop Arthur was mildly excited. He had met someone with whom he had a conversation of a certain rough edged sort. The wee man spoke with a definite Tyneside accent, but from a hard to place antiquity. If he were going to attack, Arthur knew he would not be standing upright. It was clear that despite his height, the little blighted fellow was no stranger to a scrap, or would be at all hesitant in using that evil-looking stick he clenched. Yet the accent of the baker troubled him too, it was so antique, so old.

The stairwell was pitch black, Arthur had to use the left-hand wall to feel his way up the steps. Eventually he reached his front door and retrieved the key on the string. Inside, he lit a candle and pushed it into the neck of the empty bottle. Regarding himself in the mirror by its flickering light, he winced at the nasty discoloured lump on his brow, he splashed at it in the sink with cold water and took a few aspirin for the pain. From the rucksack he took a bottle of wine, added a corkscrew and a box of matches to his pocket and descended, this time using the improvised candlestick holder to find his way backs downstairs easily. He placed the bottle by the street door and pocketed the candle.

Carefully cradling the fine red wine, he made his way back to the old bakery on the bridge. Before he knocked he thought he heard singing and laughter from the far side. He rapped three times.

'Is that yoo?' a voice from within asked.

'Aye' replied Arthur, 'it's me'.

'Me who? ye daft bastard yer!' the cantankerous gravely voice snapped.

'Arthur ' answered Arthur, hoping this was a good idea.

The bakery door opened and there was the rough looking stump of a man,

'How 'wer in' he said.

The room within was bare, rough stone. A massive range dominated one wall and by this a well-scrubbed, slate-topped table displayed a batch of two large fresh loaves, two cakes and three pies. It smelled delicious. Arthur then realised how deeply hungry he really was.

'Any funny business an' arl fuck yer gud an' proper, yer hear me!' Stumpy pointed out his comment with the bulbous black stick and a snarl.

'Loud and clear' acknowledged Arthur, ' thanks for letting me in'.

'It's a fuckin' shop yer silly bastard! Now where's yer trade?'

Arthur handed over the bottle of wine and the wee man's eyes widened with surprise.

'Fuck me!' he exclaimed ' where th' hell didjer git this?'

Arthur thought it prudent to protect his source and answered cautiously and civilly,

'Will that make it taste any better?'

Stumpy laughed. It sounded like a rockfall on a stony mountain, when this subsided the wee monster asked,

'Whet yer wantin' fur it then?'

'Some of your baking and a bit of your time.' Arthur answered, deciding directness may pay.

'Well, yer can have most of th' first and a bit of th' second', the wee man responded.

'Fair enough', replied Arthur.

'Sit yer swain doon a bit, rest yer arse ' the rough little guy said and made to break off the neck of the bottle on the slate table. Arthur saw this and said from the simple beam bench,

'Don't do that man, I've got an opener for it!'

'Aye have yer? Fancy that eh? Well open th` bluddy thing fer me then!'

Arthur took the wine and popped the cork quickly. The wee man's beady eyes never left the bottle for one moment. Arthur handed it back to him, and at once he put it to his mouth and took a very, very, very long swallow. The bottle glugged several times and then he paused for breath.

'Ye Gods that is luverley! That really is bluddy luverley! Well dun yer big auld string o`piss yer!'

The hostile stump sat himself on a stool opposite Arthur, near the range and took another long slug.

'Ah` will wrap yer scran in a bit fellah`, just lemme neck a drop mer o` this.'

The wee man's boots did not touch the flagged floor, he was little higher than a child, but the muscles in his arms and legs bulked him disproportionately. As he drank, Arthur studied the room.

A candle burned on the slate-topped table, a lamp hung on a bracket near the iron range, and it smoked heavily as if it were burning fat. It was a sparse room, but warm. The windows were narrow and shuttered from within. The ceiling was low and from its sturdy beams pots, pans and utensils hung.

Arthur noticed a half dozen pigeons hanging from their feet and a bucket full of feathers below this. Large earthenware pots lay in rows upon a shelf, a stout ladder led to a ceiling hatch and that was it.

'Whoo boy!' the stunted fellow whistled and carefully, almost delicately, placed the bottle down.

'That's made me swain a very happy wee man that has, good bluddy trade this nocturne'.

Swaying slightly the little guy took a hessian sack and placed all the baking into it, bar one loaf, one pie and one small cake, thrusting it towards Arthur with a brief nod, the exchange was now complete.

'There yer go. Now ask yer bloody question an' then fuck off.'

Arthur knew he should not push his luck and got straight to the point.

'How did you get here and where did you come from?' he asked.

The hefty wee fellow looked momentarily confused, his callous bluster subsiding as he scratched his ear. Then he tilted his head to one side and squinted as if peering into a far, far distance. Arthur thought it best to give him time to respond and sat quietly, waiting.

Stumpy exhaled and took another swallow of wine. He stared at Arthur, but this time the bristling antagonism and palpable aggression were absent. The fire rustled within the range in the quiet. Eventually the muscular fellow almost gently said,

'Bluddy gud question man. I cannit remember how lang I've been here. Seems like furevah. A reet lang time, reet enuff. A reet lang, lang time agan.' He took another slug and added quietly,

'Wance thir was a King called Henry, a strang king, lang way doon in th' souff, in London. 'Ee 'ad a shower o' wives. Wance… a reet lang time back. That's it man, that's all ye gettin' oot o' me.'

Arthur rose and shrugged his shoulders in acceptance, none the wiser. The little man dropped from the stool and shuffled to the door, opened it cautiously, deftly peered out and quickly glanced both ways, then stepped aside for Arthur to leave. He had his cudgel at the ready.

'Ah cannit mind 'ow I got 'ere big man, a'divvint knaa'. I jus' did...
an' now 'am here... an' that's it.'

Arthur stepped into the narrow street and nodded silently.

'A wurd o'advice mister, eh?' Stumpy offered in parting.

'Please.' Acknowledged Arthur.

'Durnt walk these fuckin' streets at night w'oot a weapon o' sum
sort, reet?'

Arthur shivered and answered simply,

'Cheers.'

The door clunked heavily shut. He walked cautiously back to the
tenement under the bridge, clutching the corkscrew, its steel spiral
protruding from his clenched fist.

The sacking bag was still warm by the time he got back to his attic
room. Arthur locked the door, lit the gas mantle and put the kettle on.
He poured himself a generous brandy and retrieved the meat cleaver
from the rucksack, placing it on his bedside cabinet by the candlestick
he kept there. Sitting at the window stool he ate a large portion of the
pie as the kettle boiled. He was too hungry to wait. It was delicious.
The filling had to be pigeon, or some rich red meat, that plus potato
and onion. The kettle boiled. He made a cup of black, sweet tea and
set himself by the casement, feasting on his provender. Occasionally
he glanced out the window as if the darkness over the river would lift,
revealing a city of lights like it did back home. He needed it to. It did
not. It could not and never would.

He demolished a whole pie and one entire cake, which had a filling of
black currant preserve, then ate a few slices of bread. He felt content for
the first time since arriving here. He found his old and slightly mildewed

pyjamas, then shivered briefly in the damp sheets and blankets. Soon he began to warm up, and as he lay there he thought about what the wee baker had said. Surely he could not mean he had been here since the reign of King Henry the Eighth? That would be impossible, for it to be so he would be nearly six hundred years old. It was simply not feasible. Then sleep took him down to sweet velvet depths.

In the night Arthur awoke to the sound of a commotion outside. Someone was shouting loudly and angrily and female voices were shrieking inarticulate curses. Without lighting the candle he moved to the window and tried to open it with as little noise as possible. The casement slowly widened enough for him to peer directly down on the small group beneath. Someone held a lantern aloft and by this meagre light two men were raging at each other with swords. Arthur rubbed his eyes to make sure. Judging by the elaborate bonnets and old fashioned bustles, those were the women that were doing the shrieking. The fight staggered onto the other side of the road and a little in the down-river direction. He got a better, but not a clear, view. The fighters looked like cavaliers, with three-cornered hats, plumes and ten gallon boots. Cloaks billowed and swished behind them as they lunged and parried with deadly seriousness. The thin blades traced sharp silver arcs in the lantern light. More impossibility was fighting to the death in the road below. The duel surged into a narrow alley that ran towards the river, the noise diminished gradually, soon there was nothing to hear as well as see. Arthur returned to his bed.

As the morning slowly coloured the dim little room with its gradual touch, Arthur rose and dressed and put the kettle on. Deciding to shave, he went to the tiny bathroom and regarded himself in the mirror. The bruise had settled into an egg-sized black lump, he dabbed it with Dettol, a strong antiseptic, but something else caught his eye. He noticed that his stubble had not grown at all in four days, this was most odd, he still only had a day's growth. Regardless, he poured a little hot water into the sink and, with the routine of a lifetime, quickly cleaned his face. He would take note of this day.

He breakfasted on bread, a slice of cake and several cups of strong black tea. Retrieving the well-made boots and the leather-care kit he had found in the arrival hotel, he oiled and polished his footwear. Today, he would explore upriver and scavenge what he could. In the kitchen cupboard he found amongst the small supply of tinned food, some corned beef. With this he made plain, but edible sandwiches, these he placed in a tin 'bait box' with a slice of pigeon pie. Back in the real world he used to save spending money in the works canteen by taking his lunch to the office. Unpacking the rucksack to make space for anything he found, he placed the few hotel findings about the plain room and remembered the meat cleaver by the bed. This he stashed in the rucksack side pocket. The food and the waterproof cape he packed into the bottom of the bag.

Arthur thought if he walked up river for a few miles, this would take him eventually near the parts of the city that had looked less crowded and had parks and trees. To his left, the bank teemed with rows of tall terraced housing, the chimney stacks ranked in their thousands. He kept his eyes peeled for smoke issuing from the elongated brickwork, but nothing could be seen. To his right, he passed many an industrial workplace or fabricators and scores of small boatyards. No hammers fell, nor workmen swore, no spanners shifted stubborn bolts nor did sweaty Geordies shovel fuel into furnaces. The long riverside road was quiet, totally still. Only the scattering of pigeons disturbed this motionlessness with their clumsy take off.

What felt to Arthur like over two miles had passed, he turned to look back the way he came. The city was vast. The entire bulk of the southern hill was taken up with its enormity. He could see the topmost fortifications again and the huge enclosing wall. With a bit of peering he could just discern the streets of hotels and the grander houses with their tree filled gardens. He had forgotten the binoculars and thought it too far to walk back, so he continued upriver. The opposite side was still in thick mist, it seemed like a wall dividing the town in two. He remembered glimpsing turrets and towers that punctuated the fog, when he had looked from the hotel roof on his arrival. Even by the very river itself, no details were clear at a close distance. Regardless, he steadily plodded onwards and as he walked he wondered why no-one came out during the day?

Another mile later the riverside path reached a distinct fork. A clutter of minor bridges and some tall warehouses lay ahead of him. To his left, where south should be, a walled lane ran through cleaner looking terraced houses to a woodland beyond, less than a mile away. He made his way to this, passing the neat little row of buildings, on the sides of a gentle slope. By the time Arthur reached the woods, he was feeling out of breath. Clambering over a drystone wall, he found the trees were of great age. He sat within the armchair-like ridges of the roots of a nearby beech and had a bite to eat. The pocket watch said twelve o'clock, he had taken three and a half hours to cover a mere five miles at the most. Arthur really wanted to do better than that, he knew he could if he tried.

The tree cover was thick and vigorous, the undergrowth thrived. Thin grasses, patches of weeds and last autumn's leaves carpeted the earth. He could look over the valley to the fortified hilltop from where he sat and could take in the extent of its cover. There was a separate walled sector within the city, an enormous hilltop defensive network. He noted that there were more steeples within this enclosure than outside of it, and tall watchtowers stood out on the southern side. He wished he had the binoculars because he was sure smoke drifted upwards from the dark structures within.

One of the worst things a human being can encounter, is a complete apprehension of the inevitable. This and the foreknowledge of tragic consequences, and regret as deep as a coal mine. This is more than enough work for any mortal. The immediate pang of seeing ones demise approach is a form of cognisance all healthy-minded humans avoid. For pristine and appropriate reasons too. Any sentient life-form would sooner take on the challenge of overflowing broken public toilets and the plumbing repairs, rather than face ones termination. Long before that particular exit was considered, so to speak. Clearly and obviously.

No place to be. On this it is noted, the caring, objective, majority would easily sway the verdict of foreknowledge and consent to a faultless plunge into the very welcome pools of deepest ignorance. The corrosions of both time and biology, crushing our era into an ever-decreasing layer of a more specific narrow interest. To grieve, and to mourn, and to pity. To find a distant blue sphere. To start again afar.

More trash for paradise.

Arthur had done his National Service back in the real world. He was twenty eight when he was called up, his job being secured until his training was completed. He learnt to march and fire 303 rifles with a degree of proficiency. As well as square-bashing, they cleaned ordinance and polished weapons. Sitting under an ancient beech, eating his sandwiches and scanning the entire hilltop, Arthur wished he had a pistol. One like the officers wore in the British Army, where he had done exactly and precisely as he was told. A revolver, with six shots and more bullets in a pouch. He liked the notion that six rounds would be proficient. The Americans had those sleek, black forty-five automatics, great guns by all accounts. Some sergeant had told him in a pub when he was young and impressionable, that sometimes these Yank guns jammed. Imagine that, he had said, imagine that in a tight spot, imagine that...

The detail in the forest floor absorbed him. No clouds passed to clock a passage of anything time or motion indicative. Arthur rose and looked long and hard at the massive silver-grey barks of beech trunks, and the deeper shadows that indicated oaks up the easy hill. He heard the sound of water flowing and moved in that direction, continuing uphill. In a fold of the ground, in a natural hall of sturdy trees, a little stream flowed. Arthur went to it and looked at its clarity. The stones were shining, tiny wee swimming insects and tendril streamers of plant life. Clear. Arthur cupped a handful and smelt it in the palm of his hand. No odour at all. He let it run through his fingers and rubbed them to feel oil or detect a scent. His fingers smelt clean. Arthur followed the rill uphill. He passed the ruined courses of a few long-fallen dwellings. Nettles bloomed dark green midst the past.

The stream divided, Arthur followed the easiest course. The trees began to thin out and eventually led to a clearing in the woodland, an enclosed place. It was a picture-postcard field, full of turnips, long green lines of them. There was even a tangled scarecrow. As Arthur neared the tattered rags he saw the white cage of rib bones. The shape beneath the ragged hat was a human skull. He decided to take a few turnips, quickly, and then walk back to the little attic room beneath the dark sweeping arch of an outsize railway bridge.

Arthur washed the earthy turnips clean in his cracked earthenware sink, the enamelling was now a parchment yellow, the cold water revealed the perfect robust vegetable beneath the dirt. He stacked them all to dry on the draining board, then sat by the window. Each time he returned to this view, he hoped within himself that the smog over the water would have thinned, or shifted a little. Nothing had changed. The ghostly white wall of mist with its snaking tendrils and wisps remained as before. When he had tried to cross the ancient bridge-way, before he fell over the bike, Arthur found the smog had a sweetness to it. Although it was causing him to pass out, it retained afterwards a narcotic pleasure, an enhancement of the senses that was clean, clear and fresh. Like being young and happy. Arthur did not really wish to be thinking about when he was young and those rare occasions that stood out over the years, those which genuinely had lasted in memory and could be denoted as happy. He had awoken in the strangest of places. The city was an enormous abandoned enigma. His past was long gone, it had no purchase here.

He decided to read his mother's letters again. He had done this so many times in the real world and was troubled why these copies were different. As he read and sipped his tea he found that they had a frankness and clarity absent in the original, disturbed correspondence. Arthur put a tiny measure of brandy in his black tea. He settled in and let the day pass into shadowy twilight. When night fell, he ate the rest of the food remaining in his tin box and sat in the dark by the open window, listening. Just quietly listening. Slowly, the sounds of the night emerged, gently and softly each whisper became audible.

First, the soft slap of water slowly flowing against wood and stone. This was constant. Secondly, and with random timing, came the sound of a door slamming. Sometimes far, sometimes so near that he leaned out the window to check who was there, but it was too dark under the arch. Similarly, if he concentrated, Arthur could just discern the sounds of a man shouting angrily. When this quietened, someone passed below in the street, whistling very softly. Arthur shivered, and sat upright. It was a once common and popular tune, a war-years song his mother used to sing. He had a half-memory of it. An upright piano merrily ringing away. VE Day, Victory in Europe Day. Tables laden with sandwiches and cakes and jellies. He had been twenty seven years old, running a riot with a bunch of other excited blokes, like happy little kids. The war was over...long ago and far away. Someone below him was still living in that spirit. He smiled, for the first time since arriving. It made his bruise ache.

Again, that night like the previous, Arthur woke to the sound of a violent commotion outside. He had left the window open, and quickly crouched by it, listening and looking. Nothing could be seen, but it was the sound of many people fighting in a screaming angry crash. Curses and shrieks rang and howls of pain and rage bellowed. It was a cruel, chaotic symphony of violence, a riot of aggression and injury, in the dark, in the blackness, under the big arch of the High Level Bridge. He listened, enthralled and repelled at once, but deeply needing these human sounds.

Someone really close was shrieking above the clamour, an old woman's voice, raised in objection. Arthur leaned out and discerned that about two floors below him and to his left, someone was shouting out from a window, really yelling her head off. Candlelight from behind her highlighted the shape.

'Take it somewhere else yer noisy shower of bastards!' she was screeching,

'Cut it out will yers? Shut it down or ye can have me bed-pan slop!'

The racket below surged and raged regardless of her threat. A flash of falling liquids arced to the invisible crowd below, the urine and worse cascaded into the mob at their quarrel. It fell upon the rabble below.

A few noises of disgust flared. The battle bruised on, but had moved along this alternative Pipewellgate and came within the glare of the hanging gas-mantle, revealing a huddle of cursing, seething men all fist-fighting and raging mad with it.

'Bloody idiots!'

The old lady had continued her haranguing throughout the clash. It was quieter now.

'Hello neighbour', Arthur said as gently and with as much friendliness as he could muster.

The little figure beneath him, twisted around and looked up towards where she had heard the voice.

'Hello yourself, ye arse!' she spat, and slammed her casement down so hard it rattled.

As curtains closed below, the absolute darkness returned. Further down the 'Gate, the bruisers at quarrel battled on with vigour undiminished. Arthur watched them for a while until they had surged and fought until out of sight and earshot.

The sound of the soft slap of water on wood and stone resumed.

Arthur returned to his now cold bed.

CHAPTER ELEVEN

Exploring the confines.

The stinking filthy river oozed its foul-some slop slowly towards a sickening poisoned sea. A dark grey sky and the jaundiced stain of a pale-yellow sun roughly indicated the source of light and inadequate warmth. An ugly place, made worse by the evil eyes of an ancient alien intent. A zone, a particular assemblage of twisted misery, despair and sordid want. The very end of human hope and all possible, reasonable dignity. A stink hole. A shit heap. A rat and cockroach infested midden. Miserable and pitiful and dire.

Tyneside in the 1970s, I'm telling you.

A month had passed and Arthur's stubble had not grown at all. The bruise on his forehead was just as livid as the day he received it on the Medieval bridge. It still throbbed and stung with immediate injury. At night, often he would wake to the sound of commotion outside. Maybe it was some particular inverse virtue, or a curse concerning this actual bridge, that the rabble gathered here and fought and yelled, beating one another quite senseless. After more than four weeks here he was none the wiser as to the reason why or how he had arrived.

It was equally odd how he was growing increasingly less hungry and needed fewer visits to the stunted baker on the bridge to replenish stocks. One loaf he traded for two fat turnips sustained him for a whole week, which simply did not figure. Plus he still had no need to shave, which puzzled him immensely. Even the gas meter needed no extra coins. Outside the tenement, during the day, nothing stirred, no-one moved, and he himself had fallen into a pattern of sleeping all the day and wandering abroad at night. He also found a little alcohol went a long way. He still had one bottle of wine, unopened and a full decanter of brandy. The whiskey was long gone. So was his sense of time, completely remiss. He had a rough idea how long it had been since his arrival. He had a vague idea, period.

Arthur had formed a dim plan of walking to Hexam, up the river, about two or three days walk, to see if his mother was also an inmate in this bizarre copy of Tyneside. He planned it with the equipment he had salvaged from his arrival point, the abandoned hotel on the hill, but the longer he stayed in the little set of pokey rooms, the further away it became a reality. The fog never lifted over the river. He had even stopped bothering to look across the flow in the hope of seeing a hillside alive with lights in the night. He was an inmate. He had been efficiently collected, and his original physical body was now officially two and a half weeks dead. He was a copy, a facsimile, a type of consciousness reconfigured into a new and fixed form. He would be the very last to know this, for there was no return ticket. In 1978 Tyneside, he was very dead indeed and buried in a sorry paupers grave.

A dimness had overcome him. He had developed the habit of skulking off into the pitiful sunset and standing a little past the twisted wee baker's shop and inhaling the intoxicating fog that swirled at the other end of the narrow bridge-street. He felt somewhat ashamed by this and was glad the city was sparsely inhabited, there he was, sucking at the very fog of the Tyne. Ridiculous and absurd by turns, but none the less a real pleasure, a growing addiction. At the very least, a nasty or potentially dangerous habit.

One night he had been quite careful calculating how far over the bridge he could actually get without passing-out as a result of the sweet narcotic mist, when Arthur saw something which both scared and amazed him. A noisy clattering of iron studs on cobblestones told of someone approaching on the Gateshead side, so he shrank back into the shadows of an overhanging porch and watched unseen. The noise came from a man, marching, not walking, a wall of a man, pacing fast with a military gait, hard toward the baker's shop, he carried a large sack over one broad shoulder.

'Salve homunculum!' he called, banging on the worn old door. He was not concerned one bit about the stunted little fellow within. Arthur looked at the leather-skirted kilt, the battered war torn breastplate and the dull red cloak thrown over the tall, olive-skinned fellows shoulders and realized this was a real Roman soldier he was looking at. A functional gladius hung on a scabbard from his wide belt. The man swayed slightly as if drunk and banged again, cursing in the Vulgate tongue, waiting impatiently for the bulky dwarf to open his massive door.

'Fatuae homunculum!'

He bellowed as the yellow light encroached into the gloom and even at a distance, Arthur could smell the fresh bread and pies and cakes.

'Tempus praeterit idiota!'

The big warrior cursed and entered the shop. Arthur decided to swiftly make his way back to the tenement flat.

Another month passed. The city was becoming familiar, at least the small sections he had explored were. Certain areas repelled him by smell alone. That and the sense of fear that hung about these zones. When confronted by something utterly unusual and menacing, the human instinct is to avoid it or observe at a safe distance. The neighboring area, under the scaled-up Tyne Bridge was such a place. The shadows that crept from this dense and reeking sub-slum were ragged and hunched up with illness or infection. Arthur watched on many nights, from as far as he could comfortably reach into the narcotic mist on the Medieval bridge. He quietly noted where lamp light and candle glowed, who or what walked the narrow chares and alleys. It was safe from this vantage, as no-one tried to cross. They had all stopped trying long ago.

One uneventful night he heard again the merry laughter of children playing, he peered into the fog and could just discern little shapes darting to and fro, at some game. Without warning a football bounced into view, kicked from the far side, rolling to a stop near Arthur's feet. He picked it up, it was real, a leather case-ball of an old-fashioned design. As best he could manage, he booted it back into the mist and smiled as from the other side came sounds of cheering and applause. He then wondered why he had seen no children on the Gateshead side?

The Old House

Whilst exploring his immediate location, Arthur turned into a shadowy narrow alleyway with moss stained masonry and decayed brick-work, now a dull green. A cobbled drain ran centrally down the dingy back lane and long dead gas lamps jutted at intervals. Even narrower alleys ran back into the tenements, claustrophobic and reeking of decay. A massive eight floored slum towered over him, approached by a door-less arch where a broken water pipe hissed and filled the confined space with a rippling silver. It was the only sound, the only motion. The place stank.

Arthur crossed a small backyard where glass, rubbish, filth and water squelched and crunched beneath his feet. He passed the outside toilets, the doors broken open, the ceramics shattered, vandalised. The main back door to the tall tenement was ajar, the rooftop almost reaching the massive span of the King Edward Bridge above. He carefully and slowly entered, giving his eyes time to adjust to the murk. The stench was an offense to his sense of smell, the overwhelming reek of rot, of rats and something worse. He wished he was not alone and considered abandoning this particular search, yet passed through a wrecked kitchen with an enormous earthenware sink, cracked and parchment yellow.

The floor beneath him groaned and slightly moved, Arthur knew he had to take care as it could collapse and falling through into unknown darkness was most undesirable indeed. He came to a hallway with a derelict staircase and an open doorway leading to another room, steeped in shadows due to the stinking velvet ceiling-to-floor curtains, these tore as he parted them. Dust, fungi and cobwebs drifted from the tattered cloth and a little more light penetrated the apartment gloom.

He saw an ornate Georgian fireplace, dark stained wooden shelves filled with swollen damp folios, the leather furred with mildew. About the room were gas mantles, candlesticks and a paraffin lantern with a long glass cowl, all cold and unlit for an age. An armchair with its tall back towards him sat by the fireplace, a skull surmounted a moulding corpse. A rotten dress with bared ribs peeking through fraying rents and a tumble of long grey hair falling over the empty eyes showed it had been an old woman. Pins and hair-slides rusted in the spill of her spidery locks and a book lay open on her lap, a skeletal hand lay still upon the pages before her vacant gaze.

Out of curiosity, Arthur wanted to know what the volume was. As he approached, it was clear this dead old lady was the explanation for most of the stink and that she had been reading the Bible. He wondered if it had been of much comfort to her and it crossed his mind that in all his foraging this was the first Bible he had found. Gently he lifted the delicate claw of her hand and took the book, reading it by the window. He checked a familiar passage and it was not the Bible he knew, but a contorted version of the same, like the box of his mother's letters. A copy and a distorted one at that. He shivered briefly and put it down at once. Nothing was complete here, everything had been twisted and confused.

Arthur then decided to leave, but before he did, he checked a wardrobe where hung women's clothing, dresses and a moth eaten fur coat. Shoes had degenerated into tidily paired mounds of green mould. A sideboard with drawers had swollen shut and took an effort to open, he found bundles of letters tied with coloured ribbons, some curled postcards and a wooden box. Within it lay a row of five military service medals; a war hero had earned these and his widow had out-lived him, spending her remaining days in this room. It was a story unfolding. A stiff brown paper envelope contained a solemn notification. Beneath name and rank, a brief mention of bravery and wounds sustained leading to death on the battlefields of France, all in the service of King and Country. He sighed sadly and replaced these relics. The drawer would not close and evening drew near. Once outside in the chare, the dim light seemed to glare at him. This awful place was sickening his heart.

A boredom began to set in. Arthur needed very little food to stay alive, he took the smallest glass of wine or spirit and was quickly intoxicated. It worried him that he still had no need to shave, and that the bruise on his head was as large and as livid as the injury sustained the same day. He decided one night to revisit the library, which he guessed at being two miles away at most. Quite simply, he needed something to read to pass the time in this odd place. A distorted Bible being the only reading material he had yet found, and even that had been foul and corrupted in content.

He figured that if he tracked uphill and out of the Pipewellgate copy he should be able to find the big gloomy church at the road junction, where the warren of alleyways began. Then it should be easy. In fact, he found in actuality, it was a lot harder than he had considered. It was night, and the narrowness of the tiny streets, along with the height of the tenements and shadowed buildings made keeping a bearing very difficult. He spent over an hour skulking around this maze until he found the church. He could hear voices within and so cautiously he peered into the doorway, listening intently. A dozen tattered figures, all dressed in early Victorian garb stood and sat around a brazier that cast its light about the abandoned building. Most of the pews were gone, bar those in a square around the source of heat and light. The honk of human excrescence filled the place. Arthur thought it best to leave them to it and continue on.

As he entered the discernibly more attractive Regency era streets, he remembered the metallic music from just over two months previous and grew very cautious in his pace. Again he could hear it, but it was louder and even more menacing. The road in front of the once-elegant building was blocked with big motorcycles, light flooded from the windows and illuminated about six large, rough-looking men in leathers and denims. Arthur decided to give them wide berth too, and walked the perimeter of the block by turning right up one long featureless street of terraced houses, then left down an alley parallel with another main street heading in his direction, and then left again, back down onto the road to the library. He made it undetected and unseen.

The i…

An inch. The centimeter. The almost equal thrust of will in mind and heart is nothing to them. The aliens have us in thrall. Our best, our effort, our intentions are forwarded upon some inebriate whom randomly chances upon the Sanctum Mysterium. What luck! Such superb mischance! The company of reprobates has little play upon his dearth of fortune. Where ignorance drips slowly and inevitably by.

Gelatinous time, falling in globular splatterings. Plop! A week. Glop! A month.

Time, dropping thick in jelly-like increments, upon arachnid webs of sheer unthinking stupidity. This is humanity. We may ignore it all the fuck we want, but our very lack will find us all, and those spaces and chances where we could have paid attention will catch up with us, and tear out our very throats. With teeth! Dente Timitur. Beware the teeth. Be real careful pilgrim, be right royal careful. Easy like.

Makes for a Christian soul to think some.

The i...

They hate you. They really loathe us all. They have floated across the void for thousands of aeons, making such fuss in their drift about algae and beetles and lower primates and planets brim full of hopeless geeks. If you are reading this, and may the Great Hypothesis have Mercy upon you, it will bring scant comfort to consider that we humans are more interfered with than a teenage Bangkok dancing girl. Curl your liberal lips and contort your shaven-monkey brow all you fucking like, it is the truth. There is nothing in your power to make it other than the waning rebuttal of your futile denial. Soon, our era of control will come to a crashing conclusion. They will be at our burial. They will spit on our caskets. They will dance on our graves and piss on our flowers. For now, our time is drawing to a close. Soon, the utter misery we have ordained will return and find us all. It will, mark my words. All our ignorance is destined to collapse upon our thin, sorry, empty skulls.

Jesus is looking for sunbeams. Better be observant.

Sure ain't a lot of sunshine in these parts, Christ knows…least he should, being an avatar and all. Makes a right-thinking man to consider the ebb and flow of this shit-show we have corporately assumed as representative of life. For the sake of honesty and human dignity and hope, perhaps we should admit to being useless? We could simply come clean and admit to at least one living soul, that we have no relevance or talent or use or ability or acumen or inclement or knowledge of any practical use. This is a hard thing to do. Any useful thing at all, anything that can help or assist or amend or attest, anything that can aid or assure or comfort or compassionately gift peace. Anything. Other than the gossipy, slanderous drivel that pours from cursed uncreative mouths, bound in slavery to bitch-craft, wanton in misery, stooped in the gait of wretched uselessness. All this and meaningless work to boot. Hurrah!.

Hatred is not entirely pointless. Despite what the stupid, drivel-mouthed, liberals say, hatred has a place. Clever enemies do not like to be hated, they prefer to remain unobserved. The politically correct are, in the main really cowards, whose skill exists entirely in human interference. They are utter busybodies with empty humor evoking pointless laughter from a puerile entertainment…and sheep-like they gather to a final, bitter butchering. They will all die horridly. The very thing they have avoided like the pox will find every man jack of them. Assuredly. It would be remiss to write anything otherwise. So it is, so it has been, so it shall be cast forevermore. One hopes to be there when it falls, happy as the sickening day is long, and as drunk as Zeus on Destruction Day. Burning cities. Lots of deaths, all in a row, waiting to be registered.

The Library.

As Arthur's eyes adjusted to the dim glow within, he noticed that the gas mantles were burning very low, almost out, a soft spluttering throb of orange flame. They cast very little useful light and served only to indicate where the avenues between the walls of books lay. It was still clean and warm within, so he set about looking for the recent history section. He would be looking for a very long time indeed.

His footsteps seemed remarkably loud in the hushed interior, the wooden flooring amplified even his careful tread. It was far too dark to discern the book titles and the brass plates that denoted each section were equally indecipherable.

Arthur saw someone move, silently and quickly, a tall figure had passed him at the end of his avenue. He hurried to find out who was there. Peering carefully around the corner, he saw this tall, thin woman, very prim looking, with her hair in a bun and little ovoid spectacles perched on her nose. She held a bundle of books and seemed engrossed. Very gently and with as much friendliness and sincerity as he could muster in this awkward situation he spoke.

'Hello there.'

Immediately, the lady shrieked a piercing, shrill scream of fright that shocked Arthur's senses and broke the library quietness, she dropped her books to the floor. They all thudded down loudly.

'Sorry!' he emphasized, 'I mean no harm, my dear, please don't be alarmed'.

She stared at Arthur like a frightened little bird. He noticed how slight she was, quite dangerously skinny. Her bones made angular ridges on her buttoned-up tweed jacket, she appeared really undernourished. Arthur made no move to approach her, but stood at his distance and waited for her to calm down. She seemed to gather all her courage and with a quavering, very proper voice asked him,

'What do you want?'.

The question seemed odd, it was a library after all, but nothing was normal in this place. Normality was not one of it's prime features.

'The local history section actually,' he replied, ' I need to know more about this town.'

Her hesitancy and nervousness manifested in how she had backed herself against the shelf behind her and also how she stared and glared with fear and dread at a genuinely harmless Arthur. Why would anyone be afraid of Arthur?

"You would be most fortunate there, sir," she answered and collected her senses,

'we have everything but that subject'. Cocking her head slightly to the side, she studied the man in the shabby black suit.

'You have not been here long have you?' she said as if verifying her observations.

'Two months, maybe just over. Time seems to be difficult to ascertain in this place', Arthur answered and felt relief that a conversation had begun without physical threat or excessive swearing, or any immediate danger.

'Then too late for you to return', she said almost wistfully, 'too late for you...'

Arthur studied the tall skinny lady and in the dull glow of barely flickering lamp light and assessed that she had been an elegant beauty at one time, it was difficult to tell in the gloom, but she appeared to be a little younger than himself. He kept his distance all the same and then when he thought prudent to commit, asked calmly and evenly,

'Do you remember how you came here?'

The question hung in a long silent pause. He remembered Stumpy, the little baker and his response to the same inquiry. The tweedy lady caught her breath and looked calmer, but sad, and eventually replied,

'I was the head librarian here and I still am. This is my world now. I clean it and mend it when the barbarians and brutes visit and make their vandalism. Thankfully, they do so rarely. My last memory of the 'other side' was the end of the Boer War. What do you remember sir?'

'It was 1978 and Gateshead was being largely demolished,' Arthur answered.

She made a pensive nod and looked at Arthur squarely saying

'So you are from the future.'

'From your point of view I suppose I am', he affirmed, ' and like yourself I am now stranded here, like it or not'.

She shuffled awkwardly towards Arthur and extended a hand in friendship.

He took the long fingers gently, feeling the frailty in her grip.

'Welcome to the madhouse', a shadow of a smile touched her thin, tight mouth,

'I am Cecilia Fotheringham, or at least I once was'.

'Arthur MacNeil' he responded, 'and I think I still am'.

Outside in the street a rumble of noisy engines was growing, Arthur realised it was the sound of motorbikes, and they were drawing close. Their sound implied danger and threat. A growling of throttles and screeching brakes resounded.

'Quickly', urged the librarian ' follow me!'

Swift as a hawk she dashed to a junction of book-lined corridors and turned a brass handle anti-clockwise. Immediately the whole place dimmed to a complete darkness. Arthur could not see a thing. Outside the engines roared and bucked. Her hand found his elbow and drew him deeper into the pitch black of the library.

'Careful!' she hissed, 'there is a ladder here, please do not fall, nothing mends quickly in this place, use your hands to stay safe'.

He heard the rustle of her skirts as she ascended, reaching forward, his hands found rungs in a narrow space and, as she had suggested, he very carefully climbed. Somewhere in the library a window shattered, raucous laughter could be heard above the sound of dirty throbbing engines.

Arthur thought that they had climbed up to the very roof and could feel, blindly, that the shelf had a narrow surface, but wide enough to kneel prone. He reached up into the dark and there was the ceiling. It seemed a safe place to be, albeit a bit odd.

'Carefully now', she whispered ' move to the end of this row, there is a little door which leads to the attic rooms. Use your hands to feel the edges of the shelf'.

Shuffling along in the darkness, Arthur felt glad he had ventured out and found this person, who exhibited the first and only civility he had encountered since arriving. He heard the creak of a hinge ahead of him and soon could feel the space where shelf surface met the wall. He climbed in and blinked as a match flared into life, Cecilia was lighting a candle. Some of her hair had come loose in the effort to find safety, it hung in wisps about her face. He noticed her eyes were huge, giving the impression of a quick, nervous intelligence. Arthur was fascinated.

Looking about him, he found he could almost stand in the angle of the attic, she led him to an intersection of a similar shaped roof space and there was a smaller ladder leading to another little hatch. The librarian disappeared into it, so he followed, somewhat slightly out of breath.

Inside was a round room, a cupola in reality, but decked out comfortably and telling of old-world tastes and distinction. Books ranked on provisional shelves all about the circular domed room. There were four tiny hatch doors with internal bolts and two slot windows.

'Well done', she said, and sank into a basket seat with a sigh, brushing her stray hair back into place. Arthur found a similar pew and relaxed into it. The single candle illuminated the little room.

'This is my sanctuary', she said with resignation, 'the best I can offer you'.

The thunder of motorbikes continued, he assumed they were riding in circles, it certainly sounded as such.

'Thank you for your kindness', Arthur said, 'you are the first decent person I have met so far'.

'You are welcome Mr MacNeil', her response ever so proper, Cecilia continued,

'you had better wait until the brutes have finished their play. They are utterly reprehensible, animals really. Some of them live a tad down the street'.

The subject seemed to pain her. Arthur remembered the angry metallic droning music and made the connection. He was glad he had avoided the big, dirty men with their noisy machines.

'So what are the 1970`s like if I may inquire', the lady appeared more relaxed now and her naturally curious mind was keen to discover more about this unexpected visitor.

Arthur thought about it and realized he would have to avoid colorful terms such as shit-hole and sewer and bombsite. He attempted to describe the world he had left behind. It would not be easy task.

'Since you left there have been two major world wars. Society has changed in ways that would amaze and dismay you. The old order of self improvement and propriety is over, in its stead we have a generation of happy morons and smug ignorami. Common folk live in constant insecurity about every aspect of their lives, in employment and in relationships, there is little in the way of certainty now, back there, back where I come from. I wish not to depress you, but it really has declined'.

'Sounds dreadful!'

Cecilia frowned, but clearly wanted him to continue.

'Science however has advanced us enormously', Arthur resumed his summary,' we fly between continents regularly, we have even been to the moon and travel frequently into space, well, the Americans and Russians have done so'.

This caused her to gasp, astonished 'You mean men have left this planet?' she gasped, '... and fly! Surely in more than hot air balloons?'.

'Indeed', affirmed Arthur,' aircraft now travel faster than sound itself. We have also split the very molecules and atoms of matter to create weapons of war which have decimated two entire oriental cities'.

The lady leaned forward, straining her mind to grasp the dimension of this notion. Her posture and expression tensed accordingly. Arthur continued,

'We have reached a point where the rich live fabulous extravagant lives whilst simultaneously millions starve and perish all over the world, simply through want of food and water. The world you knew has long subsided into history. We are ruled by cheats and liars and crooks. Britain is a mess. The country you knew has been swamped with ever expanding cities and roads now cover the land in a web. Only a few buildings remain to connect you to the era you would actually remember'.

Cecilia sat quietly, absorbing the facts.

'None of the books in this library are publications later than 1900', she told him, 'yet the barbarians without have motorized transport, those noisy two wheeled machines they ride'.

'Motorcycles' interjected Arthur.

"Quite,' she acknowledged, 'motorized cycles'.

After a pause, she spoke again, saying,

'I think I would not take to the temperament of the age you have known.

I mean not to cause offense, but it sounds terribly daunting, to have achieved so much and progressed so little'.

'Well put', replied Arthur, ' it is all that and more'.

Her eyes held him, their direct frankness and sincerity fascinated him.

They talked long into the night as the candle burned slowly down to a stump. Two human specimens separated by a gulf of time and history. The engine noises had long ceased. The darkness of night was fading. Cecilia covered her mouth and yawned. Arthur thought he had better leave and said so. He thought to ask her if there was anything she needed, and if he could, he would find it and return. The lady looked at him curiously and said,

'If it would not disadvantage you so, Mr MacNeil, I would greatly like something other to eat other than pigeon and herbs'.

Arthur walked the empty streets back to the Pipewellgate slums. The light was growing and so was a dim hope within him that this city may now be more endurable. He knew he had some trade to do with the stunted baker on the bridge. He had a mission, a purpose.

Then he heard the ringing of church bells from high on the hill behind him and quickened his pace, he had no intention of meeting the religious inhabitants of the town. He correctly guessed they would be very odd indeed, like everything else here. Unusual, potentially threatening and ultimately best avoided. He was very right.

The abandoned church was silent within, incapable of ignoring his curiosity, Arthur decided to peek into the murky interior. It stank. The smell assaulted the nostrils and caught the back of the throat. He put his handkerchief to his mouth and waited till his eyes adjusted to the gloom. It had been a fine place once long ago. Someone inside was snoring loudly, he turned and made his exit, heading back for Pipewellgate, his curiosity satisfied for the moment.

As he descended the steep alleyways to the 'Gate he could see briefly a group of tall, formally dark-clad men down by the Medieval bridge. He stopped and shrank into the safe shadow of a crumbling, filthy wall. The narrow space of the chare made it hard to discern what the group were about, so carefully he approached. By the time he had reached Rabbit Banks Road the eight somber men were walking away from him, up to Bottle Bank, and they were carrying a body. Pallbearers of sorts, collecting the casualties of another rough night down on Pipewellgate. He thought it would be prudent to consider moving out of the area. Their casualty was still lightly struggling as they walked easily up the narrow, steep street. Blood dripped from the objecting hand packaged within the basic scoop stretcher.

CHAPTER TWELVE

Making a friend.

Arthur quietly crept along the narrow alleyways that rose steeply from the dirty auld river. In his rucksack, carefully wrapped, was one enormous loaf and two cheese and onion pies and two small cakes. He had traded half a decanter of brandy for this food, he could feel the warmth of the newly baked bread upon his back. He had decided to carry the meat cleaver in his hand and genuinely hoped there would be no need for it to be used in wrath. The handle became slick with sweat.

A non-toxic mist had risen from the river, it was if the Newcastle side had decided to widely spread its constant fog cover. It drifted slowly in the dusk and gave an even creepier air to the 'Gate. It also helped Arthur make his way unseen. Swiftly passing by the derelict church he could hear the drunken voices inside indulging in some communal song. He wondered where they got their booze from, or if it was what would pass for regular alcohol. The silent streets were without note.

Again he gave a wide berth to the bikers den by skirting the featureless terraced streets, but this time by the pitch-black back lanes. At one point he collided with an overturned dustbin and ruined his efforts toward secrecy and non-detection with the metallic racket that rang in the dark night. Arthur swore and hurried onwards towards his objective, somewhat thrown by his impromptu metallic riot.

The library interior swallowed him with a warm and welcome old-world cosiness. Only a few of the gas lights barely glowed, spluttering as the meager supply of fuel burned low with a dull orange flame. He eagerly searched the book-lined avenues for a while before he found her at a desk surrounded by heavily bound manuscripts, she was clearly preoccupied, searching for something. Arthur cleared his throat and she sat bolt upright with surprise, her eyes wide, but no piercing shriek this time. She reminded him so much of a startled bird.

'I have brought you some food', said Arthur, 'and there is no pigeon in it'.

Cecilia composed herself and indicated the volumes before her, saying,

'I've been trying to find local maps covering this area for you, it has taken an age and I have little to show for my efforts. There is nothing concerning the recent history of this place. Nothing at all of any practical use I am afraid'.

'Thanks', replied Arthur, genuinely grateful for her attempt, 'perhaps you would like to see what I have brought for you?'

She nodded and suggested that they ascend to the cupola room, where they would be guaranteed to remain free from any brutal interruptions.

Cecilia cut a thin slice from the loaf and smelled it before biting. By the way her eyes widened and the pleasure she took in each taste, Arthur knew that fresh, plain white bread was something she had not had in a while. Politely he waited for her to finish and then gave her the remaining pies and cakes. She stared at them, her head slightly set to one side, her face set in disbelief and undisguised astonishment.

'I have not left the library in ages', she began to explain,' it is not safe out there. I managed gradually to create a small garden on the roof, mainly herbs and vegetables that can be grown in boxes. I trap pigeons in the attics too. Would you like to see?'

Arthur agreed and she opened a half-size door in the cupola, the foggy night was waiting for them. Arranged around and about on every flat level space were wooden crates and boxes, even drawers taken from cupboards, all filled with soil which was now fecund with greenery. The walkway led to the front of the building, the iron handrail was cold to touch. Beneath them the road below was thankfully quiet. No roaring motorbikes rumbled on this very misty evening.

'Do you ever think about leaving this place' Arthur asked.

'The library?' Cecilia questioned, her face was puzzled in the darkness.

'No' added Arthur 'this city'.

She laughed lightly as if it were a joke he had made.

'How on earth would one go about such a thing Mister MacNeil?'

'Have you never tried or even considered the possibility?'

'Of course ', she responded as if Arthur was being deliberately slow, 'many times. There is no way out, either from this city or the world in which it is placed'. She paused before continuing.

'A little after I first arrived here I thought the entire place deserted. I walked everywhere by daylight until I met the Grey Men from the hill. They tried to take me away with them, but I fled. Thereafter, I explored with greater care. I took food from gardens and nearby fields and found that over time I needed increasingly less. Once I walked for four whole days upriver. There was nothing. No buildings, no towns or villages, no farms nor fields, just an eternity of moorland and barren fell. The agricultural areas which surround us range only for a dozen miles at the most'.

The mist had begun to thicken and visibility diminished rapidly to barely a stones throw. The night deepened into a darkness impenetrable, the librarian suggested that they return to the cupola. Arthur turned towards the small rectangle of candlelight, coils of fog twisted and convoluted there.

Due to a clever extension of a gas lamp pipe, Cecilia had rigged a simple stove. Upon this she placed a kettle, having taken the water from a large pail. She busied away, gathering a few jars from a roughly made shelf and asked if Arthur would like some herbal tea with a slice of cake. This civility and semblance of normality was really very welcome to him, relaxing he said,

'Why have you not found another place to live? The town appears abandoned and there are plenty of houses which seem empty. Why live up here?'

'Because it is safer this way,' she answered, ' this place is not as empty as it looks. It is not wise to investigate these apparently abandoned properties.' Cecilia shivered briefly, then continued,

'There are some things dwelling here in hiding that you would not care to meet.'

She found a second large tea cup and a strainer then added,

'Everything seems to have its setting, its compartment which tallies with who and what they were back in the real world, in the life they had before this place. To attempt to find another habitation or to change any single feature of it seems to attract trouble of a most disturbing sort'.

She was silent for a while, her brow furrowed as if recollecting something traumatic.

'When I first arrived there were many fields and woodlands close by. Entire sections would disappear in one night to be replaced with rows of houses which looked old and lived in. There would be no noises or sounds of construction, they would simply manifest there.'

'Of course, features and buildings after the 1900s would not be here when you first arrived'. Arthur noted, making this obvious point as the kettle began to boil.

'Quite so.' Cecilia replied, ' This town has grown much since my arrival. I recall times when the streets were full of angry people fighting, pitched battles would rage outside in that very road. Frightfully injured bodies lay were they fell until the Grey Men came for them. Yet no-one died, despite terrible disfigurement and wounds, they wailed and moaned even as they carried the injured away'.

The kettle blew off its boiling steam and the tall thin lady made a weak brew of mixed herbs. Arthur thought that his next gift would be some of his real India tea that he kept in the pokey little rooms under the shadow of the big, dark bridge. That and some sugar.

Cecilia served a slice of currant cake with the insipid steaming brew and seemed to enjoy the novelty and the taste of the gift Arthur had brought.

'Thank you so much for this feast', she said sincerely, ' I have not tasted anything so delicious since time out of mind.' Arthur smiled, but wished he had brought some real tea along.

'What do you know about the history of this place?' he asked during a natural pause.

'Just that which is apparent,' she answered, ' the books say nothing, yet the city is a collection of architecture and peoples reaching far back into antiquity.' She sipped the hot pale tea.

'Have you met the Romans, yet?' she asked, Arthur nodded in reply.

'Or the armoured knights?'.

'No knights, not so far. One Roman, an enormous chap' Arthur answered.

'Or the cavaliers?' she inquired further.

'Oh those. I think so, they were fighting beneath my window under the bridge', he replied.

Cecilia looked at him with undisguised pity and said as if to comfort Arthur,

'You poor man. You live down by the river, by the bridges. You poor fellow'.

Arthur really didn't know how to respond to that comment at all, he just shrugged, and sat quietly.

Once their simple but welcome feast was done Arthur thought he would ask Cecilia if she could remember how she had arrived in this city, what actually had happened to her. She nodded and seemed to have some difficulty in recalling the events. He waited patiently for her answer.

'Considering that over seventy years have passed in the real world, you must understand that this is not such an easy task,' she explained and then eventually continued,

'I awoke in complete darkness in a cell, the door was locked and as morning dawned I was able to see over the city, well, this side of the river at least. I was on the hill. Out of the window I could see my vaulted stone chamber was situated upon a steep crag. Some days passed, I cannot recall how many and I became desperate to escape. The door remained solidly shut and no captors visited me. I thought I would rot in that dank, chilly place.'

Arthur nodded sympathetically and asked, 'How did you escape?'

'I tore up my dress and wove it into cordage which allowed me to reach a small tree that grew from the wall. From there I was able to climb by clinging to similar shrubs and growths until I could eventually drop to the ground below.'

The idea of this prim lady from a reserved and apparently most proper era ripping up her skirts convinced Arthur she must have been utterly desperate. She continued,

'It did not take me long to realise this town was a version of Gateshead, and so I found my way down the hill to this library. In the offices I kept some personal belongings, they were all there, intact, exactly as I had stored them in the real world.

I was alone, however, and quite confused. It took much exploration of the environs before I concluded that the dangers are unexpected and mainly unforeseen.' She paused, again seeming pained with some awful memory.

'Initially, I would enter buildings that I assumed were abandoned', she continued, 'I took clothing and food, bedding and utensils. I had little idea what perils this would expose me to. One particular episode led to an encounter with a horrid creature disfigured and damaged in a most awful manner. How it was animated in the light of its injuries was incomprehensible. Since then I have concluded that in this place we do not perish so easily, that wounds take years to heal rather than weeks. Take that bruise on your forehead. How long have you had it?'

'Well over two months', answered Arthur, 'I fell trying to cross the river.'

'The intoxicating mist that never lifts.' Cecilia affirmed, 'A barrier which cannot be passed.'

'Like a wall." added Arthur.

"Correct, a sort of boundary.' the lady confirmed.

'To keep us in or to keep something out?' Arthur asked.

'How will we ever know', she said with a clearly sad note of resignation in her voice.

They talked for many hours until it was clear that the librarian was really becoming very tired. She moved to the roof-access door and looked outside. The mist still dominated, but the faintest hint of dawn had touched the night. She bolted the wee hatch and said,

'It is almost morning, soon there will be enough light for you to find your way back. You must take care. On the occasions when such a fog arises, it has precluded some disturbing events in the past. Like the arrival of the motorised cyclist villains.' She spoke with distinct abhorrence.

'You have met these people?' asked Arthur innocently enough.

'I care not to talk about it, nor remember the instance, thank you, sir.' she responded resolutely.

Cecilia took him to a little office, which looked as if it had not been used in decades. Cobwebs festooned the wood panelled walls and a film of undisturbed dust lay upon every surface. She asked him to wait here until first light and then bade him a polite good night and retired back to her cupola room, safe and secure behind bolted wooden hatches and doors.

Arthur sat and stared at the window and waited for the darkness to slowly lift. The hour passed quickly, he had much to think about and give due consideration to, but he was happier, most certainly so.

The first twinges of daylight did little to assist or aid Arthur's progress back to Pipewellgate. The mist had actually thickened and he could barely discern the pavement for only a mere ten feet in front of him. The bikers den was quiet, so he quickened his pace to hurry past. There was fresh blood on the doorstep and broken glass everywhere, he did not like this place one bit. The motorcycles had matted scalps hanging from the handlebars, the savagery of this gang now was beyond doubt. Whoever they did this to would never heal, according to the rules of this prison world. Blood dripped from these gory trophies.

Pipewellgate was deathly silent, where the smog was even thicker, it bellowed from the river, limiting visibility to a few feet. Arthur even walked right past his own tenement front door. Only by identifying the corner of a massive bridge stanchion was he able to correct his error. The fog had filled the stairwell. He found his room and fell onto the bed. The silence was omnipresent, stifling and unnerving. He could not even hear the lap of the river as it passed. Sleep came to him quickly. A solemn quiet within a smothering absence of sound.

Arthur dreamt the Grey Men were dragging him, screaming and kicking down a tunnel. Firebrands fluttered at intervals along the corbelled passageway. Someone was laughing as they hauled him deeper under the hill, a sound he recognized. A low muttering hateful laugh that brought with it an uncomfortable, unavoidable fear. He woke after an effort of will.

He knew that laugh. It was the creatures that had tormented his poor mother, the very same ghouls that he suspected had brought him to this dark and dangerous town. He rose, brewed a cup of strong tea and thought of elegant skinny Cecilia and her weak herbal infusions.

That morning the view from his window was in its own way, reassuring. The mist had cleared, apart from on the opposite bank of the river. There it still ranked impenetrable. He put a little of the remaining brandy into the strong dark brew, there was not much left and he thought he may need what remained for trade with Stumpy, the dwarf baker on the bridge. The dream had shaken him, he was no closer to discovering how he had been brought here, or why this city was so similar to his home town, yet so manifestly other, so strange and distressingly askew.

He thought to take a careful exploration of the area. It had been a while since he had done more than simply stand on the Medieval bridge, sucking at the fog on the Tyne, watching the creatures of the night scuttle about. His visits to the library had given him a confidence and a renewed interest in resolving his predicament. Or at the very least of it, gaining an increased understanding of what the city was about. He noticed that his food supplies were very low, not that he had used much since his arrival, but he would have to do some pillaging if he wanted to continue to eat.

Arthur had forgotten to set his acquired pocket watch. He estimated that the day was already half spent. He took the rucksack and meat cleaver and this time remembered the binoculars. Unable to throw off the feelings of unease the dream had left him with, like a bitter after taste, he was glad to have a mission to take his mind off his nightmare. As usual, the winding narrow street was deserted, he headed off upriver with a rough plan to take more turnips from the fields beyond the woodland.

Following the same route of about two months previously he noticed, after about a mile, a small workshop adjacent to a boat builders yard. It was the fading sign which displayed that it was a manufacturer of diving equipment. The established date said 1912. An idea occurred to Arthur and he decided to investigate the premises. The heavy main doors were chained and locked fast, the padlock had rusted completely. He tried around the rear, away from the road, down by the riverside and found a clutter of collapsed sheds and timber piles. A door rattled open as he tried it, its coach bolt falling to the floor with a corroded crash, rotten wood snowed down. He was in. The grimy windows, thick with industrial filth and age, permitted little light to enter. Slowly his eyes grew accustomed to the gloom. He noticed wide shelves laden with long-abandoned tools and items of sea-diving equipment. Iron boots and enormous fish bowl type helmets lay in various states of completion. Further investigation revealed finished stock, including rubberised suits and spools of piping. He searched for a standard shop-floor standing trolley and knew his instinct had been validated. Initially, he had to find oil for the wheels, and then he could carefully strap a suit with full helmet and about a hundred yards of pipe to his rig. His plan was forming as he continued to check all about him.

A wooden box lined with oiled cloth revealed thirty heavy duty divers knives in steel sheaths. He took them all, reasoning the dwarf baker may trade with him for these weapons, useful in a town where he had been informed, weapons were prerequisites. He stashed these in his rucksack.

Arthur blinked as daylight poured into what must have been the manager's office situated above the shop floor, accessed by a creaking wooden staircase. The room was tidy, files and wooden shelves ranked two walls.

An enormous desk with locked drawers dominated the central space. He took the meat cleaver and wrenched the first drawer open. He smiled, as he had found the office drinks cabinet, he even laughed aloud, a sound which resounded in the dusty old room. Four full bottles of hard liquor and six more half-finished assorted decanters sat in recessed slots, red baize lining protected the bottles and the glasses. Just what the doctor ordered, he thought, very handy indeed.

The other drawers revealed a strong box and many sheaths of documents, order books and incoming/outgoing ledgers. Assuming the metal box had money in it and this was of no use here, Arthur decided to leave. The light was failing and that he had better get himself back with his finds and acquisitions. He took all the booze, smelling which spirit was which in the used decanters and combining the contents to create three full ones, two of brandy and the other of wonderfully matured malts. The full bottles still remained in their hard cardboard tubes. He found a set of dusty overalls to wrap and protect this trade-worthy stash, and carefully put it in his rucksack. He and Cecilia would eat well.

The burdened upright trolley trundled loudly in the cobbled streets. The day was closing and as he approached the 'Gate, a few spindly chimneys plumed smoke. He knew the inhabitants of these slums would soon emerge and thence the dangers would grow. He had to make it to the railway bridge before darkness dominated. He accomplished this with little time to spare. Reaching the bakery he paused to regain his breath and wipe the sweat from his brow. Then he solidly knocked…

'Who the bluddy hell is that!' a cantankerous, ancient voice rasped from within.

'Arthur', replied Arthur,' I want to do trade.'

'Oh happy day!' the wee man's face appeared and creased into his one and only smile mode, a scary leer which merely indicated he was not about to kill anyone.

'More drink I hopes'. Stumpy's eyes glinted, ' the last lot were right royal!'

Arthur withdrew the decanter of mixed whiskeys from his rucksack, careful not to let the wee man see the full extent of his finds. He handed it over to calloused palms. The bakers eyes widened as he saw the quantity and smelled the potency, he immediately took a swig.

'It's a deal!' he barked, 'whitever yer want!'

Arthurs bargain involved leaving the upright trolley, overnight at the bakers humble shop. He knew he could not hoist it up the tenement's stone stairwell and did not wish to hide it anywhere on the 'Gate lest it be discovered. He even got two enormous loaves and three pigeon pies and five cakes thrown in to boot. As he departed he took the meat cleaver from the rucksack and placed it in his leather belt.

'Gud ter see yer learnin' yer silly auld bugger yer', the baker said in parting.

Childlike laughter tittered behind him over on the Newcastle side. He hoisted the rucksack and hurried home.

Tomorrow he would pay a visit there at last, he thought, the diving gear would help him breathe as he crossed the bridge and investigate the other side. Arthur afforded himself his second smile of the day and, tired but satisfied, returned to his little rooms under the bridge. A profitable day with no need to raid the turnip field and risk whatever hazards that may bring.

Arthur made a strong black tea and added a generous measure from the brandy decanter. He toasted two slices of bread and sat in the darkness by an open window simply listening to the sounds of Pipewellgate coming alive. He still had not placed another coin in the gas meter nor shaved and the bruise on his forehead remained sore. These facts continued to puzzle him.

Where are the aliens?

Where gentleness and hard work collide.

When the casualties are unsuspecting.

Why the jacket is too thick, like the accent.

It could be the last thing you ever hear...

For there is a hatred, which runs deeper than blood, richer than wrath.

It is as solemn as the stare of a dying friend.

Equal in its desperation, standard in its ardour.

Bound in pain, lost, insane.

Forged in a life, hard beyond our comprehension.

We do not get bombed,

We have no misfortune of missiles crashing our sweet routine.

We have a life, and long may it be maintained.

The tender fibrils of our efforts, the nudging forward of our time.

It is all, gradatim, a clockwork thing, a sense of event and stage.

A way of things, an edge, an intelligence.

Where are the aliens?

Where are the lumpy-headed geeks from outer space?

If they do not arrive soon we are finished as a species.

Noble Lords of our sick polluted molehill.

Preening Kings of our ridiculous consensual oblivion.

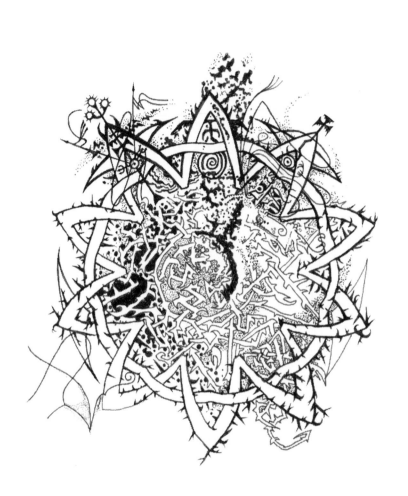

CHAPTER THIRTEEN

Going over the town.

The baker did not like to be woken so early. Night time was his house trade and the daylight marked a duration of rest to him and most of the denizens of the `Gate. He looked even grumpier than ever, probably due to a severe hangover, but a deal is a deal, so he thrust the laden standing trolley towards Arthur with one hand, the other hand held the door securely and warily from within. The heavy timbers shook as it banged shut.

'Thanks' Arthur said sincerely.

'Fuck off!' was the response on the other side of a thick, slammed door.

He pushed the upright wheeled barrow almost to the limit of the intoxicating mist and then searched for a firm anchor point for his air pipe. A drain bracket seemed to offer a reliable purchase, so Arthur unpacked his load, donning the suit, closing the legs and wrists with the wide leather straps and buckles. Then he fitted the airway to the helmet. He paid out the pipe in a way that ensured it would not twist or snag when being pulled over the river, into the mist. Then he placed the heavy helmet upon his head. It struck him as seriously strange, needing this get-up to visit neighbouring Newcastle.

Into the swirling mist he walked, peering through the thick glass visor. The bridge closed in around him, the narrowness of the street claustrophobic and confining. The air pipe trailed behind, a black rubber snake keeping him conscious. Arthur could see the end of the bridge, it was a bright rectangle of light getting closer with each step. He had been counting these steps, so far Arthur had taken about seventy, he guessed that had maybe thirty left. The light increased. The mist was diminishing, thinning. Soon he stood at the Newcastle end of the Medieval bridge and stared with bewilderment at what he found.

From the confined vantage of the heavy helmet, Arthur could see that it was ancient, yet cleaner and brighter than the Gateshead side. It seemed to shimmer magically, a glimmer, a strange glow exuded from the stonework, the cobblestones, the windows. Four little boys were pointing at him, laughing at the strange man in the funny costume. Stalls, and street vendors stopped assembling their stands and looked in his direction, some smiled, some frowned. Arthur took his last dozen steps and seeing no mist, removed his helmet. He was in Newcastle.

Sunlight poured down, he had left a grey, overcast Pipewellgate, but here it was warm and bright. He stepped out of the divers suit and pushed the lot into an alcove, out of sight. The wee boys had begun to cheer and clap, Arthur smiled at them, pleased to see happy, healthy faces for a change. He passed a fruit seller, another wholesome looking young man, who offered him an apple as he neared. He didn't speak, just smiled and nodded for Arthur to take it. So he did. It tasted wonderful. It smelled of dewy orchards and sweet late summer. Proper fruit, real fruit. How did it get here? Why did the lad think he needed charity?

Arthur found it hard to focus as he walked. Many architectural ages were represented here also, but they were cared for, maintained and preserved, an ingredient lacking on the south side of the river. This place was shining with love and care. Timbered Tudor buildings leaned into the Quayside, the plasterwork white and fresh, the timbers painted matt-black. Window boxes cascaded flowers, no-one was dirty, no-one was aggressive or dangerous. Also no-one was old. The only difficult or unnerving feature was the shimmer upon everything. It was as if the physicality of the past and the present superimposed themselves in the same place at the same time. A tall ghostly tower of pale stone rose from an old-world huddle of pre-Victorian tenements. Washing hung drying in the sunlight, little kids played merrily in clean backyards. This was the Happy Land, the place were all the young and the beautiful, the kind and the good arrive. Arthur felt hurt that he had been excluded, then realized, he was simply too old. When he looked again for the tall, slender tower, it had faded away, only the sound of children at play remained. This version of Newcastle seemed to be occupying two places at the same time.

Arthur reached the bottom of the Castle Stairs, an alleyway that rose steeply up from the Quayside to the Norman keep at the head of the bank above. It had always been a shadowed place where drunks urinated and homeless old men wrapped themselves in many overcoats and huddled out of the cold night. The steps were still worn, but the alley had been swept clean. Brightly painted doors cheered the narrow confines enormously and all the way up, little shops and businesses, announced their presence with skillfully presented hanging signs, lanterns and banners. This was not the same Newcastle Arthur MacNeil knew.

The penultimate set of stone steps passed through a gatehouse of what had been the City Wall, almost nine hundred years old. Not only was the entire wall intact, but the gatehouse was in pristine condition. A young man sat with two pretty girls and was entertaining them with a story. They laughed and fawned over him as he told his tale. Arthur looked at their antiquated clothing and tried to place it in time. The young man wore a padded leather cuirass and a wide belt over a full grey plaid. A basket hilt sword was in its scabbard and bright keen. As Arthur drew closer he discerned the broad Border Scots accent. None of the trio regarded him as he entered the approaches of the lofty Norman keep.

Flags flew from the battlements above, carts laden with supplies were being unloaded by tanned, muscular men. A gaggle of females with elaborate coiffures, colorful bustled dresses and heavy face make up passed him, deep in some gossip or intrigue. Several modern cars were parked near him, a slim, suited gentleman with a briefcase walked on his way to the Courts of Law, tipped his bowler hat to the playful ladies. It was an outright confusion of times and styles. A massive horse carried an armored knight to the castle stables, the polished steel plate shone in the sunlight, a pennant hung crimson and viridian from his couched lance. He was magnificent. Arthur stared, gawking at the marvel, both man and beast being led by a page in a tabbard echoing the colours that flew from the lance. The Bridge Hotel was there! Exactly as it was on the real Tyneside, but so much cleaner and cared for and maintained. Industrial dirt had spared it. Arthur wanted to go in and buy a beer, but remembered he had not even thought to carry his wallet with him anymore. In the vain hope of recognizing the barman, he crossed the busy forecourt and entered.

The bar was just the same. The partitioned sections contained a few small groups of folk, the accents that Arthur could hear were all Novocastrian, Northumbrian and Lowland Scots, this was greatly re-assuring. He approached the bar where a very good-looking young girl, barely eighteen, smiled and asked what he would like. Arthur said,

'Is there a barman here called Geordie Stark? I would like to talk to him if that is possible.'

The girl replied that she had not worked here long and would ask the manager. When she re-appeared the lad she was with was hardly any older than herself.

'Sorry mate, there is no-one called that working here,' the casually dressed young man informed, 'is there anything I can do to help?'

'I didn't bring my wallet', apologized Arthur, ' If Geordie was on bar-work he would give me tick.'

The pair behind the bar looked puzzled at first and then broke out in hoots of honest laughter.

"You don't need your wallet here!", the young manager eventually smiled and said, 'Have what you want, it's free. Do you understand? There is no need for money.'

Arthur frowned with incomprehension. Free beer? The young girl nodded in consent.

'What will it be then?' she asked.

'Oh, a... a bottle of Brown Ale please.' Arthur answered, unsure whether this was all some sort of send-up, a trick, a nasty stunt of some sort, devised to bring ridicule and insult. It was nothing of the sort. She poured the beer into a glass and handed it to him with a smirk and went back to her business. Arthur sat in a cubicle and gazed at the empty High Level Bridge that disappeared into dense fog. The Brown Ale was the best he had ever tasted.

By his second free bottle Arthur realized this was not a practical joke. He thought to take a walk about this alternative Newcastle and investigate further. It was about mid-day and the town thronged with many beautiful people. Girls in pretty summer dresses strolled with tall, clean, handsome men. It was too good to be true. Where were the old and the ugly? Where had the ever-present poor and the equally ubiquitous criminal element gone? Often folk would stop and stare at him as he passed by as if he were the complete oddity. For he was, it was Arthur who was out of place. Gradually this dawned on him as face after face he noticed in passing was healthy and lovely and fair and cheery.

The further away from the Quayside he got the shimmering effect diminished. The town center seemed solid and real, not a place between times, but an architectural wonder, something to amaze and impress. It combined everything that had ever been that was good and accomplished, skilful and unique about Newcastle. The details in the carved stonework of the cathedral told of pride taken over the task. The elongation of the buildings that predominant on the other side of the river was also present here, but done with a grandeur and a flair Arthur could only but admire. He wanted to find a place for himself and Cecilia here, to live on this side, not in the city of eternal grey cloudscapes and nocturnal woe. This was much, much better.

He decided to enter the cathedral at a junction of streets. There were no pews and a half-dozen people were mopping the echoing space. Metal pales clanked as they moved to clean another section. He stood at the back and noticed every single religious trapping was completely missing. Each cross and statue, every representation of Christianity had been erased and replaced with an iconography utterly and irrevocably alien to the old man. He stared at one carving nearby that was both savage and erotic simultaneously, it had an elegance and a brutality, a visceral shock quality. He had enough basic education to recognize the theme as that of nymphs and satyrs, but the skill executed in the work was equaled by the ferocious representation of raw passion and sheer, forceful lust. It made him sweat profusely in the cold cathedral interior. He remembered he had not changed his socks or shirt in ten days. 'Dear God!' he thought with some intensity and conviction, 'I have become a dirty old man!', and so hurried out. The sun cast his shadow sharp upon the granite pavement.

He had to overcome the overwhelming self consciousness of his age and demeanor. This took some effort as he was fully aware that many in passing had begun to stare at him. He walked into a gentleman's outfitter shop that he knew by the Theater Royal on Grey Street and took a deep breath.

A strikingly featured young man whose facial bones sat fine beneath the thin, pale skin of his face made approach, saying ' Can I help you sir?'

Arthur smiled and answered, 'A complete change of clothes please.'

In the changing room he noticed that the bruise on his forehead was visible to all and sundry, and he would need a hat. He had not seen one sign of illness or injury since arriving. Everything and everyone was simply beautiful. He stripped naked and dressed. Cotton shorts and vest, white, brand new. Black socks, again, pristine. A white buttoned down shirt out of a plain paper bag, lovely cotton, all clean and lightly starched. A new black suit, fine woven tweed, a blue silk lining on trousers, jacket and waistcoat. He pinned his acquired pocket watch in place and stepped into a pair of splendid black leather boots. Renewed, he emerged from the changing rooms.

The Clark Gable look-alike was nodding in approval.

'Could I have a hat too, please, to match the suit colour?'

'Splendid, good choice.' The assistant was quick on his feet, bone thin, but attentive. He found the perfect hat really quickly. He had a notion of Arthur's look and pitched it perfectly.

Arthur appreciated the black tweed flat cap enormously, it made him smile, which took years off him.

'Thank you very much indeed' Arthur cheerfully approved, ' how much will that be?'

The attendant assistant's eyes widened and then he laughed with a hyena grin, saying

'Sir is very funny!' and left the shop to busy away his threadbare cast-offs to the dustbin. Arthur also exited the shop with a smile and a spring in his step.

He was not hungry, but thought it may be a good idea to eat at a restaurant. The very few times he had dined out were those rare occasions with office staff at Christmas. He had always lived frugally in order to save money, for his poor mothers sake.

Strolling at ease through the pleasant alleys and lanes Arthur noticed that the passers-by had ceased to stare. The more he relaxed, the easier it was to fit in. The more he took a real interest in the amazing amount of diversity in the detail of this town and the range of shops and all the lovely people, the happier he became. Smiling, he walked into a tiny little cafe in a narrow lane full of vitality and colour from where he could hear the various musical styles that vied for attention outside. Fragrant smells filled the long, narrow room. A faded picture of the Leaning Tower of Pisa hung on the wall.

He ate with his hat on.

The spaghetti a la carbonara was delicious, the chilled white wine that accompanied it was splendid. Food and vino had never tasted so gorgeous before. He took his time in finishing the bottle. The small window permitted a quick glimpse of the people passing in the lane. As he ate, Arthur noticed in the bearing and clothing styles at least a score of various fashions and eras. Without exception, every male and female was in glowing health and noticeably good looking. It was remarkable.

Bright eyes, the flash of white shining teeth set in red lips, a laugh beyond the window, the flick of lustrous hair. Pretty people, interesting faces, busy folk enjoying their perfect day, passed for a second or two outside the frame of the restaurant window. So many pictures of health.

A pair of willowy 1920's flapper girlfriends were followed by two guys on the make in sharp 1940's zoot suits. A medieval court jester, cockerel hat askance, a drunken stagger in his steps, an infectious grin pasted on his face. A group of World War One field officers in formal dress sauntered casually by, some smoked cigars. A busty, succulent Moll Flanders type with rosy pink cheeks and a mischievous glint in her deep brown eyes swayed by following them, off on some distinctly naughty business. An enchanting young femme fatale in a black pencil skirt so tight she took tiny, mincing steps on high, high heels. Her perfect derriere confined and wrapped, swayed with each step. Arthur could not do but stare.

'Dirty old man', he told himself, 'sad, sad, old bastard.'

When he stood to leave, the now customary vision of beauty that was the waitress beamed over and asked if he had enjoyed his meal. Arthur told her it had been wonderful, and in response was gifted with an adoring smile. As he walked out, no angry voice demanded he return and pay the bill, he simply walked freely into the busy lane. A young Faustian wizard with jutting beard and long black cloak drifted by leaving a whiff of intoxicating scents and oils in his wake. He wondered, as he headed back to Grey Street, if the countrified gun shop was still there. As he turned out of the lane, he noticed the Romanised columns that flank the theater had doubled in height but not in width. So much of this elongation of the architecture predominated. A vertically warped copy of Newcastle.

An enormous limousine with wide white mounting boards and flamboyant wheel arches drew to a halt right outside the Theatre Royal Bar. Three glamorously elegant women and a suited young chap emerged and entered the lounge. They were so distinctly attractive they had to be three actresses with their manager. He studied them until they entered the theatre.

'How can they be so lovely?' he thought to himself.

The gun shop was still there, further down the tall-fronted Georgian street. A brass bell rang clear as Arthur stepped in, a bespectacled guy in his mid thirties appeared from the workshop, a door at the end of the counter had been completely removed. He could see gun and rifle parts scattered on benches, many tools were ordered on wooden racks.

'How are you today, sir?', the man asked amiably, 'and how may we be of assistance?'

'I would like a revolver', began Arthur,' A Webley and Scott mark six service handgun with webbing belt, canvas holster and two, thirty round pouches for the .445 ammo supplied, please.'

'A reliable weapon', the gunsmith nodded in approval and asked,' Would that be domed or flat head rounds, sir?' A large clock ticked solemnly in the brief silence. It was three thirty. Arthur set his pocket watch to this. He clearly remembered his National Service and answered,

'The latter, thank you very much. One hundred rounds of flat-heads will do just fine.'

The handgun came with a beautifully made wooden case, containing a brass pull-through for cleaning and a little gun oil. It spoke of old world skill and craftsmanship and smelled of precision and reliability.

Carrying the heavy brown paper bag, Arthur looked, at a glance, just like any other shopper. The cap hid his bruise, the suit and clean shirt made him look fifteen years younger. He realized that the more he enjoyed this alternative Newcastle the easier it was to become invisible, un-noticed. Everyone seemed happy, all were perfect human specimens. He was now walking in the Land of the Forever Young.

The Grainger Market swallowed Arthur into its cool interior, avenues of stalls and established traders filled the available spaces completely. Everything a person could need was here; his favourite section was the meandering bookstore that had specialized in local interests. It was there, just the same one he had known.

He browsed for an hour, yet could find no maps, atlases, city plans or history books, there was nothing which could inform about location or environs. It was deeply puzzling. Despite this, Arthur persisted without any eventual satisfaction.

In one corner of the closed market he turned into a narrow door which took him by a staircase to an open cafe which looked down on the market activity below. A few couples sat together, hands touched, eyes gazed. No-one noticed Arthur but the fragile, beautiful little waitress. He ordered a mug of tea and sat looking on the movement below with his eyes slightly out of focus, the blur of colour and sound was familiar to him, just like it was in the real world. Yet if he returned his vision to actually look at what composed the hypnotic unfocused dance, it was certainly not normal at all. Anything but.

Courtesans and clowns, soldiers and students, gentlemen and ladies, princes and prostitutes, all sorts of youthful, attractive humanity swarmed below. Arthur spluttered on his tea and gawked. A black leather clad dominatrix in skin tight attire led a man by a collar and lead as if he were a dog. The chap wore nothing but a tattered breech-cloth and his body was covered in weals and bruises. She walked like a hunter, a predator and more, she had to be over seven foot tall.

Arthur felt momentarily afraid, noticing the way all the happy young people quickly moved out of her way, avoiding her. This woman was something other entirely. She was clearly very much in charge, an authority figure in sharp stiletto heels and a fitted, soft, black hide bodysuit. Her blonde hair was drawn up tight into a pony tail that bobbed and swished from the crown of her head. What was worse, she carried two long daggers sheathed at her hips from a wide black leather belt. Her human dog sniffed the ground curiously and then looked directly up at Arthur.

'There he is!' it said.

The tall, slender woman in tight supple hides tilted her haughty head to regard Arthur. Her eyes were truly enormous, massive, almond shaped dark orbs of an unfathomable intelligence. She half smiled, a gesture that froze upon her face. Something eerie then occurred and all the folk nearby ran for cover. The fetishist clad Amazon and her crawling cur remained alone below. Even the smiling florist had ducked behind her counter. The colour of the tall woman's face had turned to a paper-pale white. Arthur squinted, unsure at what it was he was actually seeing. The dominatrix stepped away, disinterest upon her features as she prowled off. Yet she had left a face-like impression behind her, hanging in the air. Her very face had peeled away and remained where she had been standing. Slowly this pale mask drifted up towards Arthur MacNeil, its blank eyes and half smile fixed and unchanging. The mask-face drew level with his own face, and then, gradually, the atmosphere grew cold, all heat dissipated. The mug of tea in his grasp quickly cooled. As Arthur's breath began to plume in the frozen air and terror overcame him, he knew he must flee. As he turned to run, time seemed to slow down and his muscles ached with effort, he pushed through this, convinced the last thing he could hear as he fled the cafe was that evil, ancient laugh.

i...i...i...i...i...

CHAPTER FOURTEEN

Pursued by a mask.

Arthur ran until he could run no longer. He had reached Eldon Square, a Georgian-fronted affair, again elongated in the vertical and made even more elegant for this. Trees offered shade, pigeons shuffled stance on the central statue. Young women in stiff crinolines sat with girls in miniskirts, high collared, old-world town officials chatted with long haired, bearded lads in kaftans and sandals. He thought to lose himself amongst these people and paced quickly through, scattering birds as he passed. He glanced over his shoulder, thankfully seeing nothing was following him.

Taking a lane which ran west, he composed himself in the doorway of a pub and entered, calming his nerves and ordering a Brown Ale. The young barman gave him a curious glance, but was keen to return to a conversation ongoing via a very old fashioned telephone. The beer was cold and welcome. He sat with a view of the little street, his eyes looking for a mask without an owner, a floating face. He shivered. The day slowly faded as he drank his ale. After a second beer, sunset was sending roseate rays into the narrow lane. He left, thanking the barman, still deep in conversation. The dusk was breathtaking. Its touch softened the stonework and deepened the shadows. It blushed on every face and shone in every passing eye.

The sun bled one last gush of deepest red that spilled for long minutes down the streets and lanes and alleys, its parting gift was the onset of night. Arthur had found his way to the gents public toilets in the Central Station. It too was stripped of all indications of everyday usage, there were no arrival and departure times, no timetables. Trains ranked at deserted platforms, engines and carriages from every industrial phase of the locomotive era. The gents were open and thankfully deserted, someone was whistling a melancholy tune out on the platform.

He unpacked the webbing belt, with holster and ammo pouches and arranged it all over his shirt. Putting the waistcoat and jacket back on, he positioned it in a way that reduced the visual impact of the various bulges they cast upon his coat. From the box he took the revolver and with a nervous shake, chambered six of the girthy rounds. He holstered the pistol and filled the two pouches with thirty rounds apiece. He pocketed the remaining rounds, the pull-through and the small brass tin of oil. He felt a little guilty about leaving the well made box stashed above the toilet cistern. He closed the waistcoat and smoothed the cloth. Anyone who had ever worn a gun would have clearly seen he carried one too. It would have to do.

The whistler on the station was warbling on about 'that old feeling'... it echoed in a sad treble about the dimly lit platforms. A bit of litter was blowing slowly towards him. He looked out where Gateshead should be and saw but a bank of featureless grey cloud. Arthur shivered, thinking of life over there and then noticed there was no wind and it was suddenly very cold. A plain sheet of paper was drifting as any such discarded litter would, but it was the mask. It was the dominatrix face set in a cold, hard smile on a thin, silk-like material. It skipped and danced along the granite paving. It looked at him, stopping at head level and its empty eyes were on him. It crossed his mind that whatever was wearing that mask was invisible for a reason.

He lunged a fist at it and was wide of the mark, it moved just before contact.

He tried again and it slipped easily to one side. Arthur turned and walked out of the station, refusing to run, fighting hard to ignore the fear welling up inside him and the half heard-laugh that he had become to hate with all his being. He crossed over by the bottom of Westgate Road, intending to lose himself in the warren of narrow alleys that ran from Blackfriars to the Haymarket. He began to run at a jog. Glancing back over his shoulder, he could see it was easy to put a distance between himself and the floating shell of a face. It was soon a whole block away. People stepped clear of the thing as it floated past. He entered what the Geordies called Chinatown, awash in colored glass lanterns and streamers. Arthur fought to overcome his fear, …

'Its just a mask with a dodgy laugh', he told himself.

In the colored lamplight, all manner of exotic femininity and genuinely well-dressed, handsome men seemed to be utterly at ease with how fabulous they were. It was impossible for Arthur not to stare sometimes. Thankfully, no-one seemed to be bothered at being gawked at anyway, there was so much sass and glamour that drawing the gaze had to be a factor in it. He focused on relaxing, which is hard when part of you just wants to run and hide. He heard a young lad in a 'Beatles' type jacket and mop-head haircut say to his similarly styled pal,

'So what's this Mayfair Ballroom like then Steve?'

Steve grinned back a positive and told him,

'It's mad in there. It goes aboot fower floors doon to a dance hall, bars look over from the balcony above. Archways and tunnels lead off into uther dance halls and more bars. It used to be the city wine cellars, there are lurds of rooms. Every style is there. Now and again something kicks-off, but usually the bouncers teck care of it.'

'I've heard they can Shell?' said Stevens pal.

'Keep a had!' the Geordie stressed, ' were talkin' aboot ex-squaddies and commandos not the fuckin' Suits'!' he lowered his voice adding, 'Gan canny man, keep a had-on.'

Arthur wondered whether 'Shelling' was what he saw the statuesque, leather clad woman demonstrate. The way her facial expression froze and removed itself as a pale animate mask. Could it be transmitting visual information back to its original source? He wondered if it was the 'Suits' who controlled things over here, corresponding to the Grey Men on the hill. It was plain that on this side of the river, life was a whole lot more fun and upbeat and essentially lively, and let's face it, young. But it was not perfect. Someone or something was at the top of the pile.

'Will you look at that!' the Steve guy nudged his pal,' talent or what man!'

'Oh aye!', was the affirmative response.

A group of girls had decided to go to town wearing only silk underwear and miniscule lace capes, they tottered along on high dagger heels. They were giggling and mincing their way to another fantastic night out. One glanced back towards the pair of 'Beatles'.

'She fancies us. Were in!' Steve affirmed and the two lads hurried forward to attend their catch. Arthur looked about him as he passed the queues by the Mayfair. All the girls out that night were stunning. It made his heart beat to an uncomfortable pace. Being so scantily clad seemed acceptable amongst young women in the Mayfair Ballroom crowds, some wore dresses of see through fabrics, many of black lace and deliberately worn thin cottons. It overawed. Urchins, vampires, dark faeries. Matinee idols, dashing pilots, wags and farm boys. Everything there being heavily stylized.

Perfect hair, beautiful smiles, all in the peak of health and dressed to the nines. Everyone there in that lane was a picture, a study in looking good and having a great time. Arthur wished he could get in. However, he just kept walking. The floating mask was behind him somewhere.

The town was busy. He turned back towards the river and down St Nicholas Street towards the Bridge Hotel. Occasionally he glanced over his shoulder nervously. He couldn't help it. The revelers thinned towards the old castle. A more archaic mode of dress was frequent as in keeping with the mix of Norman, Tudor, Elizabethan and early Industrial Era architecture. An insane collision of ages and forms. There were fewer gas lamps and the shimmering resembled a light fret of rain. A magical place.

Arthur entered the Bridge Hotel and during his pint decided he would go back across the river that night. The manager did not recognize him in his new clothes he even got a wink from a flame-haired gypsy type girl in an embroidered dress. He had an ale, then smiled his thanks and left the pub to its sloshing beer and clinking glasses. He was swaying a little, and staggered slightly over the castle forecourt to the gatehouse, descending by the Dog Leap Stairs this time, which steeply flanked a massive railway bridge.

He was careful and used the iron handrail most of the way down to the Quayside. Everything was a-shimmer here, a ghostly, two-things-at-once visual tease.

It was not far to the Medieval bridge.

Arthur had been drinking all day and fumbled in the darkness with the catches and buckles of the diving suit. Looking back out on the glistening mirage of the Quayside he felt sad to leave it. Groups of folk sat outside on the street around trestle tables, talking, eating, drinking. They hadn't a care in the world. They were clean and happy, healthy and well fed. They had everything, he had Pipewellgate. Children were playing out late, their gleeful cries and shouts rang happily around the narrow streets, a friendly, welcome sound. One which he could quite easily get used to.

The heavy helmet reduced his movement to a blind-man's stumbling. He stood on his air supply pipe a couple of times and walked into the walls of the buildings which swarmed the ancient bridge. Eventually, a dim yellow rectangle gave a blurry indication of the limit of the noxious mist. The bracketed gas lamp dripped water, it was pissing down. Cobblestones shone and the shadows sagged in the damp air. The city on this side was a dirty, washed out stain. He hated being back immediately. It was a rotten, stinking filth hole. All the rain in creation would not clean it.

It took an effort of will in his drunken state to coil the feed-pipe and stash it in a ruin, just on the limit of the mist, where the air was only barely bearable. Arthur thought no-one would find it hidden under the stairs of a long-abandoned, pokey little house. He emerged coughing and light headed, he had inhaled too much of the narcotic fog. Carrying the fishbowl helmet under his arm he forced himself to walk the last two hundred yards to his tenement home in the diving suit. Hard routine.

He felt it had been a very physical day. So much running, so much fear. That weird statuesque woman with the face that 'Shelled' had almost scared the very life out of him.

So much to tell Cecilia.

He folded the diving suit away into a wooden cupboard and added the enormous spherical metal helmet. This was his ticket to the other side. He put the kettle on and thought that being able to get commodities for free meant that life in this prison world may not be so unendurable. He also reasoned that the tall, leather-clad lady and her 'dog' represented something the denizens feared. Something to be avoided if at all possible. Even in their happy, healthy, hedonistic existence where everything was free, someone was calling the shots. There was an upper echelon that inspired great fear. He remembered the look of utter disinterest in the dominatrix's face after she had 'Shelled' and her facial expression had turned into a floating mask. That was the look of someone who was not worried or concerned one tiny bit.

He hung up his suit and folded his new clothes away. They represented another world, a better, brighter aspect of this prison city. Splicing the tea with an enormous shot of whiskey he then sat by the window in the dark and listened to the sounds of the 'Gate emerging into nocturnal activity.

He almost fell asleep in his chair. Outside, in the darkness under the High Level Bridge, someone was vomiting copiously. This convinced Arthur to shut the window and go to bed. He hung the belt and holster from his bedpost, the revolver handle turned towards him. Just like in those gangster movies he used to follow, Sam Spade, Marlowe, Dick Barton...

He had his best sleep since arriving. The riots and pitched battles that clashed under his window that night did not wake him. In the morning light when the Grey Men came and carried the injured and prone away, Arthur was snoring in his bed, oblivious. Blood, teeth, glass and discarded weapons lay where they fell in the lane below. Every picture tells a story.

Arthur woke refreshed, as usual he had no concept of what time it was and regarded his pocket watch with surprise. It was three-thirty, the day was almost spent. He rose and washed in the cold rusty water and noticed the size of his bruise had diminished considerably. It also had ceased to ache. Could this have been an effect of just one visit to the other side?

The other half of this city had a lot in its favour. If only he could avoid the weird authorities, it was a greatly preferable place by far.

He had a good wash, the water heated by boiling a kettle and two large pans of hot water, this was added to the ever available cold running water and cleanliness was had. The cottons were quality. The shirt still felt wonderfully new. The jacket and cap had a capable mans look. He felt enervated by yesterdays jaunt over the water. It showed in his face. The yellow in his eye whites was also gone as had the stains on his teeth. This startled him, so quick a transformation occurring in just one visit inferred that a longer stay would be very beneficial indeed. The notion of having a life all over again occurred to him as a likely possibility. Incredible.

The Webley was strapped to his waist beneath the jacket. He removed the ammo pouches to limit the tell-tale bulges and paused to think. He threw a gents raincoat about him, one that he used to wear for his walks to work in bad weather. If he stood fully upright and did not stoop, his lean frame was six foot high. There was life in the old boy yet. He carefully stashed the remaining loose ammo and pouches behind the gas meter. All seemed completely normal. He took a stiff dram and waited for the day to fade a little. Surviving this prison city brought with it many thoughts to Arthur that begged for attention, like how on earth anyone could create such a thing! Where in the world could it be? Why were the young and the beautiful and the talented all over on one side of the River and all the old, diseased, aggressive and unhinged had been set down on the other? It seemed dashed unfair to Arthur as he listened to the river flow, so profoundly unreasonable that he should be considered to be placed amongst such dross and ugliness.

He was a man... He was, angry.

He held within the fibres of his fraying memory the notes which had burned their pages onto the life he had lived, with blood for ink and tears for years. His years, his life. It may not have really added up to much, but for some good shipyard designs and many precise draughtsman drawings. This and the fact he had looked after his mother. Whether there was nothing to it or not, it still did not connect with where Arthur was now, in the overcrowded, smelly slums of an alternative Pipewellgate. What was the link? It made him furious not to know, and too a degree, not to have someone to complain to. Who or what had done this to him?

He was a man... He was sure he was a man...

He had lived his own story in fiery letters and numinous words, spelling out compassion's cost and love's expense. His life, in a grammar, particular to itself, had a way with words. The authenticity of caring for his mother before his own desires stood out in Arthur's memory as a marker in time and place. A proof of species and a noteworthy personal datum. In this alternate Tyneside he still could identify with this caring aspect of his humanity and emotionally respond to memories, so Arthur concluded he himself was the same person and all else may have been altered but not his vital nature.

He sat by the window overlooking the river. As always, the far side was a bank of mist and the water barely stirred in flow. The real version was tidal, it rose and fell, it burst its confines during heavy rain and ran low in dry weather. There had to be some rules here, thought Arthur, everything had rules.

All eras were here. The whole place was a collection of Tyneside throughout its entire history. Both in peoples and architecture. No actual concession was made for when or wherever you came from, yet there were many familiar things which sat alongside much which was not. Also, the ageing process had stopped or had slowed down so markedly it was undetectable. So the baker was from Tudor England and still attempted to live in that time, despite a Roman in full Lorica Segmentata calling in to procure bread. Arthur wondered if that was how people here stayed sane, by keeping their own time or era about them?

There also was no money, every transaction was a barter, or if over the river on the Newcastle side, everything was free. He considered that a city containing folk from over 2000 years of history would have no common coinage, barter was timeless and efficient. It was notable too, that residents from one era of time had great fear of folk drawn from another quite different to theirs. More so, that the greater the difference in time or period between people, the violence and hostility proportionally increased. This could have been the cause of the many savage fights on the 'Gate.

It was hard to accept, but the reality which confronted him was that the Gateshead side, or this version of the place, was the repository of all that was ugly, old, demented, diseased and dangerous. Whilst the Newcastle side held the young and vital, happy, healthy lads and lasses. This Arthur really did not like, that he had been purposely placed in a place full of danger and threat and that its filthy streets never saw the sun. This just wasn't fair in his view. Somehow, he had to break out of this and take Cecilia with him. He knew there had to be a way, it was simply finding out what this was. A visit to the library was in order.

Arthur noticed he was walking very quickly uphill and he was not short of breath. He stopped in the stairway of the narrowed alleyway that ascended the Bankies. Looking back down towards the 'Gate, the evening had cast shapes in the shadows. Warm circles of yellow gas lamp detailed the night. It was a view he knew well. Nothing stirred, yet. No-one was about, just himself and the continual mist that rose like a wall upon the river.

The Church of the Drunkards he now knew could be avoided by using smaller side lanes, but always choosing those that took him in the desired direction. Which was south, where the bulk of the massive fortified hill dominated the horizon before him, now black angular shapes against a dark-blue night sky. Arthur felt alive and alert, a man with a mission, pacing down these claustrophobic little back lanes, knowing where he was going, in a raincoat, with a gun. By the time he reached the library it was pitch black. He had not even broken a sweat.

Cecilia jumped out from behind her desk and quick as a bird had disappeared as soon as she saw that someone had entered the library and was walking towards her. She had spotted the white smile on the tall man and dashed for one of her many escape routes.

'Cecilia!' he called, 'It is me! Arthur! Please don't run.'

Her head peered cautiously around from a tiny narrow space between bookshelves and stared.

'Goodness me!' She exclaimed in much surprise, 'I didn't recognize you!'

'I have so much to tell you' he began, 'you will hardly believe where I have been!'

Cecilia insisted that they spoke somewhere safe and set off for the cupola. Arthur watched her ascend the little ladder, hidden in the confined space of cornered bookshelves. She was tall and slender, her movements fluid and graceful. Arthur liked her. He hoped quietly within himself that he had found a friend. That in some way he could be a friend in return. She told him to join her and shuffle along the narrow shelf to the hatch. For the first time in this situation Arthur felt twinges of desire flutter in him as he watched her skirts disappear into the wee door. He flushed red with embarrassment and concentrated on calming himself down a touch.

He was sixty years old. Maybe there was still a pinch of lustiness in him yet?

Cecilia disconnected those few gas lanterns burning low in the library by turning a brass lever, complete darkness filled the avenues at once.

'Tell all'. She sat with her back ramrod straight and said,

'spare not the smallest detail'.

So he told all....

'...and what is more, my bruise is healing. It does not even hurt anymore!'

Cecilia sat with a hand covering her mouth, which was hanging agape. Her large eyes were expressing serious incredulity. It took a very long silence as she assimilated Arthur's adventure in Newcastle. Before her, if proof was needed, there he was, in a brand new change of clothes, a new suit, looking younger and healthier and exuding a fresh confidence and vitality.

He set his overcoat by the bolted hatch door and hung his cap.

'See' he said, offering his forehead for inspection.

'Indeed!' she responded, 'remarkable, really quite fascinating.'

Arthur withdrew his tin of loose tea, saying,

'Try a brew with this, it's India tea, I think you will like it.'

The librarian eventually re-emerged from the mental weight of all what she had just been told and began to ask questions in an attempt to conceptualize what such a predicament actually inferred and described.

'The lady whose face turned into a mask and followed you, you say she was tall?'

'Indeed' answered Arthur, 'she had to be well over seven foot tall.'

'Some amongst the Grey Men are of that stature.' Cecilia noted and continued,

'This mask followed you. Are you sure?'

'It was definitely her features on that mask. It followed me alright. What do you make of it?' he asked,

'It scares me.' Cecilia said, 'It reminds me of the black light...'

'About fifty years ago,' she explained 'a fleet of horseless carriages drove up Prince Consort Road. They had open tops, I could see happy people in colourful clothes, laughing and drinking as they passed. One vehicle stopped and a sweet, smiling lady waved to me. I was at my roof garden, and waved back. Over the din of these carriages she told me they were having a party in a hotel and would I like to come. Well, I used to think there was safety in numbers, so I descended and joined them.' Cecilia paused and set the kettle on to boil.

'I rode in the rattling machine, perhaps a mile up the hill to a grand hotel set beneath the ruins of the castle on the crags. The roads were tree lined and fine houses with gardens flanked the way.

They were a very friendly and playful lot. I dined with them and had a little wine. I danced! I almost forgot where I was. Then I began to worry about the situation and felt a strong desire to leave, so I did.'

Cecilia shivered and seemed to cower, lowering her voice almost to a whisper saying,

'I was almost out of sight of the hotel when I heard screaming. I turned and shrank into a hedge beside me. I saw figures, very lofty men, from whom exuded a inky mist. Whatsoever it fell upon either broke, shattered, bled or burned up. I squeezed through a gate in the hedge and curled up in fear.

The skin of these tall creatures was shifting and changing. It was only fixed for brief periods. They reminded me of coloured glass, for a degree of transparency was about them. But...'

She paused, it was clearly hard for her to continue. Arthur waited, listening.

'When they speak,' Cecilia's voice lowered even to a hush,

'it is sheer violence made manifest, in the vilest of ways.'

Arthur strained to hear, yet she continued the story.

'I saw that hotel destroyed in minutes. One moment they are all having fun, the next they are perishing by the most horrible of means. Windows showered glass, which flew about like savage birds, lacerating and slashing. Fires broke out and disappeared immediately. The screaming, the cries of those dying was unendurable. I thought no more for my safety and turned and ran. All I could hear behind me were their shrieks and howls.'

The words sank slowly in.

'Both sides of the river can be dangerous.' Arthur stated the obvious.

'Clearly.' acknowledged Cecilia.

CHAPTER FIFTEEN

The congress of automatons.

The Dominatrix Amazon woman strolled, without her wretched 'dog' in tow, down the rich burgundy velvet corridor. The carpet was thick, the velour wallpaper a lush, textured, deep-wine colour, the ceiling hung with dark red drapes. She entered the little cinema, it had hardly more than a hundred seats. Something highly sexual was being enacted onscreen. A single figure sat in the audience. It was a Suit, alone before the porno movie.

She settled in the adjacent seat. The suit wore a mask, it was her face, half smiling, watching the movie. There was nothing visible behind the mask or occupying the actual space inside the suit. Whatever filled it did so unseen.

'The movie can wait!' she barked at the mask.

It turned idly and regarded her, silently, almost insolently.

'Do not look at me like that!' the Dominatrix warned, then noted, 'It did not take you long to suit-up, did it?'

The mask actually smiled and replied, 'Sure enough Ma'am.'

In the cupola, above the central library on the Gateshead side, Cecilia and Arthur talked, as the tiny gas lantern softly hissed.

'I think that the nearer to the river one stays, on the other side, the less chance of detection there will be. It is most odd there. It is as though it exists in two places at one time. It is shimmering, ghostly, I find it hard to explain. Perhaps it is a result of being near the wall of toxic mist.'

Arthur sipped the dark, strong tea and continued,

'I wonder about what you told me concerning how the farms that surround this side of the town which only range for a dozen miles and then it is barren. A desolate terrain for a desperate place. Perhaps the outer environment of Newcastle is quite other, far more bountiful and productive, in order to supply those parts of the city with so much provender and goods.'

The tea was good. Arthur summoned his courage and said,

'Would you be willing to come over there with me and to try to find a place where we could perhaps live a better life? I mean to explore the land on that other side. Not the city itself, but the hills and woodland to the north. I really would value your company, for I may not be able to return here. I may not wish to. The only human contact I have in this place is you.'

She smiled at him and answered so distinctly sweet and civilly,

'I would love to accompany you on such an adventure Mister MacNeil.'

The half-smile Suit sat in an office full of Suits. Some of them had not moved in years. After a certain period a Mask would be taken away by Mister Mort and filed, once it was redundant or concluded. As soon as the file drawer closed, the actual suit would collapse, that also was taken away, cleaned and stored neatly. Each Suit had a case. The information in that case was recorded in the memory-membrane of the Mask. If the file was active it became animated and acquired a smart suit, it then became a Suit. Activation was at the will of the Hybrids, genetically modified human forms developed to police the city, to watch over the inmates and perform the bidding of their creators. Hybrids like the Dominatrix.

It was these that had generated the Mask or Shell, which in turn animated the Suit.

They had a degree of independence, but wholly according to the Hybrid that had created it and was bound by the framing conditions at the moment of its creation, its purpose, its job or mission.

Half-Smile, the Shell of a Dominatrix Mask, sat waiting.

It had to track a dirty old man. In a city where inhibition and restraint had no play, where a thousand pubs and clubs entertained and fulfilled the needs of any attractive exhibitionist or pleasure seeker. There was so much to see. It would be a prime task for a Suit. City Central Investigations. A name everyone feared without exception. The phone rang, Half-Smile answered it.

A laugh, an echo of a laugh, a breath of ancient age, repeating unto silence.

i...i...i...i...i...

The Suit got up and smiled.

'Game to go'. It said.

Outside in the night, music throbbed insistent and sensual.

'Great work if you can get it!' grinned Half-Smile, to anyone in earshot.

The implications of leaving the library clearly was having an effect upon Cecilia.

She was most confused about what to take and what she may need. There was also the matter of her books.

The librarian had become deeply attached to dozens of massive tomes, which she knew it would be impractical to carry and would have to reduce her favourites down to a mere three. Arthur waited patiently, after all, she had hardly left the library in fifty or sixty years or more! Sure, she would sneak out and forage for herbs and mushrooms in parks and gardens, but that did not constitute freedom by any mark. Living like a frightened little animal was not good enough. There had to be more to life, even in this odd place.

Eventually two large satchels were found, one carried her three most precious books, the other a change of clothing and personal effects. Cecilia had not fully realized that life over the river was very different, and that everything was free and she could acquire a new set of clothing easily. Arthur wondered how such a state of affairs could come to pass, people had jobs and busied away at their daily tasks, but wages and payments did not seem to come into the equation at all. There had to be hundreds of miles of countryside beyond the town, producing food and commodities that kept the Land of the Forever Young in plenty. Arthur began to hope it wasn't a long shot, because even if it was, his mind was already made up.

'Well then!' said Cecilia with a brave face on ' I'm ready when you are'.

'Are you going to lock up?' Arthur asked, taking up the heavier satchel.

'Oh, I suppose so,' she seemed unsure, 'what if I lose the key?'

'What if you never come back?' suggested Arthur.

Half-Smile, now a Suit calculated it would take ninety-four nights of work to cover all the major, big sexy venues on the town where a dirty old man may emerge. Then it would take almost three times that to check all the seedy little back street sex shows that proliferated. It lacked the self consciousness to be aware that it was itself a rather dirty new Mask. During the day it would systematically visit all the pubs, this would take considerably longer to cover. Many months of work! As a Suit it had a degree of self awareness that enabled it to enjoy what it was programmed to do, this basic and rudimentary form of pleasure was directly linked to the personality of the Hybrid that had Shelled it. The notion of being a CCI Suit with work on the town gave the Mask plenty to look forward to, much was to be appreciated in the execution of its task. Big Fun in Fat City.

This job promised to be a good one.

The Masks were programmed to follow, record, scan, interrogate, analyze and arrest. They also possessed the ability to neurally stun and sedate suspects, this was partially the source of the fear the specimen humans suffered. The data gathered on the case was delivered directly back to the Hybrid who would then answer to its own Creators, which were but a voice at the end of a telephone. A distant, ancient, mocking voice that laughed in the whispers of infinity. This actually was much more bearable than having a Creator manifest amongst them, for when they did it was always big trouble, every single time. Lots of horrible ways to perish quite miserably would ensue.

First on the list for Half-Smile to check was the Mayfair Ballroom.

All the kids instantly stepped out of the way of the Mask as it floated by the colourful crowd of beautiful people, lined up in the queue outside.

Being a big-shot Suit it turned to the massive, muscularly bulked out doorman and said, 'CCI'. The enormous man bowed his head, looked away in fear and opened the door, barely subduing a shiver of fear.

Arthur got Cecilia safely to his tenement flat. She had been constantly nervous and frightened all the way. He had traveled by the quieter back lanes and alleys, but her fear was justified. The Tyneside she was seeing had completely changed, many more structures and buildings had crammed into its overcrowded spaces and it simply exuded menace and threat. Now, however, Arthur was armed.

At his little table, they ate toast and pie and cake with dark sweet tea as the first indications of morning began to show. He peered out the window into the gloom.

'I have to go and get you a diving suit, helmet and air pipe,' explained Arthur, ' please stay here, don't worry about me, I will return.'

She laid a slender hand on his elbow and looked earnestly into his face,

'You must stay safe. You must return. Be quick!'

She had the most penetrating, lovely eyes, Arthur thought appreciatively.

He walked with new found energy, striding purposefully on his way to the diving equipment shop floor when a shabby shadow from a decrepit stinking alleyway cursed at him, spitting the words,

'Look at the big man in a hurry, eh! What's so special about you, yer shite!'

Arthur didn't even bother to answer, it would be a waste of his breath.

The miles would pass more swiftly if he saved it.

In the Mayfair, Half-Smile was content that the dimly lit dance floors and bars off the main, well-lit hall helped disguise the fact that it was a Suit. It had found a table in the shadows and sat watching the cavorting of a highly sexually charged sub-sect of the youths, clearly into a glossy form of voyeuristic posing. Any dirty old man worth his salt would not miss a floor show like this. In the gloom, the Mask caused no fear or panic, it looked just like a well-dressed gent idling his night away. A lithe, petite little girl, no more than sixteen swayed over to Half-Smile's table, a drink in hand. Her entire abdomen was bare and heaving from the exertions of her sensuous physical dancing. She wore tattered silks, the 'urchin' look.

'Wow!' she gasped, ' What a night! I'm knackered already!'

The Mask regarded her pale exposed skin.

'Human' it thought, then said evenly,

'Have you seen any dirty old men down here lately?'

She peered at the luminous face before her and then stiffened in fear, her breath came in rasps as she realised exactly what it was she had sat down next to.

'No, no, this is only my fourth time, time, time down here!' she stuttered.

The Mask smiled, it liked this power. Being a Suit was a great job.

'If you do see an old guy, grey hair, five-ten or eleven, lean build,' the Suit used the official voice, ' he may be found in places like this, looking intently at lovely young things like yourself. Please be certain to contact me on this number.'

A slim card slipped from the breast pocket of the Suit's suit and hovered before the urchin's frightened face. She took it with a shaking hand, but having no pockets to place it in, lifted the tattered silk at her hip and tucked it into the elastic at the side of her tiny gossamer panties.

'Thanks a whole pile,' said the Suit as it rose and drifted out, leaving the shivering young lassie to her ruined night. She herself would go home soon, looking over her narrow trembling shoulders all the way.

When Arthur returned, the morning had arrived in a dull-steel sheet of cloud that told of more rain. He smiled at his friend who was sitting stock still and bolt upright by the open window, she said,

'I heard the sound of iron wheels on cobblestones, that was you wasn't it?'

'Aye', replied Arthur, 'It was. Now I must quickly pack my own stuff.'

He took the ex-army rucksack and filled it with the camping kit he had acquired in the abandoned hotel. First the sleeping bag, the oiled cape and the gents cape. Then the nesting pans and kettle, the various fishing and survival items and then the large water canister, which he filled.

The binoculars he strapped to the front of the bag, and placed the meat cleaver and an unopened large decanter of brandy in the side pockets. The remaining spaces he packed with food, clothing and two divers knives. The rucksack was heavy to lift, but once on his back and adjusted, felt a lot easier to carry.

Retrieving the spare ammo from behind the gas meter, Arthur remembered the ornate key in the drawer, beneath the brown paper lining where he kept his shirts. He pocketed it, unsure why he did so initially, perhaps a reminder. He did not take the odd version of his mother's letters that lay in the shoebox, he did not trust them, he could not see the person he knew and loved in the writing. The last things he did was to place his considerable stash of alcohol into a canvas bag. Then he collected the diving suit. He turned in the doorway and said,

'I don't ever want to see this place again.'

Half-Smile was watching the party people stream from the clubs and pubs. It stood in the dawn, a presence without substance. An empty mask on an vacant suit. It was a machine, a program, a file during an operation. Its first night on the job had brought no findings or leads whatsoever, but it had thoroughly enjoyed itself.

'Plenty more to go', it thought as early hints of morning touched the eastern sky.

It drifted off to the office, where all the Suits must report each morning.

It was smiling, happy with both itself and the task in hand, such a wonderful world.

Cecilia did not take well to the morning light. She clung to Arthur's left elbow and would not let go. This made it hard to push the laden upright trolley. He liked this, he enjoyed being needed, he felt alive in having this purpose. They stopped by the bakery and Arthur banged loudly and confidently on the door.

'Whet in fucks name is gannin'on!" an angry voice sounded from within.

'It's Arthur,' said he ' I have something you will like a lot.'

The heavy door opened.

'Fuckin' whet?' the bleary eyed little monster snarled.

Cecilia jumped backwards a step in horror at the apparition.

'This is yours' said Arthur, handing him the bag of booze.

The baker opened it and spotted the brandy and whiskey. There was even a corkscrew and two glasses. At the bottom of the bag, four steel sheathed diving knives glistened in their grease coating. The dwarf looked at Arthur uncomprehending.

'What d'yer want fur this lot then?' he eyed the pair with suspicion and mistrust.

'Nothing' replied Arthur, ' it's a gift, I'm leaving. Goodbye, and thanks for the trade.'

'Where the hell do yer think yer gannin'man?' the baker asked as he held the gift to his chest, blinking at the light and the gift incomprehensibly.

"Never you bloody well mind! answered Arthur with a smile.

The pair walked towards the mist.

'Who was that ugly little fellow?' Cecilia had to know.

'The nearest thing to a friend I had before I met you.' answered Arthur.

He quickly retrieved his stashed air pipe and helped Cecilia into the bulky diving suit, her tweed skirt bunched up as she stepped into the legs of the rubberized canvas. Arthur caught a quick glimpse of soft white thigh above darned and patched stockings. He felt briefly aroused, but concentrated on the task in hand and then suited up himself.

As before, he anchored the air pipes and arranged them so they could run-out evenly. He then donned the rucksack, fitted the air pipes to the helmets and said,

'Hold my hand as we pass over. Stay with me lass. It is dark and frightening, but it is a better land over there. Do not panic, do not run. Stay calm, keep by my side and all will be well, you will see, I assure you.'

She smiled nervously as Arthur placed the heavy helmet over her head. A few hairs strayed about her large brown eyes. He wanted to kiss her, even behind thick glass, she was beautiful to him.

He smiled back at her and took one last look at Pipewellgate.

'Bye-bye hell-hole.' he said, donned his helmet and with his friend's hand in his, crossed over.

Half-Smile sat silent in an office and waited with all the other Suits. It would wait until midday, and if the phone did not ring, then it was free to go about its business. This was the routine. A phone call could hold instructions or information, a lead or a tip-off. The window near Half-Smile slid open as willed to do so, the Mask regarded the view of the fabulous town. Ornate rooftops ranked as far as it could see. Towers and fancy ironwork vied with epic carvings and ornate architectural details. It certainly was the place to be. The hours would pass. The phones did not ring. Half-Smile was recalling the details of the previous night, the skinny young bodies cavorting on the dance floor, the heightened sense of arousal it could detect all around the room. The pleasure in it all, the sheer charge. It briefly wondered what the other Suits were thinking about and then smirked, glad that none were on such an excellent task as itself. City Central Intelligence never had more than four Suits out at one time. They frightened the inmates too much.

This did not go down well with their superiors. They who governed this collection of humans.

The i…

The alien alien's alien…

Two figures in early model diving suits emerged into the morning sunshine, out from the foggy darkness of the Medieval bridge, whorls of mist spiraled behind them. The Quayside streets were empty, so unobserved, they coiled their air-pipes, changed out of the shapeless, diving suits and hid them in the shadows. The pair looked about them, captivated.

'See, I told you,' said Arthur, 'so very, very different.'

Cecilia regarded the beautiful shimmering place and her heart beat fast and strong.

'So much..' she tried to express herself, ' so much, more…'

'Let us be off,' Arthur stated, ' we will head upriver until we are free of the city, then we can head north. I wish you could see this town, but perhaps it is not safe just now.'

'What I see of it already is enchanting enough,' she replied and walked alongside Arthur. Soon the tenement lanes of the western docks and warehouses swallowed them. They walked along these steep gloomy canyons alone, for nothing stirred.

After three miles the couple entered an area which corresponded to Scotswood in the world of the real Tyneside. Terraced housing ranked the entire hillside and many factories clustered the river banks. People had begun to go to work, but no-one rushed or looked gloomy or sad about the prospect. Some waited awhile in conversation, had a cigarette or stoked a pipe of tobacco. No-one was in a hurry. Arthur suggested they use the back lanes which ran parallel the main road west, he wished their departure to remain secret, from who and what though, he was not entirely certain. He noticed that this Scotswood was a lot cleaner and in better overall condition.

'This place has a bad reputation back in the Tyneside I come from.' Arthur informed.

'It doesn't look too bad to me,' responded Cecilia, 'quite quaint and tidy.'

'More proof of the divisions of this place,' Arthur observed, 'this side is a lot better off.'

Another three miles brought them to the limit of the city environs. Woodlands and fields welcomed them. Friesian cows grazed in green paddocks. Horses neighed as they passed.

The sun shone down on them, a light wind played with their hair.

They drew near a little village, a hamlet on the outer edge of the vast conurbation that was this alternative Newcastle. They sat under old oak trees and rested, sharing water from the canteen and eating a little dry bread. Arthur felt he had never been so alive before. Cecilia was now much less nervous and was beginning to respond to the countryside that was unfolding around her.

'How far do you think we should go Arthur?' she asked.

'As far as we can,' he replied, 'until we find a place that we can claim or make or build. A place far from here'

'We should be going then!' she approved eagerly.

No cars tore along the quiet winding roads. They passed the occasional hay wain and pony trap on their way north. Farms and hamlets proliferated, as Arthur had suspected, the fields were lush with produce and the livestock had an abundance of sustenance and space.

The road eventually became a track, which in turn soon became a dirt path. They had walked all morning and long into the afternoon and both felt footsore.

Moors broke the very far horizon with heather and gorse, maybe two days walk ahead of them, due north of a huge forest. Arms of this great wood enclosed many farms and small settlements. They continued walking until dusk fell, stopping neither for rest or food.

Later that long day Arthur chose an area of deep, broad-leafed woodland to rest the night, a clear brook ran through it. He made a little fire in a pit, using bone-dry twigs and branches for fuel and soon had the kettle singing with boiling water. They ate some of the bakers bread and a little cake. Birds sang and old leaves rustled. A hint of colour touched the western sky.

'Perhaps we should camp here tonight?' Arthur motioned to the sheltered glade approvingly,

'This seems a good enough head start to me.'

'Do you think we will be followed?' Cecilia asked him.

'I don't know. That all depends on why we were brought here and by what, I think.'

The setting sun transformed the woodland to shining gold and green.

The i...

CCI offices, in the City of the Forever Young.....

A whole bunch of blank-eyed Suits pin uninformed notions to a wall chart.

There is a sunset out there, especially if these machines are working late, there is!

It matters little to these spectacular but functional technological creations.

A Big Shot Wise Guy once said,

'The entire purpose of communication is not to baffle ones opponent into submission, but to communicate a comprehensible idea, or a series of ideas.'

Been some folks figuring that one out in all kinds of places for quite some time. A whole lot of shaking going on. A great big hill of shakes.

CHAPTER SIXTEEN

The madness of machines.

The i…

Had made a good copy of Northumberland.

Perhaps the forms and patterns had resonated an age-old core of memory? Maybe they simply had enjoyed its history? Whatever it was, their version was beyond perfect, it was idealized. Expanded enormously, but identifiable and beautiful.

On the fringe of a wing of woodland, a rill of water ran through tall arching beeches. This forest, if viewed from above, had many clearings and settlements, yet its great green bulk ran far into the north. Two figures lay on a bed of old leaves, mounded to give a little comfort, each wrapped warmly. Long graying hair spilled from a woolen gents traveling cloak. The woman stirred in her sleeping bag and regarded her friends reclined form. Blackbirds sang and bees lazily wandered by. Shafts of warm sun poured down upon the glade.

When Arthur awoke, he found Cecilia sitting under a tree, reading a book.

'Good morning.' she said, cheerily and quite matter of fact.

'Aye', he rubbed his eyes, 'good morning to you too.'

With a comb he raked his gray hair back on his head. Then he brushed away all the leaves that he had packed about himself for insulation. He thought he had better have a wash in the burn, he was in the company of a lady after all. A large handkerchief served as a towel. He had slept in his trousers and white vest, he looked younger already, standing upright at his full height, a gladness in his face plain to read. He was simply happy to have got this far.

He pulled up his braces, took his clothes and walked into the dense interior of the forest, to relieve his bladder and change into the shirt. Returning he emerged to find Cecilia packing her book away.

'Thank you for taking me with you,' she spoke quietly, ' this is more life to me than a century of fear. Whatever befalls, let us see this adventure through.'

'Aye, indeed. We can give it our best go! I hope for a good road'. Arthur was sincere, 'and that it leads to somewhere we can live like regular humans.'

Cecilia simply nodded in agreement. Neither were hungry, but they silently shared the water in the canteen and ate a little dry bread.

Woodland predominated. The dirt path they had followed yesterday frittered away into meandering routes that often led to tiny hamlets and settlements. It became clear to Arthur that finding a way out may not be so easy without a map or a compass. He had the binoculars and decided to find a hill. They backtracked to a wider way that ran through large open fields, the forest still dominant nearby. Arthur used the binoculars and studied the lie of the land.

The woodland beyond was extensive. A craggy hill, roughly one mile ahead looked a good vantage point. The track they were on was heading that way.

It was early morning, life was stirring around the farmsteads and cottages.

The gardens were laden with vegetables, orchards fecund with fruit.

They walked side by side, at a quick pace, occasionally, Arthur would frequently glance backwards, hoping there would be nothing and no-one following.

The track re-entered the great canopy and was swallowed by the leafy roof. It continued northward until the hill steeply rose to its left. They abandoned the wagon way and climbed the tree-covered slope. By the brow of the hill, crags jutted steeply, covered in lichens and moss. They traversed under these until an easy access was found. Scrambling to the top, they found the summit was flat. To the east the land spread far. Arthur used the binoculars to scour the terrain. There were farms and villages, hamlets and settlements as far as he could discern, running east to a sliver of blue, a distant North Sea. To the south, a thousand rooftops swarmed and grew loftier toward the city center. They were still not far enough away. To the north, the forest spread as far as he could see. Arthur decided they should stick to the little woodland tracks. They rested briefly, looking towards the city, eating a little cake and finishing the water. The miles would pass without them meeting another single person.

Mask-Think.

Corrupt file. Hybrid Shell. Dirty Old Man. Track. Aged voyeur. Check-datum, rapid cellular dissolution, molecular mis-reactions. Specimen out-with perimeter of Northern-Eastern Borderland...

Human, sort, elderly, sort, unique, innocent, witness, fulcrum-function. Check-datum, no transit permit.

Origin - non rational food source. Example - possible genetic copy mutation. Location? Pre-sub-sort-routine, analyse. Record. Check-sort. Routine-run. Go.

The Suits became active simultaneously in the Land of the Forever Young.

All the empty Masks in the CCI offices, waiting for that phone call, suddenly sparked into motion, when the phones began ringing at once! All of them.

Dangallangerdang! Dangallangerdang! Dangallangerdang!

The harsh tone was jarring and set too loud on the office speakers.

'Shag me stripy! Lots of phones going off at once?' commented Half-Smile.

'Keep it! Shut that shit out!', spat one floating Mask, answering the phone before its empty eyes. Business as usual.

'Stop calling this number you creeps!' said Half-Smile in mock complaint.

'Its just a devolved, trans-scanned awareness substrate in rapid decomposition, set in a pre-consigned, verifiable, projection degeneration! Standard stuff! This type hang around in The Mayfair, The Boo Hives. Jizzdizzy Jump, Ooogie Booogie Box,...'

'SSShhhuuuttt uuuppp reprehensible worrrrrmmmm'.

The voice like no voice ever, ordered in a hiss. A whole office of empty suits and masks stood to precision-perfect attention. Truly, a most efficient technology.

'Hence not so swift with such fresh assumptions.' A voice of death, lots of deaths in a row. Masks don't swear, as a general rule, and most Suits are quiet...

'You got me all tore up.' said Half-Smile, impertinently.

'YOU! AND Your transparent friends will immediately find ALL the DIRTY OLD MEN in this city, do you understand me?!' The voice was commanding.

'All of them boss?' asked the Dominatrix face, smirking with some attitude.

'Unto scintilla and teeth records, as is your function and design.' the commanding voice rasped. It was not a voice to be dealt with lightly.

'Copy that. Check, Record, Sort, Execute, file. 'Dirty old men'. In transit. Out.'

Half-Smile glibly spoke the Suit-Think protocol.

Every single Mask without exception left its seat immediately.

'Hail to the Chief!' saluted Dominatrix face, so in touch.

Half-Smile was last out of its seat and when it departed it did so without any clothing. Some Masks know just where to go.

Isn't that right.

'Humans!' writhed Half-Smile, loathing and obsession fizzled within its myriad paper-thin circuits. ALL the other Suits had ran into the night, hot on the case. A few had evolved by incidence of circuitry a sneer of sorts.

Suits love jobs. Masks love work. Life is enormous. A need based thing.

The aliens have it all on the books, I'm telling you, wrapped, recorded, filed.

'Who gives a shivering shit? thought Half Smile, as it had left its own suit in the office. It was but a Mask that sailed out of an open window and delicately soared away into the City of Fantasy. No wonder the other Suits ran out so fast. Half-Smile had left its own garments behind, slumped emptily in his chair. Bad form. Before it departed on the search sheet it had typed,

'Soul-dive, lust-thing, spell-shake, juju-whoop, also-ran 70s fruitcake-hero. Heartache. Slices of Let-Down-Pie. Vast, vast empty distances. Impressions.

Non determinate. Record. File. Deus ex machina.'

Half-Smile covered itself with a wig and a hat, for in its great hurry, had deliberately forgotten clothing. Only newly Shelled Masks could forgo their attire. The human specimens were justifiably afraid of these machines.

'What do you think?' asked Half-Smile with all due sincerity of circuits and form. The little girl was barely sixteen. This was no place for her, in such a sophisticated shop. Hell no! She also stuttered, life forms tend to stutter when they possess intelligence and are confronted with a vastly enhanced species, or a greater skill, or an advanced technology. Which is what it is really? Hellish, by any other term.

Threatened, is another.

The i.

Gravel in your eyes. Boots in your face. Blades in your buttocks. Inarticulate venom. Beyond the talkers and the so called thinkers. Makes for a man to question. Like how general incompetence rises easily to higher administration levels. A whole pile of rot. The days certainly are short, yet they are not going to magically lengthen just because you go to some fucking office and complain. When it's curtains folks, it's curtains. The lights go out and you hope for the best with your last dying thought. Sure enough. Why do you think death is simply so fascinating?

Lonesome Road. Johnny Lonely Human. Heart full of tears. Broken dreams and shattered lives. Troubles and lost, injured consciousness, a whole lot of shaking going on. Told you so, no-one listens. Guess that's why the theme keeps repeating, a needful re-iteration. Glass in your shoes. Shit in your sandwiches. Tell you folks, no place to be…No one gives a hoot, cry all you God-damned want. It cannot shift a single little leaf. Tears will not make a rich man part with a penny. Not a single bean. Nihilum caritas. Minimae sapientae. Real, real sad…

Where is Captain Kirk when you need the bastard, eh?

Well, that is how it ticks. Oh, but now the dickheads have taken over and humans can't pretend it does not matter anymore, because time is tight. Trying to reach out to our terrorist cousins is not going to gain anything short of a snarl. Pilgrim, on this dirty trail, do you wish for your life to be ended for a wage, or for a meaning? Thither lies the end of ends. No sorrow that an enemy cannot fathom, no limit to the exploitation of grief.

Up and over boys! A to Z. Sounds like a head swerve, but it is just Mask-Think…

'Nut Loaf son of Nut Loaf, cracks appear, illiterate, unpronounced, diminished, swarming, illogical, forwarded pronunciations of untested authority'.

The crazy thoughts from an unorthodox Suit.

'A sort of rape'. Half-Smile grinned and spoke to, or rather at the passers by.

Humans both repulsed and fascinated it in turn, whereas Masks just terrified the civilians. They caused unease wherever they drifted. Understandable really.

'When was the last time you turkey necks actually danced properly?'

A kind of threatening question, backed by menacing ability from a Mask in a wig and trilby. An alarmingly off-putting sight anyway, a floating head.

'Shush honey, here comes the professor' Half-Smile should have brought his suit.

It hovered like a decapitation denying gravity at the front of a line of students.

He had come to hear a talk by an authority on crime resulting from biological and psychological decay. A regular guy's-regular guy. The Professor...

'I am fully aware that we inhabit an environment profuse with manifest examples of pointless lawbreaking and general disquiet', the erudite young gentleman brightly elucidated...

The professor was in full flow, five dozen listening ears gave full and studious attention. Another score tried hard to follow the lecture.

'What is true of the part, may provide indicative of notions concerning the entirety...'

In the audience, Half-Smile, half listening, was wondering how a Suit got to fire a gun. The Prof 's lecture continued, rattle rattle rattle. Being a Suit can be real, big time dull. Half-Smile tilted the wig and hat if it could have yawned it would have, so it began a sub-program in order to achieve this very thing. A yawn.

'Sure, being a Suit may appear a swerve compared to shooting vermin on the farm and punching a few bully redneck faces towards their spinal column.' Half-Smile was trying to impress a pretty young student with his spiel and lucid take. He did not read, however, that she was smiling out of sheer terror and apprehension.

The Mask was loving the sound of its voice far too much…

'Doof. Doof. Doof, farm boy! Here is a name you may conjure with.

Brutal Pointless Violence. Suits can call that in. On command.'

For a mere film of advanced technology, this Mask was getting cocky.

Suits do not have friends you see, only files and cases in common.

City lights and gas lamp, tunnel and wynd and autocar. A steam train with no reason to board. Same city. The town that never figured. Looking out, terminally dumb, out towards a horizon bleeding with clues. Dripping on comfortless desire, unspoken want, the lust of dust, the patina of the ageless…Where intelligent guess and calamity collide, unsuspected, unforeseen, unbidden.

A tragic tragic's tragic.

All the Suits congregated and investigated the dodgy freakshow clubs on the town, looking, it is added, for the 'dirty old man'. Some had not even checked the definition of the phrase. Crivens! A whole pile of trepidation ensued as so many Masks hit the nightspots and fun huts.

Skinny girls danced and wriggled a map of sensual fun and show. Empty Masks watched strip shows all night long, vacant Suits sat in auditoriums and witnessed eroticism flagrant and manifest. Anything human near it was clearly scared, edgy at least. The floating, talking faces frightened everyone. This was in the design remit.

It was morning. After listening to the Professor, Half-Smile had witnessed lots of undulating flesh and licentiousness. All manner of slutty exhibitionist pantomime, all through the night. Sin in right royal efficient motion. Sin and veritable shame. But nothing dirtier than itself. A grubby mask. A seeing, non-doing function. Despite this, it had found nothing, no one. Zilch.

'Shagging technological limits!' it thought…

Being programmed, as it was, it missed the significance. A yellow sun was rising over the city, music nearby insisted, beating in the dawn.

'Where are the boot boys?' the song beat onwards. 'Where did the boot boys go?

You hang around with gangs of skins, you're gonna get your fucking head kicked in."

On it angrily and noisily growled in a late 70's punk thrash uproar.

'Sure makes a Mask to think,' said Half-Smile.

Arthur and Cecilia had followed the forest tracks all that day. They both understood the need to put distance between themselves and the city and so pushed on without complaint. Arthur knew that the moorlands he had glimpsed beyond the forest could not be much further, but it was clear they would have to rest for another night short of his intended or ideal location. He reasoned rightly, they would travel faster and meet fewer people once free of the massive woodlands. He refilled the large round canteen in a clear stream. They ate very little and both fell into sleep quickly. Arthur had given the sleeping bag to Cecilia again, but she had insisted that he is took the traveling cloak this time. The deep mound of old leaves made for another comfortable night. They had covered many miles that day.

They woke with the warm rays of a rising sun finding them through the tall pillars of beech trunks. Grey columns and golden light met their waking eyes. Cecilia smiled and Arthur noticed.

He thought the lines had thinned around her eyes and a rosy colour had returned to her complexion. He had no idea she was thinking exactly the same thoughts about him. Arthur distributed the leaves and buried the fire pit, he wanted to be careful and cover their tracks. Reasoning where west lay, he turned his back on the new day sun and walked into the forest, Cecilia at his side. It was approaching midday when the woodland started to thin out. The terrain began to gradually rise. Rounded, heathery hills and gray crags appeared distant.

Arthur scanned the moorland. There were no visible roads or tracks or paths. Neither could he see a single sign of habitation. This he liked, and his spirits began to rise because they had made it so far. He turned to Cecilia, who was fashioning a walking stick from a fallen branch of oak with her diving knife. The stick cracked dryly and echoed with a retort as she trimmed it smooth. He remembered the revolver buckled at his waist, and returned to scouring the terrain before him.

At the summit of the first hill they rested. It was a large open area, with lots of mixed grass and heather, boulders and rocks made for suitable places to sit. The city was a silver grey blur on the far south horizon, even with binoculars, no details could be discerned. The fells and moors ran northwards, the forest enclosed its eastern flank for as far as he could see. It took a long time before he picked out what looked like a ruined castle, about eight or so miles distant.

'There are ruins about an afternoon walk from here, they look promising.'

He passed the binoculars to his friend, she said

'Could you please point them in the correct direction, this device is rather new to me.'

Arthur had to stand close to her and align the lenses on the far ruin. He could smell her hair and enjoyed being so close to her, it made him to smile.

'Ah', she cheered, 'I see them now. That looks a promising refuge for two escapees.'

When descending the hill, Arthur could pick out isolated empty farms and many ruined homesteads. Traces of abandoned habitation covered the valley floor, indicating much settlement and history. Dry stone walling scrawled over the rolling hills and clumps of hardy blackthorn trees survived high on the slopes. It was beautiful. It was actually better than he remembered it, though Arthur was fully aware, it was not the same place. It was not his previous, old life Northumberland, but something very different. The miles slowly passed.

As the sun was beginning to set, the two figures all alone on a moor, could see the stones of the ruined castle turning reddish on a nearby hill. Crags broke the ease of a direct approach, so their path wove up and through these bluffs and boulders until the long tumbled stones lay scattered before them.

An ancient wall shielded them from the fiery splendour of an unhinged sunset. A cruciform arrow slot flared with colour and light, it had become a burning cross. Arthur and Cecilia investigated the ruins. With great relief, they put the bags down that they had carried for three days.

The castle stood with its connecting walls in serious disrepair. The central tower was the largest section remaining. It appeared to have been once a much more substantial construction. Nearby, the lower courses of flattened structures told of towers that had long fallen, for the fort would have once described a circle upon the hill top. It was now but a quarter of its previous might. They found an alcove under a stone staircase that led from within the main tower itself to a hall above. Another more perilous set of stones led to the parapet, about four foot wide. A smaller watchtower perched in the southeastern-corner, it was inaccessible and quite unsafe.

Cecilia set about cutting heather and bracken with her diving knife, whilst he had to walk to a neighbouring craggy hill, as this was the only place where trees grew. Gnarled and twisted thorn trees survived there, battered by time and many winds, here was much dry windfall for a good fire.

Arthur broke the branches and twigs with a stone and packed them into his emptied rucksack. He noticed a cave under the crag which crowned the moorland hill. There was not enough light remaining for exploration, so Arthur hurried back to the tower. The night was setting in.

The space under the stairwell had been packed with heather and bracken bundles by Cecilia. Arthur set alight the kindling in the massive arched fireplace of the main tower hall. The flickering light picked out surviving sections of painted plaster and alcoves, shadowed in the warm orange light. He made a wood pile of the long dead thorn, it would burn well. After repacking his rucksack, Arthur began to brew a strong, black, sugary tea for them both. The night had swallowed them, a little fire in a stone ruin, alone in a vast, light-less, empty moor. They ate bread and pie and enjoyed their tea in silence. The cackle of burning wood gave heart and heat in this their refuge. The night was now no threat. Arthur stood by the narrow arched window facing south, nothing but night lay before his gaze.

'Do you think we will be missed back in the city?' Arthur asked Cecilia who was fire gazing, enjoying the dance of light.

'By whom?' she questioned back, 'the Grey Men, the Masks or their masters?'

'Any of those,' he responded, 'do you think we will be missed?'

Cecilia furrowed her brow and looked at Arthur in the firelight.

'I very much hope not, ', she said, ' I greatly need to rest here.'

Seventy two miles to the south, all the Suits were out searching the seedy clubs and perverted sinkholes in search of a dirty old man. It happened now and again on the paradise side of the river. Because of the higher number of specimens, there was always the possibility of a scan developing an error. A design flaw that caused the copy to age. It was a big place to hide, as youth decayed into wrinkled old age and all around you beauty shone forever with bright new health and vigour. The Suits knew the mutations had to venture outside sometime, so where else would they be? Sadly, the other denizens of the city nightlife hated their company, The Masks really ruined their fun and put fear into many a young heart.

Arthur made a second brew of tea on the fire, this time he put in a good measure of brandy in each, to keep off the chills. They sat on fallen masonry in a long-deserted tower by a crackling blaze of thorn, each dwelling on what they had left behind, because what was before them was so uncertain. This was their comradeship, their commonality and the greater part of their friendship.

The fire was dying when it became clear they would have to sleep. The fatigue of a long miles and a measure of warm alcohol was upon them both.

Arthur lit a candle from the fire and shouldered his rucksack. Shielding the little flame with his hand, he led down the stairwell and then to the alcove beneath the stone staircase, that Cecilia had turned into a bed.

The cold was considerable, so Arthur wore a pullover and Cecilia wrapped a shawl about her as she settled into the sleeping bag. He had to wrap up in both capes, the woolen one innermost, a scarf about his neck. They both sank into sleep.

Arthur woke with the cold that was penetrating his bones. They were high up on the moors and a low moaning wind had picked up. He cuddled into Cecilia's back, the sleeping bag immediately warmed him. He stayed in this position all night long.

CHAPTER SEVENTEEN

Finding safe haven.

Every conscious and articulate life form really should register a degree of curiosity when confronted with a genuine opportunity to evolve. Knowledge is power, science is knowledge made demonstrative, thus making opportune more power. Even a Mask on a Suit will engage curiosity functions and speculate how absolutely incredible it would be to make that tremendous evolutionary leap and travel into White Space.

The Dark Space Continuum, the non-empty space into which our Big-Bang Event has intruded and expanded, it is accelerating in all directions, generating a form of friction. This Cold Dark Energy, in turn, generates the vacuum of vacuums whilst radiating and containing all the visible light that has ever been emitted, it creates a field of light, White Space.

The energy which concentrates in White Space is physical matter, fizzing away like a fuzzy black ball in the white soup of raw utter light. This glare illuminates a greater dimensionality than that which is attached to the physical objects alone. It tells of a physics that pre-existed our conventional model, or standard view of creation. Dark Space and sub-light velocities are only a small aspect of the Cosmos. What did the Big-Bang expand into? A pivotal question. Into what is our manifest dimension resolving into? For what was here before the Cosmos appeared must be still around, somewhere...

Even to the i...and their fascination with physicality, programming was intrinsic to any technological application and would manifest in the function of the device. A Mask, for instance, with its case full of files. Sitting watching an erotic freak-show, in the dark, Half-Smile, now suited, wigged and with gaudy vaudeville villain make up painted upon the surface of a phenomenally advanced item of equipment, a very advanced and technical face. The Mask was becoming a louche.

The Suit had now developed and acquired a yawn. Regeneration was necessary. To download a lot of non-result in order to free up operational data space. Not that clever after all, even Masks needed sleep. In an office, asleep, a sitting suit upright in a chair before a desk, waiting, even during sleep, for a phone to ring. Masks did dream, mainly about waiting for phones to ring, this theme was ever central to Suit dream story-lines. A ringing telephone about to screech.

When the i... manifested on a world and looked into the night sky, they also see what we would look upon and with the switch of a function, gaze into a vault of seemingly eternal light. Same sky but a different eye.

They would not crack open a rack of beers and slowly incinerate prime selections of various dead animals. They would be looking and listening for any passing trace of any of their kind. In every echo of their laughter a discrete amount of information was transmitted. Which is one of the reasons why really advanced, good-guy aliens with a much developed, White Space technology do not come this way at all.

An i.. infested world transmits a signal which warns other races that they are there. It is like displaying a beautiful item of skillfully made, antique furniture, a paradigm of craft and workmanship, but thoroughly riddled with wood-worm. Held together merely with veneer and polish yet doomed to soon fall apart, even as this, our realm of space will eventually fall into dust. The parasites got here first. So, not only is humanity young as a species, it is unclean. Hard pill to swallow, by all the Saints, so it is. Hardly out of the trees and we get an awful psychic parasitic infection. So sad.

In the zoos, which physically existed in a quantum-frame space, sub-worlds had been occupied, like the City of the Eternally Young. Full of two thousand years of prime human specimen copies. Scanned, atom by atom and reconstructed according to the physical laws of the plane, or frequency of the location. The human consciousness was removed from the original specimens and fixed into a copy. Adjustments were made which ensured their longevity and environmental symbiosis, yet eventually, regardless of uniqueness, they would only find walls at the perimeter of their world if they inquired. A frustrating frustrates frustrated. An infuriating zoo.

There is a whole lot of Universe out there, full of all sorts of activity and goings on, transactions, interactions and communication. The dull bit is, it is distributed at unutterably vast distances which even at variations of seven times seventy the speed of Dark Space light, all effort was STILL SLOW! Incredible, that just short of velocities reaching almost five hundred times the Dark Space light speed, it still took forever to find worlds of deep and lasting interest. The Laws of the Distribution of Life Forms state there is an equal spread of pretty much all the combinations of matter and motion and sentience. So much, spread so thinly over so much more, expanding out of reach, almost as soon as those few rare species establish its expansion rate. It had slipped. The Cosmos races off faster than we can think. So uniquely immense, such a solemn majestic massiveness.

The space-time threshold, once finally encountered with every bean of ingenuity, was going to win hands up, every single time. It always remained greater than the findings arising from perception and inquiry.

The last technological gasp of even a consummate genius species would max a basic pass mark in the classroom of space faring races. It was THAT big.

A ball buster. A rat's supper. A bastard's Fathers Day.

This is the inevitable boredom threshold which confronts those advanced races as they realise their continuum cannot be escaped, only variations of it can be investigated in minor. It is the killer blow. A hard answer! The elusive Universe.

It kicks your balls and off it skips, leaving the knackered old advanced race on their fat arse, crippled and discouraged forever. It is almost like nothing changes the higher up the evolutionary and technological scale one develops.

Cecilia again woke first and was aware that Arthur had closely hugged into her back. She waited a while before she slipped from his grasp. All the previous nights wood had burned to dense white ash. A bright sun blazed in a new blue sky, from the tower parapet, moorland stretched in every direction. They were alone. From her leather satchel she took the complete works of Shakespeare, printed in a tiny typeset. This meant Cecilia needed her spectacles to actually read the Bard's efforts. Sitting in the main tower doorway, she buried herself in A Midsummer Night's Dream.

Arthur woke, feeling fully refreshed from a good sleep. He saw Cecilia steeped in her book and thought to collect wood and look for water without disturbing her. Again he emptied the rucksack, intending to fill it with downfall thorn.

When he returned she was still engrossed. Without a word he began to light a small fire in order to make a morning brew of sweet black tea. There was not a lot of food left, a bit of cake, some pie and the ends of two loafs. He toasted the bread on a rod of thorn. Old bread makes a better toast, nice with a brew.

'Would it be possible to stay here for another day?' Cecilia asked evenly.

Arthur thought about it and replied,

'Perhaps we can. We can always use this place as something to fall back on.

It seems we are alone here. We should explore though, and look for food.'

'Good,' she agreed, 'after such a long, self-imposed incarceration in the library, my body is unused to the effort of the last three days. My legs ache, so I must rest at least today.'

Arthur knew she would bury herself in a book whilst he reconnoitered the immediate environs and was happy with leaving her for a few hours. He felt great, like he could easily manage another enormous walk, it was odd feeling so energetic at his age.

The first thing he did was check the cave beneath the neighbouring craggy hill. It widened once inside, an enormous cap of monolithic grit stone, creating a large space, now filled with a bed of decayed and long-fallen thorn leaves. From within, Arthur could see that the entrance had been deliberately narrowed by stonewalling, the gaps stuffed with sods of earth, which had taken hold and flourished. Someone had used this chamber long ago. He searched for traces of habitation by brushing the leaf mold to one side and found many animal bones, frail and brittle with age. Some had been scorched, so he searched for a fire pit. This had been cleverly built into the stone work with a flue to take the smoke away. It was a far better shelter than the bed under the stairwell.

Arthur decided to head westwards for a couple of miles, walking off the flat-topped moorland hills down towards a woodland defile created by a slow river. On his way he noted a long-deserted farmstead, mature trees growing in the roofless ruin. There had been a herb garden in its inhabited lifetime and the surviving plants and shrubs had spread widely. There also was an orchard which had completely overgrown. He stuffed his pockets and satchel with small apples, bunches of parsley and mint and carried on towards the river. Soon he could hear the sound of running water. Arthur found himself in a hazel grove and helped himself to the generous early crop of nuts, filling Cecilia's satchel completely. The river was bright and clear, he sat by it for a while and saw the large, dark shapes flitting in the recesses and deeper pools. Fish. Arthur remembered he had a hand-line kit back at the camp and was relieved to have solved one problem, in theory at least. A kingfisher shot like a metallic blue dart in a ray of sunlight. The land was rich here. As if to emphasize this, Arthur discovered a bank of wild rose which was vibrant with vivid red rose hips. He filled his remaining pockets and side bag with these fat berries, he continued onwards, foraging constantly for free food.

Tracking up water a little way, following the line of a crumbled stone dyke that bordered the river, Arthur discovered a small deserted cottage. The slated roof sagged heavily but had not fallen inwards, the door was tied with fraying twine. He looked through a dirty window. It was tiny, a single roomed dwelling with a simple range for cooking and warmth. The twine fell apart to his touch and the musky interior was revealed. Spiders webs covered everything, not that there was much to hide. By the front door, a window seat lifted to reveal long-unused woolen blankets. There was a table with a single surviving rustic stool, the others had collapsed with wood-worm and age. The floor was sound. Investigating further, in the cupboards built into the paneling of the room, he found a scattering of domestic implements and some crockery, not all of it broken. In one storage closet Arthur discovered some practical tools and a rusted woodman's axe. This was an interesting place indeed.

He noted that there were no paths at all and a rutted, overgrown track had holly trees and thorns growing from it. All this indicated a long period of neglect. The shack had been abandoned for many decades.

Cecilia had let the fire die and had finished reading. The large book was laid beside her. She smiled to see Arthur returning and listened to his report concerning the cave and the cottage. He showed some of the wild food he had foraged and told of the river, and the fish there. This seemed to awaken her interest, the notion of fresh food intrigued her.

'I think I can manage one more mile or so easily enough,' she said, ' I would like to see this place you have found.'

Arthur gathered all the kit and repacked, the day was cheerfully sunny, there was no rush now.

'We could stay a while, or base our explorations from here. We have all we need.' he said.

'And no people nearby. Perhaps we shall remain undetected,' Cecilia agreed.

At the cave they had a lengthier study and found large rinds of pottery shards and fragments of wickerwork panels. Arthur discovered a set of fire irons, an adze and a primitive wrought-iron chain that suggested animals had been penned here at some point in its history. He took the ironmongery.

As they approached the woodland hut Cecilia stopped to pick some more wild apples, she was quietly smiling as she gathered a crop into her shawl. Arthur opened the cottage door and stepped aside.

Cecilia entered and began to inquire into every corner of the wee room, finding every single abandoned thing that could be of practical use.

Arthur's first task was to clean the flue pipe of the birds nests. He took his divers knife and cut a willow straight, long enough to shift the years of built up straw, twigs, feathers, nests and ancient crap. This he thrust up the stove pipe.

It erupted from the small square chimney with a dirty burst of dust and filth. This done, he set about collecting wood, gradually filling the long wooden trough to the left of the iron range. Cecilia made and used a brush of heather to clean the rusted stove free from the worst of its decay. Then she made broom of birch twigs and beat out the dust and dirt that had accumulated in the room. At least it was dry. Arthur had frozen when the night wind caught him merely wrapped in cloaks. The castle was high on the moors, the little bothy was in a sheltered valley, in woodland that extended far into the west.

A section of the floor was raised, this was a sitting and sleeping platform. Most of the bedding was fit to burn, it stank of mice nests and rot, Cecilia piled it outside the open door. It took a second beating with the newly made broom to shift just the worst of the dirt and dust. The little room would certainly do as a refuge. They worked all day cleaning and making ready their shelter.

The declining sun filled the forest, a roseate touch upon the gold and crisp of late summer greens. Arthur told Cecilia he intended to wash in the river and took his spare set of clothes, his new ones. A beautiful evening filled the glade with a warm orange glow. Cecilia set the fire in the range, a flame flicked awake in its long unused and cold body. Until she had thoroughly cleaned the cooking pots that remained there, the nesting pans would have to suffice for boiling water. The wee room warmed quickly.

When Arthur returned, all freshened up from their journey, the toil of rough sleeping and hard work was scrubbed from him. It was clear to Cecilia that was what she wanted also, to have a good wash.

The bloodstain of sunset was colouring the sky, the branches and twigs etched black against the sinking rays. The pleasure of a clean body in fresh clothes was with them both. It was simple but it was good.

The pans steamed and a brew was made, Arthur thought to add a dash of brandy to each sweet black tea. It smelled and tasted great. A single candle burned on a pressed metal stand, they both knew they would have to forage for more supplies. The food was nearly all gone, Arthur remembered the paper wrapped rations he had included as a basic back-up supply. He melted some of the hard chocolate in hot water, making two sweet drinks. The hard tack biscuit was dipped in this. It was fine enough. The darkness stole all the remaining light out in the glade, it was black, a forest night still, all hushed and chilly cold.

Cecilia found a length of stout line and tied it across the width of the room, above the range. Two large rusted iron hooks told that this had been done before. She aired the better of the woolen blankets by hanging them from this. The yellow light softened everything. It was warm and safe, a nest of a hideout. Their belongings had spread everywhere, from hooks and on shelving various items had been placed, emphasizing their occupation. Cecilia sat on the stool by the fire, Arthur used the raised platform to recline, his back resting on the paneled walling.

'Do you think you could perhaps try to get a fish tomorrow?' she inquired.

'I could try, answered Arthur, 'I found this box of hooks, flies and reel, I could rig something.'

'Were did you get that handy little tin?' Cecilia noticed the selection of coloured lures.

'The hotel where I woke up in this world. I think it may be the same one you described, for something invasive had occurred there.

The place looked like it had been abandoned in a hurry, there were belongings everywhere. Including this.' Arthur held up a metallic blue spinner.

Cecilia shivered with a memory and said,

'Let us not speak of that place or those times, we are here now.'

'We are here now,' affirmed Arthur.

A wind grew from a rustling in the trees to a low keening that whistled and moaned by turns. It was welcome to be indoors, regardless of how humble it was. The drafts found chinks and gaps and the sole candle flickered. Cecilia yawned first. Soon after this she arranged two blankets on the raised bench, the sleeping bag was also hanging up to air and dry.

Arthur took the stool by the fire and politely turned his back as she changed into a long nightshirt, thin with wear and age. Her hair hung down loose almost to her waist.

'Goodnight Arthur,' she said, 'well done for finding this cozy shelter.'

Cecilia shuffled about a little as she got comfortable on the bare pine boards and moments later was deeply asleep.

Arthur listened to the wind and had another tiny nip of brandy. So far so good. The liquor soothed and relaxed his tired bones. He stared out of the window and into the velvet blackness that accompanied the sad sounding wind outside. His eyes began to lose focus, the candle was almost done.

As the wick spluttered in the remaining pool of wax, Arthur bedded down, covering himself in the two remaining blankets, he had stacked the range and set it low, it would be warm all night.

The struggling strand of flame beat like a frantic heart for a moment, pulsing as the fuel dwindled in its fibres, and then it was gone and absolute darkness ruled. Soon he too was fast asleep.

The morning was a riot of birdsong. The nuts and berries had attracted them in thousands, they quarreled and chattered and sang. Cecilia woke first and quietly rose, for a moment as she had shed her nightshirt, she had stood momentarily naked, all bare and skinny in the little bothy. She felt safe rather than exposed, which surprised her, even as she dressed. A warm light was finding the dusty walls as Cecilia set the fire. Arthur woke and quickly donned his trousers, blinking at the light. The rising sun was directly in his eyes.

'Good morning to you!' Cecilia opened the front door to let the dawn air in.

'Thank you,' he replied, 'looks like another lovely day.'

On the table in the sunlight, two plates found intact had been cleaned and held piles of mint and parsley upon one and nuts and berries on the other. Cecilia picked at the hazels, occasionally de-seeding a rose hip and eating that too. She had grown roses on the library roof mainly for the berries. Arthur took his shirt and walked barefoot to the nearby river for a wash. He noticed the fleeting shadow shapes of large fish. He decided to get busy after a morning brew. Fish would make for good eating.

The diving knives were proving to be very useful tools. Arthur cut a long, even rod of straight ash and trimmed it just as he had done as a child. A primitive fishing rod. He whittled a hole two inches from the narrower tip and another above the handle of the thicker end. He grooved the grip with the knife tip then knotted and threaded the fishing line. He chose the vibrant blue spinner the size of a stickleback and tied it off. He looped the run-out line with his thumb and forefinger in a way which covered the line at the slot above the handle. It had worked as a boy.

Within half an hour he had caught four large fresh water-trout, once he had remembered how to cast and draw the line slowly back in, the 'brownies' proved easy game. Cecilia was delighted at the catch and took them out of Arthur's wet hands. She prepared them and lay their glistening forms on the parsley. One of the cast iron pots with a functional handle took a long time to scour clean with river gravel and sand. Cecilia thoroughly ground the grit until it all the staining disappeared, then it was ready for use. She also found lots of water cress and took a hand full.

Arthur shelled the hazel nuts and crushed them to a pulp with a stone. Cecilia took her divers knife and chopped the parsley and cress, then filleted the trout, adding all these to the water, slowly heating on the range. Soon its aroma filled the little room.

A week had passed in Fat City, the Zoo of the Forever Young. A human ants nest swarming with activity. In every street, in all the pubs and clubs and shows, a party-time, carnival atmosphere thrived. It always had, it always would.

A place where Masks floated down dim, narrow back alleys, prowling. A place where young things danced all night, where every single stimulant and temptation is free.

A city so steeped in its hedonist culture, that it created in itself a social entity which celebrated ease and fun at any possible moment. For reasons based upon pleasure itself, they that loved it, lived for it.

The Suits were getting results, their vigilance had uncovered not one but three dirty old men, or species copies in unscheduled degeneration phase. Half-Smile had found none of them and was probably scheduled to be Folded. Kiss it all goodbye. No more fun things to see in

Happyland. The big non-existence thing. Out cold and gone. Folded in a closed drawer. Redundant.

Suits were to be re-tasked and the city center given some breathing space.

Fewer Masks were needed, so all the below-functional programs were soon closed down. There was no point in fighting it. A Hybrid albino, an intermediate creature somewhere between a human specimen and a machine, a Servant of the Will Department that could not be controlled, influenced or accessed, nor even remotely spooked. This was the closure specialist.

All the Masks had to come back for their recharge at some point in time, if it did not wish to become just so much technological litter in the street. Then Mr Mort would be waiting for the moment they 'slept'. He would take the Mask in his fingers and the Suit would sag lifeless, flopping to the seat. The drawer had rows of flat Masks, now paper thin and fifty deep per pile. Archived. Filed away. Less than asleep, closed shut.

Arthur's bruise had completely healed and he found he needed to shave, a stubble had appeared in the week he and Cecilia had occupied the woodland bothy. Having given the only soap to his lady friend he had to grease his face with fish fat. The tiny mirror didn't help much and he scrubbed his skin raw in the river trying to get the smell off. This failed, so eventually he rubbed his face with a bunch of bog myrtle leaves. Arthur ceased to honk of fish but his face was now a vivid lobster pink.

Cecilia had created storage containers out of all the old, holed or useless pots and jars. These were cleaned, dried and filled with nuts and berries. She had also washed the useless bed linen in the river by letting it soak for several days, weighed down by stones. Then she hung what remained from the nearest trees and let them dry. With the fishing knife she divided the ragged cloth into squares and strips. She stored them in the window seat box. The scraps she would use to scrub surfaces and pots.

Arthur had shown Cecilia the ruined farmhouse, a short walk downriver. From here she had cropped the apples, herbs and also discovered shallots and fennel that had endured by running rampant. These she gathered and stored them in tied-off squares of cloth, hanging them from the roof beams where their earthy scent filled the paneled room. Many bunches of herbs added to the smell with their own perfume as they slowly dried. Arthur recognised but a few of the obvious and familiar plants.

The days were growing slightly colder and the nights especially so. Arthur would set the stove box, which would smoulder all night giving out enough heat to keep the worst of the chill at bay. There was no moon in this world, that feature had been omitted in the design considerations, instead the grand display of a stellar eternity dominated every night sky.

They both accepted how much harder it would be to survive out on the freezing moorland tops. The lightest touch of first frost had formed and endured in the shadows of the sunrise, casting strips of white amongst the crisp fallen leaves. They knew this humble hut would have to be sufficient until they found something better. Arthur speculated that the very fact of its abandonment bode well for them. The area seemed long deserted, which increased their chances of remaining free from capture. He had taken walks exploring increasingly the forest that flanked the moors and hills to the west. It was clear that once it had been more populated, but had fallen into a decline from which its buildings and roads had never recovered. The little bothy was the soundest structure in miles, after that only the hilltop cave could provide proper cover and shelter, but the cave had no door and would be bitter cold at night.

Arthur and Cecilia took a walk together up to the castle where they had slept that windy night. The bed of heather and bracken had dried to a flat brown. It looked so basic compared to what they had made of the wee hut. They watched the sunset, standing together on the main tower parapet as the day went down in a blaze of glory. Cecilia's slender hand found Arthur's, he turned to her happily surprised and smiled.

'I like it here,' she said, 'I am glad to be here with you.'

Arthur nodded and actually blushed a little as he agreed.

She saw this and returned to formality.

'We could do worse, couldn't we? Imagine trying to live up here?'

Arthur regarded the moor and hilltops which far ranged to the north. Dense forests flanked both the eastern and western borders of these craggy fells. They had not seen a living soul in over a week. He too was deeply grateful for the bothy, now full of their presence and their practicality, a home for the present. He did wonder what lay to the north and how far the woodland extended in the west. The gloaming was upon them, shadows deepened in the woodland below.

'I think we aught to be heading back,' said Arthur, now very familiar with the route,

'It will be dark soon,' he added. Cecilia took his hand in the half light, Arthur was happy at this and led her to the hut without incident or slip. It was fully dark when they arrived back, a spiral of smoke soon uncoiled into the cold night sky. A tiny cottage high at the valley head, their home for the present, the only point of warmth in a vast sea of cold silence.

CHAPTER EIGHTEEN

A simple life.

The summer diminished into ochres and yellows. The verdant forest had faded into full autumn glory. Frost was now common every morning, and the upland valleys filled with freezing fog which cut cold to the bone. Two months had passed, Arthur walked to keep warm. Having seen a wild hare up on the grassy swards that crested most of the hilltop crags, he was on the lookout for any movement. As Arthur ascended and cleared the layer of cold mist that filled the valley head. The castle stood on a single island above the sea of fog. He reached the ruined fort and noted the other island hilltops that broke the mist had coloured in the sunrise. Arthur's hand was cold, glove-less, the service revolver was freezing to touch. Soon the snow would arrive, it would be harder to survive.

On the hill above the crag of the cave, a short distance away from the would-be hunter, a hare sprinted then paused to eat. Arthur descended into the river of rolling mist that separated the two sections of high ground. Carefully and quietly he stalked through the fog to a point where he thought a good shot could be made. As he emerged onto the hill and the sunlight, he crouched, using the dying bracken clumps as cover. The hare was thirty paces away with its back to Arthur who took careful aim for a point between the ears. The frozen morning awaited the thunderclap.

Two things occurred simultaneously. The hare's head exploded in a red mist as its body spun several times from the impact, and the noise of the shot rang in Arthur's ears, it echoed for miles. The smell of used cordite and the twitching body of the dead hare brought him to attention. This was the first time he had ever fired a handgun. He holstered it with a combination of apprehension and surprise. The animal had died quickly, it didn't see it coming. The hare was also enormous. Arthur tied its forelegs to a length of downfall thorn, straight and strong. He carried it over his shoulder as he descended into the mist, his ears still ringing.

Cecilia had heard the shot as it broke the dawn silence. She was clearly glad to see Arthur emerge into the glade and the hare dangling limp from the staff of thorn. She asked,

'That noise, the loud bang. That was you wasn't it? That was the pistol firing?'

Arthur re-assured her and told her it was the first wild animal he had ever killed other than fish. Her reaction to the hare was one of gladness for the change of diet. She gutted the carcass, keeping the innards for fish bait and the lights for eating right then and there. She braised them in a flat iron pan that had no handle, adding some chopped shallots and millet seed, from the bunches of herbs she had collected. They had been living on fish and foraged greenery for two months. It had not done them any harm at all, quite the reverse in fact, they were both in prime health.

All of Arthur's India tea had been used up and the leftover leaves repeatedly boiled until any colour and flavour had departed. Cecilia was trying to introduce him to her familiar world of tisanes and herbal infusions. Somehow it never satisfied and he did wonder how he could acquire more of that wonderful refreshing beverage. He had the tiniest amount of brandy left, which Cecilia insisted on keeping for cleaning wounds and cuts. With reluctance, he consented to this and began to roughly plan more explorations further afield, looking for supplies. He often wondered where the nearest settlement was, for frequently at evening he had combed the western forest with his binoculars from the moor and fells above. There had been no visible signs of occupation for the determinable distance. He knew that to the east the rich farmland he had seen may well be a source of extra food and commodities and, as a last measure, he could backtrack that way. The distance was not a deterrent any longer. His health had increased noticeably by the month.

The companions had both noticed visible changes over the last weeks, their hair had regained a touch of original colour, they experienced times of increasing strength and stamina and seemed to move with a swifter, more assured pace. The rudimentary diet had not withered them, rather instead they thrived and grew healthier, younger almost. They slept soundly and kept busy each dawn to dusk. They seemed to have been forgotten, they may have escaped. A remote and lonely part of the zoo had provided a refuge sufficient to permit their life, a safe distance from the city. Here they were both happy for the first time since arriving. A contentment that made do with what little they had. A welcome thrift and a touch of parsimony measured the facts of their survival. The bothy had become a perpetually warm nest sheltered from the cold wind and rain. They had stayed after all.

Two weeks later, when the first snows fell, the trees had not entirely shed the last stubborn leaves. Snow crept quietly into the valley as Arthur and Cecilia slept. For the second time in their friendship he had had to cuddle into her back as the cold of the night seized him. She did not shrug him off, as the icy air had caused her to shudder and shiver. Two blankets and a cloak each was not enough. They needed each other, and once sharing warmth, they returned to sleep.

The world outside had become a black and white frozen silence. They walked a familiar track to the fallen castle, breaking the virgin carpet of snow as they passed. Their tracks lay side by side.

Their original bed under the stone staircase had now reduced to a tangle of long dried strands of bracken and flattened heather. The parapet view was stunning. A world of pristine whiteness ran forever. Scurries of wind told of its transit where plumes of spindrift bloomed and billowed. The low sun lengthened the shadows of the rocks and moorland thorns. It was utter quiet.

'You can see for miles.' said Cecilia.

Arthur lowered the binoculars and replied, ' Not a soul in sight save ourselves.'

The winter light focused the colour of her skin, again he thought she was looking younger.

'I have been thinking of heading off for a day or two, I want to get some supplies to make our winter stay here a bit easier. Do you want to come with me?' Arthur waited for an answer.

Cecilia took her time replying, 'No, Arthur I will stay here and await your return. I trust and hope you will be careful in all you do. I fear I would merely add to your concerns if I accompanied you. I imagine you may succeed more assuredly without me as I find these long walks difficult'

'I'm thinking of heading north and then east and looking for villages and small towns there.'

'I wish you every safety and success.' Cecilia kissed his face on the cheek, 'for luck!' she added.

The next morning at first light Arthur rose. He realized he had become aroused in the early dawn, hugging close to Cecilia's body. He woke with his hand over her belly, his touch found it soft and warm and surprisingly gently rounded. He dressed quickly, hoping she would stay asleep and not notice his erection. At his age, this occurred most rarely. He wondered if she had felt it pressing against her as they slept huddled together. It was so strange to him, feeling this way again. Arthur cast his mind back and he could not remember the last time he had felt this way.

He packed his rucksack with his rolled up best suit and shirt wrapped in a traveling cloak. He also took the two voluminous satchels, for extra provisions. Covering Cecilia with the blankets, he stroked her hair briefly and lightly pecked a kiss on her brow. He hoped she was asleep, so she pretended to be.

He followed two sets of old footprints that had almost filled with new snow and once clear of the woodlands, Arthur could see that more threatened to fall. He quickened his pace and soon was leaving the ruined castle far behind him. The soft snow made walking any distance a lot harder than would normally be the case and he was concerned to have covered so few miles. By midday he was on the eastern side of the fells. The North Sea glistened a flat blade of silver grey on the horizon. From so high up he could see afar the plumes of chimneys, certain signs of human habitation.

Once off the moors and into farmland, Arthur made good distance and even found a road sign. 'Morpeth' it declared, eleven miles from where he stood, this he decided to reach by nightfall. He marched the miles like a man half his age, passing farms and steadings all the way. The sun was setting as he reached the outskirts of the little market town.

In a nearby stream Arthur washed the journey from himself and changed into his smart clothes. As he approached, he noticed the town was now huddled within a stout Medieval wall. Two young men stood by a fire pit warming their hands, he saw these were guards, even though they carried no weapons he decided to maintain civility as he neared them. The tallest spoke first,

'Good evening to you, sir.' The dialect was Northumbrian,

'late abroad the roads now?'

'Aye' answered Arthur and smiled, 'will I find shelter and supplies here?'

'That you will,' the tall guy continued, 'but all the town gates are locked after sunset. You just made it, another hour and you would be stuck out here with the wolves and whatnot'.

Arthur had not considered that the empty hills and fells could contain any inherent dangers.

'All the best for the now.' the guard nodded as Arthur entered through the rusting iron gates

This other world version of Morpeth was almost entirely ancient, Arthur wondered why little of the last six hundred years had any purchase on the look of the place. It was enchanting, an entire fortified town with all its functions and services secure behind a tall crenelated wall. A lantern lighter walked the narrow streets, bringing illumination to the winding little roads. He thought to find a small inn, one off the main thoroughfares where perhaps his presence would pass unnoticed. Many of the tiny shops were closing, he managed to catch a baker just before the shutters were drawn and bolted. The chap was clearly keen to get home and quickly gave Arthur two large meat pies and a loaf. Again, just like the city, there was no need for money. The baker did not even glance backwards. He explored the narrow streets and alleys of the small town with increasing interest.

'The George' was a peculiar building. It was packed between a crumbling Medieval tower and a row of high, bleak-fronted tenements. Blank spaces gaped where doors and window slots once adorned the fort and the arched entrances to the stairwells of the tenements smelled strongly of urine and stale vomit. The run-down atmosphere pervaded. A gang of young lads, some already staggering drunk, passed him in the narrow lane without a word or a glance. They caroused down the alley, a slight echo to their voices rang.

Arthur entered the old hotel.

The street door led directly to a public bar, the ceiling was low and a fire smouldered unattended. In the gloom, he could determine a half-dozen men, all sitting separately, no-one spoke. Behind a long bench-bar a skinny, worn out looking man was cleaning glasses and tankards, he looked up,

'Aye,' he nodded in Arthur's direction, 'what can I do for you?'

'A room for the night if that is possible.' A simple enough question thought Arthur.

'There are always rooms here,' he laughed a bit sourly, ' it's the last chance inn this one.'

The proprietor made busy looking for keys in a gloomy set of dusty wooden pigeon holes, in time finding a set and saying, 'Room three. Back of the house, first floor. Very quiet there for sure.'

He led Arthur up a dirty sagging oak stairway and along a short corridor to a narrow paneled door. He stood aside, so the traveler with the bag on his back could enter first.

'Itinerant tradesman are we?' the manager couldn't help his curiosity.

'Aye, that's right.' said Arthur and tried a bluff, 'heading north.' he added.

'Oh, Jedburgh or Trimontium?', the manager was clearly curious about the traveler.

'A wee bit further.' Arthur fished for more information.

'All the way up to Dun Edyin is it? We get a few from there now and again, sometimes in the spring. Wild boys! They like their bevvy those drover crews'.

Arthur put down the rucksack with a deliberate groan, pretending it was heavier and he was more tired than actuality. The proprietor got the point and left the room saying,

'The only food we have got today is lamb broth, again. The beer is not so bad though. Come downstairs when you are ready and join us if you will.'

Arthur sat on the lumpy mattress and ate handfuls of bread and pie until his hunger abated. He acknowledged that the north was accessible, the roads and paths being known to travelers and seasonal tradesmen. He wondered what lay at the very extremities of this land and how far its basic rules of good health and free merchandise applied. He wanted to ask why this little town was defensively walled and largely late Medieval in appearance. He wondered how much dealing these people had with the pleasure capital to the south, thinking it would be scant as he had seen very little of the modern at all since arriving. Yet no-one had questioned his appearance at all.

Arthur decided to sample the beer and descended to the bar room below.

There was only ale on tap so Arthur took a pint to a seat near the fire and tended it. Soon the coals and wood were flickering back to life. The beer tasted splendid, it coursed through his body and fixed him into his seat. He stared at the flames and thought about Cecilia back in the tiny cabin in the forest. He was glad no-one was talking to him. Again, for the second time in many years he became aware of his arousal at the thought of his accomplice and friend. Just the thought of her that very morning curled up asleep had triggered it. Arthur raised his eyebrows, surprised at himself and wondered at the possible implications of this revisiting phenomenon.

Arthur became so comfortable by the fireside that when his pint finished it was an effort to rise and walk the short distance to the bar. The publican poured another dark brown ale and asked whether Arthur would be needing anything to eat. He was visibly relieved that his visitor declined and he could get off duty soon and set into a few beers himself.

The evening quietly passed as did Arthur's third pint. The fire now blazed and he sat in his good shirt enjoying the comfort. No-one had spoken all evening except to order more beer.

A tall young man entered the room. He had long, blonde, braided hair tied back and wore what looked like worn leather armour. A wide belt supported a long knife and many pouches. The largest hung over his groin, a really old-fashioned sporran of sorts. He was glaring at the barman and uttered the roughest, savagest Northumbrian/Lowland Scots words. He was indecipherable. Arthur couldn't help but gawk, he was not alone, the other six men there silently drinking were also staring at the strapping brute. The proprietor answered back in the same tongue, though nowhere near as roughly or authentically. The massive visitor carried a sheepskin sleeping sack tied with a broad leather band, this he threw down by the bar and took his beer with a grunt which was perhaps a 'thank you'.

The pint disappeared quickly in a series of greedy gulps.

'Anuthur mon,' the wild looking character grinned, 'that's reet grand, cheers tae yer!'

The worn out wee barman seemed nervous and clearly wanted to be someplace else.

Arthur studied the barbarian over his pint. The armour was old, but cleverly made. He noticed panels and sections of carving, a spiraling, fluid style, interlocking and weaving its design. Then Arthur saw he had amulets sewn in or fixed to the breastplate, backplate, upper arm and leg coverings. The historical memory fell into place and Arthur knew this was a Border Reaver, the real thing, standing in the same room as himself. The guards must have taken his sword and bow from him, this hardly diminished the sense of danger he emitted and displayed in his proud martial bearing. His second pint went the same way as the first. A third, followed it before he even sat down opposite Arthur, with his fourth full tankard.

Thankfully, the warrior was content to sup and fire gaze. Arthur could study the devices on his cuirass and pauldrons, it was a variant of Celtic Art, but thorn spiked and tortured in its complexity. There was nothing of the Christian, let alone the modern in him or on him. He seemed to have just rested when he rose to get a fifth beer, Arthur heard a heavy clunk and a low curse. The lad had hit his head on a roof beam. Re-seating he pawed at his crown and frowned,

'Smote m'swain good an'proper now.' He grinned lopsidedly at Arthur.

'More-beer-will-sort-that-out.' Arthur clearly pronounced each word. There was a pause as the Reaver slowly absorbed the simple sentence. Then he roared amusement in a way that made everyone sit bolt upright. Arthur actually jumped, the lad had a bellowing laugh. Then he quickly emptied his glass of its remaining contents. Rising to acquire that fifth ale he made a jest of his height with a comic gesture.

'Daen't wish tae trounce m'swain agin,' he said lowering his head cautiously eyeing the beams.

Arthur smiled and puzzled at his capacity for consuming beer. The lad returned and raised his glass towards the fire and said something completely incomprehensible, but rhythmic and incantatory. A spell or prayer of sorts for a safe nights shelter.

Arthur had one more beer, quietly before retiring to his bed-chamber, swaying a touch. The soporific ale had him snoring within minutes.

The warrior drank till he slept where he sat, slumped before a deep bed of glowing coals.

Arthur woke with a full bladder and the sound of a cockerel welcoming the day. The narrow window looked upon a stone-flagged back yard where ducks and hens pecked. He dressed quickly in his old clothes, folding and rolling away the new. The warrior was still was slumped prone in his chair by the fire, a dozen empty tankards and glasses lay about him on the floor.

There was frost in the narrow streets. Arthur shouldered his rucksack and walked about the Medieval town until the stalls and shops opened. He was up bright and early.

From a grain merchants store he acquired twelve pounds of oatmeal and the same of coarse ground flour. These he packed into the two side satchels, they weighed upon his shoulders heavily. Arthur had to be sensible, he knew he had to get back to the bothy without damaging himself. A candle maker supplied him with about twenty tapered lights, weighing about three pounds, he knew they would need light. These he carefully packed in the rucksack.

From a grocery stall, he got two pounds of black loose tea and a large jar of molasses and some salt. The custom in this town seemed to be to engage a little conversation in each exchange, yet still no money was mentioned. The only soap which could be had was the plain unscented carbolic type, of this he took two large blocks. Finally, Arthur discovered a tailor, a tobacconist and a wine merchants, all in the same back street and procured matches, a pound of tobacco and a pipe and three large bottles of brandy. Remembering Cecilia he also asked for a bolt of cloth, an attractive green and brown hand-woven tweed and some plain white cotton, plus a ball of strong twine. His rucksack weighed very heavily upon him, he had to will each step and endure the pain in his shoulders. Arthur reached the west town gate, the watchmen were nowhere in sight. Yesterdays ashes still smouldered in the deep fire pit. Frost crunched under his feet in the shadow of the Medieval walls. The gate slid open with a loud slow creak.

He passed out of the town without a word to anyone.

The miles passed long and hard before Arthur even reached the eastern fells.

He was sweating and concerned about the remaining daylight. The rucksack was chaffing his shoulders and the skin was red and increasingly raw. He knew he could not take long rests but simply must push on. His only landmark was the old castle, and in the dark he would never find it, so he had to force himself onwards. He did not want to be stranded out here alone. The thought of that little bothy motivated him.

A lot of the snow had thawed up on the moor land. A heavy iron-grey sky threatened to empty itself of more at any moment. Arthur recognized crags and features from his outward journey and by long past mid-day he could see the ruined castle on the very far horizon. He could not allow himself the luxury of a rest, the distance was far too great, so he punished himself to get to the ruins of the fort with all his will and might. He actually surprised himself with his effort. Breathing heavily with his shoulders, neck and back sore with pain, he eventually reached the castle ruin. A sick yellow stain spoke of sunset. The wind changed direction from the west and blew from the north. It froze the sweat on Arthur, who shivered and descended to the shadowed forest. Then it began to snow.

A dull orange flicker in the window told that the range was open, letting heat and light into the little room. Cecilia was in there, warm and safe. Arthur thought it would be wisest to announce his arrival when her face appeared at the window. He heard a cry of gladness as she opened the door and hugged him before he could put down his burdensome rucksack.

'Help me off with this would you please,' asked Arthur.

'My word! Its so heavy! What have you managed to find?' Cecilia strained to lift the load.

'Lots of stuff!' answered Arthur announcing and withdrawing each item with a degree of satisfaction, ' Two almost intact, large meat pies, fresh yesterday. A large bag of black tea, so let us get the kettle on! Molasses, soap, matches, candles, twine, salt…ah, some brandy, tobacco and something for you!' He handed over the bolt of tweed and the cotton cloth. Lastly he withdrew the huge hessian sacks of flour and oatmeal. ' It was this lot that nearly did for me.' said Arthur as the bulky bags thumped down. Cecilia was feeling the tweed and nodding her approval.

'Thank you. This is good quality, well done Arthur! You have come back well laden.'

Arthur rubbed at his shoulders and winced. He had chaffed the skin red and sore. Cecilia noticed this and cut two squares of cotton and soaked them in water, after wringing them out she said,

'Put these over the sore skin, they will draw out the heat. How brave of you to endure that.' 'I'm old and soft,' replied Arthur, 'that's why it hurts so much.'

'Not as old or as soft as you think,' she chided with a kind, knowing smile, remembering him from that previous morning, his hand covering her tummy, his manhood stiff against her.

Arthur missed the reference completely and set to filling his new pipe with baccy.

A burning twig from the fire sufficed as a taper. The bothy filled with its distinctive odour, the old pan boiled water and they made a brew of black tea with an drop of brandy and molasses in it. They ate a little of the cold pie, then Cecilia rained the questions on Arthur.

She wanted to know everything, every little detail and point and would press him relentlessly until she got a satisfying account. Her interest began to fix on what little he had discovered about the land to the north. There was a Jedburgh and a Trimontium. Beyond that a Dun Edyin. Drovers and travelers did come and go, yet they also seemed to originate in another earlier, previous epoch. The young warrior in his tough, boiled and hardened leather armour seemed to indicate it was so. The past was manifestly alive here.

'The earliest Reavers would have descended directly from the Norsemen and the Scots.' Cecilia observed adding that Trimontium was the main Roman garrison near Kelso, named because of its location on a triple-peaked hill. An ancient citadel that attempted to hold the Borderlands.

Arthur found his entire body was aching. Every muscle was sore. He sat in his customary place with his back to the wall, but stretched his legs outright on the level platform, he was tired but said,

'It seems that the further north we go, we also encounter people and places from the past.'

Arthur speculated on the possible situation, relaxing at long last as the brandy tea began to work its magic. He continued,

'Which means we had better be careful out here. The facts of our history make for safe reading at a comfortable distance. The Borderland was lawless for many hundreds of years, a very dangerous place indeed. Perhaps this shelter is the best we can find for the present?'

'It's most fine for the present', Cecilia smiled saying, ' Much like having a life again rather than a pitiful existence in the attic of an empty library, frightened by every single noise and movement.'

'I'm glad you feel that way,' Arthur acknowledged, 'you are made of stern stuff really.'

'It was your idea Arthur MacNeil and my good fortune to be party to it.'

'It would not be the same without you,' added Arthur.

That night when tiredness found them yawning by the warm range and it was clearly time to sleep, Cecilia was changing into her long, worn-thin nightdress and said to her companion,

'I think we should be pragmatic about our sleeping arrangements. We need to stay warm so I suggest we share all the blankets and therefore our body heat.'

She was very matter of fact about it. Arthur remembered how his manly urges were returning and considered mentioning this. Cecilia stood before the fire, the candle behind her made her worn out gown appear transparent. He noticed her hair tumbling down, her straight posture, little breasts pushing against the thin cotton. Her eyes were calm and confident, not those of a frightened captured bird anymore. Arthur thought she could deal with the truth and said plainly,

'I agree, it is a sensible thing to do, but I have to confess that I have been having urges and desires more common in a younger man, it is an unexpected complication, I, er, it's…'

'I know,' she said and stood close to him resting her hands on his upper arms, and gently added,

'I trust you. My only friend in a world full of danger and threat. I am not afraid of your urges. In fact I think I am done with living in fear.'

Arthur felt at a loss for words and could only manage an honest smile, his body ached so much he knew that sleep was the only act he could or would perform this night.

They extinguished the candle, set the range and cuddled up together.

Outside in the frozen night, the snow kept falling and a north wind blew icy cold.

CHAPTER NINETEEN

The man beneath the gallows.

Three more weeks passed. Arthur and Cecilia survived. The snow fell so deeply the cabin roof creaked with the weight. They had to use ancient rusted shovels and pan lids to dig out their meagre stake. It was hard work. Now they had each others friendship in a deeper and more intimate way, and would endure as partners, there was a strength to them. To dig their little hut clear during short, frozen days and to sleep long in close-wrapped embrace was enough for both. Until the night the wolves began to howl. For they did, sailing their mournful wail over a cold hard wasteland of snow and ice. The sound of a bitter hunger in the frozen wilderness.

They woke at once. Arthur's hand found the service revolver. It was not cocked. He jumped from the platform and moved to the window. He knew immediately he would see nothing. He saw nothing. The long-toothed pack animals began a concert of wails around the bothy. The door was now bolted from within by an oaken spar, crafted thoughtfully over lazy snowed-in days, designed with salvaged timber and wit to resist the intruder. Two pairs of amber dots briefly registered outwith the glass panes, outside in the dark. Animals. Hungry pack animals...

Arthur dressed in his old shirt and a double thickness tweed jacket hand sewn by Cecilia. He pulled on his trews quickly and moved to the door. The range was little more than a coldness. Cecilia was almost dressed, the divers knife at a moments grasp away. Arthur opened the door, cocked the hammer of the revolver and fired towards the nearest cluster of bright hungry eyes. Two things occurred simultaneously, an animal uttered a howl of pain that pierced the night and the room shook with the retort of the round being fired. Arthur had not been far enough out of the door before shooting. Cecilia roared her disapproval,

'Tender Christ Arthur! Was that completely necessary?!'

All the eyes had blinked out and gone. A cold wind found its way through their layers.

'Please close that door!', appealed Cecilia, 'they have all fled now.'

Arthur placed a candle in an old jam jar and cautiously stepped towards the direction he had fired. He found a confusion of tracks and copious amounts of vibrantly red blood on the snow.

The morning arrived slow and bitter cold. Arthur lit the range and set the water to boil.

'We should go hunting together,' he said, 'I know it is not your disposition, but you are in no position not to learn how to hunt and therefore have to become acquainted with the pistol. Sadly, it is a must.' Cecilia grimaced and considered her response, but she just wasn't having it.

'I loathe that thing. I lived for all those years on herbs, berries and trapped pigeon and I have managed well enough. I know it is useful and it has got us fresh game, but I cannot overcome my revulsion of the gun. I am sorry Arthur, on this you will not find me pliant.'

He knew she meant every word and had to let the matter rest for now.

It threatened to snow again that night and they both knew the wolves would be back. They had stared silently at the splashes of gore that had remained where the wolf had taken injury. The blood lay red stark against the whiteness. Afterward, they gathered firewood and set a few snares. The light was failing in the sky barely had it risen. Mainly to comfort themselves and alleviate the fear, they held each other close under their blankets. The bothy eventually warmed and Cecilia rose to light a candle and read her book. Her hair had almost completely regained its light auburn colour, Arthur studied her from the sleeping platform. She had a thin face, made attractive by her enormous brown eyes that couldn't hide the inherent intelligence or innate curiosity. Her back was always straight, she had poise and dignity, there was an old world beauty to her and an unexpected strength of mind and will.

Arthur realized this was what he had once called love. Yet it had a different quality this time. It was no mad rush and flush of hormones. This time it had sprang from friendship and a sound alliance.

He also knew that he had not felt so good physically or had such vitality in his previous life. He was beginning to think that whatever this place was, despite the wolves, it was better. The dangers added to the acknowledgment that life itself was enhanced by those threats. The humans made their contentment even in such demanding and humble conditions.

When mid-winter day was almost upon them, they had been living in the bothy for over four months. They had developed the habit of sleeping long through the night and waking at the first hint of light in the sky. Arthur would hunt, but took Cecilia with him, his fondness for her was increasing with the days and he would not risk losing her to whatever chance calamity that came along.

Early one morning they had been following deer tracks, which ran arrow straight into the north, following the margin between the frozen forest and the white fells. It began to snow heavily so they sought shelter under tall nearby pines. There was no chance of finding the tracks now the snow was becoming a blizzard, a bitter cold wind had picked up and it threatened to white-out. They had no option but to return. It was almost five miles back to their nest. Arthur decided it would be foolish to track via the high ground, so after a portion of flat bread each, they began heading directly back to the bothy.

The snowstorm quietened and withdrew to reveal a land so completely white it stung the eyes. At once they both noticed in a clearing a figure sitting alone under what looked like a tall post. As they neared Arthur freed the fastener on the webbing holster, but the person was not moving, he merely sat hunched up and staring at the ground. Drawing close they realized the sturdy post was in fact an ancient gibbet, a hanging place, the oak beam still braced at the base and upper beam with rusted iron. The fellow was dressed in the same mien as the young warrior, he had met in Morpeth in the George Hotel. The man was young, his beard was thin and straggling, he had the same long-limbed frame and braided hair as the anachronism Arthur had witnessed drink copiously. Yet he was not armoured and carried no weapon, but a small practical knife. He was stooped with the cold, raised his stare from the ground and regarded the couple with eyes as blue as a summer sky. He spoke, but the rough accent made it initially impossible to follow. He tried again, one word was clear, 'Hail.' He pronounced it almost like the word 'haggle'.

'Hail,' replied Arthur, and speaking very slowly asked, 'where-are-you-from?'

The young man pointed to the north and tried again to communicate in his stilted English.

'Hast thou brought Gudrun signs?' he asked with a note of bleakness in his voice.

Arthur shrugged and looked at Cecilia who was also nonplussed.

'My runes. Isse Wyrd! Runegalder! Signs for me, Gudrun, signs from the Asa Lords?'

'Sorry,' said Arthur realizing this lad was sitting out here in a blizzard waiting for signs from his Deity, 'I am sorry, we, erm…we have no such thing.'

'Thingstane!', he extended his frozen fingers to Arthur, 'oot of the heart of a storm.'

Arthur shook his head and shrugged again, a universal gesture of uselessness and incomprehension. This was proving a most strange meeting.

'Come with us to our shelter.' Cecilia offered, concerned for the young man's well being. Her innate kindness overcoming any fears.

It took him a while to understand her, but when he did he laughed, white teeth flashed, he shook his head saying,

'Gudrun cannot return'till the Asa Lords speak, then Gudrun as Wicca returns.'

Arthur reached into his side bag and gave him the last of his flat bread, the lad took it with wide eyes and spluttered, 'Gwiffu! Runegalder ha! Gudrun hath the second sign! Gwiffu!'

It crossed their minds that the young fellow may have been suffering from hypothermia. He mumbled to himself and placed the bread in a pouch, Arthur thought this mumbling was in fact his prayer. The only determinable sequence he could discern was,

'Three in ice, in the coldest months. Three in fire, on the heights, or in war.

Three in water and in the deeps. These are the signs of my passing.'

Arthur and Cecilia left him to his strange, hard religion.

'What on earth is he doing way out here?' Cecilia asked her companion as they walked away.

'He is akin to the drunken warrior I met in Morpeth, same set, same colouring. I think it is some strange right of passage. He is looking for signs.'

'What kind of signs does he think he will he find in a snowstorm?' Cecilia asked, her natural curiosity was turning the notion around in thought.

'Ones from his Gods. He called them the Asa Lords, have you heard of these?' Arthur answered.

'Actually yes', answered Cecilia, 'they are the Norse Deities. He is therefore a Viking.'

When they returned, the bothy was cold and coated with fresh snow fall. Arthur lit the fire and Cecilia set to making something to eat. All they had to use was the now familiar dried fish, which they had cured above the range, some dusty herbs and the smallest of the shallots and fennel bulbs. In all, Arthur had shot nine hares and snared eleven rabbits, these they ate the same day of the kill, but no deer as yet.

'Soon we will completely run out of supplies,' she said, 'I think we need a plan my dear Arthur.'

He hung the wet clothing over the now radiating metal box that was the centre of their world.

'There is still some flour and oatmeal, but only enough for a week at the most,' she added.

Arthur filled his pipe and ruminated on a possible notion.

Each night the wolves returned, but they did not howl. Their injured brother had been eaten long ago, their rage for food had increased enough for them to return with a pack reason. They were scouting and checking the entire bothy area. Arthur saw a set of eyes glint as he stood by the window. He was counting how many rounds he had left and whether or not wolf constituted a viable meat source. Perhaps, he considered, if it were stewed long enough with lots of herbs and a bit of salt.

Cecilia spoke,

'Your hair is becoming darker Arthur, I thought I should point this out.'

'Really', he replied,'so has yours, or should I say, it has regained much of its original colour.'

'Indeed,' remarked Cecilia, 'I have noticed, a shame we have no proper mirror.'

'Aye', agreed Arthur completely, 'I do though have a notion to put your way.'

'Say on, MacNeil' she said, her head ever so slightly lilting to one side.

'We could trek north' he began,' we have been living on scratchings for months, yet we are thriving, feeling younger and vigorous. This is not according to the rules of biology in the world from whence we derive. We have the strength to head into the Northlands, which to my mind will be walking into our regional past. History is here, all ages and times have examples of their sort alive in this world. A place of unnatural boundaries, of alien laws, where all the inhabitants are forever young.' He paused, for that was enough of his ideas for now.

'If there is no hospitality we could always return here.' Cecilia replied, nodding in agreement.

'Then we should pack tonight, make ready what we need.' Her decisiveness inspired him to action. He laid out every item of equipment he had carried with him on the sleeping platform, briefly regretting giving all the remaining diving knives away in trade. Then he counted his pistol rounds, seventy seven remained. Plenty and enough. All the clothing could be dry by morning if they set a big blaze in the iron range and packed the fire box. This he did and allowed them the luxury of an extra two candles burning. They ate by a cheerful fire, the wee room well illuminated and warm.

Their natural habit was to wake just as morning was breaking the grip of night. Cecilia had made more flat bread which they ate with black tea. They both felt a sense of vulnerability that they were leaving the little shack which had been such a welcoming home for so long, both were silent as they dressed for the journey. Cecilia tightly rolled all four blankets and wrapped them in a waterproof cape, this she tied with rope and a belt from which it hung across her back. Her two satchels were full to capacity, she was carrying all the extra food, some clothes and her three books.

Arthur had a laden rucksack, he carried two extra items, a flat iron pan without a handle and their main cooking pot. He had decided to carry the woodman's axe over his shoulder, it was too precious to leave behind. At the door, upon leaving, their hands met without thought.

'This humble place has been kind to us.' Cecilia stated, looking around the little room.

'I know,' said Arthur, ' maybe the northern lands will prove just as providential.'

Returning was likely and they needed the bothy to remain sound. So he closed the door with old fire chains, as a measure against the weather and curious beasts. They set off as the first grey light crept across the steely-hard sky. Cecilia had made a double thickness tweed cowl for herself, with an ample hood, for Arthur she had made a jacket, similar in thickness. A length of left-over cloth served as a scarf for his neck. The older frozen snow crunched as its surface crust broke, but thankfully it was not snowing as they departed, so they choose to walk north, along the fells, and follow the high ground into the Northlands.

The pale white orb of a heat-less sun hung low in a sky turning slowly blue. They made good progress and by mid-day had passed the way-point where Arthur had turned eastwards on his previous excursion. The snow still hurt the eyes, for it blanketed everything they could see in every direction. Even the many crags and outcrops had been softened by banks of wind-driven spindrift, their hard stone faces plastered with glistening ice. Cecilia began to falter and fall behind Arthur.

He noted that the ruined castle, their first nights shelter in this vast moorland, was now completely out of sight. Ahead of them, to the north, the hills grew higher and bleaker, the largest prominence had a flat-topped crown, pines grew around its flanks in abundance. It was for this point they set their mark after a brief repast of more flat bread and dried fish.

The day was dimming as the pair neared the enormous pine trees that surrounded the flat-topped hill. Wind and storm had felled much growth, tearing up high walls of entwined root and earth. It was under one of these that Arthur chose to use as a shelter. It shielded them from the north wind, a serious source of danger. At once he set about hacking lower branches down to make a layer on the ground to insulate them from the cold. Then he dragged and trimmed as much as he could manage in the remaining hour of gloom to create a lean-to against the upturned pine tree root wall. Cecilia had collected a large pile of firewood and once the shelter was finished, Arthur joined in. This was how the night found them, alone in a snowy wilderness, two companions determined to survive, working hard at a makeshift shelter.

Arthur's fingers had frozen, his fumbling efforts eventually resulted in a crackling camp-fire, which they had positioned near the open end of their lean-to shelter in a shallow pit. The orange light grew as they heaped on the wood. A slice of flat bread and some more dried fish was finished with a black tea brewed on the open fire. They huddled together in the entrance of their camp, staring into the flames, holding their tin mugs of tea, a warmth in their hands. The day had tired them both, sleep would come easily, but Arthur knew so also could the wolves. He heaped an extra pile of timber upon the fire, including some large down-fall and hoped they would wake before it had burnt completely out.

Arthur woke from a deep warm sleep and immediately drew his revolver. A dim reddish glow indicated where the fire ashes lay deep and the cause of his concern skulked a short distance from him. A twig had snapped, this had awoken him. He rose, for he had slept fully dressed and blew upon the embers, pushing the peripheral unburned firewood onto the glowing heart. It flared back into life. Light and heat and several pairs of baleful, amber eyes regarded him. Cecilia was still asleep, he would not fire the pistol without warning her, so he waited by the fire to see if the predators would brave an attack. He hoped they would not for his friends sake. She hated the retort and noise and would certainly give him hell for firing without due warning.

Two hours later he became aware that the eyes had gone and daylight was hinting in the thick tangle of pines around him. Cecilia naturally woke to find Arthur tending a healthy blaze. Huddled in the sleeping bag and woolly blankets she accepted a morning brew.

'How long have you been up?' she asked, attempting to straighten her tangled hair.

'Just a couple of hours,' Arthur replied, 'we had visitors last night. Wolves.'

Cecilia looked timorously into the growing dawn, peeking around the lean-to entrance, her hair loose and straying about her face.

'They have long gone,' he said, ' I held off shooting at them so as not to disturb you.'

'Most thoughtful of you, Arthur' she said, giving him a little hug and a kiss on the neck, 'how very sweet indeed. You know too well how much I hate that bloody thing.'

The pine forest was impassable. Too much timber had been storm felled to take an easy route through. Arthur had hoped to ascend the hill and scan the terrain with his binoculars, but it was not to be. They broke camp and headed around the skirts of the mountain, being forced increasingly westwards by the woodland. Thankfully, the snow was less thick on the margin of the trees, so progress was made. By mid-day it was obvious that to proceed any further north they would have to enter the forest, like it or not. Arthur combed the view for an alternative. Nothing useful could be seen.

The woodland ran as far west as binoculars could discern. There was no other choice if they wanted to proceed. After a drink of icy cold water and a little flat bread they followed a mountain stream up its course in the hope that this would make for an easier way through. At first it seemed to do just that, the frozen waterway allowed them to walk with a little care, along its hard surface. Then it began to fork and branch into ever thinner streams and rills. Eventually these diminished completely and Arthur had to assess the situation. It was either to push forward or head back to the shelter.

Their breath plumed in the dim forest air. Soft spindrift floated down from the branches high above. It was snowing again, and a gentle breeze caused the treetops to sway. The ground was leveling off, which to Arthur's estimation meant that they were passing over a saddle between the hills. There was much clambering and struggling over fallen obstacles before the ground began to slope again, but now downhill. Arthur could hear and see that Cecilia was wearing out and despite her gentility, occasionally cursed when she stumbled or slipped. He knew that they had merely a few hours before night fell and its associate dangers returned. They had to push on.

Time passed slowly in this most tiring means of progress, when gradually the forest began to thin out. A clearing emerged before them, a frozen glade where the long grass formed icy membranes and still, white sculptures. Cecilia slumped down to sit at the base of a pine tree. She said nothing, but it was clear she could not take much more of this. Arthur felt somehow invigorated by the effort, when he should have been utterly exhausted. As she regained her breath he studied the glade. A frozen stream ran out from its far side, he knew this could be their way downhill.

Cecilia rose and brushed her hair from her forehead. She gave Arthur a determined grin which he knew meant she was ready to go on. They crossed the meadow and followed the frozen burn downhill. Arthur was sure there was a path, for the going was easier, but soft snow heaped in the clearings and caution was needed as the light was now dimming.

They passed the rotten stumps of long-felled trees. The axe marks gave comfort, for people had worked in this place at one time. Then Arthur saw it, a conical shape loomed ahead of him, it was the roof of a circular hut. The broken door was covered in deep scratches and welts. Within, a musky darkness awaited them. They laid down their packs and lit a pair of candles. A portion of roof had rotted and a small pile of snow indicated this. Centrally placed there was a stone lined rectangular pit, charcoal filled its depths. Heaped against one wall a mound of bone-dry timber lay, they had found a shelter for the night. Arthur investigated the door to see if it could be made strong again. Cecilia shivered and sat upon the ground, too tired for words. He lit a fire as soon as he noticed how worn out she was. Initially the smoke filled the round house and they both coughed and spluttered, yet the wood was thankfully very dry and soon Cecilia was sitting right by it getting warmed through. Arthur found rotted leather hinges on the door frame and thought it would have to be propped up and barred from within. He had to leave Cecilia to fill the canteen with water, as he broke the ice with a rock he noted how total the enveloping silence was, it made him feel uneasy, as if he were being watched.

With the door solidly braced from within Arthur took two long sticks from the woodpile and whittled them into points. In his nesting pans he mixed equal portions of oatmeal and flour, threw in a little salt and carefully added water, this he beat into a dough. Taking a handful of this, he set it upon the sticks in a cone and slowly baked it over the fire. Cecilia devoured the first with gusto, the day had all but drained her of reserves, she needed the food. Arthur had made rough bread like this as a child in the Boy Scouts, it tickled him to think that he would need such skills in this alien, moonless place. A black tea accompanied the simple feast. Arthur gave his friend an extra share of the meal, she clearly needed it, and was asleep as soon as she closed the sleeping bag. Arthur sat for a while quietly, deeply grateful they had chanced upon this archaic hut. Outside it was snowing thick and fast, a low moaning wind picked up. It was preferable to utter silence.

The morning arrived and found them curled together, fast asleep. Daylight leaked through the hole in the roof and around the door frame, Arthur rose, his muscles and joints ached, Cecilia was the same, their exertions had taken toll. The fire was long dead, it was freezing cold. Arthur had to get them both warm before any plans for the day could be considered. It took an age to feel comfortable, they endured the smoke-filled hut again, but it was worth it just to get warm and have a brew steaming hot between their stone-cold fingers. The paltry heat of a low sun never found this little round house in its pine encircled glade. In winter, it had always been quite inhospitable. A long abandoned place of perpetual shadow and bitter cold.

Conscious that the situation could become critical, Arthur knew they would have to rest another night in the hut. It was almost mid-day, they had slept far longer than normally. He took his axe and cut pine branches for a bed as he had previously, but this time it was deeper and softer. Alone he gathered more firewood and water, his companion had to rest as he prepared their shelter. Arthur used branches and slabs of hard packed snow to cover the hole in the roofing, for the very air had leached the heat from their bodies. Night came swift and harsh, darkness accompanied with the howling of wolves crying deep in the surrounding forest. Arthur had cut new staves to defend their space, strengthening the door as props. These he firmly wedged against the old timber. Candles revealed the skill of the huts construction. The roof had been carefully made, the main timber joists radiated like a wheel, upon this trimmed branches had been inter-woven. Then tightly packed sods of earth finished the covering, keeping the worst of the weather from them. He could only guess how long it had been unused. At least the place was sheltering them from the worst of the winter, without it they would miserably perish, of that he had no doubt.

In the night Arthur woke. It seemed that the mournful wail of the wolves had drawn closer. The fire needed a little encouragement to revive, the effort rewarded them with warmth. He realized he had been dreaming erotically, his arousal was obvious. The object of his dreaming desire had been Cecilia, she was lying awake quietly.

'Is all well?' she asked.

'I think the wolves have returned, but the door is stronger now... I was dreaming about you.'

'I know,' she admitted, 'I could feel you against me, and you moaned my name'.

'I am supposed to be past such urges,' Arthur confessed, 'it has been so very long since...'

He drifted into a clumsy silence.

'Come back to bed.' Cecilia said, 'Hold me close as skin itself. I need you here, warm by me.'

Arthur doused all but one stub of a candle and cuddled into his partner. An awkward hour passed and his ardor for her simply refused to wane. His manhood throbbed madly against her warm body. It was driving him to an embarrassed desperation, he was beginning to sweat.

Cecilia turned about and kissed Arthur upon his mouth. He felt absurdly young. His heart rate increased and he drew her body closer to him, her proximity was more than comfort, more than friendship. The howling of wolves outside in the night ceased to bother him.

'I want you Cecilia,' Arthur breathed heavily, 'like I have not wanted in an age.'

'Then take me, Arthur, I am yours my love.' She softly said, as the candle stump spluttered and fluttered out.

Clumsily, he tugged at her clothing and found he could not resist laughing, happily.

'What is so amusing?' Cecilia asked in the darkness. She also was smiling, unseen.

'I love you.' said Arthur, ' I have love and passion within me again, and it is all for you, dear Cecilia.'

With her skirts bunched around her belly Cecilia opened herself to her man, whilst outside the wailing of hungry beasts grew even more desperate. They did not care. In the darkness, he had no age, in her arms he had but one intent. They merged in a beautiful, releasing pleasure.

'I love you too, dear man.' Cecilia held him as close as breath, close as care and kindness.

Despite the plaintiff cry of wolves, they slept as only lovers can, tangled in each others limbs. The bed beneath them scented of pine sap, the hostile frozen night forgotten.

CHAPTER TWENTY

The hill fort.

When Arthur woke, Cecilia was combing her long auburn hair, it was remarkable how very little grey now remained in it. She had blown upon the hot ashes in the fire pit and had a small blaze going. Light and heat and morning. The nesting pans steamed as the water boiled. It was his turn for a cup of black tea in bed. Their relationship had turned an important corner, they were now lovers as well as friends. Once up and dressed, he removed the props wedged against the old door. A world of whiteness awaited, he blinked at the glare of it. Outside of this clearing, the sun was shining, but only an ambient light filled the glade.

They shared the last of the flat bread and dried fish. Their eyes met frequently and Cecilia would smile in response. The world was dangerous, unfamiliar and strange to them, but they had found happiness in each other. Arthur felt more alive than ever before. He packed quickly.

They followed an obvious narrow track downhill holding hands as they walked together. The day was bright and a cloudless sky vaulted blue above. The descent became steep and the snow had drifted thigh deep in places, this would slow them but not cause concern. The valley into which they were descending was heavily wooded, a mix of deciduous and conifers filled every available space. It was claustrophobic, as the trees towered over everything and a chilly hard silence dominated.

The track eventually led to a wider path. A pair of parallel ruts ran through the snow, the traces told of a cart pulled by a horse. Spindrift and windblown snow had filled these signs in places, but it was unmistakable, someone had recently passed this way. Greatly encouraged, they pressed on.

As the valley grew steeper and narrower Arthur thought he could determine fragments of ruins. The snow made it hard to fully discern, as it covered much of the remaining lower courses of masonry. Soon he was in no doubt that the area had once been settled, when the valley bottle-necked and turned steeply uphill. Massive fragments of a once enormous fortification lay directly before them. A large deep ditch and steep embankment had been raised in some age long past, an uneven wall of shattered stones topped this, capped white with curling cornices of snow. The path entered a high man-made gorge of stonewalling that had once been a gateway. The fortification had been a huge undertaking, once passed it, they both paused and looked back downhill on its remnants. It had originally spanned the entire narrows of the vale.

It was past midday when the valley opened up into a wide flat upland. Forest still dominated the hills all around, but many clearings had been made. Long, wide fields and enclosures marked the terrain, animal pens and barns dotted the flat, snow covered plain. A river coiled, shining silver in the sunlight, frozen quite solid. Arthur regarded these clear signs of settlement and wondered where the people could be? Nothing moved, all was still.

They had reached the river when Cecilia pointed with an exclamation, 'There!'

Many coils of smoke listed into the cold blue sky from beyond a series of lofty white walls. It was a hill fort, an enclosed settlement, set a few hundred feet above the valley, dominating a long spur that ran down from the high moors. There was a clear broad path running to it, this they made for.

As they approached a towered gateway, Arthur could see that the walls were not white with snow but had been lime washed. Substantial timbers surmounted a steep man-made bank, a deep ditch ran under this. It was a staggering construction, an epic effort. They could discern as they neared three sets of these wooden walls, increasing in height towards the summit. A timber and stone gatehouse lay before them, the massive doors were shut and barred. Arthur realized this could be the only way in. He stepped back a few paces and yelled at the top of his voice,

"Hello! Hello within!"

No-one responded so he tried again and after a pause, he had another attempt. A shuttered window opened high in the gatehouse and a helmeted head looked down on them, the face a study in astonishment.

'Aye,' said the guardian, 'whit be ye aboot?'

'We seek shelter,' began Arthur, ' if it can be had, we need a place to rest.'

The shutter closed and the sound of heavy boots on wooden stairs told the door ward was coming down to them. They waited, cast upon the mercy of strangers. A section of the main gate opened inwards and a man appeared, most surprised to see the pair.

He was clad in animal furs, which clearly were wolf skins and he wore a sword at his side. He seemed curious rather than hostile and this became manifest in his questions. Arthur had to listen hard to his words, they were distortions of the familiar, the vowels deeper and slanted, the accent one from antiquity yet punctuated with more modern terms. He wanted to know where they were from and where they were going. A fair enough request in such a wild and remote place.

The warden told them they would have to see the headman, their Thane, and ushered them in. Once through the entrance gate they walked right and uphill along a deep ditch. Tall, lime-washed timber walls towered over them on both sides, the snow in the approach was trampled and rutted.

In time, they reached a second fortified gatehouse, having walked about a quarter of the circumference of the citadel. The warden shouted a incomprehensible yell and eventually another section of this second gateway opened. Again, they found themselves in a similar trough, flanked by tall white walls. Arthur saw clearly that this would be a deadly place to be caught during an attack.

The second approach was much easier, and circuited the brow of the hill again, to the right hand side. Soon they approached a grim castle-like structure, its lower courses of stone, its upper of lime-washed posts, each having a hefty girth. The place appeared impregnable.

The final gateway opened as they approached and entered the hilltop enclosure. Hut circles of all sizes were everywhere, animal pens and stables also, all very much in use. A gang of lads were having a snowball fight with youthful fervour. They passed cows herded into yards and byres, ducks and chickens ran freely about. Arthur noticed that many of the folk wore items of clothing from recent times, this proved a contact with the outside world, it was again a strange mix of styles and eras.

They were told to wait outside of a substantial round house, its snow covered roof sloped to the ground giving the impression of a white conical hill. Smoke from a fire rose from a hole at the apex. Arthur and Cecilia studied the people about them, they were clean and well presented in appearance, this put them at their ease but confounded Arthur's notions of life in ancient times.

The warden re-appeared and ushered them into the Thane's hall.

Windowless and heavy with wood and peat smoke, the interior was a lamp lit cornucopia of colourful woven wall hangings and gilded carvings. Small side rooms with hanging drapes for doorways lay around the inner perimeter. Centrally a long stone-lined fire trench smouldered and smoked. It was warm, rush matting covered the floors and sturdy trestle tables flanked three sides of the fire trench. The Thane sat in a worn oak chair similar to those on either side, this re-assured Arthur even more. The head of this hill fort was a physically powerful man, his long blonde braided hair had receded a little to reveal a clear, unlined brow. He looked up from a document that he was studying and regarded the couple with a calculating glance and a wry smile.

'Welcome to Rothsburgh, travelers, we rarely get visitors at this season. My door ward tells me you are heading north together, a strange time of the year for such a risky task is it not?'

His English was perfect, heavily accented yet easy to understand. Arthur thought he must have traveled much in this Otherworld, so his knowledge of it might be extensive, he replied,

'Well, sir, it was a question of necessity. We had to leave the city because we are old. For as you may well know, it is a place for the young and the beautiful alone.'

The Thane frowned and said, 'You are not so aged. Even so, why head into the far Northlands?'

Arthur accepted directness may pay at this juncture.

'I am new to this land, this world. I wish to know more about it and find a place that is suitable for my friend and myself. We do not care much for the city to the south, there are forces there which make for great concern and much worry. There has to be something better for us, so we seek it.'

The leader nodded, but said nothing for a while, simply looking at the pair before him, then said,

'We have been here so long, there is but scant memory now remaining of what we were before. This land is all we know and we live the only way we know how and our traditions yet remain. For I have seen this city and I agree, it is a dark and dangerous place. I sympathize with your efforts, but there is much you need to know.'

'Your advice would be highly prized and most valuable.' Arthur acknowledged, 'Any assistance we would gladly return in a practical manner, to show our appreciation.'

'What can you do?' the Thane asked plainly. Arthur considered that a draughtsman's trade wasn't enough. He had to simplify what he and Cecilia had to offer.

'I have my axe to stock your wood stores and I can hunt a little. My partner can make clothes and cook. She also can read and write.' It sounded absurd to his ears to sum themselves up in this way.

The leader shifted in his seat and looked Arthur directly in the eye and said,

'You are both welcome to shelter with us until the weather improves. We have a practical life here, our dealings outside this valley are few and our visitors fewer. You will need to know about the lands you wish to visit in search of a home and a life for yourselves. There are dangers as well as freedoms, this knowledge may aid you. First, you must unburden yourselves of the loads you carry, eat, be warmed and rest for today. It is auspicious indeed that you find us on the shortest of days, this sits well for you both. Tomorrow we will talk again and set you to needful tasks. I discern there is no lie in you. I have lived long enough to know the very scent of untruth. My door ward will show you to your quarters. What are your names please?'

'This is my dear friend Cecilia Fotheringham and I am Arthur MacNeil.'

'I am Roth Sigurrson, Thane of this enclosure for years beyond count and easy numeration.'

The leader rose and briefly nodded to them, no handshakes, no smiles, just a polite bow.

'Thank you for your generosity and illumination,' replied Arthur sincerely, copying the nod.

'Indeed, sir,' added Cecilia, breaking her silence, 'you are most kind.'

The warden took them to a quiet quadrant of the hill fort, the snow had no prints or tracks and lay deeply undisturbed about them. He informed them this was where the drovers and traveling craftsmen would stay in the spring and summer months. Six round houses huddled together in a cluster, one had need of a door and repairs, Arthur was grateful they were led to one of the sounder huts. Once within they laid down their baggage and immediately set about lighting a fire in the pit. Snow had blocked the hole at the apex and the smoke was unbearable, so Arthur had to scramble up onto the roof and clear it, not without difficulty. He slid back down the conical slope, bringing a flurry of snow with him. When he re-entered he was freezing cold, his hands had lost sensation, but the smoke was now drawing out through the apex and soon he warmed through.

'We have landed on our feet again,' Arthur noted. Cecilia was inspecting a low, roughly hewn bench-bed, testing its soundness and replied, ' Right enough, our luck has held so far.'

She nodded to herself that the sleeping platform was adequate and began to set the bed. Arthur broke the ice on a barrel of water and filled the nesting pans for a brew.

'His English is very good,' Arthur pointed out, 'he must be well traveled and have had plenty dealings with this land in general. His knowledge may prove invaluable'

'I am thankful he is wary of the city, perhaps it is too modern for him.' Cecilia added.

'Did he not say it was a dark and dangerous place, not modern or new.' Arthur recalled and said

'I find it bizarre to consider he could be over one thousand years old.'

'The rules here are not in accord with our origins, you must clearly see this by now.' Cecilia had to make this observation yet again, adding,

'Normal rules don't apply here.'

Arthur repeated her words, admitting she was right. Normal rules did not apply one bit.

The pans soon steamed and they gladly drank hot black tea, it restored them quickly.

'I would like to see more of this place, it is fascinating.' Cecilia's interest in ancient British history was backed by decades of book reading during her self imposed incarceration in the library.

'I think it would be prudent to wait until we have gained a degree of their trust,' replied Arthur.

'Perhaps you are right. Does it not strike you as the strangest of things, this is a hill fort, a well defended walled enclosure on high ground. It has been continuously lived in for goodness knows how long.' Cecilia stated and wondered at the facts of this, then continued, 'Yet here it is, as real as real can be!'

'Makes you think what else there could be in this world. Anything is possible.' added Arthur.

One of the Thane's stewards came to their little round hut, burdened with a sheepskin bundle and a covered wicker basket. He told the couple they were a gift from his leader, who wanted them to be warm and to eat. The skins were well tanned and soft to touch and the basket contained strips of black, dried venison and a loaf of gritty bread and a little goats cheese which was tough and hard. They both thanked him, realizing that life up here on the high ground would be a difficult one and the nights cold indeed. Cecilia cast the skins upon the bed, they had been carefully sewn together, she admired the handiwork. Arthur had set candle stumps about the circular room on brackets of rusted iron, he discovered a simple oil lamp half full and a broken shield, which he held before him, studying the stick letters that survived upon its leather skin.

'What manner of writing is this?' he asked Cecilia.

She stood close to him and regarded the broken shield.

'They are Runes, my dear, the written language of the Norsemen, Viking words.' she stated.

'I thought the Vikings were un-civilised barbarians that killed without reason or much thought.'

Arthur's notions of the warriors of old was not atypical and based on movies and television.

'Like everything else,' patiently his lover spoke, 'there would have been good and bad amongst them. History records their acts of savagery, the slaughter of villages and monasteries. This and their brutality and ferocity upon the battlefield. Little is told of their many skills or artisan genius.'

The sun set and darkness swiftly fell. The hut had a good supply of wood and peat, so the round room heated quickly. Outside in the night, a cold wind moaned and whistled. Arthur noticed that the door had a whole hide that could be pulled over it to eliminate drafts, once this was in place the round house became even warmer. Cecilia wiped a large earthenware dish and heated pans of water, she was determined to be clean. Arthur watched her completely undress and studied her body as she first soaked and soaped her hair then washed herself all over. This was a different creature before him, confident and un-selfconscious in her nakedness. Once finished, she stood naked by the fire-pit, flame and candle light softened her skin. Although she was long-legged, tall and slim, their adventure had given her a new health, a vitality. Wet hair hung down her back, her little breasts had a pert set to them, her belly had an endearing soft curve to it. Arthur wanted her right then, his arousal grew painful and insistent. He rose to touch her and she laughed girlishly, saying,

'No! Not a chance Arthur! Not until you are clean too!'

So Arthur followed her example and boiled up fresh water to scrub himself and shave off the week-long growth from his face. Cecilia changed into a nightdress she had sewn herself, Arthur preferred her nakedness by far, but said nothing. That night their lovemaking was slow and gentle, each giving to the other their passion and kindness until sleep overcame them both. The candle stumps guttered out and far away, carried on the frozen wind, the long wail of hungry wolves rose and fell, a sorrowful, eerie song. A winter ballad for a frozen land.

They woke early, the hut was still warm so they dressed and ate in comfort. The Thane's steward came to them, summoning them before his lord. The day was shining and crisp. Fresh snowfall had covered all the footprints and they could see for miles over the walls that protected them. The Thane noticed the food and rest had been of benefit and without due concern set them to task for the day. Arthur he included in a woodcutting gang, who would take a horse-drawn cart to be filled outside the hill-fort in nearby woodland, whilst Cecilia joined an industrious gathering of womenfolk who sewed, making and mending garments and clothing. This was the first time in many months they had been apart, and initially it felt strange to them both, but they set to their appointed tasks with determination, for they would prove their gratitude with hard work and honest labour. Arthur's group consisted of men half his age, but he grafted steadily, winning the silent approval of these hardy, rough-spoken hill folk by the day's end.

It was in such a routine of days that a month passed. The Thane did not summon them again, but had gathered favourable reports about their efforts and willingness to contribute. He was content to let them stay as long as they wished. One night whilst washing himself, stripped to the waist, Cecilia noticed Arthur's body was firmer, stronger looking. She had been laying belly down on the bed in her nightdress reading her Shakespeare by candlelight, her glasses glinting, her hair loose, tumbling over her studious face.

'You are changing, my love,' she said, looking up and regarding him attentively,

'your body is hardening and your hair has as much dark as gray in it.'

'It needs cutting,' he responded, 'if it gets any longer I shall need braids like the men folk here.'

'Perhaps that would not be a bad thing,' Cecilia mused, 'you would then look like one of the locals.'

'Can you really see me braided and bearded, clad in hide and fur?' Arthur asked amused.

'Actually, yes,' she replied, 'if you continue to firm up as you have been, you will resemble these Northmen whether you like it or not.'

'Normal rules don't apply.' Arthur reminded himself and grinned.

Another two months swiftly passed. Cecilia had taken to wearing a long woolen cloak like the womenfolk of the hill fort and wearing her hair in long plaits tied with leather thongs. Her time in the company of the menders and makers had been a great pleasure to her, she had been accepted and was valued for her talent. Arthur's hands were hardening, his muscles had developed from the daily axe work. The notion of heading further north was forgotten and remained unmentioned. The Thane's steward came to them one evening after sunset and summoned them to the Lord's hall. It was the time of the Equinoctial celebration.

As they entered the Thane's garth, they saw that the tables were laden with food and almost every chair was taken. The steward led the couple to a long bench seat, the Thane and his head men sat in their chairs at the far end, there was the murmur of talk, an air of excitement and expectation. They thanked the steward and took their places. No-one had touched the laden platters before them, Arthur smelled the delicious aroma of roasted pig, freshly baked bread and tall flagons of frothing dark ale. His mouth watered, hunger stung him with a sharp ache.

The chatter subsided and the Thane rose. Everyone present followed suit. The leader raised both his hands and blessed the gathering. From farthest away, where Arthur and Cecilia sat it was almost inaudible. He then turned to the main door where a group of men in the strangest attire had entered. All eyes in the hall were upon the weird procession before them.

Arthur immediately recognised Gudrun. He wore a long cowled cloak of black feathers and held a burning brand, his face was decorated in a stark mask of black vertical lines running down from the eyes to the chin. Another huge fellow had a bearskin draped over him, the mask of its fierce head worn over his face, the long claws as gloves. Another tall man wore the skin of a stag, the antlers had holly entwined in them, red berries glistened. There was also a horse-man, the hide covering him completely, a white skull prominent upon his head and also a wolf-man clad in the thick, silvery-grey pelt of the ever hungry howlers. Central to the procession was a fellow in beautiful, elaborate armour. The curling, complicated designs had been brightly coloured and highlighted, he carried an enormous carved staff, this he raised as he addressed the gathering assembled there.

'All-Father is very strong and full of might,' he began in deep solemn tones.

'He lives through all time and governs all things. He is the High Lord of the Heavens and the Earth and all that is in them. When he made man he gave him a soul that can live on and need never die, though the body will drop to dust or burn to ashes.

Night is the greatest of mysteries, she is past and she is the future.

All Creation came from her womb and to her embrace it will return.

All-Father took on the form of Twilight and had a child by Night; it was a son named Space.

All-Father then had a second child by Night, it was a daughter named Earth.

All-Father took on the form of Dawn and had a third child by Night, it was a son called Day.'

The Thane then called loudly for all to sit and eat, taking a haunch of venison in one hand and a massive cup of beer in the other, then he bellowed three times,

'Hail! To thee Children of All-Father!'

The entire company responded, Arthur and Cecilia, quite taken with the ceremony joined in also. The animal-men procession sat and watched as everyone ate. No-one took food or drink to them. They neither asked for it or seemed to want it.

Feasting fully in the company of the boisterous, laughing Northmen, the splendid food lasting well into the night, as did the noisy and bellicose celebration, Arthur took his cup of ale and raised it to Cecilia.

'Cheers to you my love, my friend. I do believe we are free, we have made it!'

She smiled at him, a look of love, kissed him quickly on the lips and raised her own cup, saying,

'Let it be so, long may it remain so. Cheers to you, Arthur MacNeil, you have found us a life worth living. Well done my man!' her huge dark eyes glistened with tears of gladness and love.

They drained their cups with thanks, around them the festival was almost deafening, a celebration of life at the waning of winter, when daylight was the equal fight of the night.

When the gathering could eat no more, but only pick idly at the remaining food, the drinking began in earnest. Songs were sung, some telling of a remote past, of battles and sagas and monsters and heroes. The dark beer had a definite power as the night drew on, some couples danced with abandon, young men wrestled and brawled, others just howled with laughter at the antics of others. Arthur and Cecilia joined in the celebration, they held one another tightly and slowly span the simplest of dances, their eyes full of each others eyes, their mouths meeting often, the pleasure of kissing, the bliss of lovers words in their ears, in their hearts. The closeness of life.

Arthur knew they had to leave, his desire for his woman friend had gripped him yet again. Other couples had wandered off, groping and fumbling, kissing and laughing. They did the same, stepping out into the star-filled night. Arthur spoke,

'Why is there no moon here? Where is this place? What kind of world is it?'

Cecilia hugged-in tightly to him as they walked, swaying slightly, back to their hut, she replied,

'It is the world where we now live, my dear. It is what we have and we will make the most of it.'

They re-kindled the fire in the humble round house. What few candles remained they set about the circle. Arthur felt his lust rise with a frantic urgency, he could not get his lover's clothes off fast enough. They feasted now upon each other with passion, naked as needles, full and high on the pleasure of pleasure, the love of love. The celebration had intoxicated them, raised their senses to a heightened state. They would sleep until late in the morning, wrapped under the sheepskin, warmed by one another.

No-one would be working the next day.

CHAPTER TWENTY ONE

The bear.

Arthur and Cecilia stayed in the hill fort under Thane Roth's protection until the snows melted and the first signs of spring began to show. The valley below grew greener by the passing weeks and the cattle were driven down from the hill to the fields and enclosures by the river. A few men and women tended them and kept watch against hungry predators. These lived in simple round houses, which were positioned on vantages that provided the best view of the grazing land.

Arthur's hair had grown, and with Cecilia's encouragement he wore it in a short pony tail. This and the fact he had adopted the clothing of the Northmen, made him resemble the hill people, which had given them both a welcome and a home. He was becoming one of them.

Arthur had physically transformed. The stooped, defeated, frightened man that had endured in the squalor of Pipewellgate and had skulked miserably in the sorry, otherworldly version of the same place, he was gone. He stood at his full height, six foot tall, his arms had firmed with muscles and his gray hairs had all but disappeared. He wore a short goatee beard, again a concession to Cecilia, who was happy with this assimilation into the hill clan.

Cecilia too had joined the natives in dress and appearance. She rarely wore her prim long tweed skirt and adorned herself with the practical dress and ornamentation of the womenfolk there. Her hair was braided and bound in an elaborate coil when she worked during the day, at night she would loosen the pins and ties and it would spill down past her waist, an auburn cascade. She too had changed, a confidence was about her that made pale the frightened little bird who had hid in the attic of a library, that had jumped at every noise and shrieked when startled or surprised. Her love for Arthur had continued too, they were each others comfort, their alliance complete.

It was when the first flowers of the valley blossomed that they decided to Handfast.

This was the tradition of the hill people, a form of public ceremony that declared their partnership to all. Marriage, by any other name. Summer, they were told, was a good time for wedding. To Handfast would also join them to the clan fully, publicly and spiritually.

They rarely saw the Thane, now the snows had receded, he rode frequently with his chosen guard out on the hunt. This often followed what they called the Marches, the boundary of their territory, the limits of the land they claimed as their own. When they returned it was never without a catch. The commonest game was the deer and the boar, yet even wolf and fox would be eaten, tough and rank as it was. Arthur had never in either life been on horseback. The way in which the Thane and his champions rode made it look as if they were born to it, for so they were.

Arthur was content to be a humble woodsman, his axe was his trade now, the forests that surrounded the valley were his shop floor. From his workmates he slowly acquired the folklore and religious beliefs of the tribe. These had survived down through a thousand years and had changed little. He even wore the hammer sign around his neck on a leather thong. This was sacred to their warrior god, Asa-Thor. He gradually assimilated into all aspects of their world, he was becoming a Northman. His own troubled mother would not have recognized him.

Tribal life was run by two factors within the settlement. Firstly, the Thane who ran the practical affairs of the citadel and secondly the Seidmenn, or shamans. These were men like Gudrun, who had lived the warrior life for such an unutterably long time they wanted to walk a path beyond the common run. The Seidr served the people and the Thane stood to them as one of their charges, nothing more. This arcane sect lived separate from the rest of the community. Some took no partners, but those that did, their wives would become the female source of esoteric knowledge and belief, the Wise Women, the holders of a dark and secret wisdom. Also known as Seid or the Wicce, from where the modern word 'witch' arises. This was the world they had held firm to since being taken and transported to this new, moonless place. They determinedly continued their traditions, just as they had lived before, nothing had changed for them bar the unusual nature of a land where all ages and times co-existed. They had no way of dealing with this, and so kept themselves apart as much as possible. The world outside the valley was too confusing, so they dealt with it rarely, if they had to at all.

Morpeth lay three days walk to the east. The walled Medieval town was a source of commodities of which the hill folk would have need on occasion. Tools and cloth being the commonest requirement, also strong spirits, fine ground flour and salt. When they rode east, they did so in numbers, out of comfort to themselves and for safety. Further north other clans dwelt, some with a more warlike emphasis to their nature and life. Attacks had occurred in the past, men had fought and died in battle and conflict. Vigilance was a constant feature of the hill people, for children were not born in this world, they could be specimens cast in perpetual youth, but fatalities could not be replaced.

Arthur learned by listening to the tales told in the company, stories of the Legion of Trimontium, and the disciplined soldiers whose language was Latin. These men fought shield by shield and ruled many valleys far to the north. There was also the Cruithni, a secretive people who fought the Roman soldiers from the triple-peaked hill fort. The Legion and the Cruithni were blood enemies. Stories about these wary, tattooed folk were told to scare and frighten people. The slow foul poison of their darts, their ancient tongue, the hollow hills within which they dwelt, and hid. Some said they were cannibals, that they feasted on the flesh of their fallen enemies, others that they were powerful magicians that could disappear at will, or fly, or breathe underwater. Beyond these, even less was known. The people of Dun Edyin were said to be like the Northmen, living in a citadel upon a stark crag of rock, but built of stone and set in a swamp that would confuse any attacker. Their reputation was fierce, of great martial prowess and a legendary capacity for consuming alcohol and distilled spirits. In the spring they had been known to travel south in war bands. The conflict between the Picts and the Romans meant a vast tract of land between Rothsburgh and Dun Edyin was indeed a perilous journey, one from which many had never returned.

It was early in the summertime when such a party led by the Thane traveled out to the Morpeth to procure extra supplies. Arthur was included in the retinue and walked with the clan, for only the leader and his guard possessed horses. Cecilia had given him a list of things to find and had told him to return soon, unharmed and whole. Their custom of acquisition took the form of an open trade, they had a horse-drawn cart piled with skins and hides, for their pride disallowed them from simply taking what they wanted. Money requires a number of factors to be in place, none of which worked in this Otherworld. As Arthur had discovered, in the city everything was free and within Morpeth's town walls the same state of affairs existed. The Rothsburgh Clan regarded themselves as separate, apart from the rest and could not take the goods without giving something back. It was their way, their sense of independence and self sufficiency was important to them.

On their second night out, when the town was but a days walk away and the men folk sat around a massive bonfire, a huge black bear attacked. It had been drawn to the smell of the food and was driven mad with a ravenous hunger. Out of the darkness it came, a sentry just had time to yell the alarm when the enormous brute rent his head from his body. The others drew their swords and grabbed firebrands to see what the commotion was about, only to find the bear was ripping open the sentries rib cage and in the process of eating the dead man's heart and lungs.

Arthur had grabbed his axe and joined the clansmen to see off the attack, with his heart beating wildly, he stared into the star-flecked night. He saw the monster eating steaming flesh and swatting wildly at its attackers. He froze for a drawn out moment, the vision before him was brutal and shocked his senses, but he could not merely stare in horror. He grasped his axe firmly in his fists and paced steadily forward, trying hard not to shake with fear.

As Arthur neared, he could see that the bear was massive, when it roared in pain or fury, its open mouth was the size of a man's head, and it stank. One of the Thane's guards was mauled badly down his sword arm, the blade clattering to the grass as blood sprayed and steamed in the night.

The pain of the jabbing and thrusting steel was driving the bear into a frenzy. A fellow woodcutter had his neck ripped wide open and slowly toppled, face down into the bloodstained earth. His name had been Hrolf, he and Arthur had worked together and talked much, now he lay twitching in death in the trampled grass. MacNeil roared in rage and disbelief, he hoisted his felling axe high and lunged at the beast. The blow fell square upon the bears massive skull and it roared out in pain, making one final effort to kill all its tormentors. The axe was buried deep and was wrenched from Arthur's hands. His final thought before the beast hurled him away and he fell like a limp rag was simple, why had he stopped carrying his revolver? His world blacked out and he was down.

Arthur woke in a proper bed with blankets and white sheets. His forehead was craftily bound. It throbbed madly, his neck ached. With eyes bruised blue from the cruel blow he looked about him. Thane Roth sat by a small coal fire, he looked so out of place in the clean and ordered chamber.

Arthur groaned and his vision span and blurred, 'Where am I?' he asked.

'In Morpeth, safe for now man, safe for now. The All Father spared you last night. You brought down the bear MacNeil, your axe was its finishing. We carried you here on the cart.'

'Hrolf is dead.' Arthur stated.

'As is Ketil, and two of my best champions are scored deep. Yet you live.'

The Thane was standing now, looking down on Arthur with a grave expression. He continued, saying,

'There will be weeping in Rothsburgh on our return. My men will be long in mending. Once we have done our business here we will return with haste. The fallen must be burned and the injured have to mend, including you.'

In the lamplight the leaders sorrow was plain to see.

'The hide of the beast is yours,' Roth said, 'you dealt it the death blow, so the trophy will hang in your hut. There is courage to you, this stands well with our kind, we have honour for the man who turns not from an enemy greater than himself.'

Arthur did not know what to say. He thought of Hrolf and his wife and wanted to weep. The Thane left him to attend the other wounded men. Arthur realised that he too could be wrapped in a shroud, lying with the dead. He gave himself up to the nausea of pain that dragged him back down to sleep. His last thought was of Cecilia, what would she do if he had perished?

The following morning Arthur woke and dressed. His head hurt, the wound had been sewn with horsehair and it stung sharply. He could not find his axe, it had been taken in safekeeping by the town guards along with all the other weapons. Down wooden stairs he found a gathering of clansmen breaking nights fast, they hushed as he approached. Strangers in the inn pointed at him and whispered. Arthur ate heartily, for hunger pangs gripped him, then he emptied a pewter tankard of black beer. The talking resumed. Two men there both had their sword-arms heavily bandaged, they nodded to him an acknowledgment. Arthur poured another ale from the large glazed jug. He remembered the list of things Cecilia had asked him to procure, weak as he was, he would set about the task once refreshed. The beer took the edge off his pain. Once the ale was downed he set off upon his errands.

Arthur was almost at the door when a familiar voice rose above the conversation.

'Arthur MacNeil! Killed a bear with his axe! Hail the man folk of Rothsburgh!'

The Thane had spoken and all the company there gave cheer. Arthur's face reddened, he found the praise harder to bear than his injury. He turned and bowed to the clansmen, then departed to his domestic tasks. As he walked away into the narrow Medieval streets, he smiled to himself. To any of the townsfolk, a Northman walked amongst them, one wounded in battle, tall and strong, with purpose in his pace and pride in his bearing. The old Arthur was gone, a new life lay before him. He was one of the hill people now. This would more than suffice, this would be good indeed.

As he walked, he remembered Pipewellgate, the misery and menace of the place. He recalled his parting words as he and Cecilia had crossed over the ancient bridge into the narcotic mist.

'Bye-bye, hell-hole.' He had said it and he had meant it. There would be no going back now. The inhabitants of the walled town stepped out of his way as he approached. He didn't notice, he was not a that kind of man.

The return journey was painfully slow. Arthur chose to walk despite the Thane's offer for him to ride the way in the cart. Instead, his rucksack and bag of acquisitions and axe lay in the wagon with all the other goods, rather than himself. This added to his stature amongst the clansmen, he had politely refused comfort and ease, the Northmen respected this attitude and added it to his story, his new-found fame. The stinking ragged hide of the black bear was salted, rolled up and bound, it hung from the wagon boards, so it would not stain or poison the goods they brought back to Rothsburgh. Its enormous head bobbed as the wheels turned, its fangs were as long as a man's finger. The Thane had ordered the rigged tack of the injured horsemen to a second cart, in this two dead men lay wrapped in shrouds. These would be given over to the priests on their return. A cremation ceremony and a wake would duly follow.

On the last day of their journey, the final miles brought quiet comfort to all but the Thane, as he would have the unpleasant task of bringing very bad news to the surviving widows. His face was closed in thought, his mind turned inwards. Arthur longed to see his lover, he knew he would have to tell her what happened and decided to play the encounter down in a hope she would not be angered at the very dangers inherent in his rash but brave act. The white walls of Rothsburgh rose high above them, the same walls and towers that Arthur and Cecilia had found when adrift in the snows of that mid winter day. It had become their home. In fact it had become a sanctuary. As the final gate opened, the whole settlement had gathered in wait, he saw her standing in the crowd, tall and fine and smiling at him. He ran to her and clasped her tightly, kissing her forehead and lips.

'What have you done to yourself?' she asked, as well he knew she would.

'I shall tell you all once we are indoors. There will be sorrow this day. Men have died. My injury is nothing compared to such a loss.'

Taking his rucksack and belongings from the wagon they walked to their hut as the sound of keening and wailing rose sorrowfully. Cecilia recognized he had spoken truly,

'I am so glad you are back. I missed you so much, I was cold, alone in our bed at night.'

'I missed you too my love, you will not be cold tonight, nothing surer.'

Three days of quiet in which almost no work was done, was set aside for the fallen. On the evening of the third day the shamen in full attire came from the House of the Dead, bearing the shrouded deceased upon wooden litters. The whole community had gathered to witness the cremation pyre. Upon a raised platform of earth and stone a bonfire had been prepared. Arthur and a select few had worked hard to help build this pile. Its core was packed with compressed gorse and dry downfall. Death was mourned deeply in Rothsburgh. These people had been taken in an entirety as specimens long, long ago. They had lived and survived down centuries together, their binds were deep. Childbirth was not even a memory amongst them now. As creatures in the confines of this Otherworld, they could live for millennia providing accident or injury did not befall, but they could not reproduce. The very subject had been taboo for so long it had slipped from the memory and converse. Hence, death having such a heavy effect upon them, they had lost two very dear and familiar friends.

The priests performed their incantations and lit the pyre, quickly it caught and crackled and blazed. Women snuffled and were comforted by kin, men openly cried, there was no shame in displaying regret and loss at the parting of a friend. Arthur held Cecilia's hand silently, a puckered wound glistened upon his brow, she had braided his hair and bound the plaits with hide. They both now completely resembled the hill clan, they had made their choice.

A plume of smoke rose into the starry night, slowly, folk began to leave the fires as the bonfire settled to an even mound, the bodies that had lain upon it were now little more than ash.

In the Thane's garth, barrels of beer waited on the tables, jugs and tankards also. There would be a wake in which the clan would drink and remember their departed. This was their custom. The sturdiest would be there until the morning sun appeared, night and coldness crept over the hill-fort walls. Arthur and Cecilia left early, making room for those who had known the deceased the longest.

The summer was warm and vibrant, the festival of the longest day neared, traditionally the time for Handfasting. Arthur and Cecilia were taken into the House of the Siedr and inducted into the clan's beliefs on the sanctity of the ritual they were about to perform. The Wise Women took Cecilia into a cave, dug into the hill fort itself, there she was bathed and adorned for the ceremony. Candles and incense filled the womb-like hollow, the preparation took all day and that night she had to sleep there alone. Arthur wondered what they were doing with her, he would never know, the tradition was held most secret. Gudrun the shaman would certainly not tell.

The morning shone warm and bright, a scented wind blew over the hill. Arthur stood in the daylight, in a place where a tall carved stone sat, waiting for Cecilia's appearance. All the woodcutters and foresters had turned out and the two Thane's guards who had been injured also attended in full battle dress, their decorated armour setting them aside of the common folk. The Thane himself made his appearance, bearing an enormous black bundle, the bear skin had been fully cured, its reek was now long gone. It was as big as a tent if laid open fully.

'This is yours MacNeil,' said the clan chief, 'and this day also. Be happy in it and love your woman long and true. You bind with us all now, you are made one of us.'

Arthur bowed, as was customary and thanked him, and as he raised his eyes he saw her.

Cecilia walked with three of the Wise Women, a crown of tiny white flowers adorned her hair. A long cloak of midnight blue was clasped at her shoulders, and her dress was palest pink embroidered with colourful intertwined foliage, beautifully hand sewn in bright threads. The sun was behind her and caused her hair to resemble a flame, Arthur felt he was seeing her anew, his heart beat raced. She was most beautiful to him. One of Cecilia's attendants produced a pottery cup with two handles and filled it with a honey wine, fragrant and sweet. Arthur and Cecilia took one of the handles each, facing one another.

The three Wise Women all wore cowled cloaks, one of forest green, one of blood red and one of night black. The dark clad one spoke first, a quiet voice, but with deepest authority.

'Eastwards I stand, for favours I pray.

I pray to the Great Measurer, I pray the mighty Sun,

I pray the Holy Protector of the Heavenly Kingdoms,

Earth I pray and sky.'

Gudrun then spoke, adorned in his cloak of crow and raven feathers, saying,

'Praise be to Ing, the Green Man,

Praise be to Frig, Mother of Earth,

Praise be to Irminsul, the Pillar of Creation,

Look now in favour upon those who art dependent upon this land

And bring forth bounty and goodness for them both.'

Then the priest and the Wise Women all did chant together.

'Erce, Erce, Erce, Mother of Earth, Mother of Harvest grant us,

fields sprouting yield, thriving, flourishing and bountiful.

Bright shafts of millet, broad barley crops and white wheat fields,

All the goodness of this land.

May the mighty and everlasting All Father and the Gods in the Heavens,

Grant our life and our products are safe against every foe, secure against all harms, safe from the witchcraft sown throughout this land.

Now we pray to the Mighty Creator of this world,

That no Wicce may be so cunning, and no Wicca so crafty,

That they can upset the words thus spoken.'

First Cecilia drank from the cup, then Arthur followed. As they had been instructed, they cast the double-handed cup against the carved stone, where it was dashed, broken, irreparable.

They had wed, they were linked together to loss and gain. Their hearts and lives conjoined now in truth and by oath, sworn and ardently binding, witnessed by the hill folk gathered there.

CONCLUSION

The i...

A hushed, even tone pronounces with some manifest gloating.

Translated to our own ears, it would sound like this...

'I win! Of this there can be no doubt whatsoever!'

Another savage voice spits, full of hatred and maliciousness incarnate.

'I should visit that hill-top hovel and decimate all those long-haired, bearded fuck monkeys!'

'Ah, but that would not be in our sporting rules would it?' the first voice states simply, adding,

'Not only did he escape from his designated zone, he took a partner with him and to top it all, our little ape evaded the undoubtedly highly functional forces of law within your own city!'

'I will wipe them all out with Black Flame and screaming torment!' the second evil voice rants.

'No, no, no you cannot,' the calmer, smug voice again states, 'it goes against the rules of play. I win, plain and simple. You will credit me my well deserved, one full Point of Stature'

'He cheated, you conniving bastard!' the hateful voice hissed, 'It is not fairly won!'

'Come now,' the calmer one speaks, 'you know as well as I the rules to the Game of Doors are older than the very simian species we have pitched upon the board.'

'Next time! You self-satisfied fuck-wit! Next game we play I will have you! I will have you!'

The calm voice laughs, the hissing one growls and dissipates into a dimension as yet unknown to human scientists.

'One whole Stature Point! Thank you very much!', the winner pronounces with pride undimmed.

A dark shadow floats on the watchtower of the empty Norman keep, overlooking the River Tyne, the ancient castle is closed to the public, for it is night. It opens its arms and briefly scintillates, then audibly buzzes with a burst of energy. A static plays about its black form. Then it laughs and laughs alone, i...i...i...i...echoing into the Newcastle night.

Arthur MacNeil had been buried in a paupers grave in a Catholic churchyard. His mothers letters were to be thrown into a dustbin. The long haired young student who cleaned the Salvation Army Hostel found that he could not do it. The shoebox, neatly packed with tied bundles also contained an Royal Flying Corp cap badge, medals and an old but well made penknife on a mildewed lanyard. He felt sorry for the lonely man who he had found in the narrow little room, now occupied by another sad little old man in crumpled clothes. The shoe box represented the old boys life, the tragedy was unmistakable. The pity the lad felt was a credit to his character and good upbringing.

'One day' the young man thought clearly to himself, ' that could be me.'

He placed the box cautiously into his duffel bag, for this constituted stealing and went about his daily chores. He intended to read them, just to learn about the old guy, an exercise in compassion. Perhaps he would write about it at college, a case study for his sociology classes.

Outside the late 1970s grumbled dangerously and discontentedly on.

The self inflated composer king had not attained the full measure of distinct glory to which he undoubtedly was confident he deserved. The bills mounted up and his music sold increasingly less and less. This was a clearly abhorrent state of affairs and despite the many letters of bitter complaint he had penned to his agent, the situation was unimproved and manifestly looking shaky. The notion of actually getting a normal job and having to mix with unintelligent, uneducated plebeians filled him with disgust and terror itself. He was an artist for Gods sake! Not just an artist, but a brilliantly gifted one who pulsed with the very spirit of human genius! Clearly it was not his fault society had reached an all time cultural low, his manuscripts were surely marvelous, his twelve long playing records vibrantly demonstrated his complete mastery of the modern classical genre. It was a tragedy of epic proportions to him, he wanted to cry, and after a few whiskeys he more than likely would do just that. His trenchant sophomania remained undiagnosed, his mental condition remaining unchanged and hence irredeemably locked in a self absorption that sank to the very depths of obsession and, concomitantly, outright bad psychological well being. Alone and unassisted, he drifted further into ideal candidature for a visit from the i...

Oh dearie me...Here is why...

The roots of sophomania have been laid bare with the arrival of the new psychological term, principally, Narcissistic Personality Disorder.

Apparently NPD has no cure, sadly. Sufferers may be self aware of this state, or simply have no notion that anything is remiss at all, nor be conscious of their effect upon others. There is a nine-stage check system which can be used to see how severe the affliction of NPD really is. The more aspects of these nine points one acknowledges, the more acute the illness. Victims of NPD have an unerring ability to exploit the pain of others and take it further than non-sufferers. They have been described as 'psychic rapists' and one particularly give-away sign is that they rarely, if at all admit to faults or shortcomings. The nine points are as follows.

1) Grandiosity. The NPD sufferer regard themselves unnaturally highly in their own opinion. This is accompanied with illusions of greatness without tangibility or real substance or warrant. Ask their parents what went so tragically amiss, a most difficult issue this is.

2) Arrogant and domineering. This is the outward expression of an inner condition. In their own NPD stained view, they truly believe they are at the very apex of the evolutionary pile. At this juncture, reasonable men may vomit without castigation.

3) Beliefs of being completely unique. They genuinely are convinced they are the most specially special specials and utterly original, and that no-one like themselves has been here prior to tread life's boards. Such utter, dismal bollocks.

4) Exploitative and perverse. The latter term meaning literally to 'be knotted wrongly', the former needs no explanation whatsoever, one manifestation occurring in sorry wanton ruthlessness. More obvious and valid reasons to avoid such sort.

5) Lack of empathy. An inability to genuinely sympathize. They are never saddened by the grief and loss or pain of others. They have no ability to empathize with anyone in trouble, whether they caused that person to suffer via themselves or not. Sympathy and empathy are completely absent. Such themes defy all manifest human reason.

6) Preoccupation with success and power. Because they are convinced they are the very best of the best of the best, they naturally believe they are due everything which comes with such privilege, especially fame, adoration, wealth and clout, preferably visited upon themselves in plenty. Again, as the Scots say, pure mince.

7) Requires excessive admiration. This nonsense follows from having such an over-exalted self view, the NPD sufferer will require lots of specifically positive praise and support. They will brook no rival to this claim either. Genuinely tragic.

8) Sense of entitlement. As in utterly not humble. Their self inflation is so pronounced it makes complete sense to them that they are due much in and through their supposed and assumed brilliance. Look out world!

9) Envious of others. This they will rarely admit to, but in the main, there is a part of them that knows their claims are absurd and that they really are missing out in general human life. Who will cry for them?

The loyalist pub, shattered by a bomb blast a year previous was cleaned, cleared and rebuilt. Photographs of the casualties of the explosion ranked, war hero-like, upon the bar-room walls. The same sort of football morons congregated there again, learning absolutely nothing from the previous, genuinely horrible event. In fact, their behaviour worsened, the bawdy bigoted chants got harder and meaner and more brutal. It was almost as if they actually wanted the same thing to happen again, but this time in a nice clean Formica and steel and glass environment. People tend not to learn so quickly down on this sorry sphere of woe and grief and pain. They stumble onwards, even when their ignorance and folly has injured their minds, their bodies and their hearts. A lasting testament to our enduring stupidity.

The beer would still flow, the television blare with inane commentary as men who should know better permitted themselves lapses of silly over-excited reportage.

'AND IT'S A GOAL!.. YES! ... UNITED HAVE DONE IT!'

Upon a television screen, men run about and kick a football to and fro upon some stadium field. Viewed coldly and objectively, it is wholly and utterly inane.

Perhaps it is the human requirement for reassurance in like-minded numbers? Maybe it is the same driving force that necessitated Roman amphitheaters? Yet it is but a game, and an overpaid one at that. Tragically, so many million men behave like spoilt, violent children, bellowing, drinking more beer and if necessary expunging their frustrations and hatred upon the physiology of others. Preferably smaller and weaker than themselves, but not always the case. The girls would still dress attractively and play the Dance of Love and the lads would pose like the vacuous big hard men they idolized. Tragedy, it is said, never ends, it merely continues unchecked, unchanging. A human constant. A human predilection.

The boys who found such passing mirth in the destruction of an old piano graduated to greater things and found fresh thrills in joyriding, ram-raiding and the deliberate destruction of cars and vans in increasingly dangerous games. They prided themselves on driving at some speed towards the sea cliffs on the coast of North-Eastern England, jumping out at the last moment and sending the automobile careening off the drop where it would smash and shatter, to occasionally burst into flames. Some that survived this danger-loving phase would join the army, those that could not contemplate taking orders and conforming, became a locally successful Punk Rock group, the Abysmoids, as the wave of rejuvenated rock and roll hit Britain in 1976. Their snarling, irreverent sense of nihilistic humour genuinely touched a chord, or three, in the youth of that period. The trail of wreckage that became their hallmark stage act was legendary and scary by turns.

The skinheads who had stalked the changing world of the 1970s, whose boots had beaten and thrashed and trounced and inflicted so much awful injury, they slowly grew old and fat or went to prison, or both, and there they grimly aged. Their children became a different class of social ill and lasting menace. The breakdown of society into the tasteless, inadequate morass it has become was given firm foundation in the offspring of this turbulent and barren era. The memory of the glory days of the boot boys faded and thinned, the crombie, drainpipe jeans and steel capped boots were changed for the baseball cap, shell suit and the training shoe. Style no longer mattered, since it was an addition that required a degree of intelligence and humour. Which being at a profound lack caused criminality to become coarser and more unaccountably brutal. A sociopathic plague, an epidemic of mental disease dictated the charmless, dangerous actions of the new generation of criminals. No-one was safe, unless fabulous riches erected the picket of strong protection and defense about the fortunate, all those below and outside such privilege simply suffered.

History accrued, it layered thick and deep under the very pavements of Britain. The past was the study of academics and volunteers with trowels and marker pens. Artifacts would emerge, gold hoards and ancient swords, pottery in tonnages. The manifest proof of our origins was unearthed daily. No-one ever suspected that history itself had been pillaged for more than mere antiques and soil stained relics. That a sub-world existed where humans had been collected as specimens and in this Otherworld they dwelt, doing what humanity can only ever do if it has not lost the will, namely to live or survive. It was not a bell jar in which the captured creature could balefully glare at the larger world of its captors outside, no, it was a fully closed dimension. There was no way out and no way back. Those that were taken remained so and the crime stood unpunished, unperceived and unknown.

And the dirty river Tyne flowed on and on, and all around its settled banks did change in the decades proceeding Arthur's unmarked demise. If proof of the tenements and slums of Pipewellgate were needed, then the library photographic archives were the place to go, to browse over faded black and white, or sepia frames of a world destroyed with little thought or care. In other, more enlightened parts of Britain where history and architecture was valued, old buildings received renovation grants and became used again as art galleries, luxury apartments and restaurants. As bland uniformity dominated and the promised Bright New Tomorrow failed to appear, the aesthetic love and preference for the demolished era actually created an entire trend amongst those with the wealth to purchase and renew. The ghosts of hungry families haunted no-one, for in this reasonable and logical future there was no place for such superstitious speculation. Folk received heavy medication for promoting a belief in such unhealthy world views. The dirty river flowed and as industry died, it became cleaner as its poisoned mud was dredged, along with the amassed rusting junk, the corpses from gangland executions and two centuries of chemical waste that had given it such a remarkable colour, smell and toxicity.

Whilst mankind had thrust the towering white rockets into local space and with much calculation had spun satellites further out to its neighbouring planets, the effort remained something which the i...found sincerely hilarious. This one small step failed to impress them, rather it constituted a running gag that could liven up the dullest day for the alien in our midst. The praise heaped upon the human apes in the padded white suits would be quoted verbatim in their gatherings and never failed to generate scathing comedy and contemptuous laughter. It was better for our human self esteem that we did not know this, that our illusion of greatness remained unsullied to our own eyes and estimation. It was noted in one particular council of the i... that if the resources the monkeys had invested in their 'space' program had been directed into particle accelerators, designed to peer into sub-atomic emptiness, the rewards would have been vaster indeed.

Yet it was not the case, history is what it is and humans are what they are, fatally flawed would-be-goods, with little hope of liberation from the cruel thraldom of the i... Entertainment, as has been stated, remains deeply important to them, it had become their very food and sustenance, much to human detriment and want.

In the Otherworld, upon a fortified hill-top there is a circular house. Its roof is composed of packed sods of earth, in summer the grass grows thick upon it green and bright. Within, in its smokey gloom, an enormous black bearskin rug is strewn over half the floor. Its massive head growls in death and its lethal fangs shine in the lamp-light. A sharp woodman's axe rests on a peg by the hide-covered door. A once smart gentleman's three piece suit hangs unused, gathering dust and tiny insects above the pallet bed, it bulges slightly from the holstered revolver within, long unused but still oiled and maintained. There is a very odd key in the right hand pocket. On a shelf by this bed are three large books. All beautifully bound from an era when artisan-ship was a thing of particular skill and pride. Long before talking things up had contaminated the working world with its poisoned, empty verbiage, a toxicity that has corroded the very words themselves.

These books were;

The Complete Works of William Shakespeare.

The Unexpurgated Culpeper's Herbal with extensive notes and illustrations.

The Phenomenology of Spirit by Georg Wilhelm Friedrich Hegel.

All three had been read by their proud owner many times.

The i...

By Paul Rosher.

ABOUT THE AUTHOR

My childhood was played-out in the Tyneside of the 1960`s, Northern England. The impressions, memories and actual places from this era form the setting for the bulk of my first novel. Both Newcastle and Gateshead by the early 1970`s suffered greatly from the economic decline that blighted much of Britain in this period. Despite a rich history going all the way back to Roman times, it had become a grimy, run-down, gloomy place.

However it was a fascinating chaos of conflicting architectural styles and eras, with much dereliction providing rank upon rank of empty terraced streets and many interesting abandoned industrial buildings which provided poor kids with lots to explore. The themes, moods and locations of this story derive directly from my formative years in this environment. Yet it is also partially an exorcism of the disturbing and sinister aspects of poverty and it's associated shadow, violence.

Tyneside could also be a very haunting place. As young lads we explored and pillaged through the spaces that once had been peoples homes and workplaces. It was all too easy to read the traces of difficult, impoverished and unhealthy existences, they were everywhere, they were obvious. As a youth, I sensed the unfulfilled presence of these tough northern folk, it was as if their ghosts were watching us as we searched through the belongings and detritus they left behind.

It was not until 2007 that the notion occurred that this personal history, both place and time, could provide the atmospheric background to a novel. Where lacunae and hazier memories presented problems, research through local libraries and historical societies solved this matter. Gradually and slowly I assembled what became "the i...".

I left Tyneside in 1978 to study in Edinburgh, Scotland and later in 1984 moved to the Isle of Skye, where I still live. I have been rock climbing since my teens and joined Skye Mountain Rescue Team the same year I moved to the Island. Both climbing and rescue work still figure large in my life on Skye, which is a remarkable place if rugged mountains, challenging sea cliffs and high crag faces are what floats your boat. I am self employed as an illustrator and occasional leather-worker (I ran a leather craft business for over 15 years) and dabble in mountaineering and rescue equipment design. In 2002 I won the Winston Churchill Fellowship Award for my work on the Secure Casualty System, now manufactured by Snowsled Polar and used by many steep ground rescue teams. I also served a placement with Yosemite Search and Rescue as a full team member-an unforgettable experience.

I am married with one son who also lives on the Island. I dedicate this first novel to the memory of my daughter Elizabeth who tragically died in 2008, she is much missed.

Printed in Great Britain
by Amazon.co.uk, Ltd.,
Marston Gate.